HATFIELD 1677

LAURA C. RADER

FROM THE TINY ACORN...
GROWS THE MIGHTY OAK

This is a work of fiction based, in part, on actual events. Names, characters, places, and incidents are the product of the author's imagination or are used fictitiously.

Hatfield 1677

Printed in the United States of America. For information, address Acorn Publishing, LLC
3943 Irvine Blvd. Ste. 218, Irvine, CA 92602

www.acornpublishingllc.com

Interior design by Kat Ross
Cover design by Damonza

ISBN-13: 979-8-88528-078-5 (hardcover)
ISBN-13: 979-8-88528-077-8 (paperback)
Library of Congress Control Number: 2023918294

where we meet Ben and Martha, a Puritan couple caught in the middle of a tumultuous era of colonial tensions. What happens next is the unbelievably true story of their treacherous and brutal journeys, inescapable danger, heart-wrenching loss, and unexpected alliances.

Laura C. Rader's meticulously researched historical novel brings to life a rich tapestry of characters. It shows us that the power of the human spirit, prevailing hope, and the unyielding pursuit of freedom are the invisible fibers that connect us all, even centuries apart."

–Christina Hicks, '22 Claymore Suspense Award Finalist, and Author of "Baby's Breath" *The Broadkill Review,* Spring, Vol 17.2

"*Hatfield 1677* is a captivating fictionalization of an incredible true story. The profound love of family that led Ben Waite to contend with colonial officials and the associated bureaucracy (some of whom were apparently completely uncaring for their charges)—while fighting weather, terrain, and his own fear—is tremendously uplifting. The struggles he and Stephen Jennings survived to achieve this feat are derring-do of the highest order. Laura C. Rader's meticulous research and feel for the time immerses the reader in the period with authentic descriptions, language, and detail. Her treatment of the conflict between Natives and English is even-handed, fair, and without sugar-coating. It's an exciting read that will bring tears to the eyes and adrenaline to the veins!"

–Thomas Wing, Retired US Naval Officer and Author of *Against All Enemies*

"*Hatfield 1677* is viscerally concrete, taking the reader into the frontier Puritan world with recognizable, complex characters and actual historical events."

–Steven Wiley, Professor of Anthropology Emeritus, Normandie Community College, Minnesota

Dedicated with much love to my daughter, Emily

Author's Note

In writing *Hatfield 1677* I developed a deep empathy for all First Nations peoples, particularly the "River Indians" in the Connecticut River Valley: allied Nipmucs, Pocumtucks, Norwottucks, and other Algonquian tribes.

I hope I have written an authentic and unbiased story, presenting Ashpelon and his people respectfully while sharing not only Benjamin Waite's and Stephen Jennings's courageous journeys to redeem their families but also their wives' and children's harrowing survival as captives.

Fifty years after the Wampanoag sachem Massasoit welcomed a small group of English Separatists (Pilgrims) to Massachusetts, Massasoit's son, Metacomet, became acutely aware that his father's kindness to those first few colonists had opened the floodgates to a massive European invasion. So began Metacomet's struggle to push back, accepting the title "King Philip" and uniting diverse Algonquian tribes to rise up against the English colonists.

King Philip's War lasted from about 1675 to 1678 and is infamous for incurring the greatest percentage of casualties, relative to populations both indigenous and European, of any war before or since in American history. (Robert Cray: *Weltering in their Own Blood*, Historical Journal of Massachusetts, Vol. 37 (2), Fall 2009.)

Chapter One

BEN

HATFIELD, MASSACHUSETTS BAY COLONY
MAY 18, 1676

On that restless spring evening, I stood on the stoop of a house that was not mine, and held in my arms the woman who was. The dark clapboards of our friend's home glowed in the setting sun, defined by light and shadow like the feathers of a bird. There was a damp chill in the breeze and the scent of rain. I was grateful for the thick hide of my buff coat.

The house belonged to Lieutenant Allis and his family. Unlike my home, it was secure within Hatfield's stockade and garrisoned by Connecticut troops. For two months my family had sheltered here, as if prisoners in our own town, while King Philip's war raged without.

The bugle's first call summoned our troops to assemble, but I would not rush this farewell. The bonds of love forged in six years of marriage had me firmly tethered, dreading the march to an ill-advised battle. I cupped Martha's fair face in my hands, her soft lips parting to mine. She returned my tender kiss for a moment, then unlaced her fingers from the nape of my neck and met my gaze.

Her green eyes seemed somehow brighter in the fading light.

"You must go. It is not your nature to disregard the summons."

I looked past her to where my bay mare, Scout, stood saddled and waiting, and beyond that to Main Street, a ribbon of hard-packed earth lined with solid two-story houses, gray and dismal as the sky. A handful of soldiers passed. Most walking, but some on horseback, muskets slung over their backs and horns or bandoliers across their chests. Heeding the summons.

"You are afraid." Martha's frank words snared me.

"Yes."

"As though this were your first expedition as a military scout."

She awaited my explanation. I reached for a wisp of her copper-colored hair, held it gently between my fingers, and tucked it back inside her linen cap. My hand lingered on her soft cheek.

I chose my words carefully.

"The River Indians' theft of our livestock is scant reason for this venture. Negotiations with them should have been allowed to proceed."

"So you find this action unwarranted?"

I nodded. "Aye. Also, our War Council moved so swiftly I've not had time to scout the River Indians' camp at Great Falls or gather the intelligence we need."

"I thought a captive had escaped, bearing information? Reede?"

I sighed. "He thought the tribes were River Indians—Nipmucs, Pocumtucks, and Norwottucks. Scarce information on their weapons or numbers. Captain Turner trusts his report implicitly."

"But you do not."

I shook my head.

"Trust in God," she said. "He will be with you in your battle and guide you safely home."

I smiled at her words. Her faith in me was only surpassed by her unerring faith in God. Love may be blind, but at times, I longed for her to embrace my doubts, to glimpse my feet of clay. Yet I would not reveal all the shadows buried in my heart for fear I might lose her love. If I told her the Natives were likely women and children, unarmed, she would be horrified at my impending savagery. And if she knew warriors would descend on us as we retreated, she would be equally horrified at the risk I faced.

Again the bugle summoned, an urgent reminder of my duty. I settled my broad-brimmed hat on my head. Martha gently folded back the flap, pinning it to the crown above my left eyebrow.

"So your aim will be true." There was a catch in her voice. She rested her cheek against my buff coat.

I snugged her russet cloak around her shoulders and wrapped her in my arms again. She had rinsed her hair in lavender water, and the familiar scent comforted me.

The lieutenant's daughter-in-law, Rachel Allis, appeared at her door beside us, holding our wee babe, Sally. "They want one last goodbye," she said.

Our other daughters—Mary, the eldest and sweetest, just learning to read, and Mattie, always determined to be heard —pressed past Rachel and scampered to me.

I bent and hugged them, encircling one in each arm, closing my eyes against sudden tears. I kissed Mary's smooth brow and Mattie's plump cheek. I rose, patted their bums, and softly urged them back inside. Rachel held Sally up to me, and I kissed her little nose. She rewarded me with a giggle and flung her chubby arms around my neck. I held her tight before I reluctantly handed her back, and gazed after them as Rachel entered her house and closed the door.

"They should be asleep, Martha, 'tis half past six," I chided, my gruff tone not hiding the tenderness I felt.

"Asleep? With a houseful of families from beyond the stockade, and armed soldiers? There are too many pleasant distractions." She laughed, shaking her head at my folly.

"I, too, am fond of pleasant distractions." I drew her to me and kissed her once more, then pulled away before I lost all resolve. I could not allow us to fall victim to the gossip of our town's mutual watch, busybodies entrusted with enforcing our Puritan ideals and squelching all pleasure.

"Will you watch us march past?" I asked. The comfort of one last look at her.

"Of course. We'll put the wee ones to bed, then be in the dooryard with our lanterns."

Martha grazed my cheek with her fingertips, her soft touch sending shivers through me. "Your fair beard will need a trim when you return," she said. And then she was gone.

Once the door closed behind her, I turned and strode through the herb garden, brushing against the clove-scented gillyflowers. I untied Scout, patted her neck, and mounted. As always, I checked my weapons—securing my flintlock in its sling across my back and taking inventory of my pistol, sword, and ammunition.

It was a short ride to the commons. The houses lined the broad main street, facing each other like opposing armies, shielded by fenced dooryard gardens of herbs and flowers. The size and design of our homes disclosed their Puritan owners' ranks as clearly as the colors and insignia of officers' uniforms. The grandest house was Reverend Atherton's, commanding the northwest corner of the common, an extravagance of three chimneys exhaling smoke into the breeze.

Maneuvering betwixt twitching flanks and stomping hooves, I rode at a trot across the green to where the heretic

Captain William Turner sat astride his black stallion. Roughly seven score of mounted troops and foot soldiers milled about, awaiting commands. Twenty miles to the north lay our destination, the Great Falls of the Connecticut River—the Algonquian River Indians' camp— where a bank of pewter storm clouds promised rain.

The fading sun cast the captain in a skeletal silhouette. His tarnished breastplate hung loose as a tortoise's shell, and his helmet shadowed deep hollows in his pale cheeks. His black horse tossed its head and skittered about, and Turner clutched a handful of mane and nearly lost a stirrup. Prison had not been kind to him, and even after his release, he continued to fade, like one of Martha's roses kept too long in a glass.

Massachusetts Bay Colony was solidly English and devoutly Puritan, and refusing to recant his Baptist heresy had cost Turner his freedom. After a year in the Boston jail, Turner's wife fell ill. Governor Leverett had taken pity on him, setting him free on the condition he assume the undesirable wartime post commanding the garrisons of Hatfield and the neighboring towns, Hadley and Northampton.

"Ready for battle, Waite?" Turner asked as I approached. His firm tone couldn't hide the rasp in his voice.

"Yes, sir," I lied.

"Your men are well-prepared." He nodded to our volunteer troops, who mingled amidst his highly trained Connecticut dragoons. "'Twas fortuitous the captive Reede escaped. We now possess details of the River Indians' camp and their weak defenses at Great Falls."

"Insufficient details, I fear."

"Goodman Waite." Turner gathered his reins and coughed into his fist. "Do you still harbor concerns?"

"Several, in truth," I replied.

I guided Scout to come abreast of Turner and spoke my mind.

"The Algonquians' theft of our cattle and horses last week

was infuriating but hardly grounds for battle. And our council's haste in voting to retaliate leads to my three concerns."

"Get on with it, Waite."

I kept my remarks precise and unhurried.

"Firstly, with all respect, sir, you may be relying upon faulty intelligence. I would have preferred to assess the situation at the Falls beforehand."

"Well, you will simply need to be more vigilant henceforth."

One did not replace the other. His lack of battle experience astounded me.

"Secondly, the Natives at Great Falls are likely the same bands of Algonquians we've traded with and shared our cornfields with for years," I said, giving Scout her head to browse the fresh grass and show I was in no rush. "If 'tis true what Reede said, that they are aged men, women, and children, then 'tis likely they are not allied with King Philip and pose no threat to us."

"I see no reason to spare any Indians at this point, Waite."

"Attacking a peaceful village will serve no purpose," I persisted.

"It is not your decision. Nor mine. The War Council voted."

I inhaled and let my breath out slowly, reining in my anger. It had been a straw vote, at best.

"Lastly, and somewhat contrary to my other point, Reede may have underestimated the number of warriors on the islands near the main camp. Those I'd have detected had I been given more time. We could be vulnerable to ambush both on approach and on retreat."

"Your objections are duly noted. I'd say the fat is in the fire at this point. Is that all?"

"Except for a caution about—"

Turner coughed again, then held up a hand to halt me. "'Twas a brutal winter, Goodman Waite. The Indians are starving. The pox and bloody flux have left them feeble, even their warriors."

"Perchance, sir, but—"

"Besides, we have you, our famed scout, and the other one, Hinsdell, to lead the way. We march in a half hour. Take your position." He tipped his hat and rode off.

"Yes, sir," I said to the ass of his horse. Turner's cough betrayed lung sickness, likely from his time in Boston's prison. It was difficult to place confidence in a leader who fancied himself an avenging angel despite broken wings.

I went in search of my fellow scout, Experience Hinsdell, shaking my head at his ill-suited name. Although he was in his early thirties, as was I, he was green and lacked discipline. I found him at the edge of the common, mounted on his dapple-gray gelding.

"Did you speak with the captain? Any news?" he asked.

"I shared my concerns, which he summarily dismissed," I said, with fresh irritation.

"He's certainly pompous. And quite dim-witted at times. But you and I will be at the front and flanks, fortunately."

"I'm pleased we have Lieutenants Holyoke and Allis, and Sergeant John Dickinson. Veterans of many battles," I said.

The drumbeats commenced. I took my place in the second rank, behind Captain Turner and between Lieutenants Holyoke and Allis. The ensigns and sergeants took their positions, and we split our company into ranks and files. The mounted volunteers and Connecticut dragoons took the lead and the flanks, and our foot soldiers brought up the rear.

"Attention!" Captain Turner commanded. We stood impressively still, the only movement or sound the jangling of the horses' bits and the beating of the drum. "Company. Forward, march!"

We headed north up the main street. Our women stood in the dark dooryards, lanterns glimmering like fireflies. Their prayers and words of encouragement floated around us.

Feeling perhaps overly confident in our troops' abilities, the captain commanded the mounted sections to trot and the foot soldiers to march in quick time, displaying an eagerness I did not feel and a vanity I found offensive.

When we reached the Allis home, lantern light illuminated Martha's sweet face, and she waved. I would have called a halt if it had been my command to make. Instead, I smiled and doffed my hat to her, tears welling in my eyes, and she blew me a kiss.

Captain Turner signaled us back to a walk, and the chill wind bore down. Nose to tail, stirrups nearly touching flank to flank, we passed through the northern gate of the stockade. I cast a look ahead of me at my abandoned home, dark and squat in the twilight. I'd built it eight years ago, just before I met Martha. Knowing I longed to leave Rhode Island after my brother's death, my father had deeded me the land. I longed to bring my family back home to it. Once King Philip's war was over.

I smiled at my fond memories of a few months ago, before the garrisoning. Bouncing Sally on my knee, delighting in her smiles. Martha at the spinning wheel, her right hand holding the wool and her left feeding the roving to the bobbin. Mary and Mattie beside her on the rag rug, dangling a bit of yarn for one of the striped barn kittens. My family had thoroughly domesticated me, and I was not sure if my tenderness for them would be my redemption or my undoing.

I startled at a clattering of hooves and glanced to my left. Reverend Hope Atherton approached my flank. He was a young Englishman, stout and energetic, a graduate of Harvard. Six years ago, Martha and I posted our marriage banns at his first sermon in Hatfield's new meeting house, and he had become a trusted confidante.

"Woolgathering, Benjamin?" he asked.

"Woolgathering indeed, Reverend. Not the best admission for a scout. I was thinking about my family."

"'Tis hard to leave them," he said, nodding.

"You and your goodwife have a new wee babe, do you not?"

"We do. Little Joseph. I suppose it doesn't become easier to leave them as time passes?"

"No, in truth, it becomes more difficult. Still, your presence with us is a comfort."

"'Tis my duty to accompany my flock. I pray the Lord will lead us to turn the tables on the Algonquians on the morrow."

Reverend Atherton fell back into his position and a more sedate pace. I much preferred his common sense to the righteous fervor of Reverend Russell of neighboring Hadley. Our severed peace negotiations with the Algonquians had been his doing, his anger fueling the demand for troops to assail them. And now all would suffer for it.

We followed the Catawumpuck Brook, where Meekins' Mill wheel spun lazily against the darkening sky, softly churning the water. Farther north, the river rushed over red sandstone, the same stone I'd used to build the fireplace of my home.

The sun buried itself behind the old graveyard, and a waxing gibbous moon rose slowly above the Connecticut River, casting shadows across our path. To the west, the sky still glowed a dusky violet, but ahead it was black with storm. My eyesight adjusted to the falling darkness, and I watched our ensign raise our Massachusetts Bay Colony flag aloft, red and white silk fluttering in the wind.

The Great North Meadow cupped us like birds in a nest of soft grass. Ditches and wooden fences crisscrossed the pastures, empty of the cattle the Algonquians had stolen. The sheep remained, and lifted their heads and gazed at us when we rode through. Their stubbornness kept them bound together like a ball of wool, lambs clinging to their sides. Even when the marauding tribe came, they refused to budge, sparing us their loss.

I eased back in the saddle, worrying again about the wisdom of this endeavor and Turner's precarious command. Although our sworn purpose was to protect our loved ones, I feared this battle might instead lead to even greater danger. I lacked the rage required to risk so much for revenge. Perhaps the relentless assaults against our towns over the past year had worn down my spirit. Bowing my head, I prayed to the Lord to give me strength.

We approached the looming hulk of Sugarloaf Mountain, which the Pocumtucks called The Great Beaver. We'd soon reach a spring that flowed to Hopewell Swamp, where I'd lost my best friend Richard Fellowes to King Philip's War last summer. And an hour's ride beyond that, we'd come upon Bloody Brook, its former name of Muddy Brook forever corrupted by the ambush that had taken Experience Hinsdell's father and all three brothers.

The horses' dust and warm breath enveloped me, leaving no quarter for ghosts or demons, and I took solace in the murmur of champing bits and the soft squelch of leather and buff skins. Distant lightning ignited clouds above the treetops. Oaks and elms crowded the trail, wind bustling their leaves. I was grateful for their cover as we approached Deerfield. Young Reede said he'd seen some of our cattle there, and I increased my vigilance.

I guided Scout diagonally to the right, her passage graceful as any Spanish nobleman's steed. I was eager to speak with Hinsdell before we reached Bloody Brook. Spying his dapple-gray mount in the moonlight that scattered through the trees, I fell into step beside him. He gave me a weak smile.

"I thought I'd ride with you for a bit," I said.

He looked off into the distance before he answered. "You know my heart, Ben. There's comfort in that."

"They're with God," I said. Truth, but often of little comfort.

Hinsdell jerked the reins, though his poor mount was not

unruly, and his voice cracked. "'Twas a simple transport of threshed wheat. We were no threat to the Indians."

"I know," I said.

"Tomorrow will be my day of reckoning. An eye for an eye, a tooth for a tooth." He laid his hand on his scabbard.

I nodded and refrained from repeating my belief that the Natives we sought at Great Falls were likely not those who'd ambushed us before.

"Hallo, Bloody Brook," he said with a sigh, when we reached its banks.

Captain Turner and Lieutenant Holyoke signaled to our company.

"Company, halt! Dismount and water your horses."

Hinsdell and I led our mounts to the brook, where they dropped their heads and buried their muzzles in the dark water. It felt good to stretch my legs.

Sergeant Dickinson approached us, leading his horse. "A fitting spot to take a moment, hey, lads?" He removed his hat and ran a hand through his graying chestnut hair. "An unspeakable loss, Hinsdell, for you and many others. We will avenge your kin," he said, then led his horse away.

In no time at all came the commands, "Prepare to Mount! Mount! Fall in! Eyes front! Company, march!" Young Jonathan Welles took up the old tune, "The Black Nag," on his fife whilst Tom Belding resumed his beat on the drum. Fearing discovery, I sent Hinsdell back to silence them. Their simple efforts were meant to lift our spirits, but mine remained darker than the waters of Bloody Brook as we forded it and continued north to Great Falls.

We marched in the footsteps of our dead, having learned little from their sacrifice and doomed to echo their fate.

Chapter Two

BEN

The clouds burst, and rain drenched us as we rode through the abandoned town of Deerfield. The deluge overcame all sounds and washed away all footprints, obliterating any trace of the enemy. The moon cast ripples of light amongst the blackened ruins of the houses, now overtaken by juneberry, staghorn sumac, and milkweed. Only the chimneys remained, like giant grave markers to the memories of our dead. I half expected a wraith to emerge from one and ascend into the rainy heavens.

Half of Deerfield's inhabitants had been slaughtered in the war. 'Twas the most remote of all the Massachusetts Bay towns and, like a lamb separated from its flock, easy prey. Deerfield's survivors garrisoned in Hatfield, Hadley, and Northampton, and the few who could afford it had sailed back to England in defeat.

"We must reduce our files, sir," I said to Turner, dreading the commotion no doubt involved.

"Company, halt! By threes and sixes!" Captain Turner ordered.

We sorted ourselves into three columns forty horses deep, each near a furlong from the front rank to the rear. From there on out, our trail was a narrow jumble-gut lane, plunging into the woods and curving east again toward the Great Falls. Whatever light the moon and stars provided could not reach us, and we were fain to trust our horses' eyesight and agility to carry us forward.

Our drummer disregarded orders and signaled the hour with three soft beats. The witching hour, some said, when the veil betwixt life and death is most fragile. A shiver rippled across my shoulders, not only from my trepidation as we neared White Ash Swamp, where the Algonquians' scouts might lie in wait.

We forded the Green River, water lapping at our stirrups. The crescent moon reappeared above us to light our passage and resumed playing hide-and-seek amongst the rain clouds and tree limbs as we entered the thick forest alongst the great bend of the Connecticut River.

Lightning struck close by, its thunder startling Scout, and a smell like gunpowder filled my nostrils. For a moment, the flash lit our path, an ascending trail beneath rain that lashed through the canopy of trees. I fumbled with the top hooks of my buff coat and undid Martha's neat pinning of my hat, pulling the brim down over my eyes. The wind picked up, beating us with rain, tree branches crackling and hissing. The storm's fury would soften our approach.

Hours later, weary and sodden, we dismounted in a thicket of brush and pine near the falls. Our soldiers looped their reins over a branch or 'round another horse's neck before attaching feed bags of cracked corn and oats to busy our mounts until we returned. Hinsdell and I scouted the area and were relieved to find no signs of danger.

Captain Turner ordered our fifer, drummer, and the two Christian Narragansetts to stay with the horses. Once heathen, Pessacus and Pumham had converted to Christianity rather than become prisoners of war. Though they were skilled guides, they refused to bear arms against this band of Nipmucs and Pocumtucks, claiming they had no enmity against them. We should have heeded their wisdom.

Hinsdell and I led the troops up the north slope, slipping on pine needles slick with rain to reach a rocky terrace directly beside the Great Falls. The roar of the waterfall drowned out all other sounds. The Nipmucs and Pocumtucks called the cascades Peskeompskut, "The Place Where Thunder Comes Out of the Rock." A fitting name. Turner released the troops to rest.

Hinsdell and I scouted the terrace, discussing avenues of retreat, and surveyed the Algonquians' camp far below. Cooking fires flickered within circles of bark wigwams. Nothing moved. 'Twas impossible to see what lay south of the camp. If, as we feared, those islands hid warriors, our incursion must be swift and brutal and our retreat rapid. Unsatisfied, Hinsdell and I returned to meet with Turner and the officers to finalize our strategy.

"Sergeants, ensigns, be sure your men get a short rest and refreshment before our assault in roughly—" Captain Turner pulled out his pocket watch, "—two hours. On my command, you will spread out and advance silently down the hill. Then, reassemble and wait until I order the first firing. Afterwards, it is a skirmish. Every man for himself. We take no prisoners."

"Captain, to confirm our orders, we fire at will? Women and children?" asked Lieutenant William Allis, concern evident in the timbre of his voice.

His frank question bared the misgivings I hadn't fully shared with my wife. Reede's scant report implied this was a local band of families whose worst crime was stealing our cattle. We had no evidence they'd been part of any bloodshed in this war, but they were an easy target for our fear and anger. It would be my first offensive engagement.

"Our orders are to destroy this encampment," Captain Turner said.

Knowing my place, I shook off my apprehension and addressed my superiors.

"Captain, our officers must remind their troops to stay clear of the swamp upon retreat, for it is treacherous. Also, the warriors guarding the islands south of the camp will be on the move at the first volley. We won't have much time before they reach us."

"Thank you, Mister Waite. Company, take care of your needs and be prepared in two hours," Turner said.

I rejoined the men. They huddled together in weary, wet bunches, whispering, swigging cider, and gnawing on whatever victuals they'd brought. Some dozed. Rain still poured, but the thunder and lightning were fading.

Someone nudged my arm, waking me. Men rose to their feet, stuffing refreshments in their pouches. I stood and stretched. A pink haze of dawn crept across the sky, and a few brave rays of early sunlight shafted through the trees. Heavy clouds remained to the east, red and laden with water. Red sky in the morn, sailors forlorn. I looked to the west for a rainbow, hoping for luck but finding none. I joined the arc of men around our young minister.

"Men, we are here to avenge many wrongs. For years, we lived in peace alongside the Algonquians and the Iroquois. Massasoit saved our grandparents from starvation when they landed at Plymouth, but his son, King Philip, has turned against us." Reverend Atherton spoke softly, but his words seemed to ring through the trees. He stared accusingly at the two Narragansetts amongst us before continuing.

"We must not forget Bloody Brook, where Algonquians slaughtered English who'd set down their guns to pick wild grapes, nor the ambushes at Hopewell Swamp and Beers' Plain. God is with us this morning. Like Samuel, we can say, 'Thou hast given me the necks of mine enemies, that I might destroy them who hate me.' Amen."

Amen, we replied. The sergeants gave the troops their marching orders, and Lieutenant Allis added my caution. "Men, heed your commanding officers upon retreat. The route through White Ash Swamp would be a treacherous choice."

I nodded to him in gratitude.

We again checked our flintlocks, which we'd loaded when we mustered. I'd taught the men to dab lamb fat on the patches to keep the powder dry in the barrel and store some beeswax on the flash pan and frizzen. I hoped they'd remembered.

I removed the leather tied to the muzzle of my musket to keep it dry and wiped down the pan and flint with a kerchief. Then, I primed the pan and snapped the frisson shut. Such familiar preparations calmed me.

"Should be like shooting ducks in their nest," I overheard someone say. Two young Hadley volunteers, laughing. Whether it was bravado or foolishness, they were mistaken. Though women and elders might not be armed, the warriors who would be upon us in short order had flintlocks and tomahawks.

"More like firing a ship's cannon at a flock of gulls, " I said. "A flock protected by sharks."

They scoffed at my odd metaphor and continued their jests.

We fanned out stealthily amongst the ancient trees and waited like children before a footrace for Captain Turner to set us loose. I listened to the rushing of the falls. The rain lightened to scattered droplets, and the sun broke through the clouds and sent drifts of steam rising from our damp buff coats, releasing the smell of wet cowhide. Someone coughed. I bent my head and murmured a prayer for my wife and daughters.

On the captain's signal, we padded down the slope under cover of scattered trees and deep dawn shadows. The Algonquians' camp was still and silent, disturbed only by wisps of smoke from the drenched embers of cooking fires and the ever-present rush of the cascades. We took our positions and cocked our guns. I held my breath.

"First firing. Make ready. Present arms!"

I was in the front line. I knelt and aimed my musket at the nearest wigwam.

"First rank. Fire!"

I squeezed the trigger and struck the wigwam, a resounding thump sending shreds of birchbark flying. Native men and women erupted from it like sparks from a tinder.

"Reload and fire at will!"

I pressed the stock of my gun into the ground and measured powder into the barrel, my hand trembling. Rammed the patch and ball down deep with the rod, primed the pan, snapped shut the frisson, and set it full cock. Bending low, I ran into the camp, gripping my musket. My next shot took down an older man wielding a tomahawk. I froze, momentarily stunned, watching through a haze of smoke as his life bled away. Why were we shooting elders?

Before I could reload, a Native boy leapt into my path, brandishing a club. I swung the butt of my musket and knocked the weapon from his hand. I kept moving. My heart skipped beats. My breath came in deep gasps. Captain Turner roared indecipherable orders, drowned out by the explosions of musket balls.

Our enemies stumbled to the river, babes crying, women

screaming. They scrambled into birchbark canoes that over-loaded and overturned, dumping them into the rapids. A dozen of our soldiers lined up alongst the riverbanks, firing at the helpless people swimming toward the southern camp. Upriver, I heard a tremendous splash as other men heaved the Natives' forge and bars of lead into the water.

I ran low beneath the musket fire, the black smoke stinging my eyes, and passed their central smoking pit. Soldiers yanked down the ropes of dried salmon, dragged them to the river, and hurled them in. The two young Hadley volunteers stuck branches into the fire, and, when the tips burst into flame, torched the wigwams.

Three women escaped one as it caught fire, rushing at me, waving tomahawks. I'd not time nor room to raise my gun. I drew and swung my sword, a shudder through my arms as it connected. I wiped the blade clean, sheathed it, and, without warning, heaved up everything in my stomach. I stumbled to another wigwam and pressed my back against it. My hands shook violently as I drew my pistol from its holster, cocked it, and aimed it into the wigwam. For a moment, the darkness blinded me. I heard a wee babe's cries, so much like Sally's.

Dear sweet Sally. I was moved to offer comfort.

I blinked hard. The light from a small fire revealed a young woman, her skin aglow from the flames and dusky from the smoke. She stared at me with wide, dark eyes and shrank back, one arm straight out, palm flat, one arm clutching her babe to her breast. I hesitated.

"*Mahta, Toshshonte! Nuqisus, Mahta. Monto'ac!*" She was weeping.

No, Englishman, my son. No. God! I knew her Nipmuc language by heart.

"*Monto'ac!*" She staggered to her feet and thrust a book at me. Her babe wailed. Through the smoke, I read the words on the cover: *Testament. John Eliot.* Her Bible. She wrapped both arms around her tiny babe, sheltering its head in the hollow of her throat, her black hair falling like curtains to conceal it. I lowered my gun, turned, and ran. The babe's cries lingered in my mind, somehow louder than the sounds of battle.

My vision filled with fragmented images of scarlet blood, copper skin, and raven hair like shattered stained glass windows. Blood pounded in my ears. My breath came in tight bursts. I wiped away hot tears and sweat from my face with my gloved hand. Men torched wigwams and watched them burn. The mighty river swept people and canoes over the falls, and the white water sparkled in the sun, mocking the horror.

Someone shouted, "King Philip is coming! Thousands with him! King Philip! Retreat! Retreat!" Fresh canoes landed, spilling armed Algonquian warriors onto the shore. Lieutenant Holyoke took his long sword in both hands and swung it like a scythe at three of them. I turned away in horror and scrambled up the hill, heading for the horses.

Praise be to God, our mounts remained where we'd left them, milling about in distress. I grabbed Scout's reins and swung into the saddle. Around me, dragoons and volunteers mounted and raced off in all directions before I could stop them. Captain Turner commanded we follow him, and many did.

"If you value your lives, follow me!" Hinsdell shouted. He turned his mount towards White Ash Swamp. Had he lost his mind? Had he not heard my cautions?

"No, not that way, Hinsdell!" I yelled. "They'll ambush you! Men, follow me! I know a trail!" But Hinsdell was already gone, leading his band toward the swamp, leaving me to save those who remained.

"By God's blood! This way! Make haste!" I cried. I guided Scout down a steep switchback toward the river, followed by a dozen men. My route was the less obvious way, and I kept

White Ash Swamp to our north. The dense forest rose to either side, glimpses of the river to our left between the trunks of pines and firs that reached like ship masts for the sky. I wiped my face and neck with my kerchief, soiling it with blood and sweat, then cast it aside, gritting my teeth to stop from retching again.

In the breeze, the lush green foliage cast dappled shadows that fluttered and tricked the eye, making me flinch at imagined warriors amongst the trees. We trotted alongst the winding trail. A trail Richard and I knew well. Long days spent hunting and trapping. A life that seemed to have belonged to someone else, in a distant time, and a different land.

Chapter Three
BEN

MAY 19, 1676

My band of men reached Hatfield long after sunset. We were thirsty and hungry, spattered with blood, mud, and sweat, our horses stumbling and their heads drooping. Through God's grace, our injuries were minor; my worst a sprained ankle suffered when I stumbled up the hill in retreat. I remained in the barn for a quarter-hour, trying to settle my nerves, taking my time unsaddling Scout, wiping her down, feeding and watering her.

Martha met me in the dooryard and took me in her arms. I rested my scruffy chin on her bare head, not speaking, basking in her warmth. Only her cloak covered her shift, her light brown hair long and loose about her shoulders. She'd been readying for bed.

I held her tightly, overcome by both relief and exhaustion.

"Thank God you're back," she murmured into my chest, then pulled away. She stared at the dried blood and gasped.

"Are you hurt?" Her hands fumbled with the hooks of my buff coat.

I gently grasped her wrists. "No, 'tis not my blood."

Her gaze was wide and bright. She pulled me inside the house.

I limped to a stool and removed my weaponry, handing it to John Allis, who carried it away to clean and store it safely. Martha soaked a towel in a tub of water, and then wrung it out. She sat beside me and dabbed at the blood on my buff coat, biting her lip and keeping her gaze fixed on her task. I submitted to her ministrations willingly, grateful to be cared for. When she was satisfied, she unhooked my coat and helped me out of it.

Blood from my buff coat stained her white shift. I reached out and foolishly tried to wipe it clean. She shook her head.

"I'm sorry," I said.

"I have another."

She bent to pull off my boots, and I stayed her hand.

"Easy, love. My right ankle is sprained."

She gently eased off my boots and dried them, my stockings, and my buff coat by the fire. Taking a clean shift from the cupboard, she went to the bedchamber to change.

Goodwife Mary Allis was still in her cap, her wrinkled hands worrying her apron. "Goodman Waite, 'tis a joy to see you safe. John is home, thanks be to God."

She hesitated, then asked, "Do you have news of my husband or our son William?" Her expression bespoke both hope and fear.

"Goodwife, your husband and his men were close by when we passed through Deerfield on our return. I did not see your son, but we were separated on retreat. I'm sure they are still on their way." I was not sure, but it was what she yearned to hear.

John Allis and his wife Rachel conversed in hushed tones whilst she darned stockings and he gazed into the fire. He'd already changed out of his coat, washed up. Their four babes and my three girls lay strewn about the floor, piled on pallets and quilts, fast asleep. A vision rose unbidden to my mind, of the Great Falls' camp, the dead bodies of children. A sob caught in my throat, and I shuddered.

"Goodman Waite, there's porridge on the fire," Goodwife Allis said. "Also, a cauldron of fresh water on the hearth, a sponge and towel besides so you can wash."

I took off my doublet and shirt, bathed myself in the soothing water, and dried off. Martha returned wearing a fresh shift and handed me a clean nightshirt. I donned it and removed my breeches. We sat at the board, and I rested my sore ankle on a chair. The porridge of oats and samp and honey slid down my throat, hot and sweet.

The family's Bible lay before me. I opened it, seeking solace or chastisement. I found the verse I sought in Kings and read it silently.

"But the children of those that did slay him, he slew not, according to that which is written in the book of the Law of Moses; wherein the Lord commanded, saying, 'The fathers shall not be put to death for the children, nor the children put to death for the fathers: but every man shall be put to death for his own sin."

Stark proof we had sinned. Though I'd spared the mother and child, the bloodstains on my coat and my wife's shift bore witness to the battle and the innocent children slain. I closed the Bible and reached across the table, taking Martha's hands in mine. "I love you," I whispered.

"And I, you," she replied, and then, "The blood . . ."

"Hush, I'm here. I'm safe."

We lay by the hearth on a pallet stuffed with corn husks and goose feathers, and she pulled the woolen blanket over us. I wrapped her in my arms, breathing the soft scent of lavender at the nape of her neck. I prayed for the safety of the men who'd followed Hinsdell, Turner, and Holyoke, and fell asleep to gentle sounds of snoring and the whisper of flames on the hearth.

&

I awoke to the patter of little feet and the laughter and wailing of children. I was relieved to find Lieutenant Allis had returned in the night, though he was exhausted and bore a nasty bruise on his upper back from the blunt head of a tomahawk. He'd not seen his son William.

Throughout that day and the next, men straggled home to Hatfield and Hadley, bearing tales of God's providence and power, of triumph or despair. As I'd feared, Hinsdell had made a grievous error and led his detachment into White Ash Swamp, thinking it a shortcut. They'd mired in the mud, and Algonquians hiding in the deadwood and thick reeds had killed them all. Seven good men and my fellow scout, gone. Why had he not listened to my counsel?

The warriors had ambushed Captain Turner and his company as they'd forded the Green River. His riderless horse returned in the night.

Martha and I sat vigil alongside the Allis family. Whether from the exhaustion of battle or deep sorrow, I fell ill with a fever and took to bed, lost in fitful slumber, waking only to sip hot broth and shake off nightmares. I was dimly aware of the others in the house, patiently cooking the meals, sweeping the floors, and darting glances out the doorways and down the street at every hoofbeat. Martha brought rags soaked in cool well water and laid them on my forehead and throbbing ankle.

After two full days and nights, I left my bed and was confronted by the grim toll of the battle. William Allis had yet to come home. Martha's best friend Hannah had lost her father, Sergeant John Dickinson. Hannah's husband Samuel Gillette, the Reverend Hope Atherton, and our fifer Jonathan Wells were among the missing.

Some heaped gratefulness at my feet for leading my band of men back safely, but I brushed their praise aside, muttering something about God's hand. Whatever part I'd played had been my duty, and I felt more shame than pride in it. We'd been vain to think we'd end King Philip's War with one battle, yet we'd forged ahead, slaughtering women, children, and elders, and lost many good Englishmen.

On May 22, a small band of men traveled to the Falls to search for those who might have survived the battle, and to bury our dead. Filled with grief and the foreboding of more pain to come, I accompanied them.

Chapter Four

MARTHA

May 22, 1676

Benjamin left on horseback before noon alongside Sergeant Joseph Kellogg, Hannah's cousin Nathaniel Foote, Reverend Russell of Hadley, and the Narragansetts, Pessacus and Pumham. I watched from the stoop as they trotted off down the street. They took three extra mounts, saddled, bridled, and laden with bandages and poultices, canteens of fresh water, and long-handled spades. Steam rose from the road, a reminder of the evening's shower, slowly hiding them from view. I worried about the spades.

"Where is Daddy going?" my Mary asked, coming up behind me and taking my hand.

"To help some friends, love. And I must visit Goodwife Gillette and Goodwife Dickinson. You stay here and play with Abigail. Help Goodwife Allis, and mind Mattie and Sally."

Mary, ever obedient, nodded her little head, golden curls bobbing beneath her cap.

I fastened my brown cloak and put my arm through the willow handle of my basket. Beneath a checkered cloth I'd placed fresh eggs, a loaf of corn pone, a slab of bacon, and two jars of asparagus and beef soup, a favorite of Hannah's. Her family was garrisoned across the lane in her parents' house. I crossed the flowered dooryard and steeled myself for my task by reciting a Psalm under my breath, "The Lord is near unto them that are of a contrite heart and will save those afflicted in spirit." The door was already draped in black and barred. I rapped gently and heard the bolt slide back.

"Martha!" Hannah smiled weakly and pulled me inside, taking the basket. She wore her black Sabbath gown, and her brown eyes were puffy from weeping. My heart ached for her.

She peeked under the cloth. "Oh, how lovely. Your hens do lay such perfect eggs. And the men relish your corn pone! Here, take the loaf to them, won't you? Let me put the soup on, we'll have it for dinner."

Hannah's brothers, Nathaniel and John, and her uncle Obadiah Dickinson had just returned from helping families of Hatfield's slain and wounded and missing. Dirt and tears caked their faces. Obadiah washed and dried his hands, then took the loaf of sweet golden bread. I greeted his wife, Sarah, who sat by the window, her children and Hannah's gathered 'round her feet. She read to the elder ones from the Bible, and the wee babes sucked on bits of honeycomb and rags dipped in goat's milk to keep them from fussing.

Goodwife Dickinson sat at the board with her daughters, shelling fresh peas and dabbing at tears with a handkerchief. Deep in mourning, without even her husband's body to lay to rest. The four girls bent over letters they were writing to their kin in Connecticut, no doubt sharing the doleful tidings of their father's death.

I could never keep sorted the names of Hannah's four younger sisters, all youthful, all teen in years, and it was more difficult today as all wore black mourning clothes. I knew their names but mixed them up, as I was wont to do. At times, my thoughts and speech seemed at cross purposes, leading me to misspeak, especially when distressed. I took a deep breath and let it out slowly.

I sat beside Goodwife Dickinson and offered my condolences.

"Sergeant Dickinson was a brave and wonderful man," I said, taking her thin hand in mine. "I knew him to be kind to all in need. Ben spoke highly of him, and desired me to convey to you he died a hero . . ."

"Thank you, Martha, for your comfort. 'Tis hard to bear up, with my John slain in battle and no word of Hannah's husband, Samuel."

Hannah rested a hand on her mother's shoulder, then looked at her aunt.

"Sarah, thank you for keeping an eye on our wee ones. Martha and I are going out to the garden to chat." Sarah looked up from the Bible and nodded.

Hannah and I strolled to the south side of the house, where the garden flourished under her loving care. Vining tendrils and purple blossoms of peas and beans draped the fence, amid the luscious big leaves of grapes. Hannah's checkerboard of herbs was the centerpiece of the garden, and last night's rain had released their sweet fragrances into the air: mint, rosemary, thyme, and sage. Between the fence and the herbs grew carrots, turnips, parsnips, and fat round cabbages. Pumpkin vines' yellow flowers opened in the sun.

We sat side by side on an old wooden bench beneath an apple tree. Honeybees darted about in the snowy blossoms above our heads.

"Martha," Hannah began, "my cousin Nathaniel has gone with Benjamin and the others. Dare I hope for my husband Samuel's deliverance?"

I picked through my thoughts like I picked through dried beans before tossing them in the soup broth, choosing my words carefully.

"Those who saw your father and others slain did not mention Samuel," I said. "Have faith."

Hannah sighed deeply. "Perhaps he's on his way?"

"'Tis likely. The fifer Welles returned only yesterday. The dragoons have been straggling into town, one or two at a time. Perhaps Samuel will be amongst them," I said.

My clumsy words did not comfort her, for Hannah began to weep. "I feel God has forsaken me. My griefs only multiply. My firstborn, my father, my husband . . . how have I sinned? For what am I being punished?"

"Hannah, tragedy is not always punishment. At times it is a test of our faith." *Or just a tragic happenstance*, I wanted to add, but I bit my tongue on the blasphemy.

"How do you bear it, the loss of your father?" she asked me.

She knew my grief was fresh. Algonquians had slain my father in Springfield scarcely two months before.

"I know I was a good daughter to him, as you were to yours," I said. "I hold fast to my memories, and my faith that we will meet again in Heaven. But I admit I also cling to my fear and anger."

I kept my arm around her frail shoulders as she wept.

Hannah wiped her eyes and gazed into the distance. "I was a good daughter, but I am not an obedient wife, at least my husband does not think so. He . . ."

"Yes?"

She shrugged. "Perhaps 'tis wicked to speak thus, but our marriage is . . . troubled."

"No one's marriage is perfect," I said. "'Tis not wicked to say so."

"But my tears for Samuel are perhaps for . . . release, from what I endure."

"Endure?"

"He is cruel, privily. I know a wife must obey, but his

demands are often . . . excessive, and when I fail to please him, he . . . harms me."

"Oh, Hannah, I'm so sorry." *How had I not suspected such?* I sat beside her on the bench, gripping her hand in mine, my thoughts buzzing in tune with the bees above us, my head bent in silent prayer for her.

⁊⁊

Reverend Atherton stumbled into town that afternoon, pulling the longbow with his tale of deliverance. He shared anecdotes to all who lent him their ear and promised to make a proper sermon for the Sabbath.

Late at night, Ben and the others came home. They carried a few injured men on the horses, but they'd not brought back any of the dead, and Ben wouldn't explain why, only that they'd dug graves in a clearing on a hill above the falls. He said it was a peaceful place, surrounded by trees and scattered with wildflowers. Among the dead was Samuel Gillette, and I despaired how Hannah's tangled feelings might unwind when she learnt of it.

Ben and I waited until everyone was sound asleep before we made love for the first time since he'd returned from the battle. He was desperately tender at first, as though I might break under his touch. Yet I burned with desire to weld him to me, a fire melting gold, and soon his lust overcame him, the heat of our passion binding us together.

Afterwards, we lay in the firelight, face to face. Tears welled in Ben's eyes, but when I touched my fingertips to his lashes, he pulled my hand away and kissed my palm. I asked him to share his sorrow with me, but he shook his head. Closing his eyes, he held my hands in his until our breathing slowed and our hearts beat as one in slumber.

Chapter Five

MARTHA

The meeting house was overflowing and the seating committee quite vexed by complaints from those obliged to sit on stools in the alleyways or stand in the back. I smiled and glanced across the aisle to catch Benjamin's blue-eyed gaze. He gave me a wink, then ran a hand through his golden hair. The seating committee had assigned us new seats in the third row in tribute to Ben's valor in safely leading his men home from the Falls Fight. The honor pleased me, though Ben seemed uneasy with it.

Mary sat quietly by my side, her little hands folded in her lap, humming a sweet hymn. To my other side was our Mattie, worrying the braids of her cornhusk doll, sucking her thumb, swinging her feet, and driving me to distraction. Sally, thank the Lord, was soft asleep in my arms. Reverend Atherton's words flowed over me.

"I have passed through the Valley of the Shadow of Death, and both the rod and staff of God delivered me," he said in his booming voice. "On the morning following the night we went out against the enemy, a gun was discharged against me. The Lord diverted the bullet, so no harm was done to me. When I was separated from the army, none pursued me, as if God had given the heathen a charge, saying, 'Let him alone.'"

Mattie kicked the bench in front of us, and Goodwife Billings turned around and glared.

"Mattie, hold still," I whispered.

"The next day, I was encompassed with enemies . . . I expected they would have laid hands upon me, but they did not. I believe they were restrained by the hand of God from doing the least injury to me. God always can, and sometimes doth, set bounds unto the wrath of man."

Reverend Atherton raised his arm above his head and held up two fingers.

"Two things I must not pass over that are matters of thanksgiving unto God; the first is that when my strength was far spent, I passed through deep waters, and they overflowed me not, according to those gracious words of Isaiah. The second is that I subsisted for three days without food.

"God's providence hath been so wonderful toward me, not because I have more wisdom than others, nor because I am more righteous than others, but because it so pleased God."

"Amen," I whispered.

Had Reverend Atherton waded the Connecticut River? Surely not. Yet he had survived three nights in the wilderness and the battle at Bloody Brook eight months ago. Perhaps he *was* more righteous than others, as befit his calling.

Sun streamed through the small clear windows, etching brilliant diamonds on the white-washed walls. We sang the Psalms from the Bay Psalm Books. I loved to sing and was pleased with the reverend's choices. The Psalm of David refreshed my heart.

"Lord, I'll praise, with all my heart, thy wonders I'll proclaim.
I will be glad and joy in thee, most high, I'll sing thy name.
In turning back my foes, they'll fall and perish at thy sight.

For thou maintain my right and cause, in thrones fits judging right."

The morning sermon concluded. The men and boys rose and filed out first, followed by the women and girls. Dinner was held on the common within the stockade. Men laid boards atop barrels and trestles, and women placed linens upon the boards and refreshments atop the linens. Despite the lovely day and the uplifting morning sermon, our hearts were heavy, for we knew the afternoon's sermon would honor the many men who lost their lives at the Falls Fight.

I wanted Ben to tell me more of what had happened there, but he was uncharacteristically silent. I'd heard that our men and soldiers killed hundreds of the River Indians. We mourned many: Samuel Gillett, Sergeant John Dickinson, Will Allis, Captain Turner, John Colfax, John Church, and Ben's fellow scout Experience Hinsdell. In addition, the River Indians had slain a dozen or more men from Lancaster, Springfield, Hartford, and Northampton. Ben's fears before the attack had been well-founded.

My thoughts worried Ben's secrets in the same way Mattie worried her doll's braids. My heart tried to fill the empty silences between his words and the gaps in his telling. Those ghosts and shadows frightened me, for they'd opened a chasm between us.

Chapter Six
THE SACHEM ASHPELON

THE FLOWER MOON

Let me tell you a story. Our people tell stories to offer wisdom. I have read some of your John Elliot Bible, and I know your Bible also tells stories to offer wisdom.

I am Ashpelon, brother of Mugwump, and a cousin of Metacomet, who was renamed by you as King Philip. I once traded furs with the French and English, and hence learned their languages, both spoken and unspoken. I was chosen to be the Sachem of my small band of Nipmucs, Pocumtucks and Norwottucks; "River Indians" as the colonists call us, and my cousin has convinced me it is now time to join him in his war. Listen to my story. Then you may better understand what will happen today and in days to come.

Long ago, the Chief of the Squirrel Tribe was passing through the woods to see how all the little squirrels were faring, and if they were laying up their store of nuts for the winter. One of the squirrels he visited was Jonisgyont, who lived all alone in a hollow tree. On one side of him lived Frog, and on the other side, Woodchuck.

Jonisgyont was puzzled, for he saw that his stock of nuts was growing smaller, though he worked hard to gather his nuts from the big hickory-nut tree, which was far away, because it had the sweetest nuts. When he returned from his trips to the tree, his cheeks full of nuts, he found fewer nuts in his storehouse than when he had left. He began to have suspicions.

One evening, Jonisgyont said to Frog and Woodchuck, "Neighbors, there is a thief about. Someone has been stealing my store of nuts." Frog and Woodchuck could not imagine who would do such a thing.

The Chief of the Squirrel Tribe overheard this conversation, and he began to have his suspicions, too. That night, when Jonisgyont was asleep, the Chief saw Woodchuck digging a hole and filling it with hickory nuts, which he was taking from the hollow tree where Jonisgyont kept them. Then the Chief went to the marsh, where Frog sat on the mossy bank. As he watched, Frog lifted the moss and tucked a quantity of nuts underneath it, and then returned to the same hollow tree to get more.

The next night the Chief of the Squirrel Tribe held a council, and all the forest people attended. He told them what he had seen, and they said they would look for themselves to see if it was true. So they all went to the hollow tree, and saw Jonisgyont's small pile of nuts, and then the large piles of nuts in Woodchuck's hole and under Frog's moss, and asked them to explain, but they refused.

So the Chief of the Squirrels said he would judge. "I pronounce each of you guilty of stealing from Jonisgyont. You are both fat and lazy and must be punished. Frog, all you must do is stick out your tongue to catch food, yet you stole from Jonisgyont. Your punishment is that you will lose all your teeth, so that you can no longer eat nuts."

Frog hopped away, and with each hop, he lost another tooth, until they all were gone.

"And Woodchuck, you sleep through the winter and do not even need the nuts you stole from Jonisgyont. Your punishment will be that you will now live only on plants. Both meat and nuts shall be forbidden to you."

Woodchuck lumbered home in disgrace.

"Jonisgyont," the Chief of the Squirrels said, "the forest people are sorry for you, so I shall give you a gift that will help you move swiftly from tree to tree, so that you can gather more nuts, and hasten home when you are in danger."

Then the Chief of the Squirrels spread a web of skin from Jonisgyont's forelegs to his back legs, to form wings when he leapt, so that he could fly. And so that is why we have flying squirrels. That is also why those who work hard and treat others honestly receive their just reward, but those who are greedy and selfish are punished.

As English often do not understand, let me make my meaning clear, like the sunlight on snow or the water flowing in the river. I am like the Chief of the Squirrels, and my people work hard to survive. You are like the Frog and the Woodchuck, lazy and dishonest, taking from us what is not yours. But soon, you will be punished. And then we will fly away, like Jonisgyont. You will not hurt us again.

Chapter Seven

BEN

May 30, 1676

"Blasted crows!" Samuel Foote exclaimed. He picked up one of the stones our plow had overturned and heaved it at the flock. They flew off, cawing, to the old elm tree, where they perched and scolded us.

"Aye, we barely plant the corn seed, and they swoop down to eat it." I reined in my brace of oxen, removing my hat and mopping my brow.

"We need scarecrows," Samuel said. "When we go home for dinner, I'll ask my goodwife to make some."

"If the crows aren't afraid of us, what makes you think they'll be afraid of stuffed rag dolls on posts?" I said, laughing.

"May be worth a try, is what I'm saying," Samuel said.

We were keen to plant the last of the corn in the next few weeks so we could harvest before the first frost, which by Poor Robin's Almanack would be early this year. But today the weather was glorious. The sky washed blue from last night's showers, big puffs of white clouds like a flock of sheep making their way south. It was good to be out in the fields again, to put the horror of the massacre at Great Falls behind me.

Our families were secure within the stockade, mine still with the Allis family. Men hadn't ventured out to work the fields until today, and most of us carried a pistol or musket. Some of us—myself included—continued our petition to enlarge the stockade, but many in Hatfield and Hadley thought the expense and labor unnecessary. They chose to believe all the Native tribes had fled to Canada or been killed at Great Falls barely ten days ago, despite evidence to the contrary. After the battle, our search party saw at least a dozen Nipmucs at the ruins of their camp. Like us, they were burying their dead, and at my request, we let them alone.

I gazed at the horizons around us, the shimmer of the river to the east, ribbons of stone walls crisscrossing pastures of green to our west, and the cooking fires' smoke rising above the stockade of our little town. I was ever watchful, a trait born of years sailing in Rhode Island, studying the weather and the tides, watching for reefs, heeding the thunder of the surf at night telling me I was too close to shore.

Just by, my neighbors planted corn, wheat, and flax, tilling furrows in parallel arcs following the gentle rise and fall of the land, their plowshares releasing the smell of rich, moist earth. I'd earned praise for my scouting, fighting, and well-executed retreat at the Falls, but I took pride in what I'd sought to protect—land of my own to farm, a loving family, true friends. A peaceful life.

'Twas kind of Samuel to help me sow my crop, especially as my ankle still had me limping, but he was distractible. I was obliged to halt my plow at times so he could catch up. He threw more stones at the crows than corn into the furrows.

"The sooner we cover the seed with soil, the sooner the crows will leave," I said to him. "Maybe less complaining and more sowing so we can get done in time for supper."

"They'll leave, but they'll be back once *we* leave. Clever rascals know just when we aren't watching them," Samuel said.

I glimpsed a flicker of movement, something or someone creeping on the far side of the nearest stone wall. The flock of crows startled and burst from the elm tree in a flurry of wings and caws. I eased the oxen to a halt, hissed at Samuel and put a finger to my lips, bidding him be silent.

To my dismay, I spied a second shape through the fence rails. I drew my pistol, cocked it, and pressed my back against the broad, warm flank of my ox. Samuel crept to the other side of the team. I listened to the huffing of the oxen and the whisper of the breeze.

"I saw movement," I whispered to Samuel, "behind the wall and the fence. I hope 'tis but foxes."

We waited a few minutes. Whatever I'd seen had vanished, but I was ill at ease. I half-cocked my pistol and holstered it. "Let's drive these two beasts back to the pasture and head home early. We can tend to the hogs and spread some manure in the gardens. Maybe I'll take Scout for a ride beside the Connecticut."

"You're that bothered? Seems a shame to cease our labors, with the weather so nice." Samuel shrugged and climbed up beside me on the ox cart. I slapped the reins, and Brownie and Patch ambled toward the pasture.

The corn could wait or go to the crows for all I cared. If any trait made me a valued scout, it was an awareness of my surroundings. The sudden silence of crows. Shadows darting behind stone walls. The increase in the faint scent of smoke. And then I saw it.

A roiling black cloud churned above our town, consuming the fragile wisps of smoke from lazy cooking fires.

Samuel and I leapt from the ox cart, abandoning the oxen, racing home on foot. *Dear God*, I prayed, *please protect us. Please spare my wife and girls*.

Our lungs were fit to bursting, and my ankle throbbing, as Samuel and I scrambled over the last fence and stopped dead at the highway to Northampton. A line of Algonquians blocked our way. Even from a distance, I knew them from their tribal dress—Nipmucs, Pocumtucks, Norwottucks, and a few Narragansett. River Indians. My pistol was drawn and cocked. Their muskets were aimed at our hearts.

Hundreds more Natives circled the burning stockade, armed with tomahawks and guns, many astride horses I recognized as ours, driven off a fortnight ago. They wanted to hold us at bay, forcing us to watch our homes and the stockade burn as we feared for our wives and children. More Englishmen joined us, but none dared draw against muskets cocked and aimed.

"By God's wounds!" I swore, angry tears springing to my eyes. If the fire destroyed the stockade and the enemy breached it, all would be lost.

Although we'd mourned, we'd wasted much time since the Falls Fight basking in our presumed victory. Bragging at our sermons, eagerly sending the troops back to Connecticut. How quickly we'd moved on from what happened. From the unarmed people we'd slaughtered. And now, our righteous God would punish our prideful satisfaction. In our arrogance, we'd thought the worst of it over. But the Algonquians had not forgotten nor forgiven.

MARTHA

"Mommy, is it over? Is the fire all gone?" Mary asked, putting her thumb back in her mouth. She hadn't sucked her thumb since she was weaned.

It seemed years had passed, but 'twas only an hour, and the silence the attack left behind was like the pause between a flash of lightning and the clap of thunder, when one holds their breath, counting and waiting. I peered through the thick panes of the Allis's front window at the empty street.

"Yes, love, 'tis gone," I said, though I was not certain.

The Footes and Dickinsons sheltered with us at the Allis's home. Our own house was likely burned. It was the farthest one to the north, still beyond the stockade despite Ben's petition to protect it. The thought deeply saddened me.

God had sent the Natives to punish us. For the failed peace treaties and our cattle in their cornfields and whatever horrors we committed at the Falls Fight, those secrets that woke Ben from his dreams, shaking, and clouded his eyes when I asked about it.

Mary Foote, the newly widowed Hannah, and I comforted our little ones with maple sugar loaves and cider, and sang lullabies to them whilst we kept our eyes riveted on the front door, waiting on our men. Obadiah Dickinson and Lieutenant Allis helped draw buckets of water to put out the fires and posted guards at what remained of the stockade.

A pounding on the door. I leapt from my stool, a lump in my throat.

"Martha!" Ben called, his voice hoarse and tight.

I lifted the bar and threw open the door. Ben stumbled inside and into my waiting arms, Samuel Foote behind him. I clung to my husband, buried my face in his shirt, and wept.

A sob caught in his whisper. "Oh, dear God, Martha."

"Ben," I managed before I choked back my tears and looked up at him. His blue eyes were bright with fear. His face streaked by ashes, tears, and sweat. He held his dark felt hat, his blonde hair tousled. Holding him tight, I kissed him deeply, as if it were night and the children asleep.

"Ben, how fare the other men? Is anyone hurt?" I asked as I led him by the hand to a chair at the board and fetched him a pint of cider. He gulped it down and wiped his mouth on his sleeve. Samuel Foote, his wife Mary, and Hannah clustered by the hearth.

"The enemy blocked us, we tried to come for you, but they'd already drawn on us. We couldn't . . ." Ben's voice caught again.

"Men from Hadley crossed the river," I said. "They forced the Indians to retreat before they could breach the stockade. The enemy never came within the fence." I took his hands in mine, our fingers interlacing.

"God was protecting us, Martha." Ben took another swig of cider.

"Was this revenge? For the Falls Fight?" I asked gently.

Ben shook his head. "If so, God's hand restrained them, or they'd have not turned back at the stockade."

Chapter Eight
MARTHA

June 5, 1676

Dear Mother,
Thank you for your letter.
God spared our lives once again, yet much work must be done. The men are sifting through the ashes of the homes outside the stockade, gathering up cooking kettles, tankards, ploughs, anvils, and whatever other bits weren't consumed by fire. This morning, they began rebuilding the houses and barns. Our barn was destroyed and our home well-damaged. We lost our oxen—the River Indians slaughtered and dismembered them in the field. Thankfully, our horse Scout was safe in the Allis's barn.
Benjamin says this might not be the last of it—some things most wicked must have happened at the Falls Fight, yet no one will speak of it. The Governor of New York set aside land near Albany for the River Indians, hoping they'd join with the Mahicans to protect New York from the Abenaki. I pray that will put an end to this war.
Major Pynchon is sending his Hartford troops to garrison our town again, which seems a case of "once the steed is stolen, bolt the stable door." I pray daily for our village, our kin, and you and my brothers and sisters in Springfield.
Your loving daughter, Martha

AUGUST 20, 1676

My Dearest Mother,
Thank you for your letter in July. Rebecca continues my lessons on the
cittern, and I can pluck out a few songs to sing—"Over the Hills and Far
Away" and "The Water is Wide." I also am learning to dance, as our
selectmen are loosening their strictest laws against it. I know you still
frown upon dancing, yet it is becoming popular in Boston. Times change.
It is a time of rejoicing—King Philip was killed! May he pay forever for
his sins. Some have traveled to see his head displayed on a pike, but I have
no stomach for it.
Benjamin and our friends have rebuilt our barn and repaired our home.
We now have stairs to a full second story overhanging the front and a
lean-to behind!
Our girls are growing as quickly as the corn. Mary is learning to read,
and Mattie is learning to control her impish spirit. When mischief over-
whelms her, she and Benjamin have foot races in the lane. He allows her
to win from time to time, which causes her much glee. Little Sally is now
toddling about and chattering like a magpie.
I miss you. Please write again when you are moved to do so.
Your loving daughter, Martha

Chapter Nine

BEN

HATFIELD
A YEAR LATER—MAY 15, 1677

After a full year of uneasy peace, the wedding of Martha's best friend, the widow Hannah Dickinson Gillette, to a new member of our congregation, Stephen Jennings of Connecticut, was a much-anticipated celebration. I was curious to make Stephen's acquaintance. Martha had met him a fortnight ago. She commented on his red hair and gentle manner, and found him pleasing. But then, Martha tends to see only the best in everyone.

Hannah and Stephen planned to marry at Hannah's home. Rumors—spread largely by my wife—hinted there might be music and dancing. It remained to be seen if the selectmen would allow it. Having declared the wedding a feast day, it seemed they might.

Martha bustled the girls and me about in the morning, fussing over clothes and hair until I'd laughed and reminded her that vanity is a sin. She countered that she merely wanted us to appear respectable. I washed up, trimmed my beard, and wore my red leather doublet. Martha had sewn herself an indigo-blue frock, adding a bit of lace on her cuffs and collar and laces that tied down the curve of her back. All of these were vanities I found quite charming, although I hoped they'd not cost me a sumptuary fine from the censorious Puritan watch.

"Will there be music, do you think? Perhaps even dancing?" she asked hopefully.

"If Goodman Partridge has sold as much of his fine Portuguese wine to the Dickinsons as he claims, I'd think it a sound wager."

"Mary, Mattie, time to leave!" Martha called. "Ben, carry Sally, please?"

Hannah's house was newly freshened for the wedding. Sunlight poured through sparkling clean windows onto the gleaming planks of the sand-scrubbed floor. Tapers burned cheerily in silver candlesticks on the mantle, which was draped in garlands of ivy and roses. Someone had covered the boards in checkered blue and white linens and centered them with sprays of pink cherry blossoms in pewter tankards. The air smelt of vinegar, spice, and flowers.

Despite our attempts to arrive early, quite a few people had already assembled, and cheerful conversation permeated the room. I set Sally down, and she toddled off with Mary and Mattie to listen to Hannah's sister Rebecca playing a lullaby on a lute.

Hannah and Stephen faced each other before the hearth, and Selectman Belding took his place by the flickering embers. Hannah was nearly as tall as Stephen, so they gazed directly into each other's eyes.

"Does she not look beautiful?" Martha whispered in my ear. "Stephen traded with one of John Pynchon's men in Springfield for the watered wine grogram for her gown."

I raised my eyebrows in question.

"Grogram. Spun silk and wool."

"Ah," I said. "Yes, she's lovely. It brings to mind the vision of loveliness you were on our wedding day."

Martha smiled at our shared memory. "The Reverend Atherton's first Hatfield wedding banns, his first sermons in our new church. Seems only yesterday."

Martha had retrieved Sally from Rebecca and gently bounced her in her arms, making those soft cooing noises only doves and mothers seem to know.

"You wish to speak?" Selectman Belding asked the couple.

"A few words," Stephen said, and took Hannah's hands in his. "Hannah, my heart thou hast had before, now here's my hand, to continue yours till death. Be assured my love and loyalty shall be inseparable."

"And the bride?" Belding asked, almost in a whisper, a frown tightening his lips.

Hannah nodded, and in a gentle voice, she spoke. "Be thou that art my better part, a seal impressed upon my heart, may I my finger's signet prove, for Death is not more strong than Love."

Murmurs of surprise, some in approval and some not, spread through the assembly. The bride and groom were breaking with tradition, veering toward heresy, by speaking their own vows.

"Do you, Stephen Jennings, take Hannah Dickinson Gillette to be your wife?" asked Belding, back on more familiar ground.

"I do."

"And do you, Hannah Dickinson Gillette, take Stephen Jennings to be your husband?"

"I do."

Selectman Belding waited expectantly. Stephen slid a gold ring on Hannah's finger.

"Then, by the laws of Massachusetts Bay Colony and Hampshire County, I now pronounce you man and wife."

Rebecca played the old English tune, "A Shepherd's Holiday," and the Reverend's big voice, halting but still resonant, read the Song of Degrees. I spoke the words as Martha sang them, her voice lovely as always.

> *"Thy wife shall be as the fruitful vine, on the sides of thine*
> *house doth grow,*
> *And thy children like the olive plants round about thy table, lo*
> *Surely thus shall the man be blessed,*
> *That feareth in the Lord."*

As our voices faded, Obadiah Dickinson, Hannah's uncle, proclaimed, "A toast to the bride and groom!" He lifted a glass of the Portuguese berry-red sack. The rest of us poured ourselves a glass of whatever we fancied. A few even dropped in a crumb of toasted bread before they raised it. We hallooed, clinked our glasses, and drank to the happy couple.

Stephen Jennings and Hannah asked us to sit across from them. As Martha said, Stephen had a bit of Irish about him, kind green eyes and dark red hair he wore in the longer fashion. He was humble and soft-spoken, like his new bride. I liked his straightforward manner as he told me about his trade as a shoemaker in Hartford and his hopes for opening a shop here. We spoke of our horses, the farm chores we'd yet to do, and last year's attack on our town.

Hannah's sisters brought 'round platters of ham and fowl and mutton, and we passed trenchers of creamed corn and peas, hearty brown bread, and tankards of ale and apple cider. For dessert, we enjoyed the traditional bride's cake soaked in rum and spiced with cloves, nutmeg, and raisins.

When we'd done feasting, we pushed the boards and trestles off to the sides of the room, rolled up the rugs, and musicians took their places. Rebecca poised her fingers on her lute,

Tom tucked his fiddle under his chin, and Jonathan Welles raised the piccolo to his lips.

Obadiah appointed himself host and dance caller and stood up from his table.

"Though our faith be steadfast, our outward expression of it may change over time. Feel no shame in dancing today, rejoicing in the Glory of God and this happy occasion!"

Martha smiled and said, "Hannah told me Stephen bought the Playbook at a little shop in Springfield. 'Tis called *Playford's English Dancing Master*. My Mother calls it 'Church of England nonsense,' of course. I cannot wait to write and tell her of dancing today!"

"But we do not know the steps," I said, feeling out of my depth. The last time I'd danced was to a sea shanty onboard my father's boat.

"Obadiah will call them," she said, squeezing my hand reassuringly.

"I suppose it cannot be more difficult than our mustering drills," I said cheerily. "My dear lady, may I have this dance?" I bowed and held out my hand. Martha handed Sally off to Mary and curtsied.

"This first tune, 'Argeers,' four together," Obadiah called out. "Form two lines, facing your partner! Musicians, half time to start, hey?"

The steps formed patterns in lines and circles, and we joined and rejoined in trios and four squares. What we lacked in grace, we balanced with our enthusiasm.

"Meet all, take each other's Woman by both hands, two slips to the left, and two to the right!" Obadiah called out. "Change places, turn your own once and a half! Meet again, turn each other's Woman to your places, then turn your own!"

Martha's cheeks flushed, and the smile she gave me was radiant. 'Twas a trait I most loved, her joyful nature, despite all the hardships we endured in this frontier town. I was happy to join her in this rare but simple pleasure of music, dancing, and friends.

When we finally finished all the wine and cider and all the dances had been danced, we gathered our little ones and bid our friends good night. Walking home, little Sally asleep in my arms, Martha carrying a fussing Mattie, and sweet Mary skipping to keep up, I thanked God for my family and friends and prayed He would give us many more days such as this.

Chapter Ten

BEN

SEPTEMBER 19, 1677

"I'm off to the corn fields, my love." It pleased me greatly to be settled in our own rebuilt home. To grab my hat from the peg by our own front door.

"A kiss before you go? And do not forget your costrel of water; 'tis hot out o' doors for September," Martha said.

I kissed her, holding her longer than I first intended, my hands roaming her back, her hands stroking my hair. The swell of her belly pressed against me, our fourth child.

"'Tis hot inside, too," I whispered gruffly, breaking free before I forgot myself.

Martha smiled and handed me the water pouch. I considered whether to take my musket or leave it hanging above the mantle. I resolved Martha was safer with it there, and I had my pistol. Despite over a year of peace, I prepared daily for the worst.

My last look at my family saw Martha hand Mary a broom and explain how to sweep the floor properly. Mattie and Sally sat nearby, playing pat a cake.

"Look, Daddy, I'm brooming!" Mary called proudly.

I tipped my hat to her and smiled, closing the door and waiting on our stoop until I heard Martha latch it behind me. Heading to our barn I admired our squash and pumpkins, ready for picking, some as big as Sally and twice the weight. I'd promised Martha I'd harvest them when I returned for dinner. It was unwise for her to toil in the gardens in her condition, though she'd already gathered most of the cabbages, turnips, and parsnips for pickling.

Our new barn was better than the one the River Indians burned the year before. It had a stall for Scout and plenty of room for our hay, shelter for the cows each night, and in the winter for the sheep. When she heard me unlatch the barn door, Scout raised her head from feeding and nickered a greeting. I brushed her dusty red coat as she finished her morning oats, harnessed her, and hitched her to our new wagon.

Sergeant Graves and John Graves, my old friend Timothy's brother John Cooper, and another carpenter from Hadley waved to me as I set out. They were building a house next door for Sergeant Graves' son and bride-to-be. The town had raised the frame two days before, and now the men were attaching the common roof rafters from the purlin to the plate, hammering in the treenails.

"Looks shipshape!" I called up to them, where they clung to the beams like sailors to a ship's masts and boom.

"Does it? Perhaps we'll build an ark next!" John Cooper shouted.

I laughed, accustomed to being teased for my seafaring expressions, the habit born from being raised in Rhode Island by a fisherman. Many here in the valley had never seen the ocean. I sometimes missed the briny smell of the sea, a bracing breeze, and a boat's calm rocking lulling me to sleep. Sadly, those memories were tangled up with the drowning death of my brother Joseph, so I let them rest.

My house and all those south to Middle Lane remained

beyond the stockade fence. It vexed me that my home remained exposed, but since King Philip's death a year ago, most believed all threat was gone. Of course, most lived within the stockade. They'd fallen back to the habit of leaving the gate open during the day, only shutting and latching it on the coldest winter nights to keep the wolves from our doors. I had half a mind to close it myself, but Samuel Foote and Stephen Jennings were waiting for me.

I reached them, and they walked alongside the wagon. We turned right onto Middle Lane and headed through the fence gate, securely latching it behind us. I'd forgotten once and paid a considerable fine, understandably, as we did not want our cows in the corn, so to speak. It seemed we should have a law about the stockade gates, too.

We turned south, the morning sun casting long, crisp shadows beside us. Our lots weren't adjacent, but we helped each other with the harvest, and today, we were working my corn field. It lay just beyond Middle Lane and stretched south to the curve of Millbrook. We met many other men of our town, also on their way to harvest their crops.

"Mary is looking forward to the husking bee, hurried me out the door this morning with strict orders to pick bushels of corn," Samuel said.

"Hannah also," Stephen said. "She's making cornhusk dolls for Holly and Sammy."

"There'll be enough husks for her to make a bushel of dolls," I said. "Have her make one for our new bairn. Martha's expecting this winter." I smiled at my tidings.

"Good news, Benjamin, well done!" Samuel slapped me on the back.

"My wife said Hannah's also with child, Stephen?" I asked.

"Aye, in the spring."

"Happy news!" I smiled at my friend and punched him on the arm for good measure.

"So, do you wish for boys or girls?" Samuel asked.

"Another girl and I'll have to take up pirating to raise the dowries," I said. "Ol' Captain Moseley made a good living at it, and I know my way 'round a boat." I laughed.

"But Captain Moseley isn't right in the head," Stephen said, frowning. "Turning a pack of dogs loose on that Natick Praying Indian, watching as they tore her to pieces."

Stephen's words quieted all of us, and opened up my wounds from what had happened at Great Falls. I was glad Stephen hadn't lived in Hatfield then, and so hadn't been at the Falls Fight to witness similar deeds. I shuddered as though a cold wind blew.

"Which do you fancy, Stephen?" Samuel asked, pushing through our sudden silence.

Stephen smiled. "I'm happy to have a wee one of my own, lad or lass, no matter."

We reached the fields, Mary Foote's trio of scarecrows grinning at us from a rustling sea of the corn's green blades and purple tassels. The first hints of yellow on the ash trees mottled the distant hills beneath a bright, clear sky. It had been a bountiful season, and we looked forward to plenty of food for the winter.

"A shame Reverend Atherton is no longer with us. I was looking forward to having him baptize our new babe," I said.

Reverend Atherton had passed away in June, a few weeks after Hannah's wedding. We had a new minister, Reverend Wise, but I missed Atherton. I hadn't realized to what extent the strength I took from my faith had come from the joy Hope Atherton took in guiding it. I felt somewhat at sea, spiritually, since his passing.

"He never recovered from the Falls Fight," I said. Nor had I. In body, yes, but not in spirit.

"His widow and Mary have become good friends," Samuel said. "The new reverend told her she might stay in the house as long as she needed."

"And she with the two wee babes," Stephen said, shaking his head.

I thought of a hellish world where Martha was left alone with our babes, and my mood darkened.

But the ripe corn beckoned, and we fell to picking, not talking. I eased into the rhythm of the labor, blotting out the world around me. *Reach into the blades, find a plump cob, bend it down, snap it up, and toss it in the sack.* After an hour, we stopped to rest.

By mid-morning, we were deep in the field, surrounded by a corn forest as tall as us. We hauled the full sacks back to the wagon two at a time to save trips, wearing a little path through the cornfield. Each time I heaved a load into the wagon, I stopped to look toward Hatfield.

I will forever regret that I assumed the distant cries I heard were the screams of hawks.

Chapter Eleven

MARTHA

SEPTEMBER 19, 1677, MORNING

Sally was napping, but Mattie and Mary followed me down the little path through the orchard. Just beyond our garden wall, the Graves brothers and the two carpenters clambered about on the new house like squirrels in a tree. Another wedding soon to come, Sarah White and young John Graves Junior.

Ben had promised to help me harvest the pumpkins, but I needed carrots for the soup, fennel seed, and sprigs of thyme to pickle with the cabbages. Mary and Mattie pulled up the carrots whilst I gathered the herbs, our garden graciously offering up its final bounty before slipping into slumber and then death beneath the winter snow.

It was growing near to Michaelmas, a day of rejoicing for the Church of England, but one we did not celebrate. I still used some feast days to mark the time. My habit came from stories my father told me when I was but Mary's age, stories his mother told him when he was a lad in Wales. Her parents —my great-grandmother Lady Plowden and my great-grandfather Sir Richard White—had lived in a splendid manor house and celebrated many holidays, and one of the grandest was the feast of Michaelmas.

When I listened to my father's stories of long ago, I imagined living in England at the time of his parents and grandparents, a lady's maid to help me don my beautiful silk and satin dresses. To sit by the fire and read Shakespeare's newly published sonnets. And to celebrate Michaelmas in late September, the board bearing a plump roast goose stuffed with quince, grapes, herbs and spices, fresh bannock bread, and blackberries. Doubtless, all were prepared by the cook and served by the servants. Lady Plowden had probably not picked as much as a sprig of rosemary in her high-born life.

When we returned to the house, little Abigail Allis was waiting at our door, asking for Mary. They skipped off happily together, hand in hand, and I looked after them, envying their childhood and missing my father.

I chopped up the carrots and onions, tossed them in the soup pot, and set the feathery carrot tops aside for the hogs. Mattie asked to help with the cabbages, so I sent her to the lean-to for them, put the pot on for chamomile tea, and set out my herbs, a few precious peppercorns, and the salt cellar. Mattie reappeared carrying one cabbage and rolling the other in front of her, nudging it with her shoe.

"Clever girl," I said, "Were the two of them more than you could carry?"

"Yes, Mama, so I rolled one!"

Laughing, I washed the cabbages, shredded them with my best blade, and sliced more onions. I poured vinegar into the pot on the fire, and Mattie added the herbs, salt, and pepper. Pungent aromas tickled our noses and made our eyes water, and Mattie scrunched up her face in a silly manner that made me laugh. When it was ready, I spooned the chopped cabbage into four ceramic pots, poured the hot brine over, and covered them in scraps of damp hog's bladder.

Sally awoke, and I sat her and Mattie on the rug to eat the

last of the summer's dried berries soaked in milk, then checked the soup. When I lifted the lid, I blinked at the warm steam, redolent with parsnips, onions, carrots, and bacon scraps. 'Twould be just right when Ben came home from the fields bringing his wagonload of corn.

The pot o'water bubbled, and I poured it over the chamomile blossoms in my cup. Hannah said the flowery tea would balance my humors and keep them from going topsy-turvy whilst with child. As I waited for the tea to steep, I heard a scream somewhere in the distance. Most likely a hawk. My pregnancy at times led me to imagine sounds.

I felt the baby quickening. The fluttering within was delicate as a butterfly's wings drying in the sun. I was eager for a new life, and hoped it might be a boy. Ben would need a son to help in the fields someday.

Mattie and Sally finished their berries. I gave Sally her rag doll and sat Mattie on my lap to read to her from the new book, "Orbis Pictus," that Mary Foote had lent me. As we settled into the big chair—Ben's chair—I was startled by a loud banging sound close by. No doubt the carpenters.

Mattie wanted to learn to read as her big sister could. The Bible was rife with tales of murder and mayhem, so I was grateful to have the loan of this new book from London.

"Mattie, we're going to read about animals today."

"The book with lions? No lions, Mommy, they're scary!"

"No, love, no lions." She was terrified by the tale of Daniel in the Lions' den. "But look, here are pictures of all the farm animals, and all the letters and the sounds the animals make."

Mattie snuggled closer to see the crudely drawn animals.

"I know the first one. 'Tis an ass!" Mattie cried excitedly.

"Yes, the letter A, for ass. And a horse whinnies, but an ass brays. That is what it says here," I explained, pointing to the words, "The Asse brayeth. Can you make that sound?"

"Hee-hah!" Mattie exclaimed, laughing.

I was startled by a pounding of little fists. I set Mattie in the chair with the book and opened the door. Mary and Abigail stood there, eyes wide, cheeks flushed from running.

"Mama, there's smoke, look, and loud noises, like dogs howling!" Mary said, pointing down the street and scampering inside.

"Or wolves!" Abigail added, pushing past me.

"Wolves?" Mattie cried. "Mommy, wolves are scary, like lions. Look, look, it is a picture of a wolf in this book!" Mattie said, climbing down off the chair to show me.

I stuck my head out the door and smelled smoke. Not the whiff of cooking fires; this was denser, with the scent of iron and burnt paper. My whole body trembled. I peered down the lane and saw black smoke roiling above the rooftops.

Over the shouting from the carpenters next door came the dreaded and all too familiar battle cries.

I slammed and barred the door, then pressed my back against it and closed my eyes. Sweat flushed my brow. I took several deep breaths. Nearly all our men were in the fields, as usual. The Natives knew our predictable English ways.

"Mommy? What's the matter?"

My eyes flew open at Mary's voice.

I ran and closed the shutters on the two front windows. Scooping up Sally, ragdoll and all, I gazed about my home as if angels might have descended to rescue us.

The musket! Ben had left it hanging above the mantle. At the end of every mustering day, he had me practice loading and firing it. I hadn't needed that knowledge till now.

"Mary, Abigail, take Mattie and Sally to the lean-to. We're going to play hide-and-go-seek. Hide in the empty cupboard in the lean-to where we used to keep the jelly before we ate it all," I said, failing to keep the tremor of fear from my voice.

Halfway there, Abigail stopped and looked at me. "But, if you know where we're hiding, 'tis not fair, and—"

I cut her off. "Abigail, do as you're told," I said sharply.

"Will you count to twenty?" Mattie asked. Mary grabbed her hand, and Abigail took Sally's.

"I'm counting to fifty. Now, go!"

Mary had seen the smoke. Like Abigail, she knew the seeker doesn't choose the hiding place. I thanked God for Mary's virtue of obedience. She asked no questions, just hurried all of them to the lean-to.

"One, two, three . . ." I counted aloud. I stood on a stool, took down the gun, and reached for the powder, balls, and rags. Ignoring the blood pounding in my ears, I talked myself through the steps, remembering Ben's words.

Place the butt end on the floor and point the muzzle at the ceiling.

"Four, five, six . . ." *Measure powder from the horn, pour it into the barrel, then ram a wad of cloth and the musket ball down.* "Seven, eight, nine, ten . . ." *Replace the ramrod. Push the frisson forward, add a pinch of powder to the pan, and close the frisson. Finally, cock it halfway.*

"Eleven, twelve, thirteen, fourteen . . ." I made the flint-lock ready in the time it took to recite the steps. Slinging the powder horn around my neck, I stuffed the pouch of musket balls and wads into my apron pocket. I grabbed the picture book and my little Bible, too.

"Mommy?" Mattie called, "You aren't counting!"

I skipped ahead. "Twenty, twenty-one, twenty-two . . ."

Pointing the gun, I unbarred the door and cracked it a few inches to look up and down the lane. Smoke poured from houses on both sides, so I couldn't see farther than the black-smith shop. But I knew the stockade gate was open, as it had been during the day for the past few months. *Dear God!*

The fires were moving in our direction. The Natives were heading this way. Repeated gunfire shattered the air. The lane filled with people screaming, crying, yelping, and scattering. I pulled my head back inside, slammed and barred the door again, then let out a gasp of air I hadn't realized I'd been holding. "Thirty-five, thirty-six, thirty-seven . . ."

God had spared us once. I prayed the girls would stay hidden, that we could flee. I prayed that I would hit my target if I fired the gun. Tears sprang to my eyes, and I brushed them away. My hands trembled as I aimed the musket at the door and continued counting.

"Forty-eight, forty-nine, fifty! Ready or not, here I come!"

The game had served its purpose. I'd loaded the gun, calmed my breathing, strengthened my resolve, hidden my girls, and formed a plan. We'd run, not wait here for them to fall upon us. I set the flintlock down and went to the lean-to.

"Now, where could they be? Are they in the root cellar?" I opened the door to the small earthen room. "No . . . are they amongst the cabbages?" I heard giggling. "No? They must be in the jelly cupboard!" I threw open the door.

A shot rang out, quite close.

I swung Sally up on my shoulders. "Put your arms around my neck. There's a good girl! Hang on tight!"

I grabbed Mattie by the hand and held the gun in the other.

"Mary, Abigail, hold tight to my skirts!" I said, hastening to the back door.

As we reached it, I heard banging from behind us, the sound of the front door splintering, and a crash of broken glass.

"Indians!" Abigail screamed.

I pulled open the back door. I shoved Mary and Abigail into the garden as the shutters gave way. I glanced back at a blurred face peering through the window, distorted by the cracked glass. I ducked and ran through the back doorway, a death grip on Mattie's wrist, pulling her after me. *I must keep my children safe.*

I'd hoped to hide in the barn, but to my dismay, it was consumed by flames. Two warriors raced towards us from the orchard, bearing arms. I pushed the girls behind me and pressed them back against the wall of the lean-to. Pulled Sally from my shoulders, and tucked her behind the rain barrel. The warriors closed the gap dangerously fast.

I knelt, cocked, and aimed. The warriors stopped in their tracks. I had but one bullet to fire. My hands shook uncontrollably.

"Leave us be!" I screamed and squeezed the trigger. But someone clubbed my arm with something hard, my shot went wild, and I dropped the musket. Cradling my wounded arm, yelping in pain, I whirled to face my attacker. I kicked out at him and beat him with my fist. Wrenching me around by my shoulders, he pinned me to him with one strong arm—a sharp knife blade pressed against my throat. I froze.

"Do not move, or I will kill you." His breath was hot as fire, his voice like ice.

My girls and Abigail were whimpering and weeping, and out of the corner of my eye, I saw warriors grab them and carry them off. Tears sprang to my eyes. Where were they taking them?

My captor took the knife from my throat. I gasped for air but dared not move. He tore the powder horn from me and pushed the barrel of his gun into the small of my back.

"Go. Run. Follow your babes."

I stumbled after the Natives who carried my girls. My captor prodded me with his gun, forcing me forward, reminding me there was no escape.

I held my bruised arm against me as I ran. It ached and throbbed in pain, bringing vomit to my throat and a veil across my sight. I looked back only once to see our barn, house, and town ablaze. Burnt offerings to our God or a glimpse of the seventh circle of Hell, I knew not which.

Chapter Twelve

BEN

"I count twenty sacks of corn," I called over my shoulder, admiring the plump ears in the wagon. "And we've room for more!"

I took off my hat, wiped my brow with my handkerchief, swigged water from my costrel, and "looked upon a hedge" or, more literally, a stone wall. I had to concede, the scarecrows seemed to be keeping most of the crows away.

I heard Stephen and Samuel parting the blades of corn, rustling towards me.

"Are you having a smoke, Ben? I didn't think you had that vice," Stephen called.

"No. Why?" I asked, buttoning my pants. Then I smelt it, too, and wheeled around to find the source.

Above our town, above our women and children, rose thick, dark smoke.

Dear God, give me wings! I unhitched Scout, fumbling with her harness in my haste. Then, I slashed the driving reins with my knife, shortening them. Seeing what I was about, Stephen gave me a leg up onto her back.

"God be with ye, Ben!"

"I'll see to your loved ones!" I said.

"We'll be just behind you."

I punched my heels into Scout's sides, and she galloped toward the stockade like she had Satan behind her.

Scout did her best, clearing ditches and thickets at a gallop and even the latched fence gate. The closer we came to Hatfield, the denser the smoke grew and the more I despaired. I eased up on my encouragement to Scout till we finally slowed to a trot. When we came but a few rods from Middle Lane, Scout reared and shied away, refusing to go farther. I dismounted, undid her bridle and harness, and dropped them in the street. She cantered off to the pastures by the burying ground, as far from the fiery town as she could go.

The smoke rose like demons from Hell, black and hot, blowing wind, embers, and ashes upwards and down, turning the sun red. All around me, women and children were fleeing to the meadows and the river, staggering and gasping for air, for a strange moment calling to mind a haul of cod flopping about on the deck of my father's fishing boat.

I knew my neighbors and friends needed help, but I looked neither right nor left at their burning houses and closed my ears to their screams and cries. I ran towards my home. Damn us for not enlarging our stockade and not locking the gates during the day. Convinced the threat was over. That we were safe. *God, please spare my family, in Jesus's name. Amen.*

I ran through the wide-open north gate. The framework of the Graves' new house was untouched, bare as birch trees in winter. But where my home once stood was naught but a bonfire. The roof was gone, and the new second story Martha loved so well had collapsed. The stairs lay crumpled in a pile, like smoldering remnants of Jacob's ladder. Only the chimney remained above the gaping maw of the hearth.

I doused my hat with water from my costrel and pulled it down over my brow, then doused my sleeve and shielded my face, dodging flames that licked and spat at me like bewitched cats. I circled the ruins of my home, calling out the names of my wife and children, sparks scattering at my feet like bees from a hive, stinging me. I coughed on the smoke and cursed the embers burning through the soles of my boots.

Squinting through the smoke, I spied nothing but useless bits: cooking tools, tankards, hearth irons, door latches and bars. I kicked the brass chamber pot in a fury and sent it banging off the hearth. I found my musket amongst the charred flowers, too hot to touch but otherwise spared. Martha must have tried to defend herself and our girls. I felt a clutch of both terror and pride.

I held my pistol in my gloved hands as I continued my search. My barn was but a heap of blackened timbers. I had one second of thankfulness I'd driven Scout to the fields, sparing her. My family was gone. I stumbled to the garden, fell to my knees beside the blackened pumpkins, and wept. I prayed they had found someplace to run, someplace to hide.

My eyes stung from the smoke and my tears, and my breathing was ragged. I rose to a crouch, my hands on my knees. It hurt to breathe. When I stood, my vision grayed around the edges, and the soles of my feet pained me. Still, I jogged up the road towards Deerfield, following fresh footprints and hoofprints but seeing and hearing nothing but the fading screams and fiery tumult from behind me. The enemy and their captives were gone. Exhausted, I limped back to see how I could help.

Samuel Foote's front door was torn from its hinges, but no smoke poured from it. I searched inside but did not find Mary Foote or her children. Then to the Jennings' home, but Hannah and her children were also gone. Vanished . . . I nearly tripped over Goodwife Russell and her little boy, who lay in the street, blood pooling under their heads. Her cap was gone, her hair and scalp torn away. Kneeling, I held her wrist, then his, but there was nothing.

"Goodman Waite!" a woman's terrified voice rang out.

I could barely see through my sweat and tears, but I

thought it was Sarah Welles, stumbling down the front path, dragging her little one behind her.

I gathered Sarah in my arms, carried her to the middle of the street, away from the fires, and then returned for her child, wounded but alive. I put my costrel to Sarah's mouth.

"The Indians, Ben, they came so quickly. They . . . killed my wee babe . . ." Her voice trailed off, and her eyes glazed over as she drifted away.

"Our men are on the way," I said, wondering where the hell they were. I left Sarah on the rough road beside her crying child, and that image was replaced in my mind by the specter of Martha kneeling beside a wailing Sally. I reached Samuel Kellogg's house, a smoldering carcass on the corner of Middle Lane and Main Street.

"Goodwife Kellogg, are you there? Can you call out to me?" But there was no answer, only the crackle and spitting of the fire.

Sobbing and wheezing, I crossed Deerfield Lane. *Was everyone killed or taken? Where were the rest of our men?*

"Ben!"

Stephen Jennings and Samuel Foote found me, and I collapsed in Stephen's arms.

"They're gone! Martha, Hannah, Mary, our children, everyone gone or dead!"

"Ben, here, drink this." Samuel handed me his costrel. I gulped the cool water. My dizziness eased, and my breathing slowed.

"Stay here. Catch your breath. We'll be back," Stephen said.

"No, I'll come with you."

Samuel Foote's wife Mary and two of their children were missing, but he found his wee babe and remaining children safe with Mary's cousins and stayed to care for them. Stephen and I searched again in vain for Hannah and his children. As he had done for me, I embraced him when he wept, but there was no way to soothe these wounds.

Finally, the other men returned from the fields, some rejoicing in God that their families were spared, some shattered by grief. Stephen, a few other men, and I staggered off to see who could be saved and whom we must bury—a daunting task. I was barely aware of my actions or my words. Stunned as I'd been the day my brother died in my arms. No, far worse than that.

Yet others needed me. There were so many injured, and without care, even more would die. We had to help them. And so I walked the town again, searching for survivors, gathering clean linens to bind wounds, carrying wee babes in my arms, some dead, some hanging onto life. It was a horror beyond nightmares, and I no longer tried to hold back my tears, for they seemed the only way to release my pain.

Chapter Thirteen

MARTHA

I couldn't spy my daughters through the throng around me. I stumbled down the path, searching for a glimpse of them, praying they were not injured, knowing they were terrified.

I struggled to get my bearings, trapped in a grim fog where I could only stumble forward to meet my doom. I'd been north of Hatfield only a few times and now searched for markers to show me where I was, wayposts to tether myself to my world. My arm throbbed with each rapid beating of my heart, and my clothes reeked of smoke.

The Natives drove us like frightened sheep alongside the Pocumtuck path to Clay Hill by the Connecticut River. Through the willows and aspens, I caught glimpses of Mount Warner. Ben had traveled this same trail to Great Falls over a year ago. I found comfort in his passing here, as if he'd left a whisper of his spirit to protect us.

We stopped after we crossed Cow Bridge Brook. I screamed as my captor pinioned my arms behind my back, pain shooting through my injured left arm. He stopped and tied my wrists together in front of me instead, muttering angrily. My elbow and arm ached, but my shoulder was spared more agony—a small kindness.

At last, I spied my daughters. A warrior guarded Mary and Mattie as they knelt at the brook to drink, and a different warrior cradled Sally in his arms. He wore a deerskin kilt, moccasins, and a headband with a single feather. He filled his hand with water, then cupped it to Sally's mouth. I longed to go to my girls, to hug and comfort them. I took four steps toward them before my captor pulled me back, shouting at me. Tears burned behind my eyes, and I choked them down. *The Lord is my shepherd. I shall not want . . .*

I knelt and dipped my face into the stream, took a few gulps of cool water, and then managed to stand without losing my balance. The Indian who'd taken me shouted to the others in his language, and they sprang to do his bidding. I trembled at the sight and sound of him. He was tall, but not as tall as Ben. His hair spilt over his shoulders like black ink, held back from his war-painted face by a wampum band sprouting a handful of eagle feathers. He carried an English musket slung across his bare back.

My captor walked amongst his people, giving commands. Surrounding us was perhaps a score of warriors, evidenced by the single feather each wore in a band around their head. Also, three women—one elderly and two young—an older man with a sagging paunch and silver hair, and a couple of young boys.

So many of the captives were children. I counted five English children without parents, including Abigail Allis. Had their parents been killed? I spied Hannah Jennings' boy and girl, two of Mary Foote's children, Obadiah's son, and my three girls. A baker's dozen. We four adults were bound and separated from our children. Knowing who'd been taken begged the question of who'd been left behind. What had become of the others? The bitter taste of bile rose in my throat.

Suddenly, I was pulled to my feet and spun around to face my master. Indeed, that seemed the word to use. We were enslaved now, like Israelites to the Egyptians or the Native people captured and sent to Barbados during King Philip's war.

My despair gave way to fury. I wanted to spit at my captor or kick him, to hurt him as he'd hurt me. But that would serve no purpose, so I bowed my head in submission, fighting to keep my tears from falling.

"Your *kasuk* is Benjamin Waite, yes?" he asked.

My husband, my "kasuk." I knew some of the Algonquian languages the Nipmucs and Pocumtucks spoke. The tribes we called River Indians. How could I not? As recently as four years ago, we'd shared land, traded goods, and cleared the trees together. Algonquian tribes had learned English and Christianity from Reverend John Elliot and the Bible he painstakingly translated.

Would I endanger Ben if I named him my husband? I knew not, so I said nothing.

"You are silent, but I know it is true," the Native said. "And you are *neechal*." He reached out to touch my belly, and I recoiled, pressing my bound hands over my middle protectively.

"I am Ashpelon, Pocumtuck, and Sachem of this band of Nipmucs, Pocumtucks, and Norwottucks. 'River Indians', you call us. Your kasuk killed many of my *Neetompassag*—my sisters —at Peskeompskut. Killed *nokummus* also," he said.

That cannot be. Women? Grandmothers? Wouldn't Ben have told me?

"No, at Peskeompskut, our men killed wos-ket-om-paog," I struggled to pronounce each syllable of the strange word, remembering it, having heard Ben speak it. "They killed men, warriors."

"No! Many women, and also *wunneechâneunk*!" He pointed toward Sally.

I gasped as if he'd struck me. Wunneechâneunk was their word for children.

"Children?" I asked, my voice trembling.

"Yes! Children! So, we killed your people and took your women and children. It is only fair. It is a trade. We kill, and we take, same as English!"

My friends and kin in Hatfield. Killed if not here with us. *All of them? Who?*

"Where are you taking us?"

"To Canada."

So very far. I had not a moment to pray to my God for our lives before Ashpelon yelled at the tribe and shoved me ahead of him. My feelings and pain swirled together, hot anger mixing with fear and confusion. Burning bile rose in my throat, and when Ashpelon ceased prodding me for a few moments, I bent and heaved it up.

Had Ben killed children? Elders? What could I believe of Ashpelon's words? Did he speak of what scarred my husband's heart? Was our blood now shed in trade for blood shed by women and babes at the Falls Fight?

We passed the Great Pond and veered away from the Connecticut River through thick saplings, ferns, and vines. Why weren't our men coming for us? What had become of them? As best I could, I kept my eyes on my daughters, glimpsing them for moments before losing them again. My silent prayers for them were as constant as my breathing.

We crossed First Brook, then Sugarloaf Brook, after which the Natives drove us out of the valley, and we plunged into dense woods, following a narrow trail up the south slope of Sugarloaf Mountain, southeast of Deerfield. My feet were cold and sore in my wet shoes, and my left arm throbbed. Ashpelon walked behind me but, mercifully, ceased his shoving and pushing.

We came to a little clearing, no more than four rods across, where we finally stopped. Here the warriors and Ashpelon left us in care of the older man, the women, and the boys. The afternoon sun was broken up by clouds and trees, casting its gold on the meadow grass. The loveliness of it gave me a strange moment of peace and comfort.

No longer under tight guard, I went in search of my daughters.

The warriors had given them to the care of one of the Native women, perhaps my age or younger, lean, her muscular legs showing below the hem of her deerskin skirt. Sally curled in her lap, and Mary and Mattie drifted off to sleep beside her. Praise God, they seemed unharmed. Approaching cautiously, I held my bound hands outstretched in a silent entreaty. She shook her head but patted the ground, so I sat beside her, watching my children sleep, aching to hold them.

Sensing my distress, Hannah came and sat beside me. Her cheek was bruised, her eye swollen, and her upper lip split and puffy. Her cap had fallen, and her twist of dark hair was undone.

"Your poor face, Hannah." I made a clumsy attempt to caress her wounded cheek. The tears I'd been holding back fell freely now.

"I tripped on the way," she said, fixing her gaze on me, her good eye widening in alarm. "And your arm is swollen—"

"The sachem, Ashpelon, struck me," I said. "I fought back when they came for us. I had the flintlock, but when I aimed, he clubbed my shoulder." The memory made me dizzy.

"'Twas brave of you," Hannah said. A shudder shook her then, and she bit her lip. "I'm afraid they murdered Elizabeth Russell and her son, Stephen. The Indians drove me away, and she was screaming, running. A warrior swung a tomahawk, and she fell in the lane . . ."

"Elizabeth? Lord help us," I said. Goodwife Russell and I

had shared many a pleasant chat at Sabbath dinners. Her husband Phillip was Reverend Russell's kin, and as calm and kind as Reverend Russell was severe and bitter. Reverend Russell had been the most fervent in his demands that our men attack the Natives at Great Falls.

We sat in silence for a moment, stunned.

"Where are your children?" I asked, looking for Sammy and Holly.

"Yonder with one of the warriors who claims us," Hannah said. She jerked her chin to her right, toward the edge of the clearing where a young warrior gripped the hands of her son and daughter. Near them, Nate and Molly clung to their mother, Mary Foote. The older man and his wife guarded them.

Hannah blinked back tears, keeping her gaze on her children. "My cousin Mary Foote had to leave her babe. Uncle Obadiah saw his wife Sarah clubbed in the head just before he was taken and doesn't know if she's dead or alive." Images of the aggression seemed to strike Hannah like waves, each spoken in a gasp.

I took a slow, shaky breath before replying, "And naught for us to do now but pray for them and the others."

"I fear for Stephen," Hannah said. The dam broke, and tears coursed down her dusty cheeks.

"And I, Ben." He'd been in the fields when our town was attacked. *Had the Natives fallen on our men in the fields?*

We grew quiet then. The distance between us created by exhaustion, pain, and terror was as daunting to ford as the Connecticut River itself. Mattie awoke and came to me, put her little arms around my neck, then curled up in my lap like a kitten, whimpering. I wrapped my bound arms around her, squeezing her tight. The Native woman allowed it, and for a few moments, I knew an uneasy peace.

"I fear the warriors have gone to Deerfield," Hannah said, peering at the forest around us. "My cousin Benoni and a few men from Hadley went there last week to start rebuilding."

"Benoni spoke of taking young Sam Russell with them," I said. "Who else?"

"I think Sergeant Plympton, Goodman Stockwell, and maybe John Root?"

"Oh dear, what will become of them?" I asked. More poor souls.

Hannah shook her head. She had no answers to my questions.

We weren't the first English captives taken in my lifetime. Thomas Reede, of course, had escaped just before the Falls Fight. Mistress Mary Rowlandson, the wife of Lancaster's reverend, had been taken last year and redeemed when her ransom was raised, but I was not sure what happened to the rest. I'd heard that at times, the tribes kept their prisoners—a ritual adoption—and, other times, demanded wampum or guns in exchange.

A whistle pierced the forest, and the Nipmuc woman watching my children whistled back and took Mattie from my arms despite my protests. Presently, the warriors emerged from the trees, some astride horses, with captives from Deerfield. I recognized young Sam Russell and two of the three men Hannah had named. Our captors urged us to our feet, then placed the youngest children on the horses and swung up to ride behind them.

I found myself walking beside Quintin Stockwell. I did not know him well.

"What happened at Deerfield?" I asked.

"The enemy fell on us swiftly, catching us unawares. They captured Benoni and Sam Russell first." Goodman Stockwell spoke slowly, his voice monotone.

Benoni Stebbins was Hannah and Mary's cousin. Sam Russell wouldn't know yet that the Native Americans killed his mother and wee brother in Hatfield. I prayed his father still lived, followed by a chilling thought that it wouldn't matter much if we never saw our homes again.

Dread descended on me, the full weight and hopelessness of our plight. I reached for Stockwell's arm to steady myself.

Stockwell patted my hand. "Sergeant Plympton and I tried to hide in the swamp, but they found us. Took us and the horses. John Root was wounded; he fell and couldn't rise. They shot him. He's dead."

The sun was low in the sky, the forest growing dark and damp. We followed a trail twisting into the woods like a snake, then finally stopped for the night. Our captors had a camp, a cluster of wigwams, and they herded our children inside them. I thought we must be somewhere on the western slope of Sugarloaf Mountain, but I was too tired and grieved to care.

Chapter Fourteen

BEN

HATFIELD
SEPTEMBER 19, 1677, EVENING

We gathered in sorrow within the homes still standing and reviewed our missing and wounded. Our bereft women comforted the orphaned children, tended to the injured, and minded the cooking fires. Half-mad with grief, men carried bodies from their ruined homes to the meeting house, remaining there in desolation. Our new Reverend John Wise did his best to offer solace.

I caught Scout when she came trotting home and hitched her to a wagon, then handed it over to a couple of lads and told them to gather buckets and bring water from our wells. Water to douse the embers, to wash the wounds, and to bathe the dead. John White and his brother Daniel hitched up their oxen and did the same, delivering water to the meeting house.

Once we'd put out the fires, a small band of us searched the ruins in the half-light of dusk. The ground still smoldered, so some areas were impassable. I looked for Martha and my children at each house and barn still standing or burnt to ashes. Perhaps they'd not been taken but had found shelter with a neighbor. Or one of them might have slipped away and still be cowering in fear within a water barrel or in a meadow thicket. For one whose life was spent scouting and hunting, I could not fathom my inability to find them. My chest filled with emptiness, like a hollowed-out tree.

Stephen Jennings and I found the body of Sergeant Isaac Graves, lying on his back, his dead eyes fixed and staring at the unfinished rafters of his son's new home. His mortal wound was a musket ball to the chest, and a pool of dried blood spread beneath him. His face and arms were stiff and his skin strangely cool.

And in his face, all at once, I saw Martha's. For what if we found her dead? The hollow in my chest filled with unspeakable terror, and as I took the sergeant's shoulders and Stephen his legs, I willed my mind to be still, to think of nothing beyond the moment.

We carried Sergeant Graves to his unscathed home within the stockade.

His wife Mary, his son John, and John's beloved Sarah looked up hopefully when we came through the door. John fetched a pallet, and we laid his father on it.

"Is he still alive?" his son asked, laying a hand upon his father's throat.

I saw his face fall as he slowly withdrew his hand. He cast one last hopeful glance at me. I shook my head.

"He's gone. I am so sorry. John was a good man and a brave soldier."

The newly widowed Goodwife Mary stroked her dead husband's cheek and bent to kiss his pale lips. I left the little family kneeling around his body, the women weeping and his son choking back sobs.

It was after dark when all were accounted for. The men gathered on their side of the meeting house, conversing in urgent yet hushed voices, whilst our women ministered to the injured and orphaned. We moved like players in a Shakespearean tragedy, acting out roles we'd already rehearsed in our nightmares. Even with all the lanterns and candles burning, it was dim and shadowed inside.

Selectman Belding penned a list of our dead and missing. He handed it to me. "Mary was killed, Ben. She's on this list. I cannot read this, can you . . ." He wiped his eyes.

"Of course," I said, although I was unsure how I'd manage to speak the names of my missing wife and daughters.

I walked to the pulpit. Leaning against it to steady myself, pushing the faces of my friends and kin from my mind, I recited their names.

"Persons Killed: Sergeant Isaac Graves; John Graves; John Atchinson and John Cooper, both of Hadley; Phillip Russell's wife and his son; John Coleman's wife and one of his children; Samuel Kellogg's wife; Samuel Belding's wife and a child; Goodwife Allis; a child of John Welles."

Each name elicited fresh weeping from those assembled. I paused to take a deep breath, then continued. "The remaining names are of those missing, presumed taken: My beloved Goodwife Martha Waite and my three babes, Mary, Mattie, and Sally . . ." I choked down a sob, and a wave of dizziness swept through me. It seemed forever before I could go on.

"Missing," I repeated. "John Coleman's two children; Goodwife Foote and two children; Goodwife Jennings and two children; Obadiah Dickinson and a son; a son of Samuel Kellog; a daughter of William Bartholomew; a daughter of John Allis."

"Persons Wounded: John Coleman's child; Jonathan Welles's wife and his daughter; Obadiah Dickinson's wife—in all four."

I set the list down with a trembling hand, and the room erupted in anguished cries and violent cursing.

Samuel Foote stood. "I say, at dawn on the morrow, we

send a search party after our wives and children!" His voice echoed from the meeting house walls, and a chorus of "Ayes" followed.

The women paused for a moment, listening. They were not often privy to the decision-making of our men, and now they hung on our words.

"Men, let's discuss this, shall we?" Samuel Belding said to the crowd, joining me at the pulpit. "Reverends Wise and Russell and our War Council have sent messengers to Major Pynchon at Springfield, Governor Leverett of Boston, and Governor Leete of Connecticut, demanding troops. We should receive their assistance within a day or two at most. I'd like to hear what our scout says about this wicked assault. Goodman Waite?"

I did not feel like much of an expert. I'd let my guard down like the rest, and my loss and grief spurred only rage within me, not rational thought. Every fiber of my being urged me to grab my musket, mount my horse, and race after the kidnappers and their captives. I knew which way they'd headed. I could hazard a guess at what they wanted. But I was one man, and rash decisions would only result in more deaths.

"I fear we must wait for the troops," I said, steeling myself against the chorus of scoffs and jeers. "We are needed here, to tend to our orphaned children and our afflicted."

The women nodded in assent, but the men still grumbled.

"If we follow the enemy now, it may further endanger our kin. If we apprehend them, our foes won't hesitate to kill their captives. They may have posted men at their forts and sent scouts to the wilderness to ambush us."

John Coleman stood. "They killed my wife! Killed our wee babe Bethia, knocked our oldest son stone-cold, took my children Sarah and Noah! I have nothing to lose by going after them!" John's voice was raw with pain, his face gray with exhaustion.

Selectman Belding held up his hand. "Gentlemen, let's try

to do this in an orderly fashion. Raise your hand if you wish to speak. I will call on you in turn."

Several hands shot up. Belding called on young John Graves.

"Could they have been Mohawks, not River Indians?" Graves asked, "Last night, a family of Mohawks was in town with a few Natick captives. They camped south of here on the other side of Mill Creek. Might they be responsible?"

"Mohawks? That should have been reported!" Belding frowned, shaking his head, then called on Stephen Jennings.

Stephen stood. "Reported or not, the Mohawks prey on the French and Mahicans and side with us, correct?"

"That has been the case, yes," I said.

"The Mohawks have always been friendly to us," Reverend Wise agreed. "They're enemies of the Mahicans and River Indians."

"Friendly?" Samuel Foote jumped to his feet. "The River Indians may have been friendly once, but no longer. We cannot trust any of the Natives! What difference does it make which band did this?"

I sighed, wanting to break down and striving to be rational in my responses. "Because it determines where they're headed, their tactics, and how we should proceed," I said.

"Then, tell us, Goodman Waite, from which quarter came this blow?" Reverend Wise asked.

"An Algonquian band. Possibly River Indians—Nipmucs, Pocumtucks, and Norwottucks. The last remnants of warriors faithful to King Philip. Possibly some of those who attacked us after the Falls Fight."

Goodwife Sarah Dickinson raised her hand. Belding nodded to her, and the room hushed. She was breaking a long-held convention, but we all knew desperate times called for desperate measures. Her head was wrapped in bloodied bandages, her fair hair loose and matted. She held her wee babe, Eliphalet, in her arms and leaned on Rachel Allis for support.

"Gentlemen, please bear in mind your women suffer great loss, too. My husband, Obadiah, and my son, Daniel, are captives. I was all but scalped," she paused, trembling, lightly touching her fingertips to her head, "and this wee babe of mine tossed across the yard like a sack of onions. We cannot endure more pain. We cannot bear to lose more men. With all due respect, I think you should wait for the troops." Sarah sat back down.

John Allis raised his hand, stood, and nodded to his wife, Rachel.

"My mother was slain," he said, his voice rough. "She's with the Lord. My goodwife and I have a little girl, Abigail. We've not seen her since she left to play at the Waites' house this morning. She's on the list of captives. We want her safe. Whether or not that means we go now or wait for the troops."

"Are we ready to put it to a vote, then?" Selectman Belding asked. "Any more discussion?"

"My wife and children were also taken, and I say we wait for help from the United Colonies' Troops," Stephen said. "Our despair is deep. We cannot be rash."

I nodded my gratitude to him.

"Anyone else?" Selectman Belding asked. "No? Let's put it to a vote. All those in favor of waiting for the troops say aye."

The vote was taken, and by a small margin, waiting won out. Timid dogs bark worse than they bite, and few of us were ready, in body or spirit, to undertake a rescue mission of any substance.

Once more, I passed the night in the Allis home, a melancholy and desolate place. Lieutenant William Allis was not there. He remained in the meeting house, sitting beside the washed and shrouded body of his wife, Mary. She'd been felled by a tomahawk, protecting her grandchildren, no doubt.

John Allis and his wife Rachel sat by the fire, barely speaking, their three children asleep on a mattress at their feet, their twin babes, Eleazor and Eleanor, taking turns nursing. Their little Abigail was somewhere in the wilderness with my wee girls, wife, friends, and kin, lost to the darkness and the enemy.

Chapter Fifteen

ASHPELON

CAMP
SEPTEMBER 19, 1677, NIGHT

I could not rest, so I paced about our camp, watching the exhausted English sleep. We had staked them down, as we would for several nights, until they no longer knew where they were and no longer dreamt of escape. We staked only the men and the women. The English children we kept by our small cooking fire. They were our wampum, our gems for trading. Whether ransomed back to their English parents or sold to the French to the north, they would bring a high price. Or perhaps we would keep some. To replace the ghosts of our children, slaughtered by the English at Peskeompskut and in so many other massacres.

A few of our warriors stalked the forest, calling to me and each other in the sounds of owls and wolves. They scouted for signs of the English and the Mohawks. From their hoots and howls, I learned we'd not been followed. Not yet. And still, I walked amongst the captives. They lay on their backs, arms spread wide like their angels, but pinioned to the earth. Unable to fly.

It was good we had taken their women. At least one, the Waite woman, was with child, which increased the price we could ask for her. The men were a mistake. They were a foolish risk, especially the elderly warrior Plympton. Old but not weak. A possible danger to us. But some of our women had asked for men in retribution for husbands and sons killed by the English.

The English might not be following, but I was not sure about the Mohawks, our ancient enemies. They were like fawning English dogs, begging for scraps in trade for hunting down our people. The English think they can trust them, but in our language, their name Mohawk means "flesh-eater."

Likewise, Mohawks will soon learn, like we have, that the English cannot be trusted. They ask to share the land but build fences, walls, and stockades and use guns to tell us we are no longer welcome. The English will feed you one day and whip you the next.

The French treated us fairly when they wanted beaver furs, and some of us bowed to their God. But now that beavers are scarce, the French may resolve they no longer need us. Still, Canada is our safest refuge now. Even our former enemies, the Abenaki, have opened their clans to us since Metacomet's death.

The forest hides us well. The moon is just a sliver of a raccoon's whisker, a harvest moon no more. We lit only one small fire for cooking. It was a warm night, and we needed the concealment of darkness. The moon would grow again and would soon be round and full as the Waite woman's belly—the Leaf Falling Moon. By then, we would be far to the north, where neither English nor Mohawks could find us.

Chapter Sixteen

MARTHA

North of Deerfield
September 20, 1677

Somehow, I slept. I awoke to a brittle dawn as a Native undid the noose around my neck and pulled the stakes from the ground. I was stiff, my hands and toes numb, my arm still throbbing. A Nipmuc woman led me and the other women behind some sumac bushes, where we relieved ourselves. "Gazed upon a rose," my mother had called it in a gentler time.

They unbound my hands, put me on a horse again, and drove us to a river they called Pocumtuck, one of the River Tribes' names. To us, it was the Deerfield River. It was deep, and I couldn't swim. Clinging tightly to my horse's neck, I was grateful the beast was steady and sure-footed. The water reached the horse's belly and soaked my shoes and the hem of my skirt. I looked about for my girls, distressed not to see them. I knew they needed me.

When we reached the far bank, we headed up a grassy hill to a small Indian village of a dozen wigwams clustered within a stockade. A couple of small fires burned there, and I smelt smoking fish. The Natives pulled us from the horses. I sat on a log and wrung out my sodden skirt, relieved to see my girls close at hand with the young woman. I rose to go to them, but again, my captor pulled me back. I realized it was part of our punishment to keep us from our children. A way to prevent our escape.

The Natives built a fire and fed us some dried corn. I crunched on it hungrily, and when it was gone, I reached beneath my collar and gingerly touched my neck, feeling the tender ridges left by the noose. I set my shoes and stockings by the fire to dry. Then I reached into my pocket, reassured by the presence of my Bible. The picture book and tiny sewing kit were there, too, and I wondered if I could put the sharp needles to some use.

My arm still pained me, so I removed my apron and fashioned a crude sling. Feeling somewhat better, fed and dry, I opened my Bible, finding words of comfort, glancing up after each verse to keep an eye on my girls. The women and older man sat in a circle, keeping the children in the center. They held the babes, and I could see Sally squirming and crying in the arms of the young Nipmuc woman. I wept, longing to comfort her and frustrated at my helplessness.

The stockade around this camp had a wide-open gate flanked by two great oaks. Ashpelon sent a warrior to each tree. They drew their knives and carved tally marks into the bark, deep gashes in the soft wood. Beside me sat Sergeant Plympton, who'd fought in the Pequot wars. I assumed he understood some of the Indian ways.

"Sergeant, do you know the reason for the marks?" I whispered.

"I believe the Indians are counting us, recording on one tree how many they have taken and on the other . . ." Plympton's voice trailed off, and he shrugged as if I should understand his meaning.

I was growing weary of men and their unspoken thoughts.

"On the other tree, what do those marks signify?" I asked.

"Those they killed, in Hatfield and Deerfield. They are bragging."

It angered me to see the value of our lives reduced to notches on a tree, but I counted the tallies. On one tree, seventeen marks clustered together, and four more above. Us. The captives from both towns. Thirteen marks were carved into the second tree. Thirteen. I gasped at the alarming number—the count of those slaughtered in Hatfield. An unlucky number, indeed. One more tally was added above the thirteen.

"What is that lone mark?" I asked.

"John Root. They murdered him when they captured us in Deerfield," Sgt. Plympton said.

Just as Stockwell had said. His poor wife, Mehitable. She'd lost her first husband, Experience Hinsdell's brother Samuel, to the Natives at Bloody Brook. Then she remarried to John Root and lost him as well. So much loss.

Three warriors leapt to their feet, shouting and threatening each other with clubs and tomahawks. They grabbed Quintin Stockwell's shirt, shoving and pulling him about. Ashpelon strode over to them and ended it, but it left me trembling.

I looked at the Nipmucs and Pocumtucks who'd taken children. Warriors held the hands of Abby Bartholomew and Abigail Allis and carried Sarah and Noah Coleman in their bare arms. I felt the quickening of my babe, grateful it was safe within me, and placed my hand upon my belly.

The consternation of the attack was lifting, like black bunting pulled from a mirror after a period of mourning. The sudden clarity revealed new horrors, as in sudden anguish, I realized these Natives had killed the parents of the children they'd taken, for no parent would have handed over their child without a fight.

And what of the babe I carried? Would it survive this? Would my girls? Would I?

With a word from Ashpelon, the warriors put the women back on the horses. The three Nipmuc women and the older man also rode, carrying the smallest children, including my Sally, and the rest of our party walked. My heart went out to Mary and Mattie as they ran to keep up. I held the reins in my right hand, and my left arm jostled in the sling, throbbing in pain.

We headed east on a forested trail between the river and a swamp full of dead trees. As though waking from a nightmare, I shuddered in recognition of this place, though I'd never seen it—the Great Falls, where the fight had been. I couldn't help but look for ghosts. Although my horse was slow and stubborn, I urged it ahead until I fell in beside Hannah.

She looked at me, her facial expression grim when she spoke. "'Tis this the place, do you think? The place of the Falls Fight?"

I was glad she'd spoken first, for I'd no desire to dig up bones. Her husband had lost his life here. I feared mine had lost his soul.

"It must be," I answered. "How Ben described it, the river turning sharply to the east, the slabs of rock jutting out of the water. 'Like the wrecks of sunken ships,' in his words."

For a moment, the memory of his voice stabbed my heart.

"I wonder where Samuel lies," Hannah said quietly.

"Ben said they chose a peaceful place north of the river."

We both looked across the river and swamp to the hills, the forests of pine and oak and maple still green in this warm September.

Gazing at the roaring falls below, Ashpelon's words rang in my head—slain children. I shuddered and considered sharing my burden with Hannah but did not. To voice my suspicions of our men's actions would give them weight, and I need not add to Hannah's already tarnished memories of Samuel. Instead, I bowed my head and asked the Lord for forgiveness and deliverance.

We climbed a steep mountain, perhaps the one called Pisgah, farther north than I had ever been. I thought again of the Falls Fight, the party of men who'd fled to this mountain pursued by River Indians, whilst Ben led his band west to safety.

When we reached the northern slopes, we stopped again for the night. The women took woven mats from the horses' packs and spread them atop crisscrossed poles as crude shelters. Warriors built a fire. Our captors took us away from the camp—first the children, then women, then men—to tend to our needs. They gave us water and staked us down. The children they took into their shelters.

As I stared at a cloudy sky, I thanked the Lord for sparing me, my children, and the babe within me and asked Him to give Ben strength to rescue us. Pynchon would send troops. I imagined them assembling now and planning their pursuit, which comforted me.

But I recalled the notches on the trees, the fourteen marks a testament to the slain. The screams of the women and children, the smoke and flames, the image Hannah had placed in my mind of Elizabeth Russell, bloodied and dying. I was selfish, for Ben and our kin must rightly care for our wounded and lay our dead to rest before rescuing the living.

We would have to wait.

Chapter Seventeen

BEN

HATFIELD TO NEAR SQUAKHEAG MEADOWS
SEPTEMBER 20-22, 1677

I slept until the sun pierced the smoky window, and the smell of the noon meal woke me. Dragging myself from bed, I moved in a stupor of grief, trying my best to be of help but unable to think clearly. When I realized I was of no use to the Allises, I pulled on my boots and joined those out a doors.

With them, I hauled water, mended fences, swept ash from stoops, rounded up strayed livestock, and harvested vegetables from gardens. We anxiously awaited the arrival of the troops from Hartford that evening, and I recruited men to join me in the morrow's search: Stephen Jennings, Samuel Foote, William Bartholomew, John Coleman, Nathaniel Dickinson, and several men from Hadley.

John Graves Junior, a cabinetmaker, and Aaron Cook, a woodworker, took on the melancholy task of coffin making. Men traveled to Springfield for black bunting to drape the coffins and the doors and mirrors of houses. Those few who could afford luxuries sent requests to Springfield for scraps of gold for mourning rings and white leather for funeral gloves.

Some younger lads volunteered to dig the graves on the burial hill.

Despite my weariness, I spent the evening searching for clues to the path the River Indians had traveled the day before. I was confident they were River Indians—Nipmucs, Pocumtucks, and Norwottucks—who had fled to the north after the Great Falls massacre but then returned. On foot, I followed footprints in the mud and trampled grass of the meadows bordering Cow Bridge Brook. The enemies' first stop would have been near Deerfield. They had a lead on us, but perhaps we could still overtake them. The troops would arrive tomorrow, and I prayed we'd learn more.

The troops arrived late the next night after a two-day ride from Springfield. We fed them and cared for their horses the best we could. The following morning, somewhat rested, we left. I rode beside Captain Thomas Watts in the first of ten ranks. 'Twas important we did not disturb the land around us, did not trample any clues I needed to track our quarry, hence we rode but two abreast.

We reached Deerfield midday. It was completely razed, the scorched earth bringing to mind a beach, the sheen of an ebb tide on bare sand hiding crabs scuttling beneath the surface. I glimpsed faint signs of what had been but now was gone. We dismounted. I walked the lane whilst the troops and the other men took refreshments. Unchanged from the year before, only blackened shells remained of most of the houses, ruins from previous invasions of Deerfield.

I found a stack of freshly riven oak, a wedge but no ax. Close by, timbers for a barn frame lay on a cleared and leveled plot of ground. The gate was open to the small field where I reckoned the horses had been penned, fresh hoofprints leading out the gate and up the trail. I looked inside the shed that served as a temporary barn. A plow hulked in the shadows, and from the walls hung a yoke, a harness, and a few saddles, but no bridles nor bits.

Behind the shed, I came upon a dead man lying face down in the dirt. He'd been clubbed in the head, but his mortal wound was a musket ball to his back. Steadying myself, I knelt and rolled the man over, revealing a face I did not recognize— a full beard and a long nose. His eyes stared blindly, the irises blackened by death. The exit wound of the musket ball was large as a pomegranate, clotted with dried blood and ruined flesh. I waited until my vision cleared and my nausea passed and then called out to Stephen Jennings and John Coleman. They joined me.

"By God in Heaven," Coleman swore. "'Tis John Root. My Anna is . . . was . . . friend to his wife, Mehitable."

He kicked the side of the barn, then gazed up at the sky as though it held salvation.

"I need to take him home to her," he said.

We lifted John Root's body onto Coleman's horse. The stiffness of death had passed, and John's body drooped across the saddle like a sack of apples. Captain Watts sent one of the soldiers with them for protection. They headed south, John Coleman carefully leading his horse and its heavy burden, the soldier walking beside, his flintlock at the ready.

Stephen and I opened our packs of victuals and sat on the unburned stoop of one of the houses. I had little appetite but forced myself to eat my ham and cheese and drink some cider. Then, seeking solitude, I wandered to the orchard. The pears and apples had ripened and fallen, and I gathered unspoiled ones from the ground. I fed one to Scout and another to Stephen's black gelding, Raven, then stowed the rest in my pack.

I thought of my children. The three of them adored Scout. I'd often put all three on her back and lead them about in the field as they laughed in joy. The Natives would have them on horses now, but 'twould be terrifying for them. They would be kept apart from Martha to ensure her obedience. Martha must be frantic. Lost. Wondering why I'd not yet come to rescue them. Alone amongst the fruit trees, I allowed myself to weep.

We tarried at what remained of Deerfield for five minutes more and then struck out again. I was greatly encouraged to find a trail of fresh horse dung and hoof prints leading east from the field and up the west flank of Sugarloaf Mountain. We followed for about a mile until I lost the trail in the undergrowth. Turning back, we continued up the valley until we came to the Deerfield River. On its muddy banks, I found more footprints, large and small, amid the horse's deeper marks. After we'd forded Deerfield River, I called a halt.

"Captain Watts?" I said. "Allow me a quarter-hour to scout this area with Jennings and two of your soldiers, if you will?"

"Did not the Pocumtuck have a fort near about?"

"Aye, and I suspect the captors may have stopped there," I said.

The four of us cocked and shouldered our guns and rode cautiously up the forested rise until we came to the Natives' fortified stockade enclosing their camp. No smoke rose from within. We rode to the gate and tied the horses to one of the two big oak trees.

There were fresh marks carved into the bark. I ran my fingers over them and felt light-headed. I leaned against the tree until my vision cleared.

"What is it?" Stephen put his hand on my shoulder.

I couldn't speak for a moment but pointed to the hatch marks gouged into the bark.

"What are those?" Stephen asked, peering more closely at the tree.

"Indian boasts, a record of those they killed and captured," I said. "They were here."

I ran into the village and stuck my musket inside wigwams in a macabre reenactment of my actions at the Falls Fight, but found them empty. The cooking fires were cold, but the smell of woodsmoke lingered. In the dirt, I found a handful of dried corn tossed away, and a few drops of blood. I was in purgatory between the past and present. Time bent back on itself, like dreams glimpsed when one drifts off to sleep and then startles awake again.

I vaulted into the saddle, and we rejoined the troops.

"They paused here for a while," I said, "I do not think for the night, but they were here."

"You're certain?" asked Captain Watts.

"Yes, sir." I told him what we'd found. "As far as I can tell, they camped the first night near Deerfield, and I'd wager they spent last night a days' ride north of here."

We rode past White Ash Swamp where Algonquians ambushed Experience Hinsdell and his team, past where we'd assembled above the Falls before the fight, past where most of us had ever traveled. We climbed up Pisgah mountain on a narrow trail we rode in single file, weaving in and out of dark mossy forests and misty open meadows, in and out of view of the Connecticut River.

Twilight cast dusty shafts through the trees, and a ray of sun illuminated a flash of white in a thicket of maple saplings beside the trail, a scrap of white linen cloth about the size of my palm. English clothing snagged on a branch in passing, from an apron, cap, or cuff.

I signaled a halt and showed it to the captain.

"I wish we'd been outfitted for a longer expedition, Mister Waite," he said, frowning.

"What is the time, captain?" I asked. My mind was racing, grasping at straws.

He pulled out a brass pocket watch and clicked it open.

"Quarter past six. The horses are tiring," Watts said.

"A bit farther. We have their trail."

"They have at least a day's lead—"

"Please, spare us one more hour," I pleaded.

He sighed. "Very well. Let's give our poor beasts a rest for a quarter-hour first."

We were north of Great Falls and a few hours south of the abandoned town of Northfield. Thirty of our Hadley men were slain there two years ago, trying in vain to defend North-field from one of King Philip's attacks. It seemed no place had escaped the war. We slung feedbags of oats on our horses and stretched our legs. Then we were back on the trail again.

I listened intently as I rode. 'Twas a calm evening, clear and crisp. All I heard was the distant humming of the Connecticut, the crunch of fallen leaves and needles under-foot, the cadence of the horses' hoofbeats.

After a half hour, Watts called a halt.

"We must camp here, Waite. Ten hours ride is enough. It is all we were ordered to do," Watts said, his voice weary.

"Then I will take a few men and go on ahead on foot."

"As you wish. We will camp here for the night and hope to see you back in Hatfield on the morrow."

I chose Stephen, one soldier, and three men from Hatfield, and we walked single file for another hour, sensing nothing but the wind and our footfalls.

Then, a snapping of twigs and a rustling in the saplings to our left. We whirled toward the disturbance, and I signaled to present arms. I knelt and fully cocked my gun, waiting and listening, and the soldier beside me did the same. But the woods were silent. We lowered our weapons and continued down the path for another hour, reckoning time from the rise of the crescent moon as a soft rain began to fall.

And then, an owl hooted. Three faint hoots and an answering trio. I held up my hand, and it seemed we all held our breath. Again, it came, three and three, from the woods ahead. Not owls.

Chapter Eighteen
MARTHA

It was our fourth night in captivity. We lay staked on the wet meadow grass, displayed like heraldic eagles, too far apart to speak to one another. I couldn't turn my head without choking from the rope that bound my neck, so my gaze roamed the starry sky. I was grateful to my father for teaching me the constellations, for finding them gave me a small measure of joy by which to distract myself.

Glancing down, I saw the Great Square above the tree-tops. From there, I traced the curve of Pegasus's neck upwards, the flying horse upside down in autumn. Downwards to my right, I spied the circlet of Pisces, and up to my left, the crown of Cassiopeia glittered, and the house of Cepheus, the Queen and King, shone bright. My father told me Sir Isaac Newton believed the stars were suns, and our Sun, a star. I missed our conversations.

It was so quiet. I missed the late-night crow of our rooster waking me from slumber, the barking of dogs, and the fighting of the barn cats. I missed the crackle of our hearth fire, Ben's snoring, one of our girls calling to us after a nightmare or asking us to walk them through the dark to the privy by the orchard.

I missed my wee babes dreadfully, though they slept by the fire that flickered just out of sight. Were they warm enough? Hungry? Around me rose whimpering cries and gentle weeping, and I strained to hear if it came from a child of mine. I ached for them like a part of me had been severed, an arm or a leg. My heart. Missing them was endless, like the night sky. I sang a gentle lullaby out into the darkness, and to the babe within me.

> *"Golden slumbers kiss your eyes,*
> *Smiles await you when you rise.*
> *Sleep, pretty baby, do not cry,*
> *And I will sing a lullaby.*

Tears filled my eyes, and I worried where Ben was now. I knew in my bones he was alive, but was he wounded? Caring for kin at Hatfield? Was he searching for us? If ever we had needed his skills as a scout, a ranger, a tracker, it was now. *Dear God, please send him to me.* But if He did, what then? Our captors surely wouldn't relinquish us willingly. Any attempt to rescue us could prove deadly.

Though I could not see them, I heard the soft footfalls of the warriors' moccasins, their hoots like owls. Where did they go in the middle of the night? I wanted to ask one of our men but dared not break the silence. It began to rain.

I awakened in the night when one of the stolen horses whinnied. There was a shifting and jostling amongst the small herd. Another horse neighed, and a faint answering call came from somewhere far off in the distance. My heart leapt with joy. A whinny from afar would hardly be a farmer's horse, not in the midst of the wilderness. I dared hope that somewhere out there, I'd heard the friendly neigh of a horse from a search party.

BEN

The whinny floated like a whisper to us through the forest, followed by another, and Scout, ever the sociable one, threw up her head, pricked her ears, and let loose a loud reply.

"Shh!" I cautioned her, "Hush!"

"The stolen herd from Deerfield, Ben?" Stephen asked.

"It must be. We must move quickly."

ASHPELON

The five men returned from the hunt empty-handed but bringing news of the English troops nearby. I'd heard the horses and knew what we must do.

"Quick! Nìbi Wàbà, Uppeshoii, Mehtuk," I called to our women in our language, "put our elders and all the children on the horses and take them east to the river." I kicked dirt on our fire, embers scattering like fireflies.

"Atian, Kòkòkòho, pull up the stakes of the English, bind their hands behind them, divide up the men and women, and lead them off to the west. Gag them so they cannot scream. Knock them on the head if they resist. I will take the rest of the warriors and divide up in the forest. We will meet at the brook near Metacomet's hill once the trackers have lost our trail."

As I spoke, it was done. My family moved quickly, silent except for the traitorous horses, who continued to neigh. They'd be silenced soon if we couldn't find game. Killed so we could survive.

In less than the time it takes to load a flintlock, we were gone.

BEN

Our small band had to stop every few minutes to pick up the trail, guided by misplaced drifts of pine needles, broken branches, and horse manure hastily buried beneath fallen leaves. We discovered the Algonquians' camp about two miles away, a half hour at most, but it was deserted. Rabbit bones smoldered in hot embers within a ring of stones. Holes pockmarked the meadow where our foes had driven stakes to secure our kin, and fresh horse manure nearby where they'd hobbled the horses. Rage burned through me at God for allowing us to come so close only to lose the trail here.

Tracks split off in four directions from the camp, like the fingers of a hand. There were footprints and hoofprints, but the different sizes and depths confused me. I couldn't tell how they had divided themselves. They likely had separated our men from our women and children, flanked by warriors. They might send some to Albany, some to Canada, and some even to the remaining Narragansett bands near Providence. Had the Natives taken our children from their mothers? I felt sick at the thought of my girls without Martha.

The six of us split up, taking the trails by ones and twos. Stephen came with me. I chose the path most trampled by horses, figuring the Algonquians would let the women and children ride. The hoofprints showed them moving quickly and erratically but gradually vanished in the woods and brooks.

"God's nails!" I said, throwing my hat at the ground.

"We've lost them?" Stephen asked.

"Yes."

The others returned, also discouraged. We'd not the provisions nor permissions to continue, the will but not the strength, and not enough men to follow each path to its end.

Worst of all, we had lost the element of surprise we needed. I reluctantly assembled my men, and we turned back to rejoin the company.

Captain Watts had stationed a sentry, who awakened him on our return a few hours before dawn. Watts repeated his orders to halt at the Massachusetts Bay Colony's northern border. I pleaded with him, but he remained resolute.

I considered taking Stephen—and any other men who'd agree to it—up the Connecticut River in the morning. God willing, we'd pick up the trail once more. Yet my experience finally convinced me my hopes were futile. The Algonquian people knew the wilderness far better than I, and neither governments nor charters, Kings nor commissioners constrained them. As long as they kept to the east of the Hudson River—away from Mohawk land—they could travel freely with an ease we could not.

We laid our bedding upon damp leaves and built a small fire. I watched the flames and thought of that last kiss two days ago. The smoky lavender smell of Martha's hair, the warmth of her in my arms, my little girls playing on the rug, Mary sweeping. They were my world, and I had lost them, alongst with any hope of a swift recovery.

Chapter Nineteen

MARTHA

WILDERNESS
SEPTEMBER 23-24, 1677

I woke slowly from a brief, fitful sleep, reached out for Ben, and jolted awake. Pain shot through my injured arm, and the noose choked me. It took several moments to remember our long, quick march last night, my fury at the gag in my mouth, the Natives forcing our horses to trot and those on foot to run and stumble in the darkness. I knew not where we were, though I dimly heard the reassuring rumble of a large river, no doubt the Connecticut.

Once released, my sling supporting my arm and a calm horse beneath me, my spirits were somewhat restored. I was thankful to God that we had rejoined our children in the wee hours of the morning, long past midnight but before the dawn. Although we remained deep in the wilderness at the mercy of our captors, my children were still safe, and I was sure Ben had come searching for us. I held fast to those blessings. But Ben had lost our trail, and the distance between us grew. I was caught yet again betwixt hope and despair.

We came midday to a place where the Connecticut River narrowed and slowed. I might have found it beautiful if my circumstances had been favorable. Deep water in the shades of a peacock's tail, shifting reflections of the silvery clouds, banks densely flanked with trees tinged in gold. Birds twittered amongst the branches, wood ducks paddled in reeds by the banks, and a cool breeze dried the sweat from my brow.

We dismounted. My captor and several warriors took a path into the forest whilst we waited. I spied my girls with the same young woman as before and approached them. Much to my joy, when they saw me they came running, and the woman made no move to prevent it.

"Mommy, Mommy!" Mary cried. She flung her arms around my legs, nearly knocking me down. I took my aching arm from the sling and wrapped both arms around her, then hugged Mattie and picked up little Sally, wincing as pain erupted in my shoulder.

"My sweet moppets!" I covered them in kisses, smoothing back their hair, studying their little faces, their chubby arms and legs. They were scratched and bruised from the roughness of our travels. Sally wore soft new moccasins sewn of deer hide with delicate, twining vines of colorful beads. Mattie had torn the hem of her apron. Mary's shoes were scuffed, the soles badly worn. I had been kept apart from them for three days.

"Are you well? Is the Indian woman being kind to you?" I asked.

Mary nodded, but Mattie pouted and cried, "No. I'm tired and hungry, and I want to go home!"

"Oh, Mattie, I know. We are truly being tested," I said, giving her another hug.

"Mommy, where are they taking us? When is Daddy coming?" Mary asked.

Before I could summon a comforting reply, the warriors

emerged from the trees, carrying birchbark canoes above their heads. The strong muscles in their arms strained beneath the weight of their load, and I trembled in fear. I had never felt such weakness before. Obedient when it was required but never weak. The Natives made me feel vulnerable, powerless to defend myself or protect my girls.

The warriors set the half dozen canoes on the pebbles at the river's shore. Ashpelon strode over and bade me climb into the nearest one. The Native woman joined me, and Ashpelon handed in my three girls. Relief flooded me that we'd cross the river together.

"I am Martha," I said to the woman. I wanted her to think me unafraid.

The woman gazed at me directly, unsmiling. Her eyes were dark embers, and her plaited black hair shone in the sun. "I am Nìbi Wàbà. 'White Water.'"

"Please be good to my daughters."

"Mary, Mattie, and Sally," she said, pointing to my babes.

She knew English, and also their names. I was disarmed by that, affronted. Yet, on reflection, she'd had more time with them than I had the past few days. My girls had told her their names, which meant they were at ease talking to her, and that both cheered and frightened me.

A warrior climbed into our canoe, holding two paddles, and handed one to Nìbi Wàbà. The Natives sat on either side of the boat, Ashpelon nudged it into the water, and the current caught us.

"This is Kòkòkòho," Nìbi Wàbà said. "Owl."

I noticed the colorful embroidery at the hem of his loin-cloth, and the beadwork of his headband like that on Sally's new moccasins. I nodded to him, then almost laughed at the absurdity of our introductions, as though I were meeting newcomers to Hatfield between sermons on the Sabbath. Despite her squirming, I held tightly to Sally, and Mary and

Mattie sat stock still before me, likely terrified of being on a boat for the first time.

The current carried us quite far downstream, but Kòkòkòho and Nìbi Wàbà rowed fiercely, and we made it safely across the river to a sandy bank on the western side. Nìbi Wàbà reached for Sally, and Kòkòkòho held out his hand to me. Though they meant to help us safely onto the bank, I kept my arms tight around Sally and glared at them, allowing only a steadying hand on my elbow.

The Natives abandoned the canoes once we were across, though I supposed they concealed them for another time. We traveled the leaf-covered trail, weaving between the trees, the mighty river never out of earshot. Overjoyed to have my girls alongside me again, my mood lightened. I carried Sally on my right hip, and though it pained me, I couldn't bear to let go. Mattie was skipping, but Mary walked shyly at my side, holding my skirt. After a time, the girls and I tired, so Kòkòkòho put me on a horse and walked beside me, holding Sally. Nìbi Wàbà rode with Mattie in her arms and Mary behind her.

To my disappointment, we turned away from the Connecticut River, the only part of this wilderness I knew. When Ben had married me and brought me to Hatfield, he told me if I were ever lost, I should find a brook or river and follow it downhill. I had laughed at the time, doubting I'd ever have the misfortune to be lost. My life was our house, garden, orchard, and the rest of our village. Only a few times had I helped with a harvest or taken the well-traveled road or ferry with Ben to visit my family in Springfield.

Without the Connecticut beside us, I felt forsaken. It distressed me not to know when this journey would end or where we were. Our trail wound up into the mountains, barely wide enough for the horses. Lost to view in the trees, a creek trickled and splashed beside us. My feet burned with blisters, my arm ached, and our provisions were gone. My stomach growled in hunger, and I fought the dizziness clouding my vision. We traveled until dusk, when our captors staked us down again.

❧

Before dawn, the warriors went hunting and returned with three raccoons, which the women dressed and skinned and boiled over a fire for many hours. They gave each an equal portion, Native and English alike. It tasted like beef, and my girls and I ate hungrily.

In the afternoon we reached our resting place, the mountain's summit. There, the forest dwindled, and we assembled on a flat expanse of silvery rock laid bare to the heavens. Miles and miles of hills and valleys rolled below like waves in an ocean. The air was sharply cold but without wind, and the place silent but for the murmuring of the brook.

I found a soft bed of leaves and needles beneath a tall fir tree. Kòkòkòho handed Sally to me. She was crying and asking for food, but I had none to give, so I rocked her in my arms until she fell asleep. Mary and Mattie helped Nìbi Wàbà and the elder woman, Neepânon, build a fire, and I watched them, relieved to see my daughters treated gently but wanting to hold them close. Several warriors strode into the trees, wielding tomahawks, and soon the clearing resounded with their thuds. The three Englishmen from Deerfield and Obadiah Dickinson carried stout branches and the felled logs to an expanse of rock, where Natives stripped them of bark.

Mary and Hannah appeared with their children. They smiled at Sally sleeping and sat quietly beside me. Their children—Nate, Molly, Sammy, and Holly—toddled away and set about drawing and scratching on the silvery rocks with twigs.

"A blessed moment to rest," Mary said, smoothing her

blue skirt and dirty apron around her. "My feet are mighty sore, and my babes are so hungry."

I stroked Sally's golden tresses. "Mary, I fear to ask, but your wee babe, your son born in March—do you know what became of him?"

Mary nodded. "When the Indians attacked our house, my sister Miriam was there. She grabbed him from his basket and ran." She looked away at the first flames of the fire.

"Then they are both safe," I said.

"I pray they are," she said, then burst into tears. "My bosom aches, and my milk has soaked my shift. I miss my wee son. I miss my husband."

I knew not what to say. I looked around for the orphans, as I called them, the captive English children whose parents had either been killed or left behind in Hatfield. I felt responsible for them. I saw the littlest ones with Neepânon's husband but couldn't find the three older boys.

"Have either of you seen Noah Coleman, Sam Russell, or Matthew Kellogg?" I asked.

"They're gathering fallen chestnuts and acorns somewhere off in the woods," Hannah said, "I hope they find enough for our supper."

"I hope they aren't eaten by wolves," Mary said bitterly.

Hannah gasped and half rose to her feet. I realized Mary was not herself, and did not know of Hannah's firstborn's death, and the impact of her flippant words.

"Hannah, she's only jesting. Please, sit," I said, glaring at Mary.

Hannah sat but kept darting glances toward the forest. "How are you, Martha?"

"I'm afraid of angering our captors, of displeasing them. Ashpelon seems to be the chief, and he is my master."

Hannah scoffed. "Two warriors are fighting over who 'owns' me. I'm hard-pressed to please them equally, for one is short-tempered and the other most calm. The angry one is called Mattagehan, and the other, Animosh."

"The woman with my girls is Nìbi Wàbà," I said. "She told me it means White Water."

"Quintin Stockwell knows a fair amount of their language," Mary said. "He told me the names of my captors, the elder Neepânon and her husband Wekoñtam. I refuse to call them by name. They are wicked heathen!"

"How does Quintin know their language?" Hannah asked. I knew she was uncomfortable with Mary's anger.

"I have no idea," Mary said.

"I think he or his father helped Reverend Elliot translate the Bible for the Christian Indians. Maybe this tribe's language is similar," I said.

"These are not Christian Indians," Hannah said. "Are they a tribe from Canada? For you said Ashpelon told you that is our destination."

"I think they are Nipmucs, Pocumtucks, and Norwottucks —River Indians—but I cannot begin to sort out all the different tribes, clans, and languages," I said. "'Tis curious how Ashpelon and a few of the others know English."

Hannah fought back tears. "We came so close to being rescued, I thought my prayers were answered, and then they gagged us, split us up . . ."

"I think it was Ben with the English, searching for us. He knows the ways of the Natives," I said. It was a sin to think it, but my faith in my husband was at times greater than my faith in God.

We fell silent then, watching the Native people and Englishmen work, until Mary spoke. "It seems we're going to camp here for a while, with all the preparations."

"That would be a small blessing," I said. "Though the shelter isn't completed."

Noah Coleman, Sam Russell, and Matthew Kellogg returned carrying a basketful of chestnuts and even a few walnuts, and the Natives hauled back a net of fish. The Native women cooked both over the fire and gave us each a morsel of slimy fish and a small handful of roasted chestnuts. I offered a prayer of thanks, but my hunger was not satisfied. I worried for the child I carried. If I did not eat enough, neither did the babe within me.

Our captors left us unbound, though they watched us closely, and finally returned our children to us. We sat together by the campfire after we had eaten. We all held tightly to our children, embracing them, smoothing and plaiting their hair, kissing their scrapes and scratches. Hannah sat farther from the fire than the rest of us, cradling her children in her arms. Even now, years after the tragic death of her infant daughter, it seemed the warmth and flames of a bonfire frightened her. The torching of our town had shaken her even more than the rest of us.

My friends and I watched the Native women and elders place walnut shells in a wooden mortar, adding a handful of rich earth and a dab of bear grease, a provision seemingly in endless supply. They smashed and stirred the mixture with a wooden pestle until it was a paste. The warriors dipped their fingers into it and smeared the dark stain on their cheeks and forehead.

The older man produced a drum, which he rested on his lap and began to beat, and the Native women shook rattles made of hollow squash. Warriors fastened circlets of bright brass around their ankles and began to dance, stomping their feet on the ground and raising their bare arms to the heavens. Their chests shone like burnished copper as they circled about the fire.

I drew back in apprehension, but my girls watched eagerly, fascinated by the spectacle.

I beckoned to Quintin Stockwell, who sat but a few yards away, and he came closer.

"Goodwife Waite?"

"What omen is this? Good or evil?" I asked fearfully.

"I cannot tell. They are rejoicing, but whether that spells evil for us or not, I do not know," Quintin said.

Long after darkness fell, the dance ended. Our captors came 'round and bound our hands tightly in front of us. My arm was numb to the pain, swollen and stiff. Though they took our children away from us, our captors did not stake us down, and it was a relief to lie on my side and not my back. I gazed into the flames and fell asleep to the smell of sweet smoke and the crackling of the green kindling, thankful the night was warm.

In the middle of the night, I was awakened by a great commotion amongst the Native men. There seemed to be division in the ranks. The anger in their voices was apparent, though I knew not the words. I searched the darkness for my children and saw them sleeping beside the Native women at a smaller fire, safely removed from the discord. It seemed Ashpelon tried to give each faction a turn to speak, but he was losing control. Their loud, strange words swooped and crashed and trampled over each other.

As none guarded me, I rose and walked to where the men lay, away from the fire near a cairn of boulders. Quintin and Benoni were awake, sitting up and staring intently at the faces of the Natives illuminated by the fire.

"Goodman Stockwell, Goodwife Foote says you understand their language?" I asked.

"Some of it. They speak not only with words but also their hands, so I watch and listen."

"What are they fighting about?" I asked.

"They're fighting amongst themselves because, like us, they are tired and hungry," he said.

"But what is their quarrel?"

"Pay it no heed, Martha."

Benoni Stebbins shook his head. "Just tell her, Quintin," he said.

"I am not a child," I said. "Goodman Stockwell, please tell me what you know."

He sighed. "Some of them wish to punish us now that they are done celebrating this place," he said.

"Punish us? For what transgressions?" I asked.

"For being English. For the Falls Fight. For breaking promises."

I could not deny any of those, but I pressed him further. "What is to be our punishment?"

"Some speak of harming one or more of us," Quintin replied, "but Ashpelon is trying to reason with them. They want to take a vote."

"'Tis more than harm they threaten," Benoni said.

"Quintin?"

Quintin sighed.

"Tell me."

"They mean to kill one of us. On the night of the New Moon."

I glanced in terror at the waning crescent moon.

"Who? And for what reason?" I gasped.

"Who can know? To ensure we're at their mercy. To boast of their strength to any Mohawks hereabouts and hope they send word to the English not to follow."

I realized I'd been easing into an acceptance of our captivity. The reminder that we could be killed set my heart pounding.

And Quintin hadn't answered the other part of my question.

I gripped his arm. "Did they say who? Which of us they intend to kill?"

"'Tis a tempest in a teacup, no doubt—" Quintin began.

Benoni cut him off. "Quintin and I heard them speak his name and Sergeant Plympton's . . . and yours, Mistress Waite," Benoni said dispiritedly.

I learned what it meant to have one's blood run cold.

Quintin shot Benoni an angry look, then gently patted my hand. "By morning, the Indians will have forgotten their anger."

The firelight showed the shelter's frame nearly complete, a rectangular cage of pine logs stripped of bark. I returned to my spot by the fire and lay back down, but sleep was a long time coming.

Chapter Twenty

BEN

Our search party returned to Hatfield the night of September 23rd, and after a day's rest, our town held another meeting the evening of September 24th.

John Coleman spoke first, voicing the thoughts of many of those present.

"Didn't Governor Andros set aside land for the Algonquian tribes near Albany? Maybe they raided our town? Maybe he knows something?"

"Andros is away in England. Captain Salisbury is in charge," Belding said. "But our War Council and John Pynchon of Springfield think we should seek Albany's aid. Waite? What do you think?"

"'Tis true Governor Andros set land aside at Schaghticoke for many Algonquian tribes, and the Mohawks run messages for him. Salisbury won't be much help, but the Mohawks might."

"Will you go? See if they will help us?" Belding asked.

I reluctantly agreed. We should consult the Mohawks. But I'd dealt with Salisbury before when he'd tried to arrest me for "illegal" fur trade. I knew he would be less than effusive in his help.

Our United Colonies' War Council composed a letter to Salisbury, asking him to consult the Mohawks and Algonquians for any information about the attack on Hatfield. My former employer, Major John Pynchon of Springfield, had also prepared a letter of introduction. I packed provisions—corn pone, dried beef, and cider—rolled up a pallet, blanket, and lantern for over a week on the road and prepared my guns and ammunition. I tucked the letters and a few pound notes in my pocket. Then, I partook of a night of much-needed sleep.

❧

"I'd gladly come with you, Ben," Stephen said, walking beside me to Middle Lane the next morning.

"Thank you, but there's no need for both of us to squander time. 'Tis best you tend to Scout when I'm gone. She's pulled up a bit lame since our search, so the way will be quicker without her."

"You do not expect much to come of this trip, then?"

"In Albany, no. I'm sure I'm correct in my assumptions. The route the Natives followed north, how they fashioned their camps—they were Algonquian. River Indians," I said. "But support from the War Council is conditional upon eliminating the Mohawks and the Schaghticoke tribes as suspect. After Albany, I will report my findings to Pynchon and go to Boston to secure final approval and funding."

We paused by the gate at the end of Middle Road.

"Funding for tracking and pursuing our kin and their captors as far north as need be," Stephen said.

He voiced it as a statement of truth, with no tone of incredulity. I put my hand on his shoulder.

"Stephen, I would be honored to have you accompany me

to Boston. Would you be willing to continue on from there? Possibly as far as Canada?" I asked. I needed a friend beside me.

"Of course. Anything I can do to help rescue my wife and children." He removed his hat, and ran his fingers through his red hair. His usually ruddy complexion was wan and gray.

We shook hands, and I strode off under a cloudy dawn sky, threatening rain. There was no easy way to Albany. The first stage retraced my steps to Deerfield. On the second day, I cut west before reaching Turners' Falls, intentionally avoiding the place of my nightmares, to spend the second night at Shelburne Falls. Late on the third morning, I found the Mohawk trail I would follow through the unavoidable mountains. King Philip himself had traveled this trail.

My thoughts strayed to home, the funerals and burials to be conducted in my absence. Friends and kin I'd known most of my life, buried beneath slabs of roughly chiseled rock bearing only last names. The Bible did not speak of elaborate funerals. Hence, we honored our dead in a simple manner.

I thought of the bereaved families whose wealth had permitted them to order leather gloves and gold funeral rings. Solemn remembrances, the inside of each gold band engraved with the departed's name and date of death, the signet with a skull or angel wings.

Mementos I would not be able to afford, came the unbidden and wicked thought.

I fell to my knees in the middle of the stony trail, removing my hat, bowing my head, and humbling myself before my God. And it was then it struck me—my guilt. The massacre at Peskeompskut Falls had most likely led to the attack on Hatfield. And I had led us there. It was my fault that my wife and children had been taken.

But no, that was putting myself before God. *Did not Job declare the mighty power of God, and that man's righteousness is nothing?*

My faith must not waver. I spoke aloud, my words mingling with the whispers of the wind in the trees.

"The Lord to me a shepherd is, want therefore shall not I,

He in the folds of tender grass, doth cause me down to lie

To waters calm me gently leads, restore my soul doth he

He doth in paths of righteousness for his names' sake leadeth me

Yes, though in the valley of deaths' shade I walk, no ill I'll fear to see."

Rising to my feet, I added a line from Corinthians as I gazed up at the lowering sky, tears warm on my face.

"Love suffereth all things: it believeth all things: it hopeth all things: it endureth all things," I whispered. I placed my hat back upon my head.

My love for my wife knew no bounds.

I had fallen in love at first sight, as they say, in a market-place in Springfield over eight years ago. I beckoned those pleasant memories to replace my fears as I traveled the next five days to Albany.

Eight Years Ago, April 1669
Springfield, Massachusetts Bay Colony
Ben

I will ne'er forget that morning in April, disembarking the riverboat in Springfield with my cartload of furs, pulling my wool scarf snug about my neck, shivering inside my cloak. The streets were icy, and I pushed my cart slowly around the fishmongers and chimney sweeps beneath a gray sky threatening rain.

There had been several lovely ladies in my life, but the

only lass I'd courted, Esther Cowles, had recently spurned me and married Deacon Thomas Bull of Connecticut. Though not yet officially betrothed, I'd foolishly thought she was mine. I went so far as to object to their banns in court, but without proof of an engagement, I had no claim to her. I tried to convince myself I was better off, that Esther had wanted Bull's land and his title of Deacon, but the experience left me sad and shaken.

After unloading my furs at John Pynchon's warehouse, the Saturday market caught my eye. Instead of going straight to the bloomery to pick up the heavy load of iron to trade with the Algonquians, I pushed my empty cart amid the market stalls. It was a cheerful place, and I hoped 'twould lift my spirits.

The air smelled of lavender soaps and beeswax candles, clover honey and fresh loaves of bread. I passed market stalls crowded with tiny, colorful posies tied up in ribbons, jars of jams and pickles, shiny copper kettles and black iron fire tongs, powder horns and bridles. I was examining a rather unusual flint tinder lighter made from a pistol, and the man hawking it was explaining how he'd taken it from the dead body of a French fur trader, when I heard her voice.

I looked to my right, and there she was, haggling in a cheerful but persistent manner over the price of a small pewter candlestick. She was young, clear-skinned and doe-eyed, fetchingly curvy, and with a laugh that brightened the day. Her dress was modest but spoke of wealth and rank—a collar of delicate lace draped her shoulders, a green overskirt matching her bodice was drawn up in a bit of a ruffle at the sides to show an underskirt of dove gray, and emerald ribbons tied at her elbows gathered her green outer sleeves, revealing lace sleeves to her wrists. I watched her for a moment, unable to look away, until she caught me gazing at her.

With a puzzled tilt of her head, she smiled at me, and my heart leapt.

"Good day, sir. Have we met?" she asked.

"No, my lady, surely I would not have forgotten a previous moment so cheering," I said, and then, before she could spurn me, "May I buy that candlestick for you?"

'Twould cost my entire month's fur trade, even if I negotiated a better price.

"I cannot accept such a costly gift from a stranger," she said, glancing away, a blush like roses on her cheeks, but then looked back and met my gaze directly. Her eyes were a dusky green, like the sage of her gown.

"Then may I introduce myself, and we'll be strangers no more. Goodman Benjamin Waite." I doffed my hat and bowed.

"Quite the gentleman," she said, smiling. "'Tis a pleasure to make your acquaintance, Mister Waite. I am Mistress Leonard." She offered me her ungloved hand, which I took as encouragement. I removed my glove and clasped her hand lightly for a moment, marveling at the softness of her skin.

"Leonard? Are you kin to John Leonard, the ironmaster with whom I trade?" I asked, reluctantly releasing her hand.

"He is my father."

"Then we are practically friends already," I said. "You may ask him about me."

"I intend to," she said, smiling. She turned to leave.

"Wait, might I buy the candlestick for you? I can imagine your lovely face is even more lovely by candlelight." The words kept tripping off my tongue. I was indeed playing the fool.

"Oh, my, you are skilled in the art of flattery, Mister Waite, but I must refuse."

"Perhaps I will buy it for myself, and burn through candles each night until we meet again." How had she done this, mended my broken heart and set it winging?

"You presume we will meet again?" she asked, her smile sparkling in her green eyes.

"I promise we will, Mistress Leonard." I gazed after her as she walked away.

I bought the candlestick and several candles.

And, of course, we did meet again.

Chapter Twenty-One

MARTHA

The men were finishing the ridgepole for the longhouse's roof, attaching long, curved saplings, forming a shape like a giant turtle shell. It seemed a more permanent dwelling than the small, quick shelters of branches, bark, and woven mats the Natives had made the past few nights.

I ran my fingers through Mattie's light brown hair, trying to sort out the tangles and dirt, searching for vermin and, thankfully, finding none.

"Mommy, why won't the Indians let us go home?" Mattie asked.

My heart ached. There was naught I could think to say other than to make light of it.

"They want to take us to Canada," I said.

"But why?"

"Because we've never been there. It will be an adventure."

"I don't like adventures. I'm hungry. It isn't nice to take us on an adventure and not feed us," Mattie said.

Out of the mouths of babes.

I set her down in front of me and looked her in the eye. "Mattie, I need you to be a big girl, and do what the Indians tell you and what I tell you and what your big sister tells you. Now, go play with Abby."

"Which Abby?"

"Whichever one you want. Or both." Honestly, Mattie was my cross to bear. But now that our captors no longer separated parents from our children, I would bear that cross gladly. And it *was* confusing to have two captive children about the same age and with the same Christian name, Abigail Bartholomew and Abigail Allis.

Many orphaned Hatfield children were amongst us. Hannah, Mary, and I tried our best to keep an eye on them, although the Natives did a surprisingly fair job. Watching out for more than a dozen children, most under six years of age, wouldn't have been unheard of back in Hatfield, but doing so in the wilderness surrounded by Natives was beyond daunting.

One of the warriors strode over to me. I froze in fear, remembering the threats made to kill me, but he held out several yards of white linen.

"You make shirt," he said, thrusting the cloth towards me.

For a moment, I was speechless. "You want me to sew a shirt for you?"

"You make shirt. Like English."

I supposed he'd looted the fabric from the raid on our town or Deerfield. I gingerly took my arm out of my sling and checked the apron pockets where I kept the tin box containing my needle and thread, embroidery scissors, buttons, a thimble, and a pincushion. The needle and scissors were gone, taken from me at some point by my captors.

I held out my empty hands to the warrior. "I need my tools." I mimed cutting and sewing.

The warrior handed me a leather pouch. Inside were my scissors and fine needles, and also larger Nipmuc-made needles of bone, and some type of animal sinew.

'Twould be unwise to refuse. I took the cloth and the pouch.

From the other pocket of my apron, I took out the small Geneva Bible Ben gave me when we first courted. I opened it to the face page and Ben's inscription.

I'd meant to read Scripture before I sewed, but my eyes filled with tears, and I could neither sew nor read. I began to sob. The warrior turned back and took a few steps toward me, a look of pity on his face. I struggled to staunch my tears, and he turned away again and left me to my sorrow.

After a time, I wiped my eyes on my apron, picked up the pure white cloth, spread it on a rock, and cut a pattern. I could not give in to self-pity. My girls needed me, and Ben would want me to be brave. I thought of Ben and the day he'd given me the Bible.

Martha
Eight Years Ago, June 1669
Springfield, Massachusetts Bay Colony

Each market day since our first meeting, I looked for Goodman Waite, searching the crowds for his tall, loose-limbed, easy stride, listening for the smoky lilt of his voice. My father had some objections to Waite courting me, one being his lack of wealth and the other, "Waite's land is in Hatfield, one of those frontier towns far beyond the borders of propriety."

But those objections could not be tested if I never met Goodman Waite again, and if I did, I knew I was my father's favorite and could sway his mind in most things.

As I left the Springfield meetinghouse that summer's day

with my sister Mary, there Benjamin stood, gazing at me from across Courthouse Square. I froze.

"What is it, Martha?" Mary asked.

"'Tis him," I said.

"The man you fancied? From two months ago?" she asked, incredulous.

"Shh! Yes."

"I must find my husband, but I dare not leave you unchaperoned," she said.

"I promise I will come to no harm."

Mary shook her head. "Very well, I'm off then. We'll be at our house. Join us for supper when you're through getting reacquainted," she said, frowning.

I snugged the ties on my cap, smoothed my apron, and crossed the courtyard. Goodman Waite stayed where he was, his eyes locked on mine, a faint smile playing on his lips. His eyes were the same clear blue as the June sky. I realized I should have pretended not to see him, been more strange, but it was too late for that now.

"Mistress Leonard," he said, again the gentleman, doffing his hat.

"Goodman Waite. We meet again."

"You do remember me!" The joy in his voice, and his easy smile, caught my heart.

"What brings you to our Meetinghouse?" I asked.

"I think it must have been divine intervention. In truth, I arrived late yesterday and missed the boat back home. I spent the night in town, and it being the Sabbath . . ." he said. Then, in a rush, as though he'd been holding his breath, "Would you care to walk with me? Do you need to be somewhere else?"

I nearly blurted out that there was nowhere else I'd rather be, but somehow contained myself and replied evenly, "Yes, let's walk. By the river?"

And so, we did. We admired the homes and shops alongst

the riverfront, Mister Pynchon's grand warehouse, and the grist mills. He purchased dried corn from a poor waif, and we fed it to a family of mallard ducks and ducklings at the river's edge. Goodman Waite told me of his family in Rhode Island, briefly of his brother's passing, his broken engagement, and of his new home in Hatfield.

I scarcely remember what I spoke of. I suppose my parents, my sister's recent wedding to Goodman Samuel Bliss, and my enjoyment of the day's sermons and readings.

"Which Scripture do you enjoy most?" he asked, as we sat on a bench and gazed at the broad, dark river.

"Oh, I suppose the verse from Ecclesiastes, 'to all things there is a time' . . ."

"Read it to me," he said gently.

"Oh, I cannot. I do not have a Bible of my own. I usually borrow my sister's or . . ."

"Well, that won't do," he said.

For a heartbeat, I thought he was displeased with me, and I began to stammer an apology. He pulled a Bible from his pocket and handed it to me.

"There, now you have one," he said.

"But this is yours!" I took the small leather-bound book in my hands like a treasure.

"I will get another. I want you to have it."

So, I read to him from the little Bible, and we talked about the meaning, the ebb and flow of the tides, the births and deaths we'd known, the cold April day we met, and the long summer days ahead. When the sun turned the clouds and the river to persimmons and roses, we headed back. He asked me to call him Benjamin, and in return, I invited him to my sister's home for supper. I could tell they approved of him.

Before he left, he asked my sister's husband, Samuel Bliss, for a quill and a pot of ink. Samuel directed him to the side table in the keeping room. Ben took the Bible he'd given me and inscribed the inside of the front cover. With a smile, he returned the Bible to me and asked if he might see me again the next time he came to town. I silently read the lines from Corinthians he'd written.

To Mistress Leonard,

Love always protects, always trusts, always hopes, always perseveres. Love never fails.

Always, Benjamin

A feeling bloomed in me that took my breath, but I closed the Bible and managed a reply.

"I would very much like to see you again." I tucked the Bible in my pocket.

Benjamin brought my hands to his lips and kissed them, then gazed down at me, his blue eyes misty with tenderness. I walked him to the door. He ducked under the stoop, then looked back over his shoulder as he put on his hat. "Love never fails," he said. And winked.

Chapter Twenty-Two
MARTHA

PUTNEY MOUNTAIN

The longhouse was finished and the moon was dark. To our great relief, nothing came of the frenzied words and dancing of two nights before. Our captors made no moves to harm us and held no more secret meetings—or none I caught. Our punishment over, we were allowed inside the new longhouse at night.

Ashpelon sought me out as I weaved a mat of rushes for Nìbi Wàbà.

"You heard of the dangers to you, spoken by some of my people?" He crouched beside me, his arms resting on his knees, his gaze not meeting mine but watching my hands whilst I continued to weave.

"I heard you had plans to kill me," I steeled my voice, but my feelings were interwoven like the rushes in my hands. Over, under, over, under.

"Some are very angry at the English, but I convinced them you are worth more to us alive than dead."

I met his gaze and stared him down.

"So kind of you to defend me. I'm sure I can rest easier now," I snapped.

Ashpelon shook his head, frowning, and walked away.

&

I began to mark the passing days on a blank leaf of my Bible, using slivers of coal from the spent fires. Tallies, counting out the time. By my reckoning, it was our fourth day on the mountain. It might have been the Sabbath day, but I had lost count, so after conferring with Hannah, Mary, and Obadiah, we resolved to mark it so.

I set aside the shirt I was sewing for the warrior Quequan, one of Quintin Stockwell's masters. He'd been one of those wishing to harm us, hence, I took great care in making the shirt, hoping to curry his favor. He was impatient for me to finish and puzzled as to why I refused to sew on the Sabbath.

The children were bolder and more at ease amongst the Natives than any of us who were grown. It worried Mary, Hannah, and me, but we could do little to prevent it. Our wee babes less than four years of age—my Sally, Mary's little Molly, Hannah's babes, and little Daniel Dickinson—were left to our care or the arms of Nìbi Wàbà. The Native women called upon our older girls to tend the fire, gather roots and nuts, and help cook whatever game the men killed or fish they caught. The elder men and the more patient warriors taught the boys to set snares and fish. Mary and Abigail Allis threaded my needle and tied the knots for my sewing.

All the children played together betwixt the daily tasks, as they had in town, with make-believe searches for faeries and sprites in the ferns and fallen leaves, circle games, and rhyming songs. The four young Nipmuc boys clambered about on the rocks and threw pinecones at each other. Eventually, they invited the oldest children, Sam Russell and Matt Kellogg, to join them.

It was a joy to hold my girls again and sleep beside them at night. I thanked God every moment for that.

That day was perhaps the first and last day we spent at ease with the Natives. It bestowed three blessed signs from God that he had not forsaken us.

Clouds gathered all morning, and a gentle northerly breeze kicked up. The air smelled softly of fresh pine and hickory smoke from the fire, and the brooks gurgled merrily. The boys, in their exploits with the Native youth, had reported back that there were, in fact, three streams, all flowing down-hill in different directions from this mountain.

All of us were full and lazy, having feasted the night before on a deer the warriors had killed. The Englishmen napped, the Nipmuc warriors played a gambling game using painted stones for dice, and the children scampered about. I read my Bible and looked up after every few verses to check on my girls and breathe deeply of the mountain air.

I sat in my favorite spot, the rocky summit's western edge, my back to the pale morning sun and the clearing. On this side of the mountain ridge, the land fell away sharply in a hemlock-covered slope to a river in the valley. If I looked to my left, I imagined Hatfield lay just beyond the last gentle row of hills, like a precious gem carelessly discarded by a giant amongst folds of fall tapestry.

Out of the corner of my eye, I saw a flicker of orange. I glanced up to see an undulating veil of bright orange butter-flies, like a field of wood lilies rippling across the gray sky. Jumping to my feet, I ran back to where the others were.

"Look, come quickly, 'tis wondrous!" I cried.

The startled warriors reached for their tomahawks, and those napping awoke in a huff.

The children came running at my words, and by and by Natives and English, children and warriors, stood at the edge of the world and watched the wondrous flight of the winged creatures.

They were heading south, I supposed, for lands with a warm winter. South farther than Hatfield. Farther than Springfield, where I'd been born, maybe to Jamestown and the tobacco plantations. Or clear to the West Indies, a brilliant sun ripening sugar cane and pineapples, where the Pynchons had traded, and Captain Moseley prowled the ocean as a pirate.

Far too soon, the multitudes of bright butterflies flew out of sight, and we reluctantly settled back into our former tasks, shaken by the wonder. My girls wanted to stay, expecting to see more butterflies, and I hoped for that as well. As I was a bit anxious having my children so close to the steep banks of the ridge, we crossed the rocky clearing to the gentle eastern slopes. These were forested in birch, maple, and oak, the autumn colors beginning to smolder.

"Like in the Bible, Mama, the burning bush," Mary said.

"When 'the Angel of the Lord appeared to Moses, in Holy flames of fire,'" I said, squeezing her hand.

As the wind increased, tattering the ceiling of gray clouds, the hawks came. Broad-winged hawks, familiar to me as birds that rid our fields of mice and our gardens of rabbits, but I had never seen so many before. Their wings were shaped like the broad paddles of canoes, their black and white striped tails like fans, and they called to one another in descending notes.

Like the butterflies, they were winging their way south. The Natives looked up, and I feared they'd shoot an arrow to gain feathers, but they only joined us in pointing and exclaiming to one another. Dozens of hawks, swooping and diving and cresting the currents of air, bringing to mind Ben's tales of dolphins riding the waves off Rhode Island. So many of them, I was sure the wind from their wings brushed my face.

When the hawks flew out of sight, I wandered back to sit alongside my kin. We spoke of how our Lord was ever present. God had surely sent those lovely creatures to promise we would someday head south as well, back to our homes and families.

I read my Bible aloud:

"*Deuteronomy 33: Blessed of the Lord is his land for the sweetness of heaven, for the dew, and for the depth lying beneath. And for the sweet increase of the Sun, and for the sweet increase of the Moon, and for thy sweetness of the top of the ancient mountains, and for the sweetness of the old hills, and for the sweetness of the earth . . . and the goodwill of him that dwelt in the bush . . . shall come to him that was separated from his brethren.*"

Quequan came to me and made it clear, in urgent words and emphatic gestures, that he was tired of waiting for his shirt, Sabbath or not. Since he insisted I harken to him, I resigned myself to the sin I hoped God would forgive. Picking up the shirt from where I'd left it, I sat on my sad little mattress of leaves and hemlock boughs.

I had only to stitch the hem of the tails and cuffs and sew the buttons whilst the sun was high enough in the sky for me to see. My girls threaded my needle and then went back to playing. Quequan left me alone.

I felt secure at the edge of the forest, downhill from the longhouse and fire. Hannah and Mary were nearby with Neepânon, learning how to tan the deer's hide. We'd a tannery in Hatfield, hence it was a task we'd not learned.

I watched as they scraped the flesh from the leather with a knife and sliced the fat with what looked like a sword. Had we not been outnumbered, might we have stolen those weapons from our captors and somehow overpowered them? It was a fleeting thought, but it gave me pause.

Young Sam Russell and two Nipmuc boys strolled over and stood before me.

"Yes?" I asked.

Sam held something out to me. "Look what I found, Goodwife Waite," he said.

It was a dull green rock about the size of his fist, and it

sparkled with jewels. Deep red carbuncles the size of cranber-ries, cleaved and hewn like the finest gems in the rings and crowns of royalty.

"This is beautiful, Sam. Where did you find it?"

"There are more of them yonder. See those large rocks near where the butterflies flew over us?" He pointed. "Wesat-timis and Oskosk and I had to use a tomahawk to dig in the rock to get this out," he said proudly.

I reached out to hand the gemstone back to him.

He did not take it. "Goodwife Waite, I'd like you to have it. 'Tis the sort of thing my mother liked, but . . . She'd a ring my father gave her, and she always wore it. It was of silver, with red stones a bit like these."

He looked down at his feet, sniffed a little, then met my gaze again. "You remind me of her at times. Would you please keep it?"

I nodded, my heart in my throat. Sam gave me a shy smile before he walked away with his new friends.

I held Sam's precious gift in my hands and said a little prayer for him, his mother, and all the orphans. The little boy's gemstone was the third proof of God's love this day.

I wept.

Chapter Twenty-Three
MARTHA

PUTNEY MOUNTAIN
SEPTEMBER 28-29, 1677

For once, we English gathered together, busy with tasks for our masters. The women sewed, the men sealed the inside walls of the longhouse with bark and mud, and the children worked at various chores. A light rain pitter-pattered on the roof. We sat around one of the two fires, the Natives around theirs at the other end. It was an impressively large shelter, at least twice the size of my home in Hatfield. Before it burned.

About half the warriors had departed that morning for Wachusett Hills, a place Nìbi Wàbà said was southeast of here, about two days distant. A remnant of Ashpelon's band had remained there throughout King Philip's War, and now Ashpelon meant to bring them here, doubling the ratio of Natives to Christians.

"What is our cousin Benoni up to?" Hannah asked.

"I am also curious," Mary Foote said. "I spoke to him this morning, and he was excited to leave to Wachusett Hills. It seemed he had a plan. Hannah, he's your cousin and mine. We have the same cross to bear."

"Benoni said his master ordered him to accompany them," Hannah said, squinting as she threaded her needle. "Perhaps for security? So, if the English found them, they could use him as barter? If so, he's in danger, which seems to be his habit."

It made us all uneasy. Benoni was young and, by constitution, rash. When he was twelve, he and another lad stole money to pay a praying Natick to help them run away to Canada. They were caught, whipped, and made to pay back the money. He'd been fined several times for various sins, including wearing his hair too long, not keeping the Sabbath, gambling, and horse racing.

"The family was hoping Benoni would make a new start in Deerfield," Hannah went on, "wed his beloved and finally settle down."

"Do you think he has some mischief in mind?" I asked.

"I couldn't help but overhear," Sergeant Plympton said. He glanced around to be sure the Natives still clustered about their fire at the opposite end of the shelter. Our children napped or played near us, which I always found of great comfort.

"I asked Benoni when we rose this morning," Plympton said, "why he was so forward to going with the Indian party. He laughed and said we'd know soon enough but did not explain."

"We saw what they do when angered," Quintin Stockwell said. "What one of us does affects the lot of us."

"I certainly do not want to hear any more threats," I said, shuddering.

I had finished Quequan's shirt. He'd paid me an extra helping of deer meat and a rabbit skin, then told the other Natives of my sewing skills. Hence, Hannah, Mary, and I had been commanded to sew shirts for several others. It was a calming task, but I resented having to serve my captors by providing them luxuries. Our littlest ones dozed beside us on a bearskin where we could tend to them: Sally, Molly, Sammy, Holly, and little Daniel, whom we often watched for Obadiah.

The oldest boys—Matthew Kellogg and Sam Russell—helped the men with the shelter, and the oldest girls—my daughter Mary and Abigail Allis—helped the elder woman, Neepânon, stretch and beat the deer hide. Noah and Nate watched Nìbi Wàbà pound dried corn into meal, and Mattie, Abby Bartholomew, and Sarah Coleman worked together to weave a mat of bull rushes.

Neepânon hung the hide from the longhouse rafters to dry when they finished. I wondered who would receive the comfort of a deerskin tunic or blanket for the long winter ahead.

The Natives allowed us inside that night. The rain strengthened, pounding on the layers of bark, trickling down the sides, and dampening the ground. Still, the shelter and fires kept us warm and dry, and the smell of smoky deerskin was buttery and dank but not unpleasant. I was divinely happy to lay on my side and hold Sally in my arms, Mary and Mattie close enough that I could hear them breathing.

Our sleep was broken before dawn when the party of Nipmucs and Pocumtucks arrived with the Wachusett tribe. A rumble of hoofbeats and shouting spurred the Natives to leap up and run out o' doors. We English emerged more cautiously. The rain had ceased, and we all waited on the rocky ground as the new band of Natives advanced up the mountain on half a dozen horses.

They numbered at least ten warriors and a score of Native

women, a few elderly men and children, and one who seemed to be a sachem, but much older than Ashpelon. Ashpelon and this elder embraced, smiling, but after a few words, Ashpelon whirled to face us, his eyes flashing.

"Your Benoni! He escaped!" Ashpelon shouted, drawing his tomahawk from its sheath and waving it in the air. He stormed over to Sergeant Plympton, standing inches from his face.

"Did you know of this? Did you arrange it?"

The poor man had to be seventy if he were a day and often bore the brunt of Ashpelon's anger. Ashpelon clearly regarded Plympton as our leader.

Plympton replied in a firm voice, "No! We knew nothing of it until now. Benoni said his master bade him accompany them, so he went."

"I do not believe you! We have treated you well, shared our food and fire, and cared for your children, yet your Benoni thinks he is a big warrior? No, he is a fool, and you will all pay for his mistake!" Ashpelon thundered.

In an instant, the warriors advanced on us, their faces fierce with anger. My girls screamed and clung to my skirts. Our men pulled us behind them, forming a human shield, and we embraced our children. I pulled Mary behind me, pressed Sally against my chest, and gripped Mattie's hand.

"Mommy, I feel your heart," Sally said, her voice quavering.

"Yes, love, I'm sure you do." I kissed the top of her head.

Ashpelon stood within feet of us and motioned to the elder Indian who'd just arrived. "Wanalancet is a sachem and my cousin, and thinks I am a fool to have kept you all alive. He says it is best to kill one or more of you to show you and your English families and troops what happens when you defy us!" Ashpelon paced back and forth.

Several warriors of the Wachusett band brandished tomahawks. Plympton's captor, Atian, cocked his musket and aimed it in Plympton's direction. Other warriors unsheathed their knives, blades glinting in the sun. Our children whimpered in terror. Hannah wept. I stood rooted to the spot, begging God to spare us, my arms wrapped tightly around Sally. Ashpelon and Wanalancet exchanged heated words with each other and the assembled Natives. Finally, the talking ceased, and our masters grabbed us roughly.

Nìbi Wàbà tore Sally from my arms and jerked Mattie by the wrist. I had never seen her so furious. She screamed at Mary to follow her to the longhouse. I stumbled after them, but Ashpelon gripped my injured arm and dragged me to the flat expanse of granite. I fell to my knees, and he pushed me down so my cheek and belly thudded against the warm rock. He pressed his hand against my neck. My chest ached, and I couldn't breathe.

"You English will spend the day bound to the earth while we settle what is to become of you!" he said, taking his hand from my neck. I curled up on my side and gulped air.

He wrapped my wrists and ankles in deer sinew, turned me onto my back, and pounded iron pegs into cracks in the rock to restrain me. My knees and cheek ached, and my injured left arm shot daggers of pain from my shoulder to my fingertips. I cursed Ashpelon as he stomped away, and then lay crying, joining the weeping and protests of my children and friends. I shut my eyes against the sun, feeling my baby tumbling within me, and prayed my fall had not harmed it.

They left a few men to guard us, and the rest of the Natives returned to the longhouse with our children. We listened to them arguing for hours. The few times we tried to talk to each other, the guards threatened to strike us, so we dared not speak. The rain resumed, drenching us as we lay on our backs, and naught to do but close our eyes against it. Thunder rumbled in the distance, and I worried we'd be struck by lightning. The damp seeped through my clothes and skin and into my very bones, my arm and shoulder throbbing in tune with my heartbeat. I was nearly as furious at Benoni as I was at Ashpelon.

After a long time in the cold rain, Ashpelon returned and strode up and down amongst us. I turned my head to watch him, grateful no thong restrained my neck. Anger still blazed in his eyes. His voice was tightly controlled when he spoke, like an arrow drawn taut in a bow.

"We have talked. Wanalancet and many others think one or more of you put Benoni up to this. Some want to kill you. Others spoke of biting off your fingers one by one. We held a court, and all spoke their minds."

Mary gasped, and Hannah began to cry. Bile rose in my throat, sour and sickening. My right eye and cheek were swollen and sore. I hated our captors, and I hated Benoni.

"I spoke last because I am the sachem. I said Benoni Stebbins was a foolish youth and likely alone in his betrayal. I blamed the Wachusett women for taking him to pick huckleberries and allowing him to escape. I convinced Wanalancet and the others Benoni acted alone and they should not hurt you. I did not allow a vote."

Ashpelon had spared us yet again. I gave thanks to God, who rescued us from our oppressors through his enduring mercy. Yet I knew we would suffer some punishment, if only so Ashpelon could keep the respect of his people.

Ashpelon kicked Quintin in the leg, knowing he was lame from the war, and sneered when Quintin cried out in pain. "This is not the first time I have stood up for you English against my people, but it will be the last! You will lie in the rain all day and night until you learn you must obey us!" Ashpelon stomped back to the longhouse along with the guards.

We suffered the night without food or fire as the rain beat down. I prayed for the safety of my children, who I hoped were warm and dry. What enduring damage might our trials have upon their minds, hearts, and souls? My poor wee babes.

With the guards gone, we called out to each other above the drumming rain. All of us swore a solemn vow we'd not dare attempt escape, nor even give our captors cause to suspect us of planning such. We believed Ashpelon when he said he'd spared our lives for the last time.

Chapter Twenty-Four
BEN

ALBANY, NEW YORK
SEPTEMBER 30, 1677

I hopped off the ferry and looked up at the city of Albany, a hamlet on the hill above the Hudson River. I'd traded here a decade ago, wampum and pewter for beaver furs the Iroquois tribes brought down the Mohawk River from the western wilderness. Now that New Amsterdam was New York, a new English fort, Fort Frederick, was being built upon the hill above State Street.

Passing through the palisade's gate, I turned left on Handlers Street toward the *Stadt Huys*, or City Hall. I took note of the Dutch church at the corner, a fat, square building, its vestibule like a little house attached to the front, tall glass windows all around, a steep, gabled slate roof and a belfry. With a stab of guilt, I realized I'd missed the Sabbath whilst hiking from Massachusetts—another sin. I mumbled a hasty prayer for forgiveness.

In the lobby of *Stadt Huys*, I was greeted by a young man seated behind a desk stacked with papers. He glanced up from his work and offered a brief smile.

"Good day. State your business." His English was heavily accented with Dutch.

"Benjamin Waite, with letters for Captain Salisbury from Major Pynchon of Massachusetts Bay Colony and Hatfield's Council of War."

The clerk rose and held out his hand.

"I must give these to the captain directly. It regards a matter of some urgency," I said.

"Very well, wait here. Your name again?"

"Waite, at the behest of Major Pynchon. Urgent," I repeated briskly.

By the clock on the wall, more than half an hour passed before Captain Salisbury opened the door to his office and motioned me in. He was a ruddy-faced Welshman and had put on some weight since last we met. He wore his brown hair to his shoulders but not powdered, and a long coat of burgundy velvet.

"Good day, Mister Waite. What might I do for you?"

I was unsure if he remembered me from a dozen years past, nor if it would be wise to remind him, but I forged ahead.

"Good day, Captain, and congratulations on your title of Commander of the Fort and Sheriff of Albany. I come bearing urgent news from Major Pynchon, sir." I handed the letter to him.

I remained standing because he had not invited me to sit. He sat in his large armchair and read the letter through twice.

"A regrettable situation," he said. "My sympathies."

His tone was brusque, his face expressionless. I did not detect a trace of sympathy.

"Thank you, sir."

"I will have to look into this. I do not think the Mohawks are behind it—they tend to take the side of the English in most matters. Your scouting party under Captain Watts believed the Indians holding your kin are headed to Canada, not here?"

"That is our belief, sir, but Major Pynchon desires we are certain before we take any further action. Major Pynchon hopes that, if not responsible, the Mohawks might be of help."

"Possibly. The Mohawks are increasingly eager to defend their territory and assert dominance over the Algonquian tribes. As I said, allow me to investigate. Can you return tomorrow morning?"

"Yes, sir," I said, though I was not eager to face the delay. Each day meant perhaps another twenty miles separating me from my wife and girls, the Algonquians driving them north and away from me. "Sir, I'm an acquaintance of Mister Timothy Cooper. We both worked for Pynchon in the fur trade. I believe he serves on your Commission on Indians?"

"He does," Salisbury said.

"Would you direct me to him, please? I wish to offer my condolences. His brother John was killed in the assault on our town."

I wanted Cooper to look into the Mohawks, knowing Salisbury likely would not.

"He's not in today, but he rents a home by the docks," Salisbury said.

"Thank you, sir," I held out my hand, but Salisbury had already turned his back on me and was searching through some files. I'd almost forgotten how much I disliked him.

I strolled down to the river, taking a moment to breathe in the fresh air and watch the boats unload their wares. Thus recovered from Salisbury's rude arrogance, I asked around for directions to Cooper's house. It was a little stone one on an alleyway. I rapped on the door.

"Well, if it isn't Benjamin Waite!" Timothy exclaimed, shaking my hand and inviting me in. He wore only a shirt and breeches, and his face was pale and gaunt. He introduced his wife, Elizabeth, to me and motioned me to sit by the fire while she left to tend to their small garden. Their fire was but embers, with no cooking pot over it. The one room was sparsely furnished, the floor scoured but bare, the white-washed walls in need of refreshing.

"What brings you to Albany?" he asked.

"First, my condolences on the loss of your brother. I'm very sorry."

"Thank you. 'Twas a blow." Timothy sat across from me. "He was buried in Hatfield?"

"Yes. His death was swift, a musket shot," I said, hoping it might comfort him.

"Well, that's something, then. If the Indian troubles end, I might make the trip to your town, to his grave."

"I came to know him quite well," I said. "The house he was working on was next to mine."

"He loved being a carpenter." Timothy gazed into the fire. "What became of your house in the attack? Your family and friends?"

I told him of my loss, the town's need for aid, and my meeting with Captain Salisbury.

"Salisbury won't be of much help. He probably won't consult me, nor the praying Indians, nor Mohawks. He likes his title but doesn't seem fond of doing his job," Timothy said.

"He has always been a cockard," I said, vexed. "So, what do you advise?"

"We both know it wasn't Mohawks, but I will find out what they know. They still come to trade, although they bring less and less beaver. Trying to get me to take muskrat and mink, but there's no market for that."

"Fur trading isn't what it was when you and I worked together, is it?"

"No, not in the least. They've moved most of the legal

trade down the river to Manhattan. I get a small stipend for serving on the Commission, and farm a couple of acres by the river. We get by," he said, "but we'll likely move back to Springfield and live with one of my brothers there."

He slapped his knee in an attempt at cheerfulness, laughed, and said, "Let's go have some rum, shall we?"

We went to a smallish tavern and had a drink or two for old times' sake. I paid. Timothy said he regretted he couldn't put me up for the night, but one of his children was ill. I think he was embarrassed he'd fallen on such hard times. If he was in debt to Major Pynchon, I pitied him, for I knew Pynchon was scrupulous about collecting debts.

Timothy headed home after a couple of hours, and I ended up staying the night at the tavern on a pallet by the fire. They specialized more in food and drink than lodgers. It was not really an inn at all, but Timothy knew the owner.

After a fair night's sleep, I enjoyed a good Dutch breakfast of *olie-koeken* spiced apple pastry, a wedge of red-skinned cheese, and some pressed apple juice before returning to *Stadt Huys*. I received the expected curt response from Captain Salisbury, who said his under-sheriffs found no evidence that the Mohawks or other Iroquois tribes had attacked Hatfield in September. I pressed him for more details, but he waved me off and handed me a sealed letter for Pynchon.

I returned to Timothy Cooper's house. He said the Mohawks he'd spoken to that morning denied any culpability. They were reluctant to help, having reached an uneasy truce with the other tribes since King Philip's War. He added that the Algonquians at Schaghticoke were under heavy guard, did not dare leave, and so were blameless.

Encouraged that my suspicions were correct but frustrated

at losing precious time, I embarked on the Old Connecticut Path to Springfield to meet with Major Pynchon. Thanks be to God I'd left the fur trade when it was still profitable and did not owe the wealthiest man in Massachusetts any debt but loyalty.

Chapter Twenty-Five

MARTHA

The Natives unstaked us at dawn and herded us inside the longhouse. I spied my daughters with Nìbi Wàbà, but the warriors would not let us join them and guided us to a different fire. Our teeth chattering, we asked our men to avert their eyes and turn their backs to the fire, and then, modesty cast aside, Hannah, Mary, and I removed our soaked caps, bodices, outer skirts, and aprons and laid them by the fire to dry.

Wrapped in blankets over our shifts and petticoats, our damp hair loose about our shoulders, we sat with our backs to the fire across from our men. They, in turn, took off their sodden garments and boots. 'Twould have been a comical or sinful sight under other circumstances, but we risked pleurisy if we remained in our wet clothes a moment longer.

The Wachusett band provided cornmeal, smoked eels, and the troublesome huckleberries, which the Natives ate at their fire. Once they finished, Nìbi Wàbà and Kòkòkòho gave us each a small portion. I had never eaten eels but was hungry, so

I closed my eyes and chewed, glad to discover they tasted more agreeable than they looked.

I noticed two young Nipmuc women sitting apart from the fire, not eating. I asked Nìbi Wàbà why, and she replied it was they who allowed Benoni to escape whilst picking huckleberries. Their punishment was banishment from the fire and no food for two days.

Had Benoni returned to Hatfield, and his information prompted a new search for us? Did Ben still search for us? I reached for any hope to cling to.

I picked up my Bible from where I'd laid it to dry by the fire.

"Please pray with me?" I asked my friends.

My wrists were caked with dried blood from the staking, and my hands shook. I searched the Bible, leafing carefully through the damp pages, selecting Proverbs 3.

"Trust in the Lord with all thine heart and lean not unto thine own wisdom.

In all thy ways acknowledge him, and he shall direct thy ways.

Be not wise in thine own eyes: but fear the Lord and depart from evil.

Then shalt thou walk safely by the way: and thy foot shall not stumble."

I'd removed my sling to let it dry, and my arm felt strangely heavy.

"We must keep last night's pact. None shall attempt escape," Sergeant Plympton said. I recognized his voice, though I still faced away from him.

"True," Quintin said. "Their threats are not idle."

"They punish their women, but it should be Benoni in the stocks, back in Hatfield, for endangering us all," Obadiah said, his tone bitter.

Mary shook her head. "Benoni is young and foolish, but I do not think he was being selfish. If he finds his way home, he can tell them we're still alive and how to find us."

"I pray he does." I took up my Bible again and turned to Matthew, reading in a stronger voice than I expected.

"But I say unto you, love your enemies: bless them that curse you: do good to them that hate you, and pray for them which hurt you, and persecute you, that ye may be the children of your Father that is in heaven: for He maketh his sun to arise on the evil and the good, and sendeth rain on the just and unjust."

&.

We had exhausted our provisions. Our party had doubled in size, and so had our needs. The deer headed down the mountain and farther south into the warmer valleys for food, and the bears gorged themselves on fish, rabbits, and raccoons and retreated to their winter dens. Our last full meal had been our breakfast of eels and berries days ago. Since then, we'd survived on dried corn and acorn meal dissolved in hot water, a bitter version of the bland samp we were accustomed to.

The warriors went out each dawn bearing guns and bows and arrows. They returned each noon empty-handed. But on this day, we awoke to their triumphant calls, victory cheers of happiness. It was raining, but we all burst from the longhouse to see what they had brought back for us.

Six warriors carried a massive black bear across their soldiers—a *mosq*. There was much rejoicing amongst us all. Presently, the Native women had it skinned, cleaned, dressed, and cut into chunks, each the size of a horse's head, boiling in kettles and roasting on spits over the inside fires. The air filled with the smell of it.

"Faugh, why does it smell like fish?" Mattie said.

"Mattie, watch your tongue."

"I think it smells like huckleberries," Mary countered.

I caught whiffs of fish and huckleberries and a fatty, gamey smell like mutton.

Ashpelon was nearby, supervising the women fleshing the

bearskin, so I asked, "Why does it smell like fish? Is it already spoilt?"

"No, not spoilt. The bear fed on fish and berries, so we will eat bear and fish and berries. The meat must cook for a long time so it does not sicken us," he said. "Be patient."

Speaking to Ashpelon made me feel more equal to him, less frightened. It was the reason I'd learned the Natives' names—a challenging task for me—so they'd see I was a force to be reckoned with, even though I was fain to submit to captivity to survive.

We waited for our dinner and then our supper; still, the bear meat was not done. The sound of rain splattering on the longhouse ceased, and the sun set, our fires the only light remaining. It was impossible to sleep with empty bellies and the smell of cooked meat, even fishy meat, filling our nostrils.

Finally, long past dark, the bear meat was declared done. The Natives brought us a trencher to pass around, and there was plenty for each of us. It tasted better than it smelled: tough, stringy, and greasy like lamb or duck, not fish. Even Mattie ate it. I prayed it was enough to sustain my unborn child and three girls. I fell asleep with one arm around Sally and my other hand on my belly, feeling my baby move.

Chapter Twenty-Six
BEN

SPRINGFIELD, MASSACHUSETTS BAY COLONY
OCTOBER 4-5, 1677

Temperance was a virtue I seemed to lack, and I chafed at having to consult another authority. Prudence, however, required me to meet with Major John Pynchon in person. He was, in all but title, Lord of the Connecticut Valley. He founded Deerfield and Northfield, and his father, William Pynchon, founded Springfield. Pynchon was a good man to know.

His marriage to the governor of Connecticut's daughter united Massachusetts Bay and Connecticut in the colonial equivalent of a royal marriage. When John's father, William, returned to England due to a falling out with Connecticut, John assumed all of his landholdings.

Pynchon worked the trade triangle from Boston to Barbados to London for a decade, fighting off pirates while shipping, trading, and selling beaver furs, sugar, rum, and Indian and African slaves. My previous work for him involved only furs, which suited me fine. Trading in people didn't sit well with me.

My need for him now was based upon his titles of assistant of Massachusetts Bay Colony, magistrate of the Hampshire County Court, and commander of the Hartford troops.

I was bone weary by the time I reached Springfield. 'Twas a rainy day, and I worried how Martha and my girls fared, as I did every day. Their journey was far more dangerous than mine, and I felt guilty for my own exhaustion.

I prayed the Algonquians had not harmed them further since their capture. Though I knew the Natives' ways better than most, it was like a sailor knowing how to read the weather. There was always the chance of a sudden storm, an unexpected change in the wind, a rogue wave. Cautions I'd learned only too well.

Rain dripped from the brim of my hat, and I was glad of my wool coat. Light glowed from the windows of Pynchon's brick mansion on Main Street. It had withstood the attack on Springfield, when Natives burned most of the wooden buildings and killed Martha's father, among others.

I rapped the brass lion head knocker, and a young African servant opened the door.

"Benjamin Waite to see Major Pynchon," I said.

"Is he expecting you, sir?" she asked.

"Yes."

She took my damp hat and coat and laid them to dry by the massive fire in the main hall. Major Pynchon descended the main staircase, his hand grazing the banister to the curved volute at the end. He was dressed for work in a long blue coat, black breeches, and a long periwig as befitted his station.

"Benjamin, 'tis good to see you! You must be weary from your travels," he said, smiling, and we shook hands. "We will retire to the keeping room," he said, showing the way. "Please, be seated. Let me get us some refreshments."

He rang a bell on a small table. Almost instantly, the servant girl reappeared. She couldn't have been but fourteen years of age.

"Anne, bring us scones, lemon curd, clotted cream, tea," he said, and off she went.

I wondered if she was employed, indentured, or a slave taken on one of Pynchon's trade ships.

Anne returned with our refreshments and then vanished. I took out the letter from Salisbury and handed it to Pynchon. I spread a scone with clotted cream and poured tea into a blue and white Dutch china cup.

"What help does Salisbury offer in his letter?" I asked.

"He concurs Mohawks were not responsible and wrote, 'I am prepared to offer whatever help we can provide without endangering our colony.' A weak promise. But I'll hold him to it."

Pynchon leaned back in his chair, steepled his fingers. "We now have in writing proof that Captain Salisbury was approached, informed, and agrees regarding the Mohawks. A mixed Algonquian band, probably Nipmucs and Pocumtucks, fell upon your town." Pynchon took a sip of tea.

"Aye." I said. "They fled to Canada after King Philip's death but have not surrendered."

"Nothing to prevent them returning, perhaps with their new allies, the Abenaki. King Philip's war upset the delicate balance amongst all the tribes, but we can use that to our advantage," Pynchon said.

"How, sir?"

"When the Algonquians struck Springfield, they took captives. We redeemed them through help from Albany and the Mohawks."

"Hence, we can leverage that precedent to gain New York's help."

"Exactly, and with the Mohawks' help, we might parley a ransom forthwith, before the Algonquians take your kin all the way to Canada," Pynchon said.

"That would be a tremendous relief." I dared hope for the first time in days.

"This past spring, Commissioner Richards of Connecticut met with me and sachems of the Mahicans and the Mohawks. They agreed to watch the Algonquians at Schaghticoke and inform us of any threat to the English." Pynchon took a bite of his scone.

"I heard the same from Timothy Cooper in Albany," I said. "I met with him after not receiving much help from Salisbury."

"Hmmm. How fares Cooper?" Pynchon asked, frowning.

"To be honest, not well, sir."

"I'm sorry to hear it but not surprised. We were wise to leave the fur business when we did."

"Although frontier farming has turned out to be more dangerous than the fur trade ever was," I said. "I appreciate your help, sir. I yearn to leave for Canada immediately."

"You know that would be reckless. You face a difficult task. I assume you have a plan?"

"Once all the obligatory paperwork is complete, my friend Stephen Jennings and I intend to track down the captives and negotiate their safe return to us. His wife and children were also taken."

Pynchon nodded in understanding.

"I will post another letter today to Salisbury, encouraging him to follow through and reminding him of our past agreements," Pynchon said. "He must confer with Albany's Indian Commissioners, who aided in the Springfield negotiations. I'm irritated he did not do so when you visited him. Not sure who's in that body. It changes."

"Timothy Cooper implied he was a commissioner, but I gather his standing is weak."

"It is," Pynchon said.

"Would you write to Governor Leverett on our behalf? We need to meet with him for funds or a letter of credit in order to negotiate with the Algonquians once we find them."

"I'll write to him. You'll also need his written authority to travel through New York and into Canada," Pynchon said, finishing his tea. "Take a petition from your townspeople when you call on him."

"I'm heading home to secure the petition once I bid you good day."

"You must spend the night, Waite, I insist. The trail here from Albany was brutal, was it not?"

I hesitated only in the name of courtesy. "Yes. Thank you."

"Is there anything else I can do for you at this point, Ben? I'm sympathetic to your straits. You must be frantic with worry."

"Aye, sir." I risked one more favor. "Can you spare any troops to accompany Stephen and me to Canada?"

Pynchon shook his head. "I'm sorry. I wish I could."

Accommodations in his mansion were a brief but blessed respite. Pynchon's servant drew me a proper hot bath and brought me a light supper in my room, where I slept soundly on a warm feathertick.

By dawn, the rain softened to a damp drizzle. I went to the new post office and posted a letter to my Uncle Gamaliel in Boston, letting him know to expect Stephen and me, thanking him in advance for allowing us to stay with him. Shivering, I caught a riverboat home.

Time pressed on me, a gargoyle hunched on my shoulder, mocking me. Martha and my girls had been lost to the wilderness for more than a fortnight, prisoners of desperate enemies, their trail growing colder each day. It tormented me that I could not yet pursue them. Recalling the book of Exodus, I prayed God would bring my family back to me on eagle's wings.

I reached Hatfield at twilight. Funerals had been held during my absence. A chill descended on my heart as I walked past the burial grounds, mounds of freshly dug earth amid the yellowing grass and the clutter of fallen leaves. On my way to the meeting house, I knocked on doors, many draped in black bunting, and requested all freemen attend a meeting of the utmost consequence.

Once a score of men was present, I offered proof the Mohawks were not responsible for the attack on our town. Hadley's Reverend Russell and the selectmen drew up a Petition for Authority to Governor Leverett of Massachusetts Bay Colony, and all signed it.

Selectman Belding passed around a tray, and every man contributed what he could. Grief and loss had crushed us, but I was encouraged that Pynchon—and possibly Salisbury— were lending support. My kin wished Stephen and me Godspeed on our endeavor and handed us the collection.

At the Allis home, I changed and packed clothes and fresh bedding. Rachel Allis served me a trencher of stew, and Stephen Jennings joined me, his provisions packed, ready to depart. The horses were well-rested, and the Boston Road wide and more traveled than the Connecticut Trail to Albany, well-suited to riding. King Philip's War had destroyed most English and Natick praying towns alongst the way, but I'd heard some taverns remained.

Stephen and I set off after dark, crossing the Connecticut River on the ferry, our horses balancing precariously. We continued east on the Bay Road, between Mount Warner to the north and Mount Holyoke to the south, both looming darker than the night. A waxing gibbous moon rose before us, helping to light the way, and as a shooting star streaked across the heavens, I made a wish out loud. Stephen, thank God for him, laughed at me.

Springfield, 6 October 1677, Just at Night
   Captain Salisbury,
   Worthy sir, yesterday morning I received your lines by Benjamin

Waite, whereby I understand your sympathy with us in our sad disaster by the Indians; and your forwardness to do what possible lies in you for us, which I do most thankfully accept from your hands.

And as to your opinion of the Mohawks being free and assuring me of their innocence, I do fully concur with you, having satisfaction from what you writ and from Benjamin Waite's relation, but to put it out of all doubt, God in his providence hath sent in one of our captive men, Benoni Stebbins which is the occasion of these lines to yourself by post.

Benoni Stebbins came into Hadley late last night, whose relation was sent to me being but an hour since I had it. Take his relation as followeth: The company of Indians was 26 in all. They came from Canada three months ago, and had been hunting. They carried away from Hatfield 17 persons and three from Deerfield, besides this man that is come in.

Being about two days' journey above Squakheag, they sent a company of them to Nashaway to call off some Indians that have been there all this time of the war, and took this Benoni Stebbins along with them thither. This Benoni, being sent with two women to carry huckleberries, ran away from them and was presently pursued, but night coming on he escaped. He says that one of the Indians from Nashaway Ponds seems to be a counselor, and with him they consulted much and talked of carrying the captives to the French and selling them to the French, which, he concludes, they resolved on.

It was Tuesday morning last that he escaped, and they had then above thirty miles to go back to Squakheag, and then near two days' journey more to the rest above Squakheag. The impassableness of the way renders it impossible for us to pursue or do any good. But conveying speedy word to the Mohawks gives a probability of their overtaking them.

Which, dear sir, is the end of these lines to you: to request, if none of the Mohawk sachems be at Albany, to send at our charge to the chief of the Mohawks, and give them an account of matters and desire their speedy pursuing these bloody villains and enemies of them, and by this means I hope this barbarous crew—who are enemies to religion, civility and all humanity and have so deeply embrewed their hands in most innocent Christian blood—may be met with on their return, before they come to the lake or at the lake, and so our captives recovered, for which we shall give the Mohawks suitable rewards.

We desire to do our duty and to wait for the salvation of God. Sir, excuse my scribbling. I am in great haste to send away the messenger to Westfield this night, because the speed in getting the Mohawks to go out upon the enemy before they get on the lake is all-in-all.

I doubt not of your helpfulness in this exigence. With my endeared love and respects to you commending you to the protection of the Almighty God, I remain, sir,

Your very loving friend and servant,

John Pynchon

Benjamin Waite is gone home before this intelligence came to me. He talked of going to Canada before and I suppose will rather be forward to it now than backward; possible he may be at Albany about a fortnight hence in reference to a journey to the French.

J. P.

These for his Honored friend Captain Salisbury: Commander in Chief at Fort Albany.

Haste post haste, for his Majesty's special service.

Chapter Twenty-Seven

BEN

Stephen and I rode the Bay Road, our mounts Scout and Raven falling into step beside each other, enjoying each other's company. We were quiet for the most part, sharing only a few thoughts of our excitement to be on our way and our fear that we were already too late. After about three hours, near midnight, we set up camp by a large lake. I was exhausted and fell quickly asleep, leaving Stephen to gather wood and kindle a fire.

The next day, I was much refreshed, and we made good time, though fording the Swift River and Beaver Brook soaked our boots and stirrups. We had a supper of sausages, parsnips, and a good ale at an ordinary near the abandoned town of Brookfield, the ordinary the only building still standing. Characteristically, it had a shed for our horses, a kitchen, a room for let downstairs, and the owner's quarters above.

We slept on two plump mattresses, dried our boots by the fire, and woke to hot cider and samp with milk. A fair shillings' worth. Late on this third day, we reached the pebbled and forested shores of Lake Quinsigamond.

"Fancy a try at fishing for our supper?" Stephen asked.

"I took you for a village man," I said.

"Doesn't mean I can't fish. Surely, you must. Was not your father a fisherman?"

I shook my head. "I'd not the patience for it. When we fished in Rhode Island, it was net fishing for the most part. I've not had much practice at freshwater fishing," I said. "I'm more of a hunter."

"I think you'd take to it easily enough. I find it calming to the spirit," Stephen said.

"We don't have tackle."

"I do. Tools of my shoemaker's trade—scissors, needle and thread, hooks and eyes, a length of lace," Stephen replied. "Just my habit, to bring them on trips, lest my shoes need repair."

We dismounted and unsaddled our horses, hobbled them, and let them graze. Stephen opened his satchel, tied some of his heavy shoemaker's thread to a hook, then tied the thread to a length of leather lace.

"Can you fetch us two lengths of willow sapling from the thicket yonder?" he asked.

While I cut the willow cane, Stephen made a second hook and line, and once I returned, he tied the hook and line securely to a notch at the end of each cane. Finally, he baited our hooks with pieces of cheese from his pack and tied on a shiny metal eye for a lure.

"We'll stay on the lake's eastern side, so our shadows fall behind us." Stephen led the way to a spot thick with pondweeds.

A stand of young maples cast red and orange reflections on the still green water. We fished in silence for about a half hour as the shadows lengthened and the sky turned from blue to pale yellow. Stephen had a nibble but lost the hook.

I felt a tug on my line.

"I think I caught one!" I cried, and Stephen helped me land it on the bank.

"Strange looking thing," I said, "like a green eel with the head and beak of a duck."

"Aye, a fair size pickerel. They taste better than they look."

Stephen gutted the fish, skinned it, and carved four filets for us, which we grilled on willow sticks over the fire. 'Twas good eating, crisp and flaky, and we still had some cider to wash it down. When we'd finished, we laid out our bedrolls, gazed into the fire, and shared stories of our younger days to take our minds off our present straits.

Stephen grew up in Hartford and apprenticed as a shoemaker. Their neighbor had been quite wealthy, and the master of the house treated his prize stallion far better than his indentured stableboy. One day, the lad, whose name was Will, came to Stephen's shop and shared a few stories of his master's abuse.

"We hatched a scheme to get back at his master. Will and I snuck into the stable at night and sheared the horse's mane and tail. Did not harm the beast but ruined his looks, which was all the master cared about," Stephen said.

"And did you get away with it?" I asked, laughing.

"Sadly, not. Some busybody saw us leave the stable, and the sheriff hauled us into court. I was fined a pound and poor Will twice that, in addition to being dismissed, of course. My father found Will a shepherd's job, which he liked much better, it turned out."

"And I thought I was the one with a wild past. Richard Fellowes and I were quite unruly in our youth."

"I would have liked to have known you then." Stephen gazed into the fire. When he spoke again, his voice trembled. "I miss my Hannah so, and Samuel's children like my own."

"I know," I said, hearing my voice crack, "I wish time passed more quickly. We will find them, God willing."

I stood and raked some leaves together with a branch, piling them up to make a place to lay my bedding. Stephen did the same. A little mink appeared nearby, its eyes glowing in the firelight. The Mohawks say mink are good luck omens, so I tossed the fishbones to it.

Our last night on the road we stayed in Marlborough, the sole surviving Natick town. A few houses stood at one end of the main street, a few wigwams at the other, a meetinghouse at the center, and an ordinary with a shed for our mounts, samp and cider, and a dusty bed by a sputtering fire. We were glad to be almost to Boston, eager to deliver the petition and forge north.

Chapter Twenty-Eight
MARTHA

PUTNEY MOUNTAIN
OCTOBER 5

Very early, Quintin Stockwell gathered us out of doors, whilst our children still slept within the longhouse. It was a cloudy, cold day, just a whisper of wind high in the tallest pines. We sat in a circle around the fire we'd built on this great slab of rock.

"I've been speaking with Ashpelon," Quintin said. "The English at Hadley caught four Natives by their mill about a week ago. The Natives knew of us and promised to parley us for ransom if the men let them go. They agreed to meet and negotiate in Hadley soon." He added more wood to our fire.

"Interesting," Sergeant Plympton remarked. "That's about the time Benoni Stebbins escaped."

I, for one, was prepared to blame Benoni for all our misfortunes.

"Why are we only learning of this now?" Obadiah asked.

"Ashpelon thought the four Natives were killed in the attack on Hatfield, but then they arrived with the Wachusett band. He learned of their promise today."

"And what does he say to it?" Sergeant Plympton leaned back, resting on his elbows, his legs stretched towards our fire.

Quintin shrugged. "He is angry they negotiated a contract without consulting him or Wanalancet. But the journey to Canada is long, and the hunting is much worse than he expected. He is thinking of sending some of his band back to Hadley to discuss a ransom with the English."

"Which English? Was Ben among them?" I asked.

"Ashpelon might tell you more, but he gave me no names," Quintin said.

"Has the War Council agreed to such a trade? Have any officials been notified?"

"I see Ben has taught you how these matters are conducted?"

I was unsure if Quintin's raised eyebrows meant he was impressed or shocked.

"Ben says the simplest decisions often involve many different men," I said.

Quintin smiled. "'Tis true, Martha, and I assume the Council has been consulted. I do not know if this will come to pass. I wanted to share it, and then we can discuss it with Ashpelon."

"I am eager for a legitimate parley. The sooner we are freed, the better." Obadiah rose to his feet and began to pace.

Sergeant Plympton shook his head. "I'm not sure we can trust either side to have our best interests at heart. Hadley men fear for their lives, as do the Algonquians. What guarantee do we have one side is not laying a trap for the other, with no intention of saving us?"

I knew the four men could bat this about for hours, like cats with a ball of yarn, until it unraveled completely. Unless we'd assurance from Ashpelon, this conversation was for naught.

"I think we need to talk to Ashpelon about this sooner rather than later," I said.

The men weren't accustomed to having women join in their debates. 'Twas fine if you chose to listen silently and ask questions later, in private, but men strongly discouraged us from voicing an opinion before an assembly.

To protect our lives and our children's, it seemed we should set aside what was acceptable. We weren't discussing fence repairs for the Hatfield meadows.

"I agree with Martha," Hannah said.

"As do I," Mary added.

My friends' support encouraged me. "I'll go fetch Ashpelon now, myself," I said, standing up and striding off toward the longhouse before the men could stop me. I pushed aside the hides covering the opening and looked for a familiar face. Kòkòkòho sat in a corner, restringing his bow.

"Kòkòkòho, I am looking for Ashpelon," I said.

The young warrior set down his bow. "Come."

I followed him out of our lodging and across the rocky clearing toward the forest. We walked down a path to the brook on the eastern slope. I trembled in sudden apprehension to be alone in the woods with this warrior. I slowed my pace, putting a good five yards between us.

The brook rolled merrily downhill over boulders, carrying bits and pieces of yellowing leaves. Ashpelon stood ankle-deep in the water, a long wooden spear in his hand. A few women searched the ground for acorns and the huckleberry bushes for berries.

Kòkòkòho pointed toward his leader, then turned and left me there.

I was afraid of Ashpelon. He had ruined my arm, bruised my cheek, blackened my eye, and threatened twice to kill me. He'd led the attack on our town, killing and wounding my friends and taking the seventeen of us captive. Yet watching him now, his calm gaze on the water, a smile on his face when he speared a fish, he seemed no more nor less than a man. I kept that thought in my head and closed the distance.

"Ashpelon, a word?" I said, hoping my voice did not betray my unease.

His eyes remained on the brook, but he replied, "Speak."

"Stockwell told us of the agreement to meet Englishmen at Hadley and discuss a parley," I said breathlessly.

"And?"

"We ask you to meet with us to hear our thoughts."

"When I am done here, I will find you."

"When will that be?" I asked.

He looked up at me, his face solemn. "When I am done here," he repeated. "Wait."

So, I walked back up the trail, rejoined my kin, and recounted the conversation.

I was grateful we camped here rather than enduring the rigors of the trail, but a spirit of gloom weighed heavily on me. I asked Hannah and her children to share my favorite spot in the shade of a giant fir tree with views south. I held Sally's hand, but we let Sammy and my girls run ahead.

Once we reached the tree, we sat beneath it. Hannah took out the deerskin moccasins she was sewing for Holly, and I worked on a shirt, this one for Atian. The only sounds were the soft, playful voices of our girls nearby and the chirping of birds in the trees.

"Do you think the War Council will allow the parley, Martha?" Hannah asked, biting her bottom lip, not meeting my eyes.

I set the shirt on my lap.

"I do. Troops came for us our fourth night, Hannah."

"Ben and Stephen with them?"

I knew Hannah was slow to trust and easily given to melancholy. I was not.

"Hannah, Ben must have led them, as he has the skill to do so. And he and Stephen have become great friends. I'm sure Stephen came, too. He loves you."

Hannah stitched the soles to the uppers—slowly, methodically, carefully— as her shoemaker husband had taught her.

"How will they ever find us?" she said, her tears falling silently onto the moccasins.

"Ben could find a needle in a haystack."

A shrill whistle reached us, and we both looked up to see Ashpelon standing in the clearing with our men, motioning for us to return. We called our children and hurried back.

"Sit," Ashpelon commanded.

Nìbi Wàbà led our children away. I was beginning to trust her with them.

Ashpelon was pacing again. "Mistress Waite says you want to know about the parley. We plan to take you to our longhouse near the fort at Saurel and sell you to the French. They pay a good price for Christians like themselves. We do not know which of our people made the offer of parley, but they made it to save their own necks. The Wachusett think the parley in Hadley is a trap. And they remind me it is a long way back and at great risk to whomever we'd send."

I should not have hoped, nor pushed Ashpelon to a decision.

He paused and shook his head. "Still, a few of my clan are weary of feeding you. They worry, as do I, that food will grow even scarcer once winter comes. They want to consider ransoming you to your families before we travel farther north. I will put it to a vote today."

"A vote?" Obadiah asked, bewildered.

"It is our way. I am the leader but not a king. Nor was my cousin Metacomet, though he was called 'King Philip' by you English, in your mocking way. My people resolve things between us."

"Women, too?" I asked.

"All people vote who are of age," he said, and made to leave.

"Wait! Do we have a say?" I asked.

"I will listen," he said.

Sergeant Plympton looked at us. "Let us vote. Women, too. All those in favor of our captors attempting to parley us at Hadley? Ashpelon has explained it could go awry, which might mean more harm would befall us or our kin."

Though we couldn't know what fate God planned for us, we voted unanimously to support a parley with the English.

"We long to return home," Sergeant Plympton said, summing up our overriding sentiment.

"I will share your feelings at our council, but you must know I will not try to sway the people of my clan. They are a forest, and I am but a tall tree amongst them, not a strong wind bending saplings to my will," he said, and walked away.

Chapter Twenty-Nine

BEN

Boston, Plymouth Colony
October 9, 1677

"I've never been to Boston," Stephen said as we rode into town, our hoofbeats clattering on cobblestones.

"'Tis our tiny version of London, without the Church of England," I said.

"Tell me more about your family, " Stephen said.

"My cousin John moved here to care for my Uncle Gamaliel. Like my father, my uncle was a fisherman and grew wealthy from it. John has a prosperous chandlery shop, according to his letters. Says he sells everything you could ever want if you're a sailor or boatwright."

"Married?"

"My uncle, yes. John's first wife died in childbirth, as did the babe. He married again three years ago. I have yet to make her acquaintance."

We passed the Boston Common, wherein a herd of black Kerry milk cows grazed peacefully on golden grass, their tails swishing flies. Children searched for frogs by the Frog Pond and chased the birds. Meantime landed gentry and successful merchants strolled alongst the paths, ladies carrying fancy parasols and men's cutwork coat sleeves revealing the costly silk fabric of their shirts. Vanities, but not punishable, since their dress befit their station.

"No brothers or sisters in town?" Stephen asked.

"Still in Rhode Island, excepting my brother Reuben in Dartmouth, south of Boston, and my brother Joseph, who died twelve years ago."

As if conjured by my words, we passed Boston's burial ground, winged skulls carved into grave markers, the slabs and the trees casting intertwining and lengthening shadows. It reminded me of the graveyard in Newport, where Joseph and my parents slept.

"How did one of the Godly end up in Rhode Island?" Stephen asked.

I rarely discussed my faith, though spiritual examination was one of its tenets. My strong-willed nature often seemed at odds with a belief in predestination. Yet I trusted that Stephen would not judge me.

"My father was never one of the saints. He came with Winthrop to Massachusetts Bay, but before I was born, he left for Rhode Island. He was a non-conformist, and I was not born nor raised as one of the chosen."

"Yet you moved back to Massachusetts?"

"After my brother's death. I felt deeply alone. I faced my mortality and sins for the first time. Father gave me his land holding in Hatfield, thinking the change might restore me."

"And has it? Restored you?"

"My adult conversion came from the depths of my despair, but I've often felt an outsider as I was not baptized in the faith. Yet Martha married me, and our girls are all full members, as is she."

Martha. Our girls. That distant Sunday, after the Falls Fight, when Martha glanced across the meeting house aisle and smiled at me. The memory warmed my heart yet made me miss her all the more. As did the image of Mattie kicking the back of Goodwife Billings's seat.

Dock Square was bustling, and presiding over it was the wooden Townhouse, three stories commanding the corner of King and Orange Streets. The bottom level was an open-walled covered market fronted by a gallery. Large, square-paned windows dominated the second story, with smaller windows tucked into the gables. A steeply hipped roof and a walkway topped it off, turrets thrusting skyward at each end.

"Quite a building, isn't it?" Stephen exclaimed.

We tied our horses to the rail and went inside, bypassing the market and heading upstairs. I spoke to a clerk to make an appointment with the governor. The stout, older man said the best he could do was arrange a meeting with the governor's secretary for October 11th.

Discouraged, Stephen and I went downstairs to browse the market stalls.

"'Twould be mannerly of us to bring a gift to my uncle's, to thank him for his hospitality," I said.

Market day in Boston was every day but the Sabbath. Freshly butchered legs of lamb and beef rumps hung from the rafters, turkeys and chickens squawked from their cages, and cod and bass swam about in several large barrels by the fish-mongers' stalls. Late harvests of pumpkins, corn, parsnips, and apples overflowed their baskets, and polished pewter and cast-iron pots were set out on boards as though in preparation for dinner. The sweet scents of freshly baked pies and brown bread mingled with the smell of fish, poultry droppings, and animal blood. Farmers and merchants hawked their wares, promising freshness and special prices.

I bought a pair of porringers and a pint of rum, and Stephen a loaf of dark brown raisin bread and a small wheel of Dutch cheese. We wrapped our gifts in brown paper and packed them in our satchels, then rode past the stocks and pillories where an unfortunate rogue silently endured the taunts and hurled fruits of passersby.

The briny salt air and the cries of gulls increased as we drew near Bendell's Cove on the bay. Shallops and ketches rocked in their berths like babes in a cradle or sliced across the sea like great white-winged birds. Nets and cages of silvery, shimmering fish were hauled from the depths and deposited onto decks and docks, and striped cats prowled the alleyways hunting rats and mewing for fish guts.

A wooden sign swung and creaked above the door of a gray clapboard shop by the water, "Waite Ship Chandlery" carved on it in large letters. We tied our horses to the post and opened the bright red door, whence a small bell rang, announcing our entry. My cousin John glanced up from behind the counter where he was sorting tackle.

"Ben? Is it you? Welcome," he said, coming around to shake my hand, then Stephen's.

I hadn't seen John since we were children. He was about my height, dark as I was fair. He kept a trimmed beard and tied his long hair in a pigtail beneath a sailor's red knit Monmouth cap. A black kerchief around his throat was knotted in a bow. Combined with flowing sleeves under a leather doublet, knee breeches, and tall boots, he looked every bit a buccaneer.

"'Tis good to see you after so many years. Your shop is just as you described it in your letter, a treasure trove for pirates," I said.

"I enjoy it. It keeps me close to the sea, without all the miserable weather and the labor to keep a boat in order."

"I still miss it. But ever since Joseph . . ."

John placed a comforting hand on my shoulder. "I was shocked and saddened to hear of the invasion of your town, the capture of your wife and children. And yours, too, Stephen."

Stephen nodded, blinked back tears, and wandered off to

browse the wares. I felt a clutch in my chest like a hand squeezing my heart.

"Your home is a welcome safe harbor on our journey to find them. Save them . . ." my voice cracked.

"Anything we can do, cousin. Take a look around. If you find anything that might aid you on your travels, please, just take it."

"Thank you," I said, struggling to talk about my family and grateful for a distraction.

I strolled up and down the aisles, exploring the treasures.

I fingered the bolts of ivory sailcloth leaning against the wall beneath hooks bearing whale oil lanterns and coils of hemp. I examined the variety of foods for an ocean voyage: hardtack, pemmican, corn pone, dried oranges and cranberries, and barrels of flour, salt, and vinegar. Most fascinating were the navigational instruments in glass cases behind the counter: English quadrants to measure the angle of the sun, nocturnals to observe the constellations, astrolabes for shooting a star to calculate latitude, and four-pointed wooden traverse boards with pegs for judging distance.

"Look what I found for you," Stephen said, emerging from behind the rolls of nautical charts and maps.

He held up a leather-bound book with an engraving of a fish on the cover.

"*The Compleat Angler—or The Contemplative Man's Recreation*, by Izaak Walton," he read aloud.

"'Contemplative' applies to you more than I," I said, smiling.

"You can borrow it if you'd like," John said. "Bit pricey, came from London, but I have another in stock."

"Thank you," Stephen said, "your cousin would benefit from contemplation."

John measured out five yards of sailcloth for me. I also chose a brass pocket compass.

"I see you found some useful items for your travels," John said.

"Aye. Cloth for makeshift shelters," I said, "and a compass for when clouds hide the sun and stars, or snow hides the trail."

John put his hand on my shoulder again. "You men should go get a drink. You've earned it."

"What's a good tavern hereabouts?"

"The Green Dragon. Union Street. A few blocks west," John said.

"Thank you. We'll see you later at your father's house."

The namesake giant copper dragon—gone green from the salty air—crouched above the tavern's oaken doors. Inside, sailors and fishmongers, privateers and commissioners sat at tables or on stools around a central fireplace. 'Twas dark, smoky, and smelled of hops and barley, as a good establishment should. We each ordered a pint of ale and a bowl of cod chowder.

"Reminds me of the White Horse Tavern in Newport. My brothers and I loved to go there after a day on the sea," I said, raising my tankard in remembrance.

"Why do you not speak of those days?"

Stephen had no way of knowing it was more than an idle question. I nearly wept, the vividness of those memories taking me by surprise. I downed half my pint. I prayed I wouldn't someday be recounting the deaths of my wife and children in some other tavern to some other caring ear. But I'd kept the tragedy to myself for too long. I had enough burdens to bear. And so I told Stephen about my brother, Joseph, and how he died.

Chapter Thirty

BEN

❧

RHODE ISLAND COLONY
TWELVE YEARS AGO, AUGUST 1665

Our father named our ketch the *Curlew* after the flocks of curlews he'd seen in the marshes of Jamestown. He kept her in Newport Harbor at Bowen's Wharf, and she was his primary fishing and merchant boat. A fifty-footer, gaff-rigged, with a gleaming white hull. We liked to fly two foresails on her long, red bowsprit. Under sail, she did call to mind a southern white curlew in flight.

The four of us took her out on a fine, warm August day for a pleasure sail. We set our course for Cuttyhunk Island, the southernmost of the Elizabeth Islands. In those days, long before King Philip's War, Cuttyhunk was a fishing spot for the still friendly Wampanoag, and a nice midday dinner spot for day sailors.

I had five brothers and one sister, and three of my brothers loved to sail: Joseph, two years older than I; Jeremiah, eleven months younger; and Tom, the youngest son at seventeen.

We had sailed often together, especially that summer, so

we fell into our self-appointed tasks as comfortably as a husband and wife divided up labors. I was at the helm and in command, winning the coin toss with Joseph. He and Jeremiah took the mainsail, and I assigned Tom to the foresails and the mizzen.

"Standby to cast off," I shouted, my hand on the smooth wood of the wheel.

"Ready!" my crew replied in unison.

"Cast off! Let go forward!"

Jeremiah cast off our forward line.

"Let go aft."

Tom poled us away from the dock.

"Joseph, standby to raise the mainsail!"

"Ready!"

Joseph pulled down on the halyards, arm over arm, and our big ivory sail sprang up the mast and fluttered as he pulled the block and tackle tight. We caught a nice breeze, and I guided us out of the harbor. Tom scampered about, pulling in the fenders.

"Heading up! Jeremiah, sheet in!"

"Mainsheet made!"

"Thank you! Center the main!"

We tacked into the onshore breeze and headed south. Other boats sailed nearby, mostly shallops and bigger ketches, fishing in the deep trenches near the shoals and reefs. Wavelets tickled the sides of the *Curlew*, and I tasted the sting of salt air on my sun-chapped lips. Underway, I kept my distance from fishing boats to not foul their nets.

After half an hour, I tacked to the east. Tom raised our fore and mizzen sails, and the *Curlew* dipped her port side into the troughs of the wavelets, kicking up spray. White foam cut a feather before our prow. Piloting a ketch came naturally to me as riding a horse, similar in the taking up and releasing of tension on sails or reins, playing with control and speed, the breeze in my face.

We reached Cuttyhunk Island midday, the summer sun high overhead, puffy white clouds rolling in from the ocean like sheep to the fold, the breeze rising from easy to brisk. I took the *Curlew* around the island's north shore and into the Cuttyhunk pond on the east side. I stemmed the tide there, and we lowered and furled our sails whilst Tom dropped our anchor off the bow. He and Jeremiah lifted our small wherry rowboat from the coach roof and set her in the water. We threw our sacks of food and gear into the boat and rowed to shore, where we secured the wherry with a grappling hook.

Collapsing on the sandy beach, we built a small fire and set our sausages and corn cobs on a small cast iron grill to roast. We took swigs from our flasks of ale and reclined on the warm sand, watching the sunlight sparkle on the waves, listening to the rhythm of the sea.

"'Tis the life, hey?" Joseph said, spreading fresh butter on his corn.

"Your wife makes a tasty sausage," Jeremiah said between bites.

"That she does," Joseph agreed, stabbing one of the sizzling sausages from the grill.

"How fares your wife and babe, Joseph?" I asked.

"Sarah is lovely, though it seems we have not slept the past few months since little Will was born," he said, laughing.

"You're both but twenty-two, you'll survive," Tom said. "I still cannot believe you were my age when you married her."

"True love and all that." Joseph smiled, removing his red Monmouth cap and running his fingers through his blonde hair. He and I might have been twins, we looked so much alike.

When we finished our food and doused our fire, we fished in the bay's shallow waters for a time, but with no luck, we gave it up and went for a ramble. We walked up the trail to the top of the central hill, through green grass and shrubs, past scattered, wind-stunted trees and thickets of wild roses. From atop the hill, we gazed far and wide, northwest clear to Newport, Plymouth to the east, and very close by, the island of Martha's Vineyard, named after the discoverer's daughter and the wild grapes growing there.

I frowned. The wind was freshening, and the clouds had swiftly transmogrified from flocks of sheep to packs of dark gray wolves. "Looks like the weather isn't with us today, boys. Shall we head back?"

"Perhaps we should wait it out? I recall there's a shack of sorts on the south side of the island," Joseph said.

"'Tis but a two-hour sail in this wind, let's just cut and run," I said.

Even the water in Cuttyhunk Pond was roughening as we rowed back to the *Curlew*, bobbing in the waves. We clambered on board, hauled up the rowboat, secured it on the coach roof, hoisted our anchor, and sailed out against the tide. The wind was blowing soundly from the northeast, and the clouds darkened with rain.

I considered sailing south out of the harbor so the island might shelter us from the worst of the storm, but then the gale would strike us full force when we rounded the western side. My other choice, heading back the way we'd come, meant sailing downwind on a beam reach but running the risk of broaching beam to a wave. I chose the latter course.

The wave crests were breaking now, white horses everywhere, and the spray was in our faces and dampening our sleeves. We sailed east out of the harbor, close-hauled to the wind, then north practically in irons, almost dead in the water before we caught the wind again. Each time I tacked, I aimed for the smoothest part of the waves, but still we took on water.

We had our storm jib up, the foresail closest to the mainmast, trying to keep the *Curlew* balanced at the center. We were fleeing before the storm, and I was racing to get out of its path, hoping it would pass behind us and not chase us all the way home. A ceiling of dark gray clouds pressed down on us, the wind whistling in my ears and about the sails. Steering was rough, the wind and waves tugging hard on the rudder.

"The storm will drown my words, so watch my arm for signals! Remember—up or down for sails, pointing to port or starboard for tacks, a raised fist for a stop or hold!" I demonstrated, and my brothers nodded. We reefed the mainsail and the mizzen.

We were less than an hour from the harbor with a following sea, and the storm was closing in like a cat on a bird. The rain started, sheets of it beating down on us, and though we donned our coats, the chill was bone deep. I'd never known a storm to come on so quickly and with such fury.

"Lower the mizzen!" I yelled, miming the motion, and saw Jeremiah respond.

The line fouled.

"Bloody hell! Tom, help Jeremiah!" I cried, pointing.

"Prepare to come about!" I shouted, circling my arm in the air.

"Ready about!"

I steered the *Curlew* downwind.

Mainsail reefed and mizzen at last secured, the *Curlew* eased up a bit under less sail. Yet, like the buzzards in the sky above us, she was still a bird in a storm, buffeted about, swooping and staggering, seeking shelter. I yelled at Tom to go below deck, out of harm's way. Jeremiah hunkered down between the main and foresails, ready if needed.

Joseph and I worked in tandem. I took the wheel, and he controlled the main sheet, tightening and releasing it, helping me steer. I warmed to the challenge of this, confident we'd make it back in one piece. We reached a point a few miles east of Newport, and it was time to tack north again.

"Prepare to tack!" I yelled, swinging my arm.

Jeremiah readied the foresails. Joseph slowly let out the boom. I turned the *Curlew* to starboard, and three things went horribly wrong all at once.

The wind shifted abruptly, a gust across our beam pushing us back to port, and with it, a rogue wave reared up and crashed down, drenching us. I tightened my grip on the wheel and yelled, "Gybe!" but the wind sucked my warning out of me like a cat sucks the air from a wee babe. Before I could raise my arm in warning, the main boom swung hard and fast to starboard.

I ducked. I know I saw Joseph duck, too. But the boom struck his shoulder, sending him flying. He grabbed frantically for the shrouds. I reached for him. And then he was gone.

A ringing in my ears, ice clutching my heart. "Man overboard!" I screamed, pointing to where I'd seen Joseph go into the sea.

Jeremiah threw a life float overboard, yelled for Tom, and pounded on the hatch.

Tom burst out of the cabin, crouched low, and worked his way from bow to stern, gripping the lines, and searching the deep water.

Tom ran, slipping and sliding, back to me to steady the boom. I struggled to kill our forward flight. I brought the *Curlew* around and headed downwind a boat length or two, my eyes on the life ring. I seized the wheel hard and brought us back dead into the wind, sails luffing, finally rocking in place.

My eyes swept the black waves and troughs for Joseph's bright red cap, a glimpse of his golden hair. Lightning found him for an instant, then took him away. Thunder and torrential rain muffled our desperate calls.

Jeremiah threw our second life float overboard, and it drifted out behind our stern, tethered but empty. The wind against him, Jeremiah finally lit our lanterns and handed one to Tom, who held it aloft to light my search.

Fractions of time had piled up into an eternity wasted.

Tom leaned over the gunwales. "I see him! Facedown, near the ring!"

"I'm going in!" I tore off my boots and coat. I took our block and tackle and hoisted it on a spare halyard. Then I wrapped it under my arms and knotted it, my fingers stiff with cold. Grabbing a cushion from the bench, I leapt over the side. The water grasped me like the claws of Death. Tom's lantern found Joseph. He was still at least a rod away, and the waves were merciless. Three times, they swamped me, and three times, I kicked back up to the surface, gasping, frantically searching the storm-tossed mountains and valleys of water, three times spotting my brother bobbing like a cork.

"Joseph!" I screamed. All this, but especially the rest, is etched in my mind forever. It comes to me in nightmares and chills my heart even on a sunny quay in Boston harbor.

Joseph face down in the water. I shove the cushion under his chest, encircle him in my arms. The tug of the rope as Jeremiah hauls us in, the lantern showing me the way back. Another wave engulfs us, shoves us down deep, deeper. I cannot see. I cannot breathe. I hold onto Joseph with one arm, reach upward for the surface with the other, and kick. I open my eyes to the cold saltwater and swim toward the paler wash of gray lantern light above the surface. My face breaks clear, and I gasp for air. The bright white hull is within reach.

"Hoist him up to me!" Jeremiah yells, dropping the tethered float, and I get Joseph into it somehow. They pull him up and onto the boat, then haul me in. The boat is shuddering, creaking, nearly splintering from the force of the storm.

Joseph lies on his back, his eyes shut. I kneel beside him and take huge gulps of precious air. He is so still. I see the bloody gash on his arm, but I grab him by both shoulders anyway, feeling his iciness burning me, and shake him furiously. I pound on his chest to force his heart to beat again. Turn him on his side and strike him on the back. Water trickles out of his mouth, but he still won't wake. Why won't he wake?

I feel a hand on my shoulder, shake it off. Now I'm lifting Joseph into my arms, embracing him, sobbing into his chest, saying his name over and over. "Joseph. Joseph. Wake up! Please, wake up!"

The storm rages, yet all I hear is the silence of my brother in my arms.

"He's gone, Ben."

Tom's voice. Jeremiah covers Joseph with a blanket, wraps another around me. I cry, but the wind drowns me out.

We carried Joseph below decks and laid him down. Jeremiah raised the main halfway, sailing back close-hauled on the following sea. The wind held steady, just shy of a gale, and we rode the white horses into the harbor. We did not speak. My face was wet with tears and rain and salt spray, and my heart was empty. It had been my decision to try to beat the storm, my one job as helmsman to keep us all safe. And now my brother was dead.

Chapter Thirty-One
BEN

Boston, Plymouth Colony
October 9-11, 1677

"Ben," Stephen said.

I had told my story all at once, with barely a pause. At some point, Stephen had ordered me a second beer, and now I threw it back in a few gulps, then ran the back of my hand across my eyes, wiping away tears but not banishing memories. Stephen's gaze was locked on mine, and it was kind.

"I am sorry, Ben."

"If I'd not won the coin toss, Joseph would have waited out the storm. His death was my fault."

"Ben, no, 'twas not your fault. You did not create the storm or swing the boom. 'Twas God's hand, not yours."

"But for what reason? Why?" I whispered.

"I wish I knew, if 'twould give you comfort," he said earnestly, "but 'tis not our place to question, only to trust in God's righteousness and power."

I almost scoffed. Instead, I put my forehead in my palms and closed my eyes.

"Some might view your tragedy as Milton's 'sable clouds with silver linings,'" Stephen said. "'Tis perhaps why you leave naught to chance and carry the burden for others. Those virtues have saved many lives."

"Perhaps too few, too late."

"You led your band to safety at the Falls and were first to help the wounded after the attacks on our town. And you have not wavered in your determination to find our wives and children."

I tried to harken to his words. Many words from a quiet man.

"Thank you, Stephen." I stared at the foam inside my empty tankard. "Yet what if we fail? What then?"

Stephen looked solemnly at me.

"You must heed what you've heard in every sermon on every Sabbath, Ben. We are but instruments of God's will. 'The Lord himself doth go before thee: he will be with thee: he will not fail thee, neither forsake thee: fear not, therefore, nor be discomforted.'"

"Did God not forsake us on my boat in Rhode Island?" I said, my voice breaking.

Stephen frowned, and I lowered my voice.

"Those who died in Hatfield, were they not forsaken?" My already unsteady faith was veering dangerously close to blasphemy.

Stephen sighed. "Enough. You're done with your beer. Let's go visit your uncle."

We left our mounts in the care of the livery stable and walked to my uncle's big, sturdy house near the Common. My cousin John introduced his wife Eunice to us. She looked healthy and fit and carried her baby comfortably. I was happy to see my Uncle Gamaliel and my Aunt Grace again. We handed them our gifts, and I put a smile on my face, for they were kin, and wanted to help us however they could.

October 11

The clerk showed Stephen and me to Rawson's office.

"Secretary Rawson, thank you for meeting with us so promptly," I said, shaking the hand of the lean, dark-haired, dark-eyed man.

"The governor received Major Pynchon's correspondence a few days ago," Rawson said.

"Then you know our plight. We brought a petition from our town," I handed it to him.

"Pynchon's letters contained news the governor wished me to share with you. They arrived after you left Springfield and Hatfield."

"He sent more than one letter?"

"Yes. Firstly, information Pynchon received from your town of Hatfield. Apparently, a Benoni Stebbins, taken captive at Deerfield, escaped and returned home the same night that you and Mister Jennings left there to come to Boston."

"What? We just missed him?" I could barely grasp the ironic misfortune.

He handed me the letter, which I read swiftly.

"Stebbins confirms our families and kin were taken by Algonquians and are on their way to Canada. Our wives and children are alive!" I exclaimed.

"Thanks be to God," Stephen said.

"Yes," Rawson said, smiling. "And then another letter arrived just yesterday. Please, both of you, have a seat."

He read aloud, "'Englishmen from Hadley captured and questioned a company of Indians near Hadley's mill a fort-night ago. They claimed they were Wachusett, part of the war party that assailed your town. The Hadley men released them on their promise others would return to negotiate the release of the captives. Please advise Waite and Jennings when you see them."

"What? Hatfield knew of this but said nothing until now?"

"I do not think your town believed the Indians would return. But Governor Leverett plans to send Captain Treat and a few troops to Hadley on October 14, the agreed-upon day, lest it was a legitimate offer of parley," Secretary Rawson said.

I was stunned. *Did this alter everything? Dared I hope? Or would this make matters worse?* I was ill at ease that others would handle these negotiations whilst I was in Boston.

"Please ask the governor to apprise me of the outcome and any other developments. Could you take down my place of abode?"

"Of course." He dipped his pen in the inkpot.

"Care of Mr. Gamaliel Waite, Sumner Street. Or my cousin, John, Waite's Ship Chandlery, Bendell Cove."

He wrote it down and placed it and the petition with other papers on his desk.

"I will have the clerk schedule you an appointment with the deputy governor as soon as possible," he said.

"Governor Leverett remains unavailable?" I asked. I'm sure he heard the frustration in my voice.

"In truth, Mr. Waite, the colony is severely short of funds. The War with King Philip cost us dearly. Sending the troops to Hadley is the best he can do at the moment. The governor hopes to have more to offer you soon."

"And I must speak to him directly, even if he can only offer me permission to pursue my course."

Rawson sighed. "I will see what I can do."

"Till next week, then, and thank you, sir," I kept my tone civil, but the moment I reached the street, I threw my hat to the cobblestones.

"By God's blood!"

I faced more opposition from my fellow colonists than the Algonquians who had taken my family. If only Stephen and I hadn't followed protocol, hadn't left for Boston on October 5, we could have used Benoni's information to pursue my family and kin that same night. I was angry at being passed from one overlord to the next. My patience was wearing thin.

Chapter Thirty-Two
ASHPELON

CAMP
LEAF FALLING MOON

"The captives believe the English will keep their word," I told Wanalancet in our language.

"Ha! And you believe the English speak the truth? They will promise, but when we send our warriors, they will fall upon them and kill them," Wanalancet said, pacing back and forth beside our small council fire outside the longhouse.

"The English are not stupid. They will not risk danger to the captives," I said.

"Because we have captives, we are safe. But imagine we do this thing. They pay us in furs or wampum or cattle or even silver. We release the captives to them, then what?"

"Then we leave the richer," I said, but I knew what he would say next.

"No, then they kill us! Have you forgotten how they betrayed the praying Natick?"

"That was two years ago, different English. Of course, I've not forgotten," I said.

"I'd think not! The English put our people on boats and

left them on the islands in Boston's harbor. No food, no shelter, no game to hunt. They imprisoned them there. To die."

"These Hatfield English are desperate to have the captives back and gain nothing by killing us." I glanced about, but we were the only ones outside the longhouse beneath a starry sky.

"What did they gain by turning on the praying Naticks they befriended?" Wanalancet asked. "Or by killing our children when they attacked us at Peskeompskut? The English kill us even when we are gathered in peace, because we are in their way, on land they lust after."

"But now we have control. It is why we raided their town, to take captives, to take back our power," I said.

Wanalancet stopped pacing, and angrily slammed his fist into his palm. "But now they know our plans. They know because of the Stebbins boy. He has told them everything, and we are no longer safe!"

"The English looked for us once before. They did not find us."

"You said they came close. The Waite man. The tracker."

"He wants his family back. He's not stupid. I think he would honor a trade."

"Like he honored your family at Peskeompskut? Like the English honored us when they murdered Metacomet? No!"

I rose to my feet and looked up at the curved piece remaining of Penibagos, The Leaf Falling Moon. "Think, Wanalancet! We are going to starve. Too many of us. Too far. Winter."

"My warriors will find some game. Or we can eat the horses."

"And then what? Once we eat our horses, how do we travel with women and children?"

"We cannot take the horses over the lakes," Wanalancet said.

"It will be dangerous taking the captives over the lakes. You are misjudging how difficult this is," I paused, shaking my head, hearing the misplaced blame in my words. "I misjudged."

"At last, we agree! *You* misjudged. Yet now you want us to listen to you?"

"We will vote," I said, motioning for Wanalancet to stop pacing.

We entered the longhouse and sat with our people around our fire, far from the captives. The vote was heavily against me. All the Wachusett sided with Wanalancet, as did half of my people. It was resolved. I woke the sleeping captives to tell them we would not go to Hadley. There'd be no parley. We would continue to Canada, and they should speak no more of it.

Chapter Thirty-Three
MARTHA

I had not thought much about the horses until they started shooting them, one by one.

The first to go was an old mare, swaybacked and loose-lipped, her chestnut coat graying about her muzzle. My girls called her Drowsy, for she was slow. She was also gentle, reliable, and trusting. I watched Atian release her hobbles, stroke her blazed face, and lead her away. I dreaded what was to come. A shot rang out in the still morning air. The rest of the horses raised their heads, pricked their ears, then returned to their corn.

Captives and captors feasted that night on horsemeat, but I refused. Ashpelon was cross with me, asking if I was too proud to eat horsemeat. No, I said, not pride, sorrow.

The days wore on. I questioned why we stayed in this place where there was no food. Perhaps it was a sacred place to them. How long had they been coming here?

I considered asking Ashpelon or Nìbi Wàbà, but I sensed they would not find me worthy of knowing, in the same way I would not speak to them of my favorite haunts. The spot by the banks of Mill Creek south of Hatfield meadow, where wild strawberries bloomed and ripened every June. The bench under the apple tree in Hannah's brothers' garden, the bees abuzz in the blossoms. My seat in our meetinghouse, the sun slanting through the high windows to caress Ben's hair as he bowed his head in prayer. Places holding meanings I would not give away to strangers.

I was marking each day with a tally in my Bible, but now I began counting the days by the killings of the horses. It seemed killing a horse every three days fed us all, and the Natives would consume even the entrails, the bone marrow, and the tongue.

At first, I tried to keep the truth from my girls, telling them it was deer meat, which they'd eaten without complaint before, both on this journey and at home each fall when Ben went hunting. Of course, as children are wont to do, they soon learned the truth from the other children and from watching the dwindling herd of horses. Sally, of course, was oblivious, and Mary resigned. Mattie, not surprisingly, was distraught.

On the day we finished eating the fourth horse, Ashpelon told us we would leave this place soon. As he'd commanded, there'd been no further talk of bargaining or parleys with the English. It was past mid-October by my reckoning, whether by tally or horse or merely the changing leaves, the shortening days, and the colder nights. A month since our capture. Again, I feared some calamity must have befallen Ben, for what would restrain him? Dread filled me like stones dropped into a jar of water, pushing tears up behind my eyes.

Nìbi Wàbà showed me many kindnesses as we made preparations to leave. She gave me rabbit skins for new caps for my girls, a horsehide cloak for me, and handfuls of dried corn and berries to keep in our apron pockets for the trail ahead. The elder woman, Neepânon, took pity on Hannah. In her fourth month with child, Hannah was keckish or vomiting most mornings. Neepânon ground up herbs, nuts, and roots and steeped them for her in a small rabbit skin pouch.

It was a miserable morning when we left, cold and blustering, sleet and rain by turns drenching us. Growing heavy with child, I was allowed to ride one of the three horses, with Sally before me, and I hoped my need would ensure the poor beast's life.

It took us a day to come down off the mountain and find the Connecticut River again. We followed it for a week. The days blurred together, each one the same. Invariably, the rolling of the horse under me, the dense forest crowding the trail, the rumble of the river, the stomps of booted feet and the patter of moccasins, the dampness of rain, the warmth of dappled sunlight.

At night, we slept beneath the shelter of the trees, lying on woven mats atop damp leaves and fir boughs, covered in scraps of deer and horse and bear hide, clustering close to a few fires we built in the small patches of earth we cleared. There was little food besides boiled roots and songbirds, and the nights were cold.

When I was able, I cared for my children, but I was sore from the saddle, and they were weak from hunger and marching. They no longer played with the other children, for the Natives drove us on without breaks or refreshments. My girls clung to my skirts, and I was cross with them over small things. We English talked little amongst ourselves, there being little of note to discuss.

Hannah's mood grew evermore dismal. As we all did, she suffered from weariness and hunger, but her morning sickness increased both. She wept silently at odd times and without provocation. I read my Bible to her each evening, the Psalms and Proverbs that offered solace, hope, and beauty. Mary Foote joined us, offering comfort, heating water on the fire, and brewing Hannah cups of the tea Neepânon had given her.

At the end of that dreary week, we came to a place Ashpelon called Squawmaug, where the Connecticut River continued northward, the Squawmaug flowing into it from the west and the Ammonoosuc from the east. The Natives built a half dozen roughly made wigwams—*wetus*—of saplings and bark and mats arranged in a large half-circle around a fire. The goodwill they'd shown us for most of our time on Putney Mountain—except for the anger we endured due to Benoni's escape—proved absent here. They treated us like the prisoners we were, often shutting us without, leaving us to huddle exposed around the fire, threatening to knock us on the head with a tomahawk if we disturbed them by seeking shelter from the cold and rain.

Hunger was ever present, yet somehow, my babe still stirred within me. I sometimes talked or sang to it to pass the time. Mary, Mattie, and Sally placed their little hands on my belly to feel it kick, which was one small way I could distract them from their hunger. And mine. Even though I'd not refused any meat since the day of Drowsy's death, as time passed I had less strength, and was constantly overcome by dizziness. Though I had no mirror, my face felt lean and haggard to my touch, and the flesh on my arms was meager.

It occurred to me that I might be slowly dying.

Chapter Thirty-Four
BEN

We sat in the keeping room of my uncle's home Saturday afternoon, a thunderstorm pounding the roof and sudden flashes of lightning ripping shadows from the darkest corners of the room. John, Stephen, and I sat around the table, and my Uncle Gamaliel rocked the baby in her cradle by the fire. John's wife, Eunice, and my Aunt Grace tended to the cooking fires in the kitchen. The house was full of the aromas of wood smoke and the beans, onions, salt pork, and molasses simmering in the pot over the fire.

I flipped through the pages of the book we'd borrowed, *The Compleat Angler*, realizing it was more a philosophical discourse than an instructive manual, at times reading aloud a particularly pleasing insight or turn of phrase.

"I've put the brown bread and the Indian pudding on to steam. Dinner will be ready in an hour," Grace said, wiping her wrinkled hands on her apron.

My uncle and aunt had a servant girl, a Natick woman named Kanti, whom they'd found begging for food in Cole's tavern. My uncle made her their servant, but my aunt wouldn't allow her to cook for them. I was not sure if my aunt enjoyed cooking or was uncomfortable with a Natick preparing her meal. If the latter, she was mistaken. Before King Philip's war, I'd been welcome at several Nipmuc meals, and fondly remembered delicious autumn stews of wild rice and onions, lily bulbs, and Jerusalem artichokes.

"I am so grateful to God that you now have proof your wives and children are alive," John said.

Alive as of a fortnight ago, that same dark voice whispered.

"We are overjoyed," Stephen said.

Why could I not have his faith?

"We held out hope for the parley," I said, "but the Nipmucs and Pocumtucks failed to appear on October 14. Captain Treat and twenty troops arrived at the mill and waited all day to no avail."

"I'm sorry," John said.

I shrugged, summoning every shred of faith I possessed. "It could be for the best. If the Natives had shown up and faced armed troops, it might have ended in bloodshed on both sides and put the captives at fresh risk."

"You must be growing impatient," John said.

I nodded. "Quite, but I finally have an appointment to see the governor on Wednesday. After that, I pray things will move swiftly. We will return to Hatfield for provisions, then head to Albany to find a guide. I hope to avoid calling on Captain Salisbury."

The scents of apple and spice mingled with the aroma of sweet beans and bread. My stomach growled, and by and by, Kanti set before us trenchers of baked beans, thick slices of moist brown bread, fresh butter, spiced applesauce, and the sweet Indian pudding.

As we bowed our heads in thanks, shame enveloped me. I was comfortable, well-fed, and surrounded by family, whilst my wife and children were trudging through the wilderness in the clutches of our enemies. I took less enjoyment in the meal than I'd expected to.

At close to midnight, my relatives retired to their bedchambers upstairs. Stephen and I stayed awake for another hour, discussing our plans and hopes for the following week. He fell asleep, but I was kept awake by a yearning for Martha like hunger, an emptiness without her that chilled my heart despite the fire and the featherbed.

&

We arrived at Governor Leverett's office a quarter-hour before our appointed time on Wednesday, October 20, and waited in the stiff-backed wooden chairs.

A half-hour later, the secretary came for us. "The governor will see you now."

Governor Leverett stood up from his massive desk, shook our hands, and asked us to be seated across from him in two blue upholstered chairs. He spent a few seconds appraising us from heavy-lidded eyes beneath dark eyebrows, and we appraised him. His shoulder-length gray hair proved his age and humility, for 'twas his own and not the ridiculous periwigs now in fashion amongst government officials and the wealthy.

"I apologize for making you wait, but the colony remains severely short of funds," the governor said.

"We understand, sir. You've read our petition?" I asked.

He nodded. "I must say I'm impressed by your bravery, Mister Waite, and yours as well, Mister Jennings. Even with the backing of your town, the colony, and New York, this will be a long and perilous journey."

I ran my fingers through my hair, and leaned forward. "We are aware of the difficulties, sir, but we are desperate to reclaim our families and kin."

"No other men from Hadley or Hatfield volunteered to accompany you?" he asked.

"Not for lack of courage nor desire. The attack devastated our town. Many were killed, as you know. When a man's wife or children are slain, he isn't in any state to search for other men's families."

"True. You can be assured I find your valor admirable and your cause more than worthy of support." Governor Leverett sat back in his chair, studying us. "I've been called contrary, even heretical, for opposing some of the strict orthodoxies of the Puritans. Neither do I bow down to the English Crown. Makes me unpopular with many, but it also moves me to assist you."

"Thank you, sir," I said.

"I am giving you two identical letters officially appointing you, Mister Waite, as Massachusetts Colony's Agent for the ransom and redemption of the twenty-one Hatfield and Deerfield captives," he said, handing them to me. "Those should grant you the power to negotiate with the Indians. You may present one letter to Captain Salisbury and the other to Governor Frontenac of Canada if need be. I also made mention in the letter of Mister Jennings as a secondary agent."

He stood then, and I was concerned he'd not mentioned funds. English and French would accept written promises, but the Natives had learned not to trust paper and ink. They wanted blood or money.

"And as to funding, sir?" I asked.

"I can provide you a letter of credit for 200 pounds, which exceeds the demand of eight pounds per captive proposed by the Natives earlier this month after Stebbins's escape," he said, handing me a third letter. "Governor Frontenac and the United Colonies should be able to raise the funds to cover it when the time comes."

The governor walked around to us and handed me five one-pound notes. "An advance against the letter of credit to assist you in securing a guide and snowshoes in Albany or

Schenectady. I hope you have funds for provisions and lodging?"

"Yes, sir, our town raised a collection," I said.

"If you require anything else, please have Captain Salisbury, Governor Andros, or Commander Bruckholds mail a request to me, and I will see what I can do," the governor said.

Stephen and I smiled at his kindness. We stood and shook his hand again.

"You have our deepest gratitude, sir," I said.

"It has righted a wrong."

"I'm unsure of your meaning, sir?"

"I appointed William Turner captain and commander at the Falls Fight. It was a mistake, and it cost many lives," the governor said. "I also did not heed your town's requests to enlarge the stockade, not understanding the severity of the threat. I hope my support of your quest somewhat atones for that."

A journey home always passes faster than one departing, but it seemed a long trip. We reached Hatfield on the afternoon of October 25th. Captain Watts and his troops had garrisoned our town once again. By order of the governor, they were extending our palisades north and south. Better late than never. We'd buried our dead, healed our wounded, and begun to rebuild our homes.

Stephen stayed with his new in-laws at the Dickinson's home across the lane, and I with the Allis family again. Old Lieutenant Allis was doing poorly, but John and Rachel's twins were plump and healthy. The family had taken in John Coleman, who'd lost so many; his wife and infant daughter slain, his son and daughter captured. I reassured John Allis and John Coleman that my wife and the other women surely cared for their captured children. Caring for others was second nature to them.

Rachel Allis washed my shirts, stockings, collar, and cuffs, and I bathed from a pail of lukewarm water before eating a supper of chicken stew. John Allis, John Coleman, and I stayed up for an hour or two, talking by the light of the fire and a few tallow candles, reading from the Bible, and sharing our grief and our hopes. I crawled under the blankets and coverlet on a soft mattress and fell into a deep slumber.

As was frustratingly expected, Stephen and I were again delayed, this time not by bureaucracy but by necessity. It was Stephen's ill luck to awake the following day feverish and nauseous, in no condition to embark on a long journey. Though I worried about his health, I was aggrieved by the delay. Rather than uselessly bemoaning my fate, I occupied the next five days by joining in the enlargement of the stockade, the final harvest of cabbages, beets, pumpkins, and apples, and the rebuilding of my home and others'.

It was time well spent, yet while I worked, the torment of my loss fully occupied my mind and heart, as did an almost maniacal desire to be on our way.

Chapter Thirty-Five

MARTHA

OTTAUQUECHEE RIVER
OCTOBER/NOVEMBER

Like Job in the Bible, I thought I'd suffered all our God intended, but I was shortly reminded of His infinite power. For three days, at sunrise and sunset, the Natives fished the river and brooks and ponds near Squawmaug yet returned empty-handed. At night, they hunted. Although we heard the rustle and cries of wild animals, they remained invisible as ghosts.

Ashpelon and Wanalancet were at odds again, and after a day of their arguing, we split into two parties. Ashpelon was afraid the Mohawks might find us and aid in our escape, hence he separated Mary, Hannah, and me from our children and the Englishmen. When it was clear we couldn't persuade him to let us keep our children, I begged him to send Nìbi Wàbà with them, and he relented. He kept with him Hannah, Mary, and me, as well as the orphans and little Daniel Dickinson, sending our own children and our men with the Wachusett band under Wanalancet. My girls' departing tears broke my heart, but I had come to trust Nìbi Wàbà and knew she'd let no harm befall them.

We kept the orphaned children in our care. The Wachusett band with our men and children took the White River to the north, and our party headed west alongst the Ottauquechee River.

Ashpelon promised our parties would meet again, but not for many days. We were all so hungry. Ashpelon said we'd kill the remaining horses once we rejoined the Wachusett party, and for once, I was glad of it. Until then, we finished all the dried corn and berries and ate whatever we found or killed alongst the trail.

The warriors had their flintlocks, bows, and arrows and continued hunting for small game near the river. They surprised cottontail and snowshoe rabbits in the underbrush, shot gray squirrels out of tree limbs, flushed ruffed grouse from fallen leaves, and silenced many black crows. Whoever was lucky enough to kill one of these animals always shared it with the rest of us. The children and elders ate first, followed by Neepânon, Hannah, Mary, and I. The warriors ate last. I was grateful for their generosity, but we wouldn't survive long on scant morsels of crow.

Ashpelon and a few young Nipmuc boys helped us forage for food. We learned where to dig in the not-yet-frozen earth for wild onion bulbs, to distinguish edible mushrooms from poisonous ones, and how to grind fallen acorns and leach the bitterness from them. Still, there was not near enough food to sustain us. I was grateful again for the horse, as I did not think I had the strength for the march.

Hannah's sickness continued, so Ashpelon spared her a horse, but poor Mary Foote had to walk. They saved the third horse for the youngest children in our care—Abigail Bartholomew, Daniel Dickinson, and Noah and Sarah Coleman—tying them to the saddle riding double, and taking turns. The three of us tried our best to care for them, carrying the little ones in our arms when they weren't riding, sharing the patties of acorn meal we cooked on hot rocks in the fire, and snuggling them under hides and furs at night.

On the third day, we started to climb. We followed a steep and twisting trail through the woods, many fallen trees and icy brooks blocking our way. The crows mocked us with their caws by day, and owls haunted our dreams at night. Daily rain became daily snow, and the higher we climbed, the colder the nights. We wrapped small stones from the fire in scraps of animal hide and tucked them in our shoes or held them in our hands at night to keep our toes and fingers from freezing. We gathered dead fiddle leaf ferns, dried goldenrod, and bark from willow trees and brewed them, inhaling the steam and pretending the hot, weak tea was soup or stew.

When we rested, I paid heed to the number and strength of my babe's kicks to reassure myself of the life within me. I had not yet lost a child. At this point, it would be the worst of all, a sudden stillness, enduring the hollow emptiness until labor came, delivering a stillborn babe. Three or four times each day, I sat quietly for several minutes counting the reassuring movements. The counts varied wildly from time to time, and I wondered if my babe slept and woke within my womb. Day and night, I prayed it would be born whole and healthy.

We were too weak, sorrowful, and hungry to speak much to one another, and in our silence, my fears increased and multiplied, poisoning my mind like maggots in rotting flesh. I'd succumb to madness if I did not rid myself of them. I found singing softly under my breath sometimes banished my fears.

On the fifth day, our trail snaked through steep gorges of rock, with cascades of water pausing and freezing in small pools. Patches of snow and treacherous ice hid in the shadows, but where the trees thinned, swaths of sunlight baked the rocks. It was a wild landscape beyond my comprehension.

Midday, the sky darkened, and the wind blew the snow so fiercely that our captors called a halt. Hacking down small trees, they built a few crude wigwams beside a jumble of boulders and rocky ledges that formed shallow caves. We all helped cover the wigwam frames with woven mats and the flat, sweet-smelling cedar boughs. We crowded into these, and they sheltered us from the howling wind and furious snow to some extent.

Hannah, Mary, and I grew wise in the River Indians' ways. We gathered stones and placed them in a circle, then stacked slender, dry branches together. After many attempts, sparks from the flint lit a small fire outside the entrance to our little shelter. We prayed our thanks to God for the heat.

After a long time warming ourselves in silence, I spoke. "What is to become of us?"

Mary sat with her chin on her knees, her arms wrapped around her. Hannah tucked her long legs to the side and spread out her skirts. Both looked gaunt and pale, their eyes dull and sunken. I knew I was equally thin, except for my belly. Hannah was beginning to show and nearing her quickening time.

"'Tis in God's hands, Martha," Mary said, "but the question burdens all of us."

Hannah nibbled on a fingernail. "What if one of us cannot keep going? What then?"

No one answered her.

The storm had eased by dusk, though I was still hungry and cold and far from slumber. I stared into the fire, lost in my thoughts and fears. Somewhere, a wolf howled, a mournful, aching sound. I pulled my cloak around me and crawled inside our shelter. My friends and the children snuggled together, their breath like mist. The warriors headed out to hunt again, their moccasins whispering in the snow. Half-hearted whistles and hoots trembled in the wind. I admired their tenacious efforts to feed us all, for they, too, grew weaker in body and spirit. This ordeal was as arduous for them as for us.

Chapter Thirty-Six

ASHPELON

I sat in the wigwam by the fire and gazed at the first quarter of the Hunter's Moon above the treetops. I had not joined the hunt. I needed time alone to think because I was afraid. *Newabes.*

We were starving—all of us. Winter was upon us, and the air grew colder day by day, night by night. Once we reached the lake, we would need canoes, which take many suns to build. We would need snowshoes. More suns. I had misjudged the risks to my people.

Anger and fear had blinded us, blinded me. The English had driven us to this. Invading our land in increasing numbers. Letting their cattle trample our corn. Giving us guns for our furs, then taking them away. Breaking promises, angering Metacomet, and slaughtering our people. Stealing everything from us in their greed. *Wusomupok.*

I feared winter's cold and starvation, the greed and madness it might arouse in my people and our captives. Evil. *Machuk.* I feared the spirit lurking in all peoples' hearts in times of desperation. When they forget we are bound to each other. When they would do anything to survive. Our parents had warned us. In turn, we warned our own children. *Keep warm in the winter. Do not go into the woods alone. Do not be selfish. Share.*

The evil, the *Machuk*, has many names. We call it the *Windigo*, but others call it *Windikouk*, *Wittikka*, or *Kewoko*. As it has many names, so does it take many forms. It is a shapeshifter. It is ageless, and it is everywhere, and it is nowhere at all. To shamans, it appears as an owl on the night of the Cold Moon, or the Wolf Moon, or the Hunger Moon. Others have seen it fly before the fierce winds of a blizzard, bringing cold that cracks the trees.

Where does it come from, this *Windigo*? From greed born of hunger and cold. It is why we always share our shelter and our food. Cold and hunger bring horrible dreams in which men see the *Windigo*. Some say it travels a pathway from the dream world to this one. Sometimes, if you see the signs, you can save those who dream these dreams. Wrap them in blankets, put them close by the fire, and pour the Englishman's firewater down their throat until they sweat, until their heart melts. Some can see the *Windigo*'s reflection in the shine of a cooking pot and banish it by throwing the pot in the fire. If all that fails, then it must be killed.

Our men go out every dawn and dusk to hunt and return hours later with nothing or only tiny things, squirrels or wrens. We dig for onions and acorns, but soon the snow will bury even those too deep to find. We will kill and eat the horses once we have crossed these mountains, and that will give us another week, perhaps two.

We flee farther and farther north to escape the English and their cattle and guns. Winter grows colder and colder. If we reach our longhouse in Canada in time, we will live. But if not? Once the horses are gone, what will be left for us to eat if there is still no game?

Chapter Thirty-Seven

BEN

NEW YORK
OCTOBER 31 TO NOVEMBER 9

We traveled by foot to Albany, a tiring six-day journey. We'd considered horseback, but the snow, ice, and lakes we'd traverse north of there would not be passable for them, and their need for food would be a constant burden.

"You realize this is *Samhain*," Stephen said as we set out.

"All Hallows Eve, yes. Is *Samhain* another name for the Church of England or Irish Catholic holiday?"

"Yes. A bewitching one. The first day of winter."

"I always marked that on the Solstice."

"Aye, but the Irish mark it by the Crone of Beare."

"Does not sound auspicious," I said, "please spare me the details."

We arrived on a Friday, November 5, and followed the same route I had taken over a month before, through the palisade gates, past the Dutch Church on Handlers Street.

"'Tis like the Netherlands," Stephen said. "The crow-stepped gables."

"You've been there?" I asked, surprised.

"No, but my parents came here by way of Amsterdam. Spoke of it."

"Aye. Nearly half the town still speaks Dutch," I said.

"Do you?"

"Not well. My French is better, and my Mohawk and Nipmuc passable."

The Stadt Huys was closed, and the sign on the door indicated it would remain so all weekend.

"Blast it!" I said.

"Might we stay with your friend Timothy?" Stephen offered.

"Likely would be an imposition. But I know a tavern."

&

On Monday, promptly at the stroke of nine, we entered Stadt Huys and rang the bell at the empty desk. It summoned the same young man as before. This time, I asked his name and introduced him to Stephen.

"Bram Jacobssen," the clerk replied, pronouncing the J like a Y. "A pleasure to meet you, Mister Jennings. Mister Waite, I'm afraid Captain Salisbury isn't here."

"He received word we'd arrive and confirmed he'd be available to see us. In fact, he demanded to meet with us as a condition of our travels," I said, feeling my temper rising.

"You are a few days late, and I'm afraid he was called away on business by Commissary-General Van Bergen," Jacobssen said. "He bade me tell you he regrets the inconvenience but could not wait for you. "

"Inconvenience?" I retorted, then softened my tone. No need to take my frustration out on the clerk. "Where is he conducting business? Perhaps we might meet him there?"

"I'm not at liberty to say . . ." Bram said, glancing about anxiously.

I struggled to keep my voice even. "Mister Jacobsen, this is a matter of the life or death of our families. Please."

Bram leaned towards us and in a voice so hushed it was nearly a whisper, said, "I do not think it will help, but he and General van Bergen are three days south of here, negotiating a land purchase from the Mohawks, or maybe it is the Mahicans, near Kaatskill."

South would be backtracking for us and a loss of six more days. 'Twas inconceivable to me that a land purchase took precedence over a score of lives. My wife's life. My children's.

"When is he due back?" I asked.

"He left last week, on Friday, and said to expect him back in about ten days. Again, I do apologize. I know you came here quite some time ago on the same matter," young Bram said, frowning.

"Did he leave any correspondence for us? He told Major Pynchon of Springfield he would speak to the Mohawks again regarding our matter."

"Yes, I believe he did. Please, take a seat."

I remained standing, as did Stephen.

"This is unforgivable," Stephen said, then added, "I wish I'd not been ill."

"That could not be helped, but Salisbury's actions have added a delay we cannot afford." I slapped my hat against my thigh in frustration. "The lakes will be passable by canoe for only a few more weeks. If we tarry too long, they will be betwixt water and ice, and we will need to wait until they freeze solid."

"And our kin will be enduring the same storms. Blasted Salisbury," Stephen said.

Bram reappeared holding a sheaf of papers, sat at his desk, and read aloud.

"Mister Jacobssen, if Mister Waite arrives in my absence, please give him my apologies. Inform him neither myself nor the Commission on Indians was able to find a Mohawk sachem to help in negotiations for the captives nor serve as a guide. Tell him he must wait for me in Albany," Bram finished reading Salisbury's note and looked up hopefully.

"Will you wait for the captain? I can arrange lodging for you, perhaps at our expense?" Bram said.

"I appreciate the offer, but no. Could I meet with someone from the Commission on Indians?"

"They only meet once every fortnight, I'm afraid," Bram said.

"I see," I said, though I did not. "Please give this letter to the captain when he returns. 'Tis from Governor Leverett of Massachusetts Bay colony, authorizing Mister Jennings and myself to secure the release of the captives taken at Hatfield in September."

Bram added the letter to the papers I assumed pertained to our matter.

"Captain Salisbury takes his authority seriously. I think it might be best if . . ."

I cut him off. "Again, Mister Jacobssen, we thank you for your trouble."

"Good day, sir," Stephen added, following me as I strode out of the building.

I threw down my hat in disgust.

"Bloody hell!" I snarled. "A land purchase?" I picked up my hat and gritted my teeth.

Stephen ran a hand through his red hair, then put on his hat. "What now? There must be something we can do?"

"I say we go on ahead to Schenectady."

"Without Salisbury's approval?"

"His approval is a formality. We have authority from Massachusetts Bay, Major Pynchon's entreaty, Governor Leverett's documents naming us the agents for release, and Salisbury was already apprised of all details. It seems that should suffice," I said.

"Then let's be off," Stephen said.

I clapped him on the back. I was relieved to be free of petty hindrances.

"'Tis resolved, then. The King's Highway will have us in Schenectady tomorrow. We can camp on the way. We should be able to find a Mohawk or Mahican there to guide us to Lake George, where we will be beyond the reach of any sheriff, governor, or law other than our Lord's."

The King's Highway was smooth enough for wagons, though only the wealthy and officials could afford them. We walked briskly alongst it, and I marveled at the sandy hills the French called dunes, and we called barrens. Patches of black-barked pitch pine and stunted scrub oaks grew beside little brooks and pools, where we saw herons and otters intent on their fishing. At sunset, bats came out, animals my grandmother used to call rattle mice; strange creatures, neither birds nor rats, flitting through the air, catching bugs.

We reached Schenectady the next day. The town was not much more than a former Mohawk fortified outpost and a dozen stubborn Dutch settlers. Four blocks laid out at right angles, surrounded by a sturdy stockade and nestled between the Mohawk River, Binne Kill, and Cowhorn Creek.

I'd met the founding settler, Arent Van Curler, during a trading expedition over a decade ago. A few years past, he'd died on a trip to Canada when his canoe capsized on Lake Champlain—a bad omen, considering our plans to travel that way.

Luckily, the town was large enough to have a brewhouse and bakehouse. The brewmaster and his baker wife lived upstairs above both. We sat by their fire, drank good Dutch ale, and enjoyed a porridge of buttermilk, groats, and raisins.

The brewmaster, Philip Hendrickse, kindly invited us to stay downstairs in his brewery. A fresh batch of barley was malting in the kilns, another batch of finished malt was soaking in the mash tub, and the liquid wort was boiling with hops in the shiny copper keeler. In the adjoining room, another fire burned softly, baking loaves of bread. The entire abode was imbued with the rich, warm, buttery sweetness of hops, malt, yeast, and molasses, and we were happy to lay our heads down on two pallets stuffed with fresh straw.

The bright light of the full Hunter's Moon spilt through the dusty window glass into the room. A wolf howled far off, reminding me how our journey resembled a hunt. Stephen and I were wolves searching for our mates and pack, lost somewhere in the wilderness, waiting for us to find them. I closed my eyes and mumbled a brief prayer before falling into a restless slumber.

Chapter Thirty-Eight
MARTHA

HUNTER'S MOON

I longed to be down from these mountains, to rejoin my wee babes. On the sixth day the snow ceased, and I was grateful again for the horse beneath me, though it struggled in snowdrifts past its fetlocks. All three horses were in a pathetic condition, their hide barely covering their ribs and haunches. It might be a mercy to kill them.

It seemed an eternity of travel. On the seventh day, we left the mountains behind us. The forests sloped to a gentle valley, where Ashpelon rejoiced in his recognition of Otter Creek. We followed it for another two days until Ashpelon finally commanded us to halt.

The warriors began to build a longhouse on the hillside within sight of the creek, felling trees with their tomahawks and digging holes in the tender earth for the posts. Mary, Hannah, and I cleared away the brush and gathered stones, laying them in a ring and piling dry tinder in the center. We placed a tripod of stout branches at each side and a long green switch between them, then struck a flint to the tinder, coaxing sparks into tiny flames. I fetched water from the brook in one of the kettles and hung it over our small fire. We sat beside it as it slowly dried our shoes and skirts and warmed our feet and hands.

"If we cannot have food, we can at least have hot water to drink," I said.

"Or perhaps, Stone Soup," Mary said, laughing bitterly.

"I remember that tale," Hannah said, "my mother told it to us when we were little."

"Of course, 'twas not the stones that made the soup, 'twas the vegetables everybody contributed." I rubbed my hands together over the fire.

"Should we go in search of food? Perhaps roots or nuts?" Mary asked.

Hannah stood. "Let's. I am too anxious to sit here waiting for our children, watching the Natives build yet another longhouse."

"We best tell Neepânon where we're going, or she'll send warriors after us."

I found the elder woman weaving a mat from rushes.

"Neepânon, we three women go to find food." I pointed to myself, held up three fingers, and spoke the Nipmuc words for "search" and "eat." *Nunnattinneateam Mechinat.*

Neepânon nodded, set aside her work, and rose. Bent with age, she was shorter than me. "I go, too. Find *Kinepíkwa.*" She gripped my woven basket and shook it gently.

"Reeds? Can we eat those?"

She nodded.

We took our reed baskets and strode across the snowy meadow toward the river. The day was overcast and cold, and the snow had melted into a slippery slush. A brief joy filled me at God's wondrous creation, especially in late autumn. The last scarlet and amber leaves clinging to trees alongside the river, the dusty rose and silver shadings of wild grasses poking through a dusting of snow, a scattering of goldenrod. The cattails by the water had gone to seed, tufts of white feathery plumes, and Neepânon pushed past us, speaking excitedly in her tongue. "*Kinepíkwa!*"

Once we reached the river, Neepânon showed us how to dig up the cattail roots.

"Cook. Fire. Eat," she said.

We dug in the muck of the riverbank for quite some time and harvested basketfuls of roots. I waded into the icy river to wash my hands and spied clusters of large, brown-shelled creatures attached to the rocks and reeds under the water.

"Mary, Hannah, Neepânon! Are these mussels? Can we eat them?" I asked, twisting one free and holding it out in my hand.

Neepânon looked at the tightly shut brown shell that filled my palm. It was shaped like wampum but much, much larger. I'd never eaten freshwater mussels, only the saltwater kind once in a Springfield tavern. Still, my hunger was so great I'd eat almost anything now.

"Good! Cook. Fire. Eat," Neepânon said, revealing all eight yellowed teeth, the skin on her cheeks crinkling.

We filled our baskets the rest of the way with the mussels. Ducks hid in the rushes and paddled in the river, hens and drakes alike in their dull fall plumage. I hoped the men might kill some later. Perhaps then we wouldn't need to kill the horses.

Soon, three pots of tubers and mussels bubbled over the fire. By now, the men had the longhouse posts in place and were hauling more logs for the frame. Neepânon spoke to them, and Ashpelon sent three younger boys off to the river with bows, arrows, and guns.

We strained the boiling water through baskets and pried the mussels out of the open, hot shells, barely chewing the slippery pink meat. The cattail roots tasted like parsnips, and the four of us greedily ate our fill.

Within a few minutes, the boys returned, laughing excitedly and shouting to Ashpelon and the other men. I caught the words "English" and "Wanalancet."

I jumped to my feet and ran to Ashpelon.

"Are they here? My children? The others?"

"They are here."

Mary and Hannah were already hastening towards me.

"They're back? Our children? Our men?" Hannah asked.

"Yes!" I cried happily, and the three of us followed the boys and Ashpelon through the forest east of the meadow. Down dale through the pillars of tree trunks and shafts of sunlight, a large assemblage of Natives, English, and several horses advanced towards us.

Barely able to contain my excitement, I waited as warriors and women passed. At last, I saw the horses and Nìbi Wàbà, Sally riding in front of her and Mary's little girl Molly behind. When Nìbi Wàbà reached us, she handed a squirming Sally to me and Molly to Mary Foote, then sprang lightly off the horse, giving the reins to a woman beside her.

"Come," she said and led us down the trail.

Hannah's Sammy and Mary's Nate were carefully lifted from another horse, and I looked about for Mattie and Mary and saw them running towards me. They leaped into my open arms, and we all but took a tumble together. I brushed off my skirts, put Sally on my shoulders, took each of my other babes by the hand, and walked up the hill to the camp.

When we reached the fire ring, all the English gathered 'round it. The Natives left us to our reunion, building their own fires to gather around. Work on our lodging continued. We shared the broth from our meal with the men and children, hoping the duck hunt was successful.

I hadn't realized how much I'd missed our kin, not just our children. Hannah's uncle, Obadiah Dickinson, and his calm, patient manner; Quintin Stockwell, always standing up to his three Indian "masters" despite his lameness; Sergeant Plympton, aged but spry, and ever ready with wise counsel, a foolish joke, or an encouraging word. Quintin complained his toes were frostbitten, and little Molly Foote had a bad cold, but our worst calamity was overwhelming hunger.

Obadiah's son, Daniel, sat beside his father, holding his hand tight and staring into the fire. Hannah held Holly in her lap, feeding her bits of mussel, murmuring endearments. Mary rocked Molly in her arms to ease her whimpering. Sally clung to me as I stroked her yellow hair, and little Sarah Coleman cuddled against me. Sammy, Nate, and Noah Coleman played in the snow. The rest of the children helped Nìbi Wàbà and Neepânon build more fires. I murmured a prayer of thanks.

"Did your hunters find any game?" I asked Sergeant Plympton.

"No, but not for lack of trying. The animals who have not gone south are wary, or in a deep slumber," Plympton said. "This cattail broth is our first good meal." He slurped hungrily.

"We've survived on shredded touchwood fried in bear grease," Quintin said. "Nasty stuff."

"They did kill one of the horses, but the poor creatures are skin and bones, so there was not much meat to go around." Obadiah nodded toward the remaining few beasts, pawing the snow in search of grass. There was no longer any need to hobble them. They were too weak to run.

"Have you any idea what place this is?" Hannah asked.

"We followed the White River across what I think were the Green Mountains. Hence we must be quite close to Lake Champlain. Notice how the river flows northwest now? It must be emptying into Canada's lakes, unlike streams we followed before that flowed into the Connecticut River and then to the ocean," Quintin said.

I had so much to learn about the world. Only weeks past, I knew little of the Natives and even less of the wilderness, but now the ways of both seemed almost second nature to me. I was adapting to survive, like all living creatures must. A new strength born of the free will the Lord had given us filled my heart and renewed my awe at the mystery of his creations.

Long past sunset, the hunters proudly presented a dozen ducks, and all the women, Native and English, set to work cleaning and dressing the birds. For this, Ashpelon allowed us knives. I turned the gutted duck onto its back and peeled the skin and feathers away from the legs, gently separating it from the flesh until I laid bare the breast. Severing the wings and tail, I set them aside for the tribe's headpieces, necklaces, and bracelets.

Once we finished dressing the ducks, a Wachusett woman took back the knives. Then she skewered the birds with sharpened sticks for spits, turning them over the fire to roast evenly.

The Natives finished the longhouse frame and built two fires within, but we English stayed out o' doors by our little ring, comfortably, as a blanket of clouds trapped the day's warmth. We had three ducks to share between the twenty of us, yet we gave thanks as though it were the grandest feast. The rich, rosy meat slid down my throat, barely chewed.

When we finished gnawing the last duck meat from the bones, Quequan brought us a few woven mats and deer hides to share, and we moved closer to our fires. I lay awake for an hour after the rest fell asleep, gazing at the full Hunter's Moon, its cold light brightening the snow. I thanked God for the food its magic had given us.

Chapter Thirty-Nine

BEN

Schenectady, New York
November 9

The brewmaster, Philip Hendrickse, agreed to help us if we gave him a hand in the brewhouse. I stirred the kettle of cooled wort with a straw broom every quarter hour, and Stephen strained the mash from the malty wort liquid and poured it into a barrel for the brewer's livestock.

"*De* Indians are all *op de rivier,* by *de jezuïet mission,*" Philip said in a mix of English and Dutch.

"The Jesuit mission near Fonda?"

"*Ja. De schildpadden* clan, at Caughnawaga."

"We need a guide," I repeated.

"*Ja, een guides.* Ask Sander Leendertse Glen. In *Engels,* his name is Alexander Lindsay Glen."

"Where will I find him?"

"*Ten noorden van de rivier, groot stenen huis, de naam Nova Scotia.*"

Stephen looked back and forth between us as we spoke.

"Some help here, Ben?" Stephen asked.

"Mister Hendrickse says we can get a guide and should ask

the Scotsman in the mansion across the Mohawk River," I said.

We washed up and headed for the docks, telling Hendrickse we'd likely stay another night. We caught the ferry and walked a short way before seeing the brick mansion named *Nova Scotia*, or New Scotland. High on a hill, it commanded a view of all the land Sir Lindsay of Glen owned. Enviable land, arable and gently rolling.

His two-story house was also enviable, the shutters on the symmetrically placed windows thrown open to the sunlight. Philip told us Sir Lindsay came from Scottish royalty, and here in Schenectady, he was a successor of sorts to Arent Van Curler, the founder, and on the same good terms with the Mohawks and related tribes.

A young Iroquois woman answered our knock. She wore a waistcoat and woolen skirt but no cap, her black hair in a long, thick plait down her back.

"Mister Waite and Mister Jennings of Massachusetts Bay, here on the authority of Governor Andros, to speak to Sir Lindsay of Glen," I said in English.

"Please come in. I will get Sir Lindsay," she said.

We made ourselves comfortable on a settee in the parlor by a welcoming fire.

I studied what seemed to be original framed oil paintings on some walls, brocaded wallpaper on others, shining tile floors, and carved furniture arranged for comfort.

An impressively dressed man with a neatly trimmed gray beard and silvered ginger locks entered the parlor, and we stood. True to his ancestry, he wore a belted plaid tartan and a pleated great kilt in shades of blue and green.

"*Gude day*, sirs," he said, shaking our hands, "Mister Waite, Mister Jennings, a pleasure. Sir Lindsay of Glen. Please, be seated. What is your *troke*?" he asked, a rich brogue in his speech. "My maid Tali says you are here on official business. From Governor Andros?"

"Yes. Major Pynchon of Springfield contacted Governor Andros on our behalf six weeks ago." I thought it best not to mention Captain Salisbury.

"Regarding?" Sir Lindsay asked. "Ah, our cocoa." The maid brought a pitcher of hot milk and another of thick cacao syrup.

"Thank you, Tali," he said to the woman.

I had never tasted cocoa or chocolate. Tali fixed it for us, pouring the rich, brown cacao syrup into our cups, and adding sugar and steaming milk. I stirred it, enjoying the bittersweet, buttery aroma.

"A band of Algonquians burned our small town of Hatfield, Massachusetts Bay Colony, in mid-September. They killed and wounded many and captured seventeen of our kin, our wives and children amongst them." I heard my voice break and glanced at Stephen, and the clench of his jaw.

Sir Lindsay stopped sipping his cocoa, set the cup down, and steepled his fingers.

"*Bi fegs*, that is terrible, Mister Waite. You have my full attention," he said.

"We're the agents for their redemption, with letters of authority from Governor Leverett of Boston. We need a guide to help us find our way to Lake George and outfit us with a canoe. Our landlord in Schenectady, Mister Hendrickse, said you might be able to assist us," I said.

I took a sip of the cocoa. Delicious. Stephen raised his blue and white china cup and smiled. The vanity of the well-to-do might be sinful, but it was certainly pleasant.

"Ah, yes, the Brewster. Philip Hendrickse, a gude man." Lindsay took a sip of his cocoa. "Is it just the two of ye? Did you talk to any of the Indian Commission people in Albany?"

"We were told they weren't available," I said.

"I know Robert Livingston. A Scot, like myself. He's the Secretary of the Commission and may be able to help you.

And my servant Tali is a Mohawk, she may ken," he said, rising.

He went through the arched doorway to the kitchen beyond. I overheard the Iroquois language, and I understood a few words here and there. *Onckwe*, men. *Rockste*, friends. *Caroo*, close by. *Johati*, a road. *Torsas*, to the north. I was quite impressed by Sir Lindsay's command of Scotch, English, Dutch, and Mohawk.

When he came back, he was smiling.

"*Gude* news, Tali knows a wee family of the Turtle clan, only a few hours away, in a village on the *carse* of the river, the only one not abandoned after that French *eejit* de Tracy attacked them a few years past. Tali said the village is on this side of the Mohawk River, where the Verf Kill flows into it. Ask there for her cousin, *Aquinachoo*."

"*Aquinachoo*? Their word for 'angry'?" I asked, smiling.

"Aye, but she said he'd help. I asked about his name myself, and she said he was an angry *bairn* but is no longer so volatile. If he cannot guide you, he may know one who can. 'Twill save you the longer trip to the mission."

"Thank you."

We finished our cocoa, chatting with Sir Lindsay about his family, farmlands, purebred horses, and the impending weather. After a quarter hour, we rose to leave. Sir Lindsay escorted us to the door.

"*Farfaa*, lads," he said, "please let me know if you meet with any trouble from the Indians."

"Thank you very much for your help, Sir Lindsay," I said.

The big door closed behind us.

"Interesting fellow," Stephen said.

I nodded. "Back to Schenectady for one more night. We'll need provisions, and maybe your hand at mending boots. I have near walked the leather bare on mine."

I looked forward to a good meal and new soles for my boots. 'Twas cold when the sun set, and I longed to be by the fire. Yet when we reached the brewhouse, Hendrickse met us in the street in great agitation and dragged us inside, his fingers to his lips urging silence. He led us to the root cellar before he spoke.

"Are *ye een crimineel? De wachter* was *hier.* Orders *van kapitein* Salisbury," Hendrickse said.

"Did you tell him we were here?" I asked fearfully.

"*Niet!* But he knew. I said you were gone, and I did not know where."

"Thank you, but if Salisbury is behind this, the watcher will be back." I sank to the floor, my back to the wall and knees bent. I considered our options whilst the brewmaster went upstairs and gently closed the door.

"We cannot stay here," I said. "The rattle watchman will stop by again on his rounds tonight, the constable with him. Damn, Salisbury! His conceit and pettiness know no bounds."

"I feel sorry for his secretary. Probably blamed for not holding us there."

We hastened up the stairs, opened the door partway, and saw only the brewmaster tending his brew. We gathered our things, bid him farewell, and thanked him for his silence.

The moon had yet to rise, and we avoided the few lanterns the best we could. The ferry ran only one boat after sunset, and I hoped they'd not been alerted to us. The Mohawk River narrowed here but was still a good 500 feet across, with a strong current and no bridge. We had no choice but to take the ferry. At least the rattle watch did not make his rounds until 9:00 p.m.

We reached the docks and saw the ferry's lantern.

"All aboard, last ferry loading!" the ferry master called.

We ran as quickly and softly as we could with our heavy packs, but our footfalls sounded like cannons to my ears. Suddenly, the clatter of hoofbeats arose behind us.

"Halt! You two! Halt now, by order of Captain Salisbury!"

A man astride a horse appeared out of the shadows from

our left, holding his lantern aloft. Behind him waited two other mounted men. Stephen and I froze where we were.

Two of the men dismounted, handing off their reins to the third.

"Benjamin Waite?"

"Who needs to know?" I said, my patience gone.

"Richard Pritty, Albany sheriff," the first man said. "And this is?" he asked, pointing to Stephen.

"Stephen Jennings, sir." Stephen's tone was more respectful than mine by far.

"You are both under arrest for disobeying the authority of Captain Salisbury and engaging in unauthorized travel and business with the Mohawks."

"What? That's absurd! We have authorization from Governor Leverett of Boston. I can show you!" I shouted, reaching into my pack, but he grabbed my wrist and roughly took my pack, tomahawk and weapons. The other man disarmed Stephen. They bound our wrists with rope, tying the other end to the pommel of their saddles. They loaded our weapons and our packs behind their horses.

"And where are you taking us?"

"Tonight, to the custody of commissioners," he said, "and tomorrow or the next, down the Hudson to Manhattan, to stand charges."

"Charges? We are British; Schenectady and Albany are British. We have broken no British law."

"We'll let the province of New York judge that," he said.

My anger faded quickly to resignation. Our haste had been a mistake. I despaired we might languish in the Manhattan jail for months.

The sheriff and his man half led, half dragged us behind their horses, through Schenectady's streets and down the long, dark road to Albany and its Stadt Huys Gaol. 'Twas about the size of the brew master's cellar but cold and rank, and the clang of the shackle bolt imprisoned us.

Chapter Forty

MARTHA

OTTER CREEK
WINTER

"Ashpelon says we might remain at this camp until the next full moon," I said.

My girls and I sat so close to the fire our eyes burned from the smoke. A weak and pale sun had climbed above the tree-tops but gave no more warmth than the moon. "He hopes we finish the canoes before the lake freezes."

"I'm surprised it hasn't yet. I almost fell this morning, slipped on the ice when I went out to 'gaze upon a hedge,'" Sergeant Plympton said.

"Mommy, it's freezing!" Mattie said, holding her little hands to her face and blowing warm air into them to take the chill away. I'd need to search for her mittens again.

"But the ice on the trees is beautiful, Mama," said my little Mary. She pointed, and I followed her gaze to a nearby pine, its boughs strung with glittering icicles.

I smiled. What a blessing my daughters were.

Quintin and Obadiah tended to our morning meal. Perhaps, our only meal that day. A ruffed grouse, about the size of a cockerel, a snowshoe hare, herbs, and wild onions. It was not much for six adults and a dozen children, but it smelled delicious, as did the newly cut cedar of the longhouse.

I led us in a prayer of thanksgiving before we ate. Once the rivers' backwaters and the ground itself froze, there'd be no more of the small game, and the frozen soil would claim the buried roots. For now, I must be content with the blessings of a bit of food and a warm, dry, sweet-smelling shelter.

After we ate, Ashpelon gathered all the men who weren't finishing the longhouse to begin work on the canoes. Not birchbark like the Algonquians made when they'd had their summer camps near Deerfield, because bark peeled easily from the trees only in the warmth of summer. They would make dugout canoes, each hewn from a single tree hollowed by fire and tomahawk.

Our men and the warriors chose giant trees. Two men standing on either side, their arms about the trunk, could barely touch fingertips. They smeared wet river muck in a waist-high band around the trunks and lit small fires beneath the trees to weaken and fell them.

Mary, Hannah, and I watched for a while before returning to our tasks. We washed clothes in the icy river and gathered the last onion bulbs. I traced my girls' hands and mine onto deerskin using a bone awl, cut the hide with a knife I'd been entrusted with, and sewed it with sinew to make new mittens. I hoped we'd have some rabbit or raccoon fur soon to line them.

The Natives wore warm, winter clothes now. In addition to their embroidered and beaded deerskin skirts and bodices, the women wrapped their lower legs in tall deerskin stockings. Combined with their moccasins, it gave the illusion, and I'm sure the warmth, of leather boots. Some had deerskin or bear hide mantles around their shoulders, worn with the fur against their body, as was their fashion.

Mary kept Molly beside her whilst she worked, wrapped in

several furs. Her little body was consumed by fever and chills, and we were all gravely worried. Nìbi Wàbà fussed over her, serving her the first and hottest broth, dipping linen in the cold brook and laying it on her forehead, making a poultice for Mary to rub on Molly's bony little chest.

Ashpelon joined us.

"The girl? Is she sick?" he asked.

Nìbi Wàbà answered him immediately. "No, just a cold. She will be fine soon."

"Good," Ashpelon replied, but he bent and touched the back of his hand to Molly's forehead. Frowning, he returned to check the men's progress on the trees.

I feared why Nìbi Wàbà kept the gravity of Molly's illness a secret.

When five or six cedar trees were felled, the men rested around the fires until Ashpelon roused them again. With tomahawks and adzes they hacked at the tree bark, slowly stripping it from the trunks. Neepânon and the other elders fed the children and had them sweep leaves from the longhouse, gather kindling for the fires, and mend shirts and aprons.

The following day, the longhouse was declared finished, and we all helped transform the trees into boats. Ashpelon divided us into teams, each assigned to a different log that would eventually become a canoe. I worked alongside Mary, Sergeant Plympton, Atian, and a warrior named Kenompāe.

Mary was peevish and distracted, having been up all night caring for Molly, who rested in the longhouse with Neepânon.

"Molly's having trouble breathing," Mary said. We lifted armfuls of curled bark and wood shavings and placed them in baskets for kindling. "She wheezes when she breathes, cries because it hurts."

"Go, be with her. We can do this without you."

"I'm afraid if I do, Ashpelon or Wanalancet will know how ill she is and knock her on the head." Mary began to weep, and I stopped working to give her my full attention. "Quintin told me that on their way here, he slipped and fell. Wanalancet told him if he couldn't get up and walk, he would knock him on the head," Mary said, wiping tears from her eyes with the back of her hand.

"Wanalancet is not your master, nor Molly's. Atian captured you; he claims you. You need only heed him and Ashpelon."

"Atian is young and impatient," Mary whispered, glancing anxiously at Atian, who worked nearby. "He spoke roughly to Neepânon this morning, and they argued. I do not know what he said, but it was about Molly."

Perhaps he heard his name spoken. Atian ceased his chopping and glared at us.

"Mary!" Atian commanded.

"Yes?" Mary's voice trembled.

Atian was frowning, but his gaze was tender. "Go. Go to your babe."

Mary nodded to her master and fled.

The sun was already hidden behind the trees when Ashpelon called a halt to our labors for the day. We had barely made a dent in the massive tree trunks, and I was curious how long it would take to finish them. Weary, we returned to the longhouse and gathered about our fire. I sat beside Mary, who held her daughter in her lap. I bent and touched my lips to Molly's brow, feeling the burning heat. I laid my hand on Mary's shoulder.

"Nìbi Wàbà is standing up for Molly. You can trust her to help you," I said.

"I am surely grateful to Nìbi Wàbà for her tea and poultices, and Neepânon is kind. They are unexpected instruments of the Lord," Mary said.

"How is the little girl?" Sergeant Plympton whispered, glancing toward Molly, who was finally asleep.

"Very ill," I said.

"She seems to be getting worse. 'Tis a sad thing, an ill child," he said.

With a heavy heart, I paused my sewing for a moment.

"Sergeant, will you lead us in prayer?" I asked. "For Molly?"

"Of course."

We bowed our heads. Sergeant Plympton said, "Almighty God and merciful Father, to whom alone belong the issues of life and death, look down from heaven, we humbly beseech thee, with eyes of mercy upon the child Molly, who lies upon the bed of sickness. Visit her, O Lord, with thy salvation, deliver her in thy time from her pain, that if it is thy pleasure to prolong her days here on earth, she may live to serve thee faithfully. Grant this, O Lord, for thy mercies' sake. Amen."

"Amen," we said.

I spoke to Hannah about her gardens of herbs in Hatfield and her knowledge of their medicinal uses. She kept it secret from all but her family and me, afraid of witchcraft accusations like those haunting my sister-in-law. Far from our kin's mutual watch and censure, I prayed her skills might save poor Molly. She was eager to help and promised to see what she could do.

That evening, the warriors killed another horse. Counting the two from the Wachusett band, we had only four remaining.

Chapter Forty-One

BEN

ALBANY TO MANHATTAN, NEW YORK
NOVEMBER 11-23, 1677

The only saving grace to the bitterly cold wind was that it blew from the north, pushing the old sloop at a fair clip with the Hudson River's current. The sooner Stephen and I reached New York, the sooner we could sort out this misadventure and be on our way.

Our guard was Dutch, a huge, burly man named Pieter Smit. He secured us to a bench on deck and hovered. He spoke English but chose not to, and we had no desire to engage him in conversation. We spent our time gazing at the Hudson River or glaring at him. Smit drew on a long clay pipe, and it seemed he intentionally stood upwind to ensure we'd cough on the smoke.

The boat was crowded with all sorts. 'Twas not designed for prisoners but passengers and cargo. A family passed by, and their children stared at us as we sat on full display. Merchants in fine coats and periwigs eyed us suspiciously. I couldn't have been more humiliated if I'd been stuck in the stocks in the Hatfield Commons. Stephen bore it better than I, remaining stoic whilst I complained loudly.

"Ben, I think you need to accept what is. Most times, your spirit suits our purpose, but not now. Leave it to God's will."

I addressed the guard, "Mister Smit, might we have some water to drink?"

The guard huffed in annoyance but produced a costrel, took out the plug, and poured a few swigs down our throats. It began to rain, and we all sought shelter below decks, finding them damp, dark, crowded, and smelling of sweat and piss. I'd have preferred the rain, but the guard gave us no choice. Perhaps he was not a bad sort, as he'd packed some bread and cheese for the three of us and freed our hands so we could eat.

We dropped anchor at dusk, and all went ashore save our surly guard and us. The crew pitched some moldy but dry straw onto the sole below decks. Stephen and I laid upon the straw and tried to slumber. I knew I should be grateful for these conditions. The jail in New York wouldn't be half as decent.

Our boat docked at Coenties Slip on the island of Manhattan. 'Twas late Sunday afternoon after four days and nights on the river. Stephen and I bowed our heads against the wind and sleet, our wrists still bound, unable to fasten our coats against the cold. Guard Smit shoved us ahead of him alongst the slippery, well-worn cobbles of Dock Street toward the imposing four-story *Stadt Huys*. It presided over three blocks and held a court, city hall, and jail.

Smit checked us in with the city clerk, where we completed and signed various paperwork, and turned our packs over to a jail guard. The guard took our belongings and dragged us to a one-room cell in the back corner of the building, where he unbound us and locked us inside. Thankfully, at least for now, we were the only prisoners.

"Home sweet home," I said, hearing the hoarseness in my voice. I had a cold coming.

"'Tis fairer than the Merry King's Whitehall Palace," Stephen joked.

"A more apt comparison might be the Tower of London. They found those poor lads' skeletons a couple of years ago, did you know?" I was being contrary, but I was weary and frustrated.

"I'd not heard. Let's hope we fare better than those two princes."

"I'm sorry, I'm in a foul mood. Whitehall Palace this is."

The cell was dank and dark, with no fire to heat it. The only light—and the rain—sliced through the small, barred window set high on the far wall. Beneath it, a pewter water pitcher and two mugs offered a hint of civility. A cot was on each wall, but the only bedding was a stack of moth-eaten woolen blankets. A chamber pot sat next to a barred opening at about knee level, through which I supposed we were to empty it into the street.

I sat on the right-hand cot, and the leather straps creaked under me. Elbows on my knees, I rested my forehead in my palms and let out a great sigh. I was so weary in both body and spirit.

"Water?" Stephen asked, pouring himself a mug.

"Aye, thank you."

He sat across from me on the other cot.

"What now?" Stephen asked.

"I'm fresh out of ideas, my friend."

"No, not you. You always have two strings to your bow."

"I think I've used up every bowstring in my quiver. I truly did not foresee so many setbacks. I knew we'd have to journey through thick and thin, but—"

"You thought it would go more smoothly."

"Aye, I did not foresee Salisbury being such an arse-head."

"He is that," Stephen agreed. "I need a nap."

He took off his boots and picked up two of the blankets.

"You'd do well to check those for bedbugs first," I said.

"Right." Stephen shook out each blanket, scrutinized them, placed one on the cot, and covered himself with the other.

I used the chamber pot, then sat and watched the rain. Finally, I resigned myself to our fate and imprisonment as God's will. I found a few bedbugs on one of my blankets and took no small delight in squashing them under my boot. I'd rest and pray God would sort it out soon. We could ill afford a long delay.

❦

As it was, Stephen and I spent a week in the jail cell. Some scoundrels joined us on various days, some staying the night, some sent to the stocks out o' doors. None of them were pleasant, and negotiating for the two cots became more trouble than it was worth. The guard threw some extra blankets in, so those who lost the shilling toss for the beds did not have to lie on the cold, putrid floor.

We learned to wolf our food if we did not want to share it with insolent rats and even less charitable cellmates. I hadn't much appetite anyway, what with my cold, and the menu was limited to bread, samp, and broth. The worst part was the chamber pot, which we could never entirely empty, so its foul stench constantly permeated our tight quarters.

Our seventh morning was blessedly peaceful, for we were the only inhabitants of our cell.

"Breakfast!" The guard shoved a trencher of lukewarm samp under the door.

"Ah, samp! A rare treat!" I said.

"I do not appreciate the sarcasm, Waite. Yer lucky ye

aren't in the stocks getting stones thrown at ye or tied to the whippin' post for a neat twenty lashes," the guard said.

"As neither of us broke any laws, that would be excessive," I replied.

The guard shuffled off. What a horrible job.

Stephen still slept, so I used the spoon to eat half the samp and saved the rest for him. I folded the blankets and paced back and forth to stretch my legs. The light through the window was gray and cold. I peered through the door's iron grate at the empty, narrow hallway with a closed door at each end, hearing voices beyond.

"Saved me some gruel, thank you." Stephen sat up and rubbed his eyes.

"I think you'll find it well-seasoned today, the texture more refined," I said.

Stephen threw his boot at me but ate his portion anyway.

A man opened the door at the left end of the hall. He was dressed in a better manner than a guard, wearing a black hat and coat, and he strode purposefully and without hesitation right up to the door.

"Benjamin Waite," he said as though he found my name amusing. "You and your friend seem to have some high-ranking gentlemen watching out for you."

"Sir?"

"You're scheduled to be heard in the Mayor's Court on the morrow. Mayor Van Cortlandt bade me convey this to you," he said. "Rather surprisingly, he also insisted I'm to ask if you need anything and tell you he apologizes for the conditions of our gaol."

I was taken by surprise but leapt at the offer. "Some water and soap? Towels? We'd like to look a bit respectable in court, sir."

"Give me a few moments with the guard," he said.

"That was unexpected," Stephen said. "Why the sudden concern for our well-being?"

"I have no idea, though it seems Manhattan may be kinder to us than Albany. Perhaps the mayor here dislikes Captain Salisbury as much as we do," I said.

"We'll find out on the morrow, thank heavens."

The guard unlocked the cell door and set a large copper bucket of tepid water on the stone floor so heavily that it sloshed. He dropped a couple of gray towels and a bar of lye soap on one of the cots.

"There ye are. Ye must be royalty. Never seen prisoners get to have themselves a bath before," he said and walked out again, slamming our door behind him.

"See, Ben. Royalty. White Hall Palace, what did I tell you?"

I let Stephen wash, then took my turn. I felt somewhat presentable afterward. Once we'd bathed, we washed our cuffs and collars and dried them under the window.

&

After our midday samp the next day, November 23, the guard led us to the courthouse upstairs in the same building. The room was much larger than our cell and less damp but otherwise deplorable. The guard forced us along a center aisle and sat us on a bench, where we faced five men seated on a raised platform like a stage, dressed in formal black and wearing white powdered periwigs.

"Benjamin Waite and Stephen Jennings?" asked the man seated in the middle.

"Aye, sir."

"I am Mayor Van Cortlandt of Manhattan, New York. You face the Mayor's Court on charges brought by Captain Salisbury, Sheriff of Albany, Commander of the Fort. The charges are insubordination of his authority under The Duke's Laws and conducting unauthorized business with Indians," he said.

I wanted to protest, but Stephen shot me a glare. I bit my tongue.

"It also says you claimed Boston governed Schenectady?"

"No, sir. I am fully aware that the Dutch first governed Schenectady, then the British, then the Dutch, and now back to the British again. And that it is under the rule of the Duke of York and Governor Andros. Not Governor Leverett. There must have been a misunderstanding," I said.

The mayor raised his eyebrows and cleared his throat. "Albany Sheriff Richard Pritty arrested you and remanded you here under guard to stand trial. If you so choose, you may have a jury trial, but that requires you to remain in prison for a fortnight more until such a trial is arranged. Does it suit you if we simply proceed without a jury?"

"Yes, sir," I said.

"And you, Mister Jennings?"

"That is agreeable to me, sir."

"Very well. I have received a letter from Lieutenant-Governor Bruckholds, who recently returned from visiting our territories at Pemaquid. He states both Governor Andros and Governor Leverett granted permission for your travels?" Van Corlandt said.

"That is correct," I said. "I have paperwork, but it was taken from me."

"He further states the purpose of your travel to Canada is to redeem captive English men, women, and children taken in a raid on Hatfield of Massachusetts Bay Colony in September. He states you have been appointed agents and gave Captain Salisbury's clerk a letter to that effect?"

"Again, correct, sir," I said.

Mayor Van Corlandt conferred with the other four magistrates in hushed tones. Sweat trickled down my back, and my hands were clammy. I glanced over at Stephen and saw him tapping his foot. Finally, the mayor gave his attention to us, and I held my breath.

"By the power vested in me as Mayor of the town of Manhattan, by a vote of this court, and by the authority of Lieutenant Governor Bruckholds, I am dismissing all charges against both of you. I will communicate my decision to Captain Salisbury and the lieutenant governor's command and instruct them to cast no more impediments to your journey."

My sigh of relief was audible.

"Thank you, sir," I said. A sweat of relief flushed my brow. "A small matter of our weapons and packs? The sheriff took those from us in Albany. Is it possible we can reclaim them?" I asked.

"For what purpose do you bear arms?"

"Protection against wild animals. Hunting. Defense against Native tribes," I said.

"I think the lieutenant governor will find those reasons acceptable," Van Corlandt said.

"Thank you, sir."

"Court is adjourned. You are free to go. Guard, please uncuff these men and return their papers and possessions to them forthwith."

Stephen and I nearly danced with glee; such was our relief and excitement to be free to continue our journey. The guard returned our packs, and after checking them to ensure they hadn't pilfered our possessions, we strode out into the cold and rain of Dock Street.

Chapter Forty-Two

MARTHA

We could hide Molly's illness no longer. Because we were to remain at the camp until we finished the canoes, her illness did not hinder the Natives, so she faced no danger from them. Kòkòkòho built a little cedar bed from scraps leftover from our canoe building, and Mary sewed a coverlet and stuffed it with duck feathers. We lay Molly in the tiny bed close to the fire, and all took turns tending to her.

Molly struggled to draw each painful breath, the sound of it like wind whistling through chinks in a door. She drifted in and out of nightmares and cold sweats and woke herself in the night with a persistent cough that shook her little body. Mary did not leave her side.

Hannah's knowledge of plants' medicinal properties indeed exceeded mine. She, Nìbi Wàbà, and Neepânon spent hours concocting teas from feverwort berries and the powdered bark of willow roots, which they patiently held to Molly's lips for her to sip. They made salves from black pine pitch, bear grease, and wood ash, and Mary gently rubbed them onto Molly's chest. Obadiah fetched cold water for the rags they placed on her burning brow.

The remaining horses were killed one by one. Numbly, I helped skin and cook them. I also took care of all the children, especially little Nate Foote. Yet I wished I could do more.

Sergeant Plympton led morning and evening prayers for Molly. Even Wanalancet laid his hand gently upon Molly's brow and covered her in a bearskin. When she was awake and lucid, Ashpelon entertained her with legends about forest creatures and the seasons and the stars. Those made her smile. We all thought she'd recover.

And yet, she died.

I awakened from a nap to a plaintive cry that shuddered through my bones and stopped my breath. Mary knelt by Molly's bed, cradling her pale, limp body in her arms, rocking back and forth, moaning and weeping. Everyone else seemed struck dumb, frozen in place. So, I went to her.

I encircled Mary and Molly in my arms, surrendering to my tears. Mary crumpled against me, sobbing in anguish.

Hannah scooped up Nate and guided her children and mine out of the longhouse and into the bright, cold November sun. Nìbi Wàbà came and sat next to us. Sam Russell, Matthew Kellogg, and their two Nipmuc friends, Wesattimis and Oskosk, silently shuffled over and stood watching, their eyes wide and sad.

"Can we help?" young Sam asked.

"Sam, please fetch Sergeant Plympton and Goodmen Dickinson and Stockwell. They're at the canoes," I said.

Sam and his friends ran off, no doubt relieved to put distance between themselves and tragedy.

Nìbi Wàbà took Molly's tiny wrist in her hand, waited, then shook her head. "Molly is with the Great Spirit."

I longed for her certainty. My religion grimly held that not baptism nor conversion nor a life lived by the commandments could ensure our place in heaven. One was either chosen by

God or not. Looking at my friend and her little child, I wished I believed otherwise.

The men came and stood by helplessly, removed their hats, and bowed their heads.

Mary's wailing faded to sobs, her fierce hold on Molly loosened, and she looked up at us.

"Why?" she asked. "Why must she be the one to die?"

Sergeant Plympton whispered, "Jesus said, 'Suffer the little children, and forbid them not to come to me, for of such is the kingdom of heaven.'"

In a daze, I helped Mary prepare Molly's body for burial. Nìbi Wàbà melted bear fat and stirred polecat flowers into it, and the sweet, earthy scent was almost like the lavender we were accustomed to. We washed her tiny body, then put a dab of bears' fat under her eyelids to keep them closed, as if in slumber. We bound a strip of deer hide around her head and tied it beneath her chin so when the stiffness of death came, her mouth wouldn't fall open in a silent scream. Last, we wrapped Molly's body in deerskin and laid her on a blanket in a cool corner of the longhouse.

Ashpelon appeared and knelt by Molly's body. He murmured something in his language and set a horsehair bracelet by her side. He rose and turned to Mary.

"I am sorry," he said. "We will find a good place for her. Dig a grave."

"No, I want a Christian burial for her! Please! Quintin, explain to him?" Mary said.

Quintin spoke to Ashpelon in halting Nipmuc.

"Ashpelon understands," Quintin said, "he offers to find a place. But we will dig the grave and say our prayers. A Christian burial."

"The cold, the marching, the hunger—Molly died because of these Indians!" Mary knelt by Molly's lifeless body, her tears an endless torrent. Anger at our captors and despair at our dire circumstances struck me anew, and I sat beside Hannah, staring into the fire, unable to speak.

Ashpelon directed our three men to a towering cedar tree on the slope near the meadow and left them there to dig the grave whilst the warriors went hunting.

"It is our manner to feast after a death," Ashpelon said. "We hope to find food."

The cold sun was low in the sky when the English and some Natives gathered around the grave. I held Sally on my hip and kept my other arm around Mary Foote's shoulders. She held her son Nate tightly. Mary and Mattie pressed against me. Both wept. Hannah stood with her two children, her head bowed, not watching.

She remembered her own daughter's death, as did I. The one moment of inattention, her wee babe's tumble into the rendering fire. The days of prayer. The inevitable end. I had been there for her through all of it. If the memory still brought me to tears, I could not imagine how Hannah endured it.

The men lowered Molly's body gently into the hole under the roots of the cedar tree. I looked around at the gathering of mourners. Nìbi Wàbà had streaks of black on her cheekbones, as did Neepânon and her husband, Wekoñtam.

Quintin spoke quietly to me, "Ashpelon said his people bury their dead sitting up, with their heads on their knees, and put their favorite things with them. It is the reason he made the bracelet for her. He knows it isn't our way. Some will daub black on their faces. It is their color for grief, as it is ours."

Sergeant Plympton took out his Bible and prayer book and read aloud.

"We grieve today for the loss of little Molly Foote, the daughter of Mary and Samuel, sister of Nate, and a wee brother still in Hatfield. Molly was a sweet and innocent Christian child. We commit her body to this ground, beneath this ancient tree, earth to earth, ashes to ashes, and dust to dust. We believe in a resurrection of the just and unjust, some to joy, and some to punishment, and we trust in God's love and mercy. Amen."

Once our men had covered the grave, we marked it with a large, silvery rock. At the last moment, Mary knelt and placed Ashpelon's bracelet on the rock. Then we walked away. The sunlight faded, and snow fell. I lay inside by the fire, cuddling my girls, and though they slept peacefully, I could not. I rested my hand on my belly, comforted by the gentle stirrings of my babe.

Long after dark, the warriors returned from the hunt bearing a couple of raccoons. Atian woke Nìbi Wàbà and Uppeshoii, and they dressed and skinned the raccoons and put the meat in a pot to boil. By and by, the aroma, like roast beef, filled the longhouse.

Although I was hungry, I couldn't think of eating—only of Molly's little body under the cedar tree, beneath the snow.

Chapter Forty-Three
BEN

ALBANY, NEW YORK
NOVEMBER 23-29

It took five days for our boat to reach Albany, fighting upriver in a blizzard, dropping anchor each night at a port. At some, Stephen and I disembarked to buy a meal or food for the next day and slept in a tavern. Other ports were too small, so we stayed on board and slept with the crew in the main cabin. I had no objection to sleeping on boats. 'Twas in my blood.

We longed to avoid Albany but had to reclaim our tools and weapons from Constable Richard Pritty. We met with him, but he sent us away again, saying it was Saturday and the paperwork wouldn't be ready until Monday afternoon. I might have struck him if Stephen hadn't been at my side, gripping my right arm. Our old friend Bram Jacobsen suggested the inn by the river belonging to Volckert Janse Douw.

"A good family," he said, "kind, a dozen children, good food and beer."

We knocked on the double door of the inn, and the upper

half was swung open by a lad in his teens, sandy hair above huge blue eyes.

"I am Hendrick Douw. You want *und kamer*?" he asked.

"And full board."

"My mother is making *Snert*—pea soup with carrots and sausages."

I sniffed the air. "It smells delicious."

"My sister Catrina does the *koken* in the morning," he said proudly.

We signed the guest book and paid, then followed Hendrick through the broad keeping room, our feet echoing off the brick floor. Sunlight spilt through two big diamond-paned windows onto two freshly made beds beneath them. A fire flickered in a little cast iron stove. I walked to the tall, carved wardrobe, hung up my coat, and removed my boots. Stephen poured us each a cup of water from the large china pitcher on the bedside table.

"'Tis quite civilized here," Stephen remarked.

I nodded. "Enjoy it. We have a long, brutal journey ahead of us, storm or not."

I put more wood on our fire and lay on the bed, my head propped up on a pillow, watching the flames. I hoped Martha and my girls were warm by a fire. Were they snugly wrapped in deerskin? Eating moose or raccoon? The more I ruminated on these things, the more morose I became.

On Monday, Stephen examined our boots and explained he hadn't the tools to repair them; therefore, we should find a cobbler who was a member of the cordwainers' guild. We found The Van Scheluyne Cordwainer house, a brick front with a stepped gable facing North Pearl Street and a clapboard sidewall facing the other. Its sign bore the guild's mark.

A bell tinkled as we opened the door and stepped inside. The shop smelled of rich leather, wood from the lathe, and smoke, mingled with the garlicky smell of stockinged feet. Mister Cornelis Van Scheluyne handed us over to one of his apprentices, a young English lad named Robert, who listened in astonishment to our tale and eagerly helped us by mending our footwear. To my relief, Van Scheluyne sold us two pairs of snowshoes at cost. The money Hatfield had raised, and Governor Leverett had advanced, was dwindling rapidly due to so many delays.

We visited a few more shops to stock up on supplies and provisions: flints, oil for our lantern, crackers and dried fruits and meat, and knitted woolen stockings. Anxious to be off, we returned to the *Stadt Huys* that afternoon to retrieve our weapons. Bram Jacobssen led us back to the room by the jail wherein Constable Pritty had his office.

"How fare you, Mister Waite, Mister Jennings?" Constable Pritty had the impudence to ask.

"As well as can be expected, having spent a week in jail on false charges." Out of the corner of my eye, I saw Stephen shoot me a look.

"Only following orders. Here for your guns?" Pritty asked.

"Two flintlock muskets, pistols, hunting knives, and toma-hawk. Also, our lead and powder."

"That will be one guilder. Storage fee."

I counted out 20 pine-tree shillings and dropped them in his hand.

Pritty disappeared for a moment and then returned, handing over our weapons and ammunition. I checked them over.

"Constable, I seem short a pound or two of gunpowder and half a dozen musket balls," I said. "You, Stephen?"

"I'm down a pound of shot for my pistol," he said, checking his bag.

"Here's the accounting." Pritty placed an official-looking document in front of us.

"Neither of us signed that, sir," I said.

"Shame. Well, we do not have a regular gunsmith in Albany, I'm afraid," he said.

"Explains why you stole our lead," I said, holding his gaze.

"Ben," Stephen said, "we can ask the blacksmith. They must have one of those."

I started to protest again, but Stephen put his hand on my arm and bid the constable good day. I shouldered my flintlock, holstered my pistol, and clenched my teeth.

"Damn him!" I said, once we were safely on our way. "He stole our shot!"

"Blacksmith, just ahead. See the sign?"

We found the blacksmith busy hammering horseshoes as the horse and its master stood by. The horse had a shiny, rust-colored coat and a black mane and tail, reminding me of Scout, reminding me of home.

When he finished shoeing the horse, the smith found molds of the correct bore. While we waited, he melted the lead and cast the balls and shot. The horse's owner, hearing our complaints, told us where to buy more gunpowder.

Our ammunition restocked and powder replenished, we visited the tavern for pork stew, honey cake, and coffee. After supper, we returned to the *Stadt Huys* to meet Commissioner Robert Livingston. Like Sir Alexander Lindsay of Glen, Livingston cut an impressive figure, but he was younger, with long brown hair that may have been a periwig and no tartan nor brogue in his speech to mark his ancestry.

"Mister Livingston, both Major John Pynchon and Sir Lindsay of Glen said you might help us find a Mohawk guide."

"Ah, yes, Captain Salisbury told me you'd be here," Livingston said. "Only yesterday, he showed me the letters he received from you nearly a fortnight ago. He said he had one from Lieutenant Governor Bruckholds but wouldn't show me that one. He said it was 'infuriating.'"

"It has been an infuriating chain of events for us as well," I said. "But no matter."

"Tempest in a teapot, really," Stephen said.

"Aye, the captain is prone to that," said Livingston, shrugging.

"Can you advise us where to find a guide? Sir Lindsay suggested the castle of the Turtle Clan."

"That's a fair bet. Are you familiar with the Mohawks?" he asked.

"Yes, sir. I traded with them for Major Pynchon a decade or so ago."

"Then, you know how to approach them?"

"Is there a special manner which works best—?"

"Visit the camp—the Castle, they are fond of calling it— toward the late afternoon. Build a fire nearby, not closer than a hundred yards or so. They will send a scout out. If they trust you, they'll invite you to their camp," Livingston said.

"And if they do not trust us?" Stephen asked, a hint of fear in his tone.

Livingston laughed. "'Tis more of a formality. Akin to knocking on their door. It should be fine. I cannot promise they'll want to spare a guide to take you so far north this time of year. You're prepared to pay?"

"Aye, we are," I said.

"They prefer wampum, but they'll take coins, flax or linen cloth, woolen blankets—I doubt not it was the same when you traded for furs."

"Yes, sir." I knew better than to tell him I'd once used rum for barter in my younger days. It had been against the law even then—in fact, I'd been fined five pounds for it—a huge sum.

Our business concluded, we returned to the inn. Frau Douw packed us oranges and speculas —crisp gingerbread cookies shaped like windmills. We cleaned and oiled our guns and prepared for our trip the following day to Schenectady and then up the river, to meet with the Indian whose name meant "angry."

Chapter Forty-Four
MARTHA

OTTER CREEK CAMP
WINTER

Day after day, we labored on the canoes. Each morning, we covered the gunwales—the smooth top edge of the sides—with wet clay and lit small fires the length of the hollows, tending them as they smoldered and burnt away the soft, damp inner layers of the logs. We removed the charred wood by scraping the interior with adzes and tomahawks. Finally, the men carved away the log to leave behind the tapered, pointed prow and stern of the canoe and scraped the hull flat.

Like blood from a wounded animal, the sap oozed where the cuts were made. Hannah broke off a small piece of the soft pitch and placed it in her mouth, handing bits to Mary and me.

"Try it," she said. "'Tis a bit better than touchwood fried in bears' grease."

Mary took the wad of sap, bit into it, and wrinkled her nose. "Tastes foul, but I'm so hungry."

"Do not swallow it," Hannah warned.

I chewed mine silently. Bittersweet.

"There is some horsemeat left, though it will spoil soon," Mary said.

Her words, spoken so frankly, gave me pause. "The poor beasts carried us safely, with but death as their reward," I said, still distraught about it.

Mary nodded. "Better theirs than ours."

I was becoming accustomed to her candor.

"The Indians gave me one of the hides and the mane and tail," Mary said. "I'm making a coverlet of hide to stuff with the hair. I'm nearly finished."

"I'm sure it will be lovely," I said. The horsehide was one of several small kindnesses the Natives had shown Mary since Molly's death.

Mary and I walked back to the longhouse together. Neepânon and her husband, Wekoñtam, were in charge of our children today, packing for the next day's travel to the lake. The warriors had left before dawn to hunt. Many hours had passed since then, though the sky was so darkly layered with clouds there was no sun by which to tell the time. Snow would fall soon.

"Mommy, Mommy!" my girls called, running to me. I hugged them self-consciously, suddenly aware of how my friend Mary stiffened and pressed her lips tightly together.

"I'm going to go find Nate," she said, darting away.

It saddened me that my happy, healthy children rekindled my friend's grief.

"Mommy, Neepânon is teaching me to weave baskets to carry our belongings to the lake," my Mary said, holding up a partially finished basket of coiled reeds.

"Wonderful! And you, my little Sally?" I ruffled her curls.

"I'm hungry, Mama. When is food?"

"Soon, love," I lied.

"When the war-yers come back?" she asked.

"I hope so, yes."

"Mommy, Wekoñtam speaks Indian, so I'm teaching him English," Mattie said.

"Mattie, I have an idea." I dug into my pocket and handed her the little Picture Book. "Molly's picture book. You can use it to teach Wekoñtam, as I used it to teach you."

"Will Molly mind?" Mattie asked, her eyes big and round.

"I think she'd be pleased to know we are putting her book to good use." I smiled, but I sniffled back my tears once she'd skipped away.

The warriors returned without meat for the fifth day in a row. Morning and evening before each hunt, they danced, chanted, and asked their Manitou for guidance. They were well-armed with bows and arrows and English muskets and well-skilled in their use. Perhaps the animals were too wary, and our large company of three score and ten frightened them away.

Ashpelon approached me. His buckskin frock was loose on him, and it struck me with an unexpected twinge of pity that he was starving. He squatted next to me by the fire. I was piercing holes in Mattie's moccasin with a bone awl, readying it for the sinews I'd use to mend it. He was silent for some time, his thin arms resting on his thighs, watching me, watching the fire.

"We need your help. You, the elderly soldier, and Quintin," he said.

"We help you every day. We have no choice," I replied.

"Different help. We need you to pray for our hunt—English prayers. Our spirits are not listening. We want to know what your English God can do."

There was no challenge in his voice, only exhaustion. I was moved to pity.

"God cannot be commanded. We can only ask," I said.

"Will you? We need food. All of us."

"Did you speak to the Englishmen?"

"Yes."

"And?"

"They agreed, but you are a mother. Your God might listen more to you."

I smiled.

"Some want to pray with you," he said.

His request puzzled me. These were not Christian people. Only Ashpelon and Nìbi Wàbà spoke more than a few words of English. We were at his mercy, and yet he was desperate enough to seek our help.

"We pray morning and evening," I said.

"So, later then. When the sun sinks."

"Won't there be snow?" I asked, looking at the black clouds.

"No, not until morning," he said with certainty.

To be sure all heard the prayers, we divided into three parties, led by Sergeant Plympton, Quintin Stockwell, and myself. I sat in the longhouse by the English fire. English women and children and several Natives gathered around me. Ashpelon spoke first in his language. He translated for me—he asked them to bow their heads and not speak unless I bade them. Then he walked away.

"Giver of all, another day has ended, and I take my place beneath my great redeemer's cross. We thank You for the blessings of this world—the refreshing air, the light of the sun, the raiment that clothes us, the dwelling that shelters, the sleep that gives rest, the starry canopy of night, the music of flowing streams, and the happy endearments of family, kindred, and friends."

I stopped and choked back my tears. For a moment, all I thought of was Ben. The Natives looked up, thinking I was done. I bowed my head again and continued.

"Suffer me not to be insensible to these daily mercies. But we lack the food that renews our strength, and we beseech you to guide us in our hunting. Your hand bestows blessings: Your power averts evil. I bring my tribute of thanks for spiritual graces, the full warmth of faith, the cheering presence of Your Spirit, and the strength of Your restraining will. Blessed be, my Lord! Amen."

I looked at the Natives and repeated, "Amen," holding my hand out to them, palm up, and they echoed, "Amen."

We prayed again the following morning, and the warriors left to hunt as snowflakes fell. They took our Englishmen with them, so hungry they trusted them with guns. All three Englishmen had hunted before, and Sergeant Plympton was known to be an excellent shot. Ashpelon was happy for the snow, for it made it easier to track the animals.

Within hours, the hunters returned, hoisting two enormous black bears on their shoulders. They laughed and whooped in joy. Never had I known prayers to be answered so swiftly. We set to work at once dressing, skinning, and tanning, English and Native women laboring together, resisting the strange urge to devour the bear's flesh raw.

My time with the Native people was changing me in fragile but definite ways. Enduring the long journey, sharing food and building canoes, the grief of Molly's passing, the morning and evening prayers, and the joys of a successful hunt had altered my perceptions slightly, giving them a new clarity.

I remembered when Ben rebuilt our home in Hatfield after the first attack, and replaced the oiled paper in the front window with paned glass. When I first gazed through it at my dooryard garden, the pink Eglantine roses climbing the white rails of the fence, I remember I gasped at the sight. The new light had lifted my spirits and filled my heart with joy, replacing the grief I'd felt when our home had burned.

As the Bible said in Romans, I was rejoicing in hope and loving with brotherly love. "If it be possible, as much as it is in you, have peace with all men." The day's successful hunt was another moment of happiness amid the darkness, a gift from our Lord. Meat to sustain us, grease to anoint us, furry hides to warm us under the canopy of night. I felt the peace that passeth all understanding.

❧

We stayed for two more days, working on the canoes, devouring all the bear meat, and tanning the hides. Heartened by the successful hunt, some Natives continued to join in our daily prayers. Yet after a time, they wearied of it, I suppose because it was not their language nor their God.

We finished the canoes, rubbing the splintered surface of the wood with sandstone, cutting and carving wooden seats and paddles, and finally sealing each canoe using pine sap mixed with hot ashes from the fires. The Nipmuc women wove snowshoes out of softened strips of cedar and lacings of watap, their word for thin threads of cedar root.

The trip to the lake took only an hour or so, following Otter Creek. The warriors took charge of the canoes, placing our belongings within them, sometimes rolling them on sturdy logs across the ice and snow, other times poling them in the shallows of the stream. The snow was not yet deep enough for snowshoes, but it soaked through our boots and moccasins despite their linings of leaves and fur. The littlest babes rode in the canoes the men pulled—Sally, Sammy, Nate, and Matt. Mary and Mattie seemed much revived by the bear meat feasting, and they trudged beside me without complaint.

Otter Creek emptied into Lake Champlain in a sweeping delta of bright, icy water and gleaming snow. The wind cut like knives, and we threw together rough shelters of bear hides, canoes, and tree branches and built multiple small fires for warmth. The warriors hunted and killed two raccoons, which we stayed that night to eat.

"Why do we not jerk the meat?" I asked Ashpelon, "so we'd have some to sustain us on the journey?"

"It takes many days. And it is not our way. Unless we have

much more than we need, we eat what we kill and share what we eat. To save meat, to us, is greedy. Wrong," he said.

The next day dawned blessedly calm, both the weather and our spirits. My babe moved like a storm within me, no longer a fragile butterfly. Hannah's sadness and nausea had lifted now that she'd reached her quickening time. We were grateful for the new lives to come yet did not discuss our hopes with Mary, who still grieved. My girls missed their little friend. Mary and Mattie knew well of death and heaven, but Molly was the only child they'd befriended in their short lives who had died before their eyes. It made them clingy and quiet and fearful of falling ill themselves.

I sat with a few others by the fire, sipping hot water and eating a scrap of raccoon. The pale-yellow clouds made a pattern in the sky like the scales of a fish against a blue ocean. I recalled Ben's phrase for it, a "mackerel sky."

"A penny for your thoughts," Sergeant Plympton said.

"Oh, the clouds. I was trying to recall what Ben says about a mackerel sky."

"Is it, 'Mares' tails and mackerel scales, tall ships carry short sails?'"

"Yes!"

"Short sails? To prepare for a storm?" Obadiah asked.

"'Tis only a sailors' proverb," Sergeant Plympton said.

"Mares' tails," I said. "Those are the wispy ones? I like that."

The clouds, by any name, made for a glorious salmon-colored sunrise as the English men, women, and children gathered for our morning prayer. I was filled with an urgent longing to be on our way. When we reached Canada, we'd be amongst Catholics, who lived in houses and villages, prayed to the same God as we did, and would not threaten us with tomahawks or murder our kin. I dared hope we'd be taken somewhere Ben might find us, a village or farm, removed from this wilderness.

The tribe gathered in a large circle, bringing out their drums, and chanted a song. I was now familiar with their language, and it no longer frightened me. I listened to the distinct sounds, a softness to them, and understood words beyond the few I'd used when bartering with Nipmucs in Hatfield years ago. *Nummonchumun.* We go. *Chemauonit.* We paddle. *Nippe.* Water. *Manitoo ken nootah.* Great Spirit, hear me.

I ensured my girls wore their deerskin mittens and warmest clothes, and we packed up our camp. Kòkòkòho and Kenompāe dragged my canoe into the water and climbed in, taking up positions at the prow and the stern. Holding Sally in my arms and Mattie by the hand, Mary clutching my skirts, we waded out, gasping at the chill water. I settled my girls deep in the bottom of the canoe I'd helped build and wrapped us in the bearskin I'd helped tan. Ashpelon shoved us away from the snowy beach and onto Lake Champlain.

Our passage gave the illusion of crossing a vast expanse of sea, as my parents had when leaving England for here forty years ago. I thought of Ben, the distance between us increasing once again, my fate in the hands of God and our captors, no longer mine to choose. A song came to me, one Rebecca had taught me to play on the cittern. I pulled my girls close and sang.

The water is wide, I cannot cross o'er
And neither have I wings to fly
Give me a boat, that can carry two
And both shall row, my love and I.

Chapter Forty-Five

BEN

Mohawk Trail
December 1

As God would have it, Stephen and I were forced to spend the night in Schenectady due to a sudden heavy snowfall. We stayed again at the brew master's, who was relieved to know we'd been cleared of our alleged crimes. His wife served us apple krullen and coffee in the morning, and the sun beat back the clouds, turning the snow into glittering diamonds. The brewmaster insisted on loading us up with loaves of bread and a wheel of cheese and filled our flagons with beer.

Outfitted with blankets and wampum to trade, wearing our buff coats and bandoliers, and carrying our great cloaks and snowshoes, I felt more confident about our endeavor than I had in weeks. Light snow showers came and went, falling from sun-silvered clouds.

As Sir Lindsay had promised, we reached the Verf Kill Brook in just over three hours. The mouth of the stream was slushy and choked with dead reeds and vines where the trail veered north into the woods. We saw no sign of a Mohawk encampment, but we cleared the fallen leaves and needles and built a small fire, as Livingston had advised. The wind picked up, blowing smoke into our eyes. Stephen and I skewered hunks of bread and cheese on willow branches and held them over the fire, toasting the bread and melting the cheese, an untidy but tasty meal.

The gusting wind made it challenging to keep our fire alive. When I was about to give up, an Indian appeared soundlessly—a Mohawk. Unlike the Algonquian tribal warriors, his head was plucked clean but for a roach of hair dyed red and adorned with several feathers. His face was wrinkled with age and ravaged by smallpox scars.

"English?" he asked.

"I am Waite," I said in my best Mohawk Dutch, a mixed language I remembered from my fur trading days. "This is Jennings. Tali from Nova Scotia said to ask for Aquinachoo."

"I am Erhar. Aquinachoo is ill. Smallpox. Many in the Turtle Clan are sick. I survived it, so I cannot be sick again." He stood close to our fire.

"I am sorry. We hoped Aquinachoo might show us the way to Lake George."

"For what reason?"

I explained to him the best I could; the attack, the captives, our mission. He nodded sympathetically.

"Pocumtucks, Nipmucs, and Norwottucks," Erhar said, shaking his head and spitting in disgust.

"Our feelings exactly," I said.

"Aquinachoo has been sick for a dozen suns," Erhar said. "If he lives, he will be cured. Come back in ten days to know."

My hopes and spirits collapsed like a weak roof under heavy snow.

"Are there no other Mohawks on the river to help us?"

"Farther north. Caughnawaga Castle of the Turtle Clan. It is by the Caughnawa mission. French priest named Father Jean."

"The Mohawks have made peace with the French?"

"For now, some have. The mission is a safe place for those who choose to give up their ways." Erhar folded his arms.

"How far?"

"A day's walk. Follow the river. You will cross Cayadutta Creek and see the castle's stockade on a hill, a bow shot from the river."

I translated for Stephen, then turned back to the Mohawk elder.

"Thank you, Erhar. Give our prayers to Aquinachoo."

We kicked snow onto our dying fire and headed north.

Chapter Forty-Six
MARTHA

Lake Bitawbagok
Winter

The first true snowstorm of the year was the most awesome yet painful of all. In the same way as childbirth, I recalled the magic each time but forgot how brutal it could be. The budding and melting and breezes of spring, ripening into the blazing bounty of the summer, easing into the crimson glory of fall and the hard-earned harvest, made my memory of the bleakest season seem like a bad dream. Now, as always, winter roared back in that first furious storm.

The icy wind churned the lake water into a choppy sea, cold spray drenching us whilst the snow and sleet sliced across the sky. Each canoe had warriors at prow and stern, and they paddled skillfully, but many times I feared we'd capsize. Neither my girls nor I could swim, and regardless, the water would freeze us to our marrow. So, I wrapped the bearskin Ashpelon had given me around the four of us, and we curled low in the belly of the canoe, hanging onto the thwarts for dear life.

We'd built eight canoes in various lengths from four to six

yards, each roughly a yard across at the center and shallow so they rode low in the water. Waves washed up over the sides, and we were fain to bail it out with a kettle or be swamped. We barely glimpsed the island we made for, although Kenompāe said it lay but four miles distant. We headed north-west, keeping the sun and wind behind us. About halfway, we passed between two small islands, neither more than a few acres, and it seemed they created a funnel effect, for the canoes leapt forward, and the waves increased in size and number. The Natives called out to one another, their voices strained, speaking rapidly.

Kenompāe, who was at the bow, turned back to Kòkòkòho and motioned with his arm to our left. *Menatche*. I thought of Ben and the drowning of his brother Joseph, and I held my girls tighter. We shifted course a bit south, and instead of making for the big island, we headed for the northernmost point of another. Once we rounded the point, we entered a small, curved bay.

Even though we'd been on the water for only an hour, it seemed an eternity. Once we beached the canoes, I scrambled out with my girls and my few belongings. I wanted to put as much distance as possible between us and the cold, deep lake. Carrying Sally, I urged Mary and Mattie toward the shelter of the woods. The storm moaned around us, the snow blowing in angry, wraith-like drifts already up to our knees. I found a cairn of rocks to sit on, unpacked our snowshoes, put mine on, and helped my girls with theirs.

"'Tis like duck feet, Mommy!" Mattie said, lifting her feet high and walking in a big circle. She promptly fell and burst into tears. "I'm cold!" she cried.

I picked her up and brushed the snow away. "Be careful, girls, how you walk in them. You aren't ducks, and you need to practice."

I searched the bare trees for branches and brush to build a shelter.

Kòkòkòho found us. "Here." He set down a bundle of boughs thicker than my arm and as long as he was tall. "Build a frame." He handed me a few lengths of watap and a knife and left us there. I stared momentarily at the sharp steel blade, feeling the weight of the antler handle in my grip. The Natives were confident we'd not harm them. We all knew we'd not survive alone.

We propped up the branches beside the cairn of rocks, wrapping their highest point in watap. I saw other figures moving through the trees and snow and heard voices barking commands. We worked together quickly to build shelters from the storm. I hacked at a thicket of bare, twiggy brush, and little Mary and I placed those against the cone-shaped frame, leaving a small hole on the leeward side. The rest we spread on the floor of our crude shelter.

The four of us crawled inside, crowding together under the bearskin. I longed for a fire, but there was no space for it within and no chance of keeping it alive without. Freezing and starving, I lay awake until my girls were asleep. My teeth chattered, and my feet were numb. I held my babes tight against me, listening to the moaning of the wind as it continued long into the night.

Chapter Forty-Seven
ASHPELON

LAKE BITAWBAGOK
WINTER

It is winter as I've not known it in all my thirty winters. Each day, it snows, the drifts so deep we cannot walk, not even in our snowshoes. We hunt and hunt, and there is nothing. My people are starving. The English are starving. Some days, we launch the canoes into the icy water, but we paddle more slowly than the sun across the sky or the wind through the trees, and so in the end, we must surrender to the winter and go ashore again.

I am reminded of the legend of times past, when people lived always in the early red morning, before sunrise. Glooskap came over the sea in a great stone canoe, and this canoe was an island of granite covered with trees.

Maybe we are riding on Glooskap's canoe. In the legend, Glooskap went very far north, where all was ice, as we do now.

Our council meets, but we cannot agree because we do not know the answers. We pray to Manitoo, to calm the wind, to keep us alive. We dance to Michabo, the Great Hare, to feed us with the deer and fish he created, but we go hungry.

My people rarely travel in the dead of winter. Winter is for long evenings by the fire in the longhouse, sharing stories of spring. For easy tracking of elk, bear, and raccoons, animals that once almost ran to us, asking us to eat them. Now, they hide. Maybe, like us, they are afraid of the English.

Wanalancet says we should abandon the captives, that we are like a canoe of too many people. He thinks we will sink and drown unless we sacrifice them. He reminds me my first duty is to our people. He says I am worse than the English, risking our lives for money. What can we do with the money?

I told him again it was not for the money. Not anymore. The captives must stay with us until we are safely away. Without them, the English, French, or Mohawks will kill us. Our prisoners are a shield, protecting us.

Though I do not tell this to Wanalancet, I also feel abandoning the English now would be a sad thing, like when we killed the horses. Like those beasts, they have done what we have asked of them. The English have walked hundreds of miles, sewn our shirts, built our longhouses and canoes, and cooked our meals. This one small band of English has settled the score.

Chapter Forty-Eight
MARTHA

LAKE CHAMPLAIN
SNOW MOON

I lost track of the days. There was only snow, cold, and hunger. And always the endless dark lake of ice and deep water. Once again, I recalculated the measure of time and began to mark it by the phases of the moon. Despite the constant snow, the full moon shone radiantly in the wilderness of night. The lake was a living thing, crackling and moaning as it froze and thawed. Breathing.

One night, by the light of the Snow Moon, Obadiah and Quintin stumbled upon a den of raccoons—a mother and her nearly grown kits in a hollow tree. They took their hatchets and killed them, and so the next day, we sat around the fire, shoving chunks of hot, red meat into our mouths until we were stuffed.

"I've had enough raccoon, thank you," Quintin said, but Quequan forced another large chunk of meat on him. He spit it out, and Quequan smacked his cheek.

I cringed.

"It is food! You eat!"

"But I will be sick. I've had enough."

It pained me to watch Quintin's masters treat him cruelly because he could not finish all the flesh they gave him.

"Racoon enough?" Quequan said. He grabbed Quintin's jaw, pried open his mouth, tilted his head back, and poured hot, bloody raccoon fat down his throat. Poor Quintin gagged, and Quequan and the other Natives laughed at him. I wanted to shout at them to stop, but I was too weak. And I remembered Ashpelon's words, to eat all when we could.

I felt the cold changing me. I stumbled when I walked and shivered so much it kept me awake at night. My toes and fingers tingled—my boots and mittens were not warm enough. I begged Ashpelon for a raccoon pelt, some of which I used to line my deer hide boots. I fashioned the rest into small capelets for Mary and Mattie.

The freezing weather affected us differently. English suffered more than Natives, old more than young. My heart worried for Sergeant Plympton, Quintin, and Sam Russell. The sergeant—thin by nature—resembled a skeleton. Quintin's war injury hindered him, and when he slipped on the ice, Quequan yelled at him and sometimes struck him. Sam Russell seemed the worst off of all the children, perhaps because he was the eldest child and was tasked with the most labor yet given no more food than the others.

The lake was bewitched between water and ice, at times too frozen to use our canoes but not frozen enough to walk upon. The islands were a mix of sheet ice, hard-packed snow, and powdery drifts. Traveling by land entailed an unpredictable agony of stumbling and slipping, dragging our belongings and children in the canoes.

Ashpelon kept driving us north, although the wind had shifted and blew against us, forcing us to bow before it, eyes closed, pulling or paddling our canoes. We never traveled longer than a few hours before the winter compelled us to stop and make our camp, utterly spent.

Hannah and I were completely in awe of God's mercy each time our babes moved within us. For such tiny lives to survive these trials was miraculous.

"You are nearing your time," Hannah said, trodding beside me.

"Late January," I said.

"God willing, we will be with the French by then." Hannah stepped gingerly over a frozen brook.

"I never dreamt I'd long to be a servant in a Frenchman's Catholic home," I said.

"Perhaps we will be governesses," Hannah said and laughed a rare laugh.

"God willing. We could be scullery maids, though."

"I hope whoever ransoms me will have a nice garden to tend," she said.

My heart turned to ice. "What if they separate us? Ransom our children to one family and us to another! I never thought . . ." I glanced behind me to where Sally rode atop the sled I pulled.

"No."

"But—"

"No! Martha, we must keep our faith that God will guide our captors to be merciful, and He will redeem us."

"With Ben as His instrument. 'Tis a blessing how stubborn Ben can be. He says God gave man free will, so he will freely do what must be done."

Yet even as I spoke these words, I felt my faith falter. My faith that was the substance of things hoped for and the evidence of things not seen.

Chapter Forty-Nine

BEN

"*Messieurs, J'ai trouvé un guide,*" Father Jean de Lamberville said to us at breakfast.

"*Merci, Prêtre,*" I said.

We sat at a great oak table with black-robed friars and praying Indians. Breakfast was a soft-boiled egg, samp, and tea.

"You will meet your guide after breakfast," Jean continued in French.

"Thank you. We are very grateful," Stephen said.

We'd arrived the evening before. Father Jean graciously welcomed us, and we communicated our story, grateful he spoke English. The friars shared their supper of chicken stew, and we slept on mattresses on a stone floor warmed by a fire.

After breakfast, Father Jean led us across the mission grounds, his long black robe sweeping the snow. He pointed out the wooden buildings: the church with timbered front and tall steeple, the friars' housing wherein we'd slept, and the two longhouses of the Iroquois.

"We have people from different tribes and clans here," Father Jean said. "Most are Mohawks of the Turtle Clan, but we also minister to Mahicans and even a few Abenaki."

"And do they live in harmony?" I asked.

"Most of the time. If they wish to stay with us here."

The Father took us to the snug barn, wherein men tended a small flock of sheep, cows, and hogs. It smelled of manure, damp fleece, and clean straw. A young Iroquois man turned from his labors to greet us, wiping his hands on his buckskin frock.

"*Bonjour,*" he said, then switched to English. "You are the men who need a guide?"

Father Jean introduced us. "Monsieur Waite, Monsieur Jennings, this is Asserie. Asserie, these are the messieurs I spoke to you about, Waite and Jennings."

We shook hands.

"Your name means 'very strong'," I said.

"You speak Iroquois?"

"Some. And you speak three languages, I'm told. We gave Father Jean blankets and wampum for your help."

"I am happy to take you to Le Lac George. I am familiar with the trail there. You will also need a casoya. A canoe?" he asked.

"Indeed."

Father Jean spoke. "Asserie keeps a birchbark canoe hidden by the shores of the Sacandaga River."

"Thanks be to God," I said, "so we do not need to make one! Can you sketch us a map, and directions?"

"I have never been farther than the southern shore of Le Lac Champlain. You have a long journey."

"A long one behind us, also," I said. We'd been going in circles for two months, like a pair of horses tethered to a grist mill, and I was desperate to break free.

"When can we start?"

I watched Asserie pitch fresh straw into the pig pen.

"Today, if you wish."

"How do we begin?" I asked.

"Up the Sacandaga River, across it and the Hudson to Lake George. Three or four days. But we should not wait. A storm is coming."

I looked out the barn door at the cloudless sky, like Delft china, blue and white. How did he forecast a storm?

"Then, let's be off," I said.

Asserie nodded. "I will finish here with the animals and join you at the gate."

We did not have long to wait. Father Jean handed us a sack of provisions before we left: pemmican, corn, dried apples, and pumpkin. We graciously accepted his Latin blessing despite our embarrassment.

Snow hid our trail, but I knew Asserie had the means to find his way. The first was the sun, which we kept to our right as we climbed the steep hill. A few squirrels scampered and chattered at us from the trees, and I spied many deer tracks on our way. After about two hours, our guide stopped and studied a stand of oak trees.

"We rest here while I find the magic tree." Asserie headed off into the woods.

"Magic tree?" Stephen asked.

"I think he's looking for a trail marker tree," I replied.

"Which is?"

"In my fur trading days, I saw a few. 'Tis clever. The Natives choose a sapling beside the trail, bending the supple trunk down and then up again, forming a right angle. They brace and tie it to hold the bend in place, and the tree grows to resemble the number four to point the way."

Asserie called to us, and we joined him a few hundred feet to our right. He stood beside an ancient oak tree, its bent trunk pointing east. We stopped two more times. At each pause in our trek, the Mohawk searched the surrounding forest to find another tree bent at right angles like the number four, then beckoned us that way. We continued on an eastern route for another three hours when we reached a frosty stream.

"Kenyetto Creek," Asserie said. "We stop here to eat."

I scraped snow off a fallen log, sat on it, and opened my pack, taking out our bread, cheese, and oranges. The brewmaster had filled our flasks with ale. I offered some to Asserie.

He accepted an orange but refused the ale.

"I do not drink. It is the law at the mission," he said. "Firewater brings visions but also much trouble for my people, so we do not drink it."

I understood. For the past two months, since losing Martha and my girls, there had been times at the taverns when I had been tempted to drink more than a pint or two. Drink promised forgetfulness and peace, and I longed for both. I also knew I would feel sick the next day, yet want more.

Back on our way, we followed the Kenyetto Creek and reached the Sacandaga River, flowing slowly and gray like melted pewter. Asserie guided us alongst the south shore until sunset when we stopped to camp about a musket's shot from the river beside a partly frozen brook. We helped our Mohawk guide chop down young trees for our wickiups. I draped the sailcloth I'd purchased in Boston over a frame of boughs and was happy it worked, making a decent tent for Stephen and me. Asserie covered his with a sheepskin he'd brought from the mission.

The next day brought more fair, cold weather, and we skirted the river through forests of bare oaks and bright green cedar and spruce. We camped at dusk. The three of us sat around the fire, sharing bread, cheese, salted pork, and Asserie's dried fish.

"My cousin, Tekakwitha, fled this way to Canada."

"Fled?" Stephen asked.

"Tekakwitha was unhappy in our Turtle clan, even at the mission. She needed to be free to pray to her Catholic God."

"She was not free to do that with you and Father Jean?"

"At first, she tried but felt trapped within the stockade. Outside of it, our people were cruel to her, and the English frightened her. So, she left to be amongst the French and Catholics."

I finished chewing and nodded. "That is why our parents left England, to worship freely."

"But you are not Catholic."

"No," I thought about how to explain. "Our beliefs are simple. No saints. Fewer celebrations."

"No sins?"

"Oh, no, we have plenty of those." I laughed.

"How long do we follow this river?" Stephen asked.

"One more day. To where I have hidden the canoe. It will be cold enough tonight to freeze the Sacandaga, where it narrows," Asserie said. "We will cross where it is the shallowest. After that, we will cross the Hudson."

"Ben? Where exactly in Canada are we hoping to find them?"

"I hope just north of Lake Champlain. We will follow the Richelieu River."

Asserie's canoe was a lovely craft. The overlapping bark reinforcing the joints at the gunwales was cut with a scalloped bottom edge, like waves, and carved with designs of little fish swimming. It carried us safely across the Sacandaga River.

We followed the river's north bank all day until we reached the Hudson. There, at the mouth of the Sacandaga, Asserie said we'd find sandbars and silt, a natural bridge of sorts. The Hudson River seemed as broad here as in Albany, but with no one to ferry us across. The shallows and beaches lay frozen beneath the snow, but we saw the flowing black ribbon of water beyond.

"Are there any Natives here?" Stephen asked Asserie as we searched for a place to cross.

"The People, here? Some Iroquois. But there have been many wars. Iroquois against Algonquian and Huron, English against Dutch, Dutch and English against French. And sickness. *Le petite vérole.*"

"Ah, smallpox. A horrible disease." For some reason, it was far deadlier for the Native Americans than for the English or other Europeans.

At last, we found a crossing. A fortuitous combination of snow-covered sand, an abandoned beaver dam, and fallen deadwood slowed the current just enough for it to freeze. We stepped delicately across the ice one at a time, Asserie carrying the canoe above his head. Once we reached the opposite shore, we made camp.

❦

The next day we donned our snowshoes and climbed hill and dale through the woods, past frozen ponds, and a few more magic trees. We reached the south shore of Lake George before noon. Ice edged the banks for a few rods before it gave way to water. Deep blue mountains hugged the beaches on the west and east.

I studied the map he had scratched for us into a sheet of birch bark. 'Twas a delightful creation of cartography, symbols, Iroquois, and French, and certainly not to scale, yet I understood it. He talked me through it twice.

"Farewell, Asserie, and many thanks." I handed him a string of wampum and a handful of shillings. "We are forever in your debt."

Stephen and I watched him walk away into the forest.

"I wonder what will become of him," Stephen said.

"Asserie? He'll go back to the mission," I said.

Stephen rubbed more of the pine pitch mixture on the

seams of our canoe. Not having bear grease, Asserie had used the last fat from the ham hock.

"I meant, beyond that. Do you think he will stay there or head to Canada?"

I shook my head. "I do not know what will happen to the Native people. 'Tis an untenable situation. Trying to hold onto this land." I swept my arm, palm up, across the vista. "Natives, Dutch, French, English. We all want it."

Stephen stood and wiped his hands on his apron. "Is it naive of me to ask why we could not share it?"

"We did, once. But the scales have tipped heavily in our favor. This land has far more English, Dutch, and French than Native people. And for the most part, Europeans are greedy."

Stephen nodded. "'*I shall give thee the heathen for thine inheritance and the ends of the earth for thy possession.*' Psalm, the prophet David."

"And yet, another Psalm, '*But meek men shall possess the earth, and shall have their delight in the multitude of peace.*' I long for an end to constant war," I said.

"Agreed," Stephen said. "Are we ready to go, then?"

"Aye. We'll push the canoe across the snow and keep checking the ice with our oars. About two canoe lengths before what looks like water, you'll climb in and make your way to the prow. Stay low and centered." I gazed out across the lake. Storm clouds were darkening and lowering on the horizon.

"And yourself?"

"I'll give her one more shove once you're settled, jump in, and we're off."

Our morning prayers were answered. God proved merciful, and the launch went smoothly. At long last, we sailed upon Lake George, paddling north.

Chapter Fifty

MARTHA

LAKE CHAMPLAIN
WINTER

"What are they dancing about now?" Mary asked.

"Not for the hunt, that's certain. 'Tis midday and a blizzard," Hannah said.

I sighed. "I hope they're asking for it to end."

The three of us sat in a large wigwam we'd built, large enough for our children and us and a small fire. Sergeant Plympton and Kòkòkòho had helped lift the heaviest boughs, but we had done the rest. Ashpelon had decreed we'd remain until the storm passed. The blizzard had drawn a veil across the world, blinding us, and the ice was not black enough to walk upon, nor the lake calm enough for canoes.

The three Englishmen had an even larger wigwam next to ours for themselves, Obadiah's son Daniel, Matthew Kellogg, and Sam Russell. The wigwams circled a central fire that flickered and sputtered in the relentless storm.

The Natives danced around the fire, their rhythms punching through the low moaning of the wind. They filled the clearing with the rattle of gourds, jingling bells, thumping drums, stomping feet, and rhythmic, sibilant chanting. All increased my headache and shivering.

Mary pulled back the flap of our wigwam, and we watched the figures circling the fire as it threw shadows at their feet. Atian sat apart from the rest, wrapped in a bearskin, his eyes closed, his legs crossed. Suddenly, he leapt to his feet, shouted in his language, and the world fell silent. Only the wind and flames moved.

Ashpelon strode to Atian, spoke with him, and then called to us.

"English, here. Now."

We all crept out of our wigwams and huddled together, terrified of what might come next.

Ashpelon stared at each of us in turn. "Atian tells me three truths: First, he sees two men, English, heading this way. Next, he says my people should fear them more than this storm. And last, he says this storm will cast the two men away and prevent them from following us."

Mary, always somewhat cynical, scoffed. "A vision?" she whispered. "It might be true that English still search for us. But how could he know how many? I do not believe this nonsense!"

"What if his vision is true? What if Ben is searching for us?" I asked.

"And Stephen with him," Hannah added softly.

"Martha," Mary began, shaking her head, "Hannah. We are hundreds of miles from Hatfield. In a blizzard. 'Tis foolish to think our kin are still looking for us."

"Mary, hush," Hannah said and squeezed my hand.

"And my Samuel? Why do neither of you ever include him as a rescuer in your magical tales?" Mary asked, her face flushed, fists at her sides.

Instead of answering her, I stepped forward from the circle and faced Ashpelon across the fire.

"Ashpelon."

He turned to me, his dark eyes locked on mine.

"Does Atian know who the two Englishmen are?"

Ashpelon sighed. "He does not know. But I think one might be your husband."

Fear and hope tangled in my chest. This made no sense, but that did not mean it was untrue. If this storm hadn't finished us, 'twould not cast away my husband.

My vision grayed, and there was a ringing in my ears. I sank to my knees, and Hannah encircled me in her arms.

Even the Great Flood in the Bible finally ended and, at last, so did the blizzard. The wind calmed, the sun broke through the clouds, and the snow ceased. Eager as baby ducklings for their first swim, we launched our canoes into Lake Champlain, feeling reborn to sunlight and open water.

The warrior Kenompāe was again at the prow of our canoe, but Nìbi Wàbà had replaced Kòkòkòho at the stern. The Nipmuc women had carved more paddles, and Kenompāe handed one to me. We added one more person, young Sam Russell, to balance the paddles and steer the canoe. Though he was but nine years of age, he was strong and said he'd watched and learned how the Natives paddled.

Despite the wind still against us, we skimmed the choppy waters off the shore of a pair of large islands the Natives called *Gitsimenahan*. My left arm ached from my labor, reminding me with a flash of anger of the moment Ashpelon struck me and took me from my home. That day seemed years ago, yet the memories were vivid and shocking even now.

Sam Russell sat in front of me, and once or twice, he turned his head to check on me or share a friendly word. My heart ached to see how thin he was, making him look even younger. How could I have sewn a shirt for Quequan, the warrior who had captured Sam and slain his mother?

"How fare you, Goodwife Waite?" he asked. His bright brown eyes were huge above his sharp cheekbones.

"I am well, thank you, Sam. And you?"

"Grateful the storm is over!" He grinned, closed his eyes, and tilted his face to the sun.

Mary and Mattie sat between me and Nìbi Wàbà, but little Sally was in Mary Foote's canoe with her son Nate. Sally seemed to ease Mary's pain at losing Molly, so I let her care for her at times. I prayed to God morning and night to keep my girls safe, for I could not imagine the loss Mary bore. To look for one's child upon waking and find them not. To reach to hold them in the night and grasp only air. To call their name in a dream and be answered by silence. Hannah had endured the same agony years ago, when her poor, wee girl tripped and fell into the fire. I shivered.

The lake was remarkable in its length and breadth, the sheer expanse of water. In the sun, it shone like a silver plate on a white linen cloth, the islands like spoonfuls of salt crystals dotting the surface. When I dared peer over the canoe's gunwale, the deep waters threatened, black and cold.

We may have been the first English to see this lake. As far as I knew—although Samuel de Champlain had explored it— Henry Hudson had not traveled this far north. If the grace of God redeemed us, we'd have tales to tell our kin, children, and grandchildren. Tales, I hoped, of courage, faith, and love.

Our camp was a bay on the northernmost of the two Great Isles. No snow meant no clouds to blanket the icy sky, and the darkness brought bitter cold. We built our crude shelters and fires close together and sat shoulder to shoulder for warmth. All the men went hunting, Native and English. They took young Sam Russell with them, as he'd been pleading to go. His first hunt.

We hadn't eaten in nearly a week. The hunger and the cold and the babe within me all dragged me down into slumber. The moon waned, the heavens ablaze with stars. A wolf howled, and then another. Sally slept in my arms, but Mary and Mattie burrowed deeper under the bearskin at the sound. The howling of a wolf used to terrify me. Now, it only made me lonesome. We crawled inside our little wickiups and dreamt of food.

❧

"Martha. Martha, wake up!"

Mary gripped my shoulder and shook me.

"What?"

"Something's wrong. The men are back, but . . ."

I looked up at Mary's pale face and saw worry in it.

Disentangling myself from my children, I wrapped my cloak around me and crawled out into the gray light of dawn. I pulled on my shoes and stumbled to the central fire, where many had already assembled. As Mary had said, something was wrong. A deer carcass hung by its hind hooves from a tree, already dressed and skinned, which should have been cause for rejoicing. Yet those around the fire were silent.

Sergeant Plympton and Quintin Stockwell buried their faces in their hands.

I sat beside Mary on an overturned canoe. A few more joined us as a cold sun rose. Ashpelon stood and faced us.

"A heart-cutting thing has happened," Ashpelon began, "to the boy called Sam."

I looked around the circle frantically. I did not see him.

Ashpelon continued. "We tracked a herd of deer near the mouth of a stream at the end of a big bay. Some of us went inland, some out upon the frozen edge of the bay. In the starlight, the ice seemed strong. We stuck it with a pike and found no water until the hole was two hands deep. Sergeant Plympton, Stockwell, Sam, and two warriors went out upon it . . ."

I waited. We all knew suddenly, horribly, what Ashpelon's

following words would be. They chilled me before he spoke them, like lumps of ice in my chest.

"Sam put a foot through the ice. Sergeant Plympton grabbed his arm and pulled him to safety, but it all gave way under them. My warriors pulled themselves out of the water with their tomahawks, crawled to the thick ice, and held their pikes to the English. Plympton and Stockwell grabbed on and held tight. Sam tried, but . . ."

My friends were gasping, sobbing. The ice in my chest rose to my throat, to melt behind my eyes as tears. I closed my hand around the jeweled rock in my apron pocket—Sam's gift.

"Plympton lay flat on the ice and reached out again to Sam, but it was too late. Too cold. Much deeper than we thought. Sam went under. He is gone." Ashpelon's voice was as dead as the deer and cold as the snow.

I felt frozen in place, buried in silence. It reminded me of Ben's desperate attempts to save his brother from the cold sea. The only warmth was the tears on my cheeks. The only sound was Sergeant Plympton sobbing.

Chapter Fifty-One

BEN

Lake George
December 7-10

"We should fish again when we camp." I peered down into the clear depths of Lake George, looking for fish.

Stephen laughed. "You assume I packed the tackle?"

"Did you not?"

"I did."

It had been a decade since I'd paddled a canoe. The skill returned to me quickly enough, although the effort it required was more than I recalled. Stephen was managing well.

"You're quite good at this," I told him.

"'Tis a bit like tilling a field by hand."

"True."

The lake was beautiful, deep blue dotted with dozens of snow-covered islands, embraced by mountains on both shores, cloaked in forests of fir and cedar, ever green. The breeze, made stronger by our passing, cut like ice, but the sun warmed my face. I felt nearly giddy to at last be free. Free of the land, free of governments, free of storms and delays. A sense of liberty spread within me as though I'd recovered from a long sickness of the soul, casting aside guilt and doubt like one throws off the heavy blanket of a sickbed when the fever breaks at last.

Although enjoyable at first, canoeing was slow, hard labor. We'd paddle for a while, perhaps a quarter hour, then stop and glide, letting the current carry us forward. I considered myself sound and able-bodied, but my shoulders and back ached after an hour or so on the lake.

Asserie had cautioned us to keep to the middle of the lake, avoiding the Iroquois tribes to the west and the Algonquians to the east. That was easy enough to do, and when the sun lowered in the sky, we found a bay with many islands and put ashore on a gentle, pebbled beach.

'Twas a tiny island, no larger than our eight-acre plots back in Hatfield, densely forested and deep with snow. Stephen searched for deadwood whilst I built a fire in a sheltered spot by several fallen trees. I dug a hole in the snow with my tomahawk, about elbow to fingertip across and deep, and when Stephen returned, we crisscrossed branches atop it and struck the flint.

We used the upside-down canoe for a bench as we ate supper. Later, we leaned it against a fallen tree for shelter, spread cedar boughs for a bed, crawled beneath, and fell asleep.

At the first light of dawn, we fished, caught two good-sized lake trout, cleaned them, and set them in a pan on the fire. They were cooked by the time our morning prayer was done.

Stephen pierced his portion with his knife and crunched on the crispy skin.

"Now, if we had a cookery book, some herbs, butter, ale," Stephen said.

"Here." I tossed him an orange. "Squeeze a bit on it."

"Ah, perfect."

Clouds rolled in by mid-morning, and we were well on our way when it began to snow. By God's grace, the breeze was light, and our hats and greatcoats kept us dry. According to the birchbark map, the lake split ahead, the left side a bay with no egress, so we steered to starboard and found ourselves amongst islands again.

Weaving in and out of the islands, we harkened back to our childhoods, when we had played with our brothers at being pirates in a great ocean, running rum and capturing damsels. Snow did not belong in our make-believe tropical land, but it was a slight inconsistency in a fond shared remembrance.

I missed playing with my girls and telling them stories. Martha and I cossetted them more than most parents, but I found my children charming and enjoyed their company. My wife said if we raised them with a gentle hand, they would grow to have a gentle nature. Thus far, it had proven to be so. I hoped with all my heart their Nipmuc captors treated them gently. The horrors of the attack and capture would leave scars on their hearts and terrors in their dreams. I prayed the Natives treated them peacefully.

Oneida Bay was where I'd set our course, Asserie having marked it on the little map by drawing an Oneida tribal head-dress, two feathers straight up and one down. Again, we banked our canoe, walked up a deer trail, and found a spot in the trees to camp. Having built our tent of branches and mats and kindled our fire, we sat down to eat our ham and cheese.

"After this, we've only bread left, and a pint of dried corn," I said ruefully.

"Let's pray the fishing is good in the morning," Stephen said.

"Or hunting? There ought to be animals about, hares or such."

"Or trapping? Isn't that your specialty?"

Thanks be to God for Stephen. Exhaustion had addled my mind but not his.

"Yes! Save a bit of everything. For bait. 'Tis too dark now to set them, but we can try at tomorrow's camp."

The snow continued through the night and the following day, and a north wind slowed our progress. Gradually, the lake narrowed, and the current increased.

"I think we're almost to the end of the lake, heading into the La Chute River. Probably best to put ashore near here, set up camp and the traps."

"Aye, aye, captain," Stephen said.

I glanced at the map again. "We should be coming to a massive rock wall, off to the port side, a sheer cliff."

In a few minutes, we reached the slab of granite towering over the lake. We paddled alongside the foot of the cliff that sheared into the water, offering no chance of going ashore. A few twisted trees clung to the rock face in desperation, rooting into cracks and crevices. I scouted the coast for a place to land and found it north of the giant rock face. The traps I planned to make, deadfall traps, required rocks. 'Twas a fair guess that when God's hand created such a cliff, he had left some smaller boulders lying about.

We put ashore on the south-curving end of a bay. We hauled the canoe onto the shore and carried it for about half an hour until I found the Indian trail Asserie had told us about. Even with the snow, I found it, for it had been there for a very long time. For centuries, he'd said. I shivered, henflesh prickling my skin, but not only from the cold. The Native tribes had been here long before the English or the French. This was their land. We were intruders.

Though it couldn't have been much later than two o'clock,

the winter shadows gave the feeling of dusk. Stephen dumped a few handfuls of snow into our kettle. Once it melted, he threw in the last of our corn and some dried fruit.

"While supper cooks, let's set those traps," I said.

I explained the types of branches we needed and sent Stephen off in search of those. Meantime, I surveyed the area for rocks. The heavier the rock, the larger the prey, and I did not fancy eating field mice, so we'd need to build the traps where we found the stones—no need to be hefting boulders about.

As I'd hoped, we had plenty of rocks to choose from. Beside a little clearing, I found a rectangular slab of granite larger than a slab of bacon that likely weighed more than a man. Our kill rock.

Stephen gathered a good-sized bundle of sturdy branches. I chose one as long and thick as my leg for the lever stick and tied the small toggle stick to it with the rope I'd brought. The Y-branch, the size of my arm, would be the fulcrum.

I placed a small, flat stone near the kill rock on a patch of frozen ground cleared of snow. Then, I set the fulcrum atop it and wedged the end of the lever in the Y-notch. Once I had the angles and measurements worked out to my liking, Stephen levered up the edge of the heavy kill rock. I jammed the fulcrum and a safety rock under the edge of it, steadying and balancing the weight until it was safe for him to let go.

I wrapped the cord with the toggle stick around the fulcrum, and then tucked the toggle stick under the rope to hold the tension. Stephen notched the end of a thin stick and jammed a few pieces of salt pork and cheese onto it. I rested the other end of that trigger stick atop the toggle stick, angled the bait end against the kill rock, and removed the safety rock with a flick of my knife handle.

We set up two more traps similarly, one near the first and the other close to the lake's edge. Stephen examined our labor.

"What do you think we'll catch?"

"I hope something furry," I said, "but it is hard to say. Fox? Muskrat?"

We settled ourselves by our fire, added more wood, and ate our samp with bread. The storm clouds cleared, and the sprinkling of stars glittered the sky like the gilded ceiling of the Merry King's palace.

"'Twill be a deep freeze tonight," Stephen said. "Best we make a decent shelter."

I chose a sheltered site for our camp, nestled on two sides by a rocky outcropping. Stephen and I took time to build a large and sturdy wigwam, digging a hole for our fire and spreading out branches for our beds of mats and blankets. I was cold beneath our two woolen blankets, even wearing my greatcoat atop my buff coat. I woke several times at night, shivering, to feed the fire. At some point, I was startled by a loud crash, a thin scream cut short, and hoped we'd caught something.

Stephen and I woke to the cold of a dead fire. He rekindled it, and we set out to check our traps. A dark mackerel sky shot through with ribbons of gold foretold both dawn and the impending storm.

"Muskrat!" I exclaimed, pulling on its tail as Stephen levered the kill rock we'd placed by the shore. "Big one."

"Good eating?" Stephen asked.

"Yes. I feared we'd get a mink or a skunk, but this fellow will be tasty."

I cleaned and skinned it, wishing we had salt so I could properly tan the hide. The pelt was rich, brown fur—not enough for a hat, but maybe a muff? We hacked the meat into pieces and put it in the pot with enough water to cover it. Then we spent an hour or two collecting as much dead wood as we could find and were able to haul back to our camp.

"I doubt we're going anywhere for a while," I said.

The wind moaned, and sleet sliced through the trees. "That storm Asserie warned of is upon us."

Chapter Fifty-Two
MARTHA

RICHELIEU RIVER, CANADA
WINTER

The world was frozen. We pushed, dragged, portaged, and paddled to the northernmost end of Lake Champlain. At the point where the lake emptied into the Richelieu River, we abandoned the canoes. The warriors dragged them up a snow-drifted hill and buried them under a latticework of branches. Ashpelon marked the spot with a tower of stones, to find the canoes in the spring when the snow melted and the river thawed.

To replace the canoes as a means of hauling our goods, the Native women laced watap and branches to make sleds, which they pulled behind them.

Every step was agony. The others felt it, too, but we dared not complain. Speaking of our torment would only anger our captors and dishearten our kin. Sharp splinters of pain in my toes and fingers traveled up my legs and arms, setting fire to my blood. My teeth rattled in my skull from shivering. I was so dizzy I used a stout branch for a walking stick and needed all my wits to keep my balance.

Ashpelon or Kòkòkòho jerked me to my feet if I stopped to rest. "Do not stop. Keep walking. If you cannot walk, we knock you on the head!"

They repeated the threat over and over, so it no longer had meaning. My little girls' noses and chins flushed red and cold, like frozen cranberries, so I wrapped their aprons around their faces until only their eyes showed. We carried the littlest ones —my Sally, Molly, Holly, and Daniel—and when they grew too heavy, the Natives pulled them in the sleds.

I did not think Sergeant Plympton was going to make it much farther. He'd lived three score years and ten and had wasted away from hunger so that he seemed but a walking skeleton. He suffered from the storms' bitter cold and from the darkness in his spirit over Sam's death. He blamed himself, and we couldn't convince him otherwise. Several times, I heard him mumbling incoherent words and sounds, and my slumber was broken more than once by the blood-curdling screams of his nightmares.

He stopped abruptly and glanced frantically around him, confused.

"Sergeant, here, come this way," I said.

"Where is he? Where did he go? I just saw him."

"Sergeant, he's not here. We need to keep walking. Put your hand on my shoulder. Lean on me."

"No, I want to stay. I will wait here for Sam."

It took both Kòkòkòho and me to get him moving again.

Thankfully, somebody killed a pair of river otters. Nobody spoke as we sat huddled around the fire that night. Grinding jaws, ripping flesh, and crunching bone rose above Nìbi Wàbà's melodic humming as she polished a tarnished kettle with a paste of salt and berries.

Sergeant Plympton sprang to his feet, hurling his piece of meat into the fire. "I will not eat the flesh of a child! I am not a savage!" His eyes stared glassily, and his breath came in short bursts. "'Twas in my dreams, and now it is here!" he cried.

Obadiah took Sergeant Plympton's arm and spoke close to his face. "Nothing is here but us and the fire."

"No, it is within me. Urging me to do unspeakable things!"

Ashpelon spoke in sharp whispers to Wanalancet and Nìbi Wàbà, pointing at Sergeant Plympton, the three arguing.

"What is the matter with the sergeant?" Mary asked me, her whisper sharp in my ear.

"He is freezing. When Ben first began trapping, Pynchon warned him about the cold. The cold can kill you, and it can also drive you mad. Trick you into seeing and hearing things that are not there."

"Sergeant Plympton," Obadiah said, "Come, move closer to the fire. Let me give you my coat—"

"No! You mean to burn me!"

"No, no, I mean no harm."

"Get away from me!" Sergeant Plympton swatted Obadiah away.

Ashpelon strode over, laid his palm on the older man's cheek, and barked a command to Nìbi Wàbà. She warmed cloths on the hot rocks by the fire, and placed them under his hat. She handed him a noggin of steaming otter broth to drink and put a bearskin around his shoulders. He flailed at her in vain.

Ashpelon asked her a question in Algonquian.

Nìbi Wàbà was silent. She rose and bent down by the fire, gazing at the bright copper kettle.

Ashpelon angrily repeated his words.

"Yes," she said softly, "I see it. Windigo."

If silence can grow even more hushed, it happened then. The Natives reacted to her words with terror, freezing like rabbits when a fox is near. The English did not dare to breathe, not understanding what this meant. My heart raced.

"What is 'Windigo'?" Hannah whispered to me.

"I have no idea, but look how frightened they are." I motioned to the Natives.

Ashpelon nodded, and Nìbi Wàbà threw the copper kettle, broth and all, into the roaring fire. We watched in confusion as the kettle glowed red hot in the flames.

Quintin addressed Ashpelon. "I will take him back to our wigwam. He will be better in the morning."

Ashpelon hesitated a moment, then shuddered. "Keep him warm. Do not let him out of your sight."

I grabbed my girls by the hands and stumbled back to our rough shelter, away from whatever it was that had plunged us all into a deeper darkness. I lay awake, worrying if the cold had driven Plympton mad or if he was perhaps bewitched. Mary, Hannah, and I stayed awake long after our children fell to slumbering, whispering tales of witchcraft in the flickering firelight.

The next day, Sergeant Plympton was worse. Hallucinations, Ben had called them, like a waking nightmare. Obadiah pulled Plympton on the sled, and the sergeant dozed fitfully, jerking awake to scream nonsensical words. It seemed he was no longer speaking English, his voice no longer his, but angry and loud.

"Hungry! Feed me! I'm freezing. I need food!" he cried, though he refused to eat when we brought him the little we had.

Several times, Ashpelon, Wanalancet, and Nìbi Wàbà spoke in Algonquian. I heard them say "Sergeant" in English and that strange word, "Windigo."

Ashpelon called a halt, and I prayed we'd finally reached Canada. It was mid-afternoon under a gray sky. We remained on the frozen Richelieu River, and I saw no dwellings, not even fur trappers' lodgings.

"Are we to Chambly?" I asked Quintin.

"No, Ashpelon said it is much farther, two or three more days."

"Are we camping here? Why is he stopping?"

"I do not know, but I find it troubling. The name that Nìbi Wàbà called Plympton yesterday. Windigo."

"What is that?"

"It is a spirit they fear," he said. "A cannibalistic demon."

"What will they do to him?" I asked.

Quintin only shrugged and shook his head.

The Natives built a mighty fire, but we did not make wigwams nor hang our cooking pots. They made a place for Sergeant Plympton by the fire and wrapped him in bear furs and deer hides, forcing him to drink hot water. Nìbi Wàbà and Neepânon took our children, built another fire some distance away from the first, and bade us follow. Mary went, and then Hannah. I refused. I was worried about Plympton.

Several times, Plympton rose to his feet, pointing at the fire, backing away from it in terror. When I moved to go to him, Kòkòkòho held me back. Quintin shook off Quequan and spoke a few words to Plympton before Ashpelon ordered him to stand back.

"Atian," Ashpelon said.

Atian walked slowly to the sachem. They spoke in Algonquian, and then Atian went to his wigwam and emerged with his gun. He loaded it and approached Obadiah Dickinson.

"Obadiah, help me with Sergeant Plympton," Atian said.

"What? No! What do you intend to do?" Obadiah cried.

"Now." Atian pointed his musket at Obadiah.

"He is an old man! He is sick!"

"No more talk. We go," Atian said.

Obadiah squatted beside Sergeant Plympton, spoke gently to him, and helped him to his feet. The sergeant looked about in confusion.

"Where are we going?"

"For a walk," Obadiah said.

"No!" I cried. "Ashpelon, what is this? Why?"

"We have no choice," Ashpelon said. "He endangers us all."

Atian and Obadiah led Sergeant Plympton away into the trees, and I remembered the morning Atian shot the first horse, the old mare. I rushed at Ashpelon and drew back my hand to strike him, but he caught me by the wrist and wrenched my arm behind my back.

"Stop," Ashpelon said.

He held me there, and I held my breath.

The gunshot echoed through the forest. I broke free of Ashpelon and ran to my girls.

Chapter Fifty-Three
ASHPELON

The Windigo took the sergeant when he, Stockwell, and the boy fell through the ice. I was not there. I was with the others. Stockwell did not see the Windigo. But some warriors said it clutched at their ankles as they struggled out of the icy water.

I think Sergeant Plympton felt its claws on him. Saw it pull Sam under the water and heard its growling and hissing. He watched it devour the boy. Afterward, the Windigo took Sergeant Plympton, filling him with the lake's dark, cold water. The water froze in his veins, and then the Windigo came to him in his dreams until Sergeant Plympton also became a Windigo.

Nìbi Wàbà is our shaman, and she told me it was so. It made her sad.

There is only one way to kill a Windigo. I chose Atian, for he is the strongest for obeying my orders, even when he does not like them. As I ordered, Atian shot the Sergeant through the heart, but the Windigo is not easily killed. So, we carried the sergeant's body to the fire. In the flames, the icy frozen heart of the Windigo melted, banishing it forever.

Or so we have been taught.

Chapter Fifty-Four

BEN

A snowdrift blocked the exit from our shelter.

"As I live and breathe!" Stephen said.

"Just as well our fire died out. Smoky enough in here as it is."

It was slow work digging our way out with only the tomahawk, but we finally cleared the way. Outside, the snow fell heavily, the wind picking up quickly. We hastened to reset the traps, took care of business, and boiled water to cook the last of the muskrat. Huge swells and ragged layers of deep gray clouds pressed on us, extinguishing the sun and any trace of its heat or light. I wrapped my woolen scarf around my face and neck to cover all but my eyes. Despite my hat and great coat, I shivered, my teeth chattering.

The remains of the muskrat had kept well in the cold, and we were grateful to have stew to eat. Even with our entry flap tied closed, the wind snuck in, wrestling with our fire, the flames fighting for life.

"A precarious place to ride out a blizzard," Stephen said.

"The best we've got. This is the place Asserie called tekon-taró: *ken*—'the place between two waters.' Look, he drew a picture of us carrying the canoe." I showed Stephen the map, pointing at the two stick figures.

"That's us?" Stephen laughed. "And what is that? An arrow and a gun?" he asked, pointing to the symbols, then handing the map back to me.

"It must be the great battle Asserie spoke of between the French and Iroquois. Champlain fought in it."

"We have not prayed in a while," Stephen said, staring into the sputtering fire.

"A good time to do so," I agreed. "Pray we do not freeze to death."

We bowed our heads in silence. I prayed for the strength to continue and for Martha and my girls to live. When Stephen raised his head and spoke, his voice quavered.

"How are you so sure we will find them?"

I stared into the fire, thinking of Martha's smile and my children's laughter. "I'm confident I know the Algonquian tribes, how they think, what they want. I have spent years amongst them, trading and negotiating, tracking and fighting. Benoni Stebbins said they resolved to sell the captives to the French, which makes sense."

"And you think we will find them near the French forts on the Richelieu River?"

"Yes, Fort Chambly. Or farther north, Fort Saurel."

Stephen nodded, took a deep breath and spoke, his voice breaking. "I miss Hannah so much."

"Undoubtedly. You are newly married. To have just joined with her, and now to lose her . . ." As I spoke, I missed Martha with all the fullness of our seven years. Love is not measured by time.

"Did you know that her first husband, Samuel, was cruel to her? I do not know if she shared her trials with Martha."

"I've naught heard of it. But my wife can keep a confidence."

"Hannah was broken when we met. Fragile and melancholy, but she put her faith in me. She said I made her feel safe. I feel I've betrayed her."

"We will get her back. All of them," I promised. I forced down the lump rising in my throat and summoned a hearty tone. A subterfuge at which I excelled.

Such a storm I had never seen nor ever hoped to see again. 'Twas not so much the wind, snow, or freezing cold, though there was all of that. The storm's strength lay in its unrelenting determination to stop us in our tracks—a final test, I think, of our faith in ourselves and our God.

All we could do was endure it—keep the fire burning, sip hot melted snow, talk, and sleep. The last of Father Jean's pemmican and dried pumpkin gave us something to chew on, though we suffered hunger, nevertheless. We checked the traps when we dared, taking turns venturing into the blinding snow and bitter cold. Nothing. The forest creatures were snugly tucked away inside burrows, caves, and hollow trees, waiting out the storm as we were. Our hunger increased until it was difficult to think.

I spent much of the time, whether awake or asleep, dreaming of Martha. I longed for her with a deep, wild passion that had not consumed me in years, if ever. Her touch, her voice, her laughter, the light in her eyes, the taste of her mouth, the embrace of her limbs wrapped 'round me in our coupling. More than love or lust, it was a burning hunger as strong as my will to live.

The storm weakened on the eighth day. The wind died, and the snow turned to sleet. Hoping to gain some distance, we broke camp and struggled to find our way, relying upon the compass my cousin John had gifted me. 'Twas still incredibly cold, and we were weakened from hunger. I looked for the Natives' magic trees and found none, but where the path seemed to fork and my map failed me, we came upon a pillar of rock. 'Twas taller than a man and too broad to wrap my arms around, and someone had carved into its smooth gray surface images so worn by time they were indecipherable. If it was a trail marker, I was unsure how to read it, but we camped there and the next morning turned to the east, traveling downhill.

At last, we found the frozen La Chute River and followed it to Lake Champlain. At first sight, the lake was all black ice and snow, but Asserie's map showed it would increase in breadth as we traveled north upon it. I was deeply grateful to finally reach it, yet at the same time, disheartened. We still had such a long way to travel. And winter was not finished with us yet.

Chapter Fifty-Five

MARTHA

CANADA
WANING SNOW MOON

"No! Why are you separating us?" Hannah cried.

Mattagehan pushed Hannah ahead of him up the river, as Animosh dragged Sammy and Holly in a different direction. Hannah struggled against her captor, and he threw her to the ground.

"Stop, or I will knock you on the head!" he shouted, raising the butt end of his musket in warning.

"Hannah, do not fight them, please!" I cried, "Somehow, God will save us. Have faith!"

Hannah looked at her children and gave them a little wave. Holly and Sam were crying, causing Animosh to shout at them, which silenced Sam but set Holly to wailing all the louder.

They were splitting us up again, as they had the first week, dividing us amongst our captors. Against all reason, I had almost forgotten we were not part of their band, but prisoners held against our will and on our way to be sold into servitude.

Perhaps Neepânon had some compassion for Mary, for she

let her keep Nate in her arms when she and her husband Wekoñtam led them away, along with Abby, Abigail, and Matt Kellogg.

Obadiah Dickinson and his son Daniel went with their master Pomantam and the young woman, Uppeshoii. Tohkoi and Atian roughly grabbed Quintin Stockwell. Mehtuk took Sarah and Noah Coleman.

Not knowing my fate, I drew Mary close, gripped Mattie's hand, and pressed Sally to my bosom.

"Where are you taking the children?" I asked Ashpelon.

"To keep, to sell. They go with those who captured them, those who own them."

"Own them? None of us belong to you! Isn't it enough for the orphaned to never see their parents again? Parents you killed?" I turned my back to him, weeping.

"Quiet!" Ashpelon said. "Or we will take away your children!"

"Mommy, don't cry," Mary said.

Nìbi Wàbà laid her hand on my shoulder. "They'll find them nice families, who will—"

I shrugged her off. "No! I hate you! I hate all of you!"

Nìbi Wàbà shoved me. "I have protected you many times! When they wanted to kill you, I told them no! I cared for Molly when she was ill, though some spoke of knocking her on the head! Silence!"

I softened my rage to a smoldering ember, ready to flare up again in an instant. It was true that, at least for now, I had my daughters.

"Bye, friends," Sally said, waving to the children.

Anguish tore from my heart, and tears streamed down my face.

I pressed my hand to my mouth to stifle my sobs.

"Will we see them later?" Mary asked me.

"I do not know, love. I pray so," I whispered.

The rest of Ashpelon's warriors and most of Wanalancet's

people divided up. Two warriors joined our party, Kenompāe and another whose name I did not know. Wanalancet himself set off with most of his Wachusett clan. He crossed the river to the eastern side and the rest of us, though separated, headed northward. I was puzzled why he chose a different way, but I would have rather had my tongue cut out than ask the question of my captors.

I never wished to speak to either of them again.

I had feared this separation from my friends, and now it had come to pass. This Nipmuc tribe had killed our kin at Hatfield, captured us, staked us down in the rain, threatened and struck us, and murdered Sergeant Plympton. How could I have trusted they might be merciful? How had I believed Ben would remain undaunted by wilderness, distance, or winter, guided by the hand of God, able to save us? In desperation more than faith, I whispered a prayer as we marched through the snow.

"O Lord, whose power is infinite and wisdom infallible, Let us dwell in Your shadow, in safe protection from the arrow that flies by day, the pestilence that walks in darkness, the fear of death. Strengthen us by Your Spirit. Amen."

I tried my best to cast off my despair for the sake of my girls. Somehow, in his benevolence, God had seen that they were not taken from me. Not yet. I carried each of them in turn whilst the others rode in the sled or trudged by my side. Nìbi Wàbà and Ashpelon wisely plodded along in silence.

A familiar bird song, a string of clear down-slurred whistles ending in a trill, erupted from beside the trail.

"Look, Mama, red birdies!" Sally called, pointing to the trees.

A flock of cardinals hopped and fluttered amongst the pine boughs.

"Yes, Sally, they are beautiful," I said.

"I want to see Abby and Sarah, not foolish birds," Mattie said, pouting. Never one to hide her feelings, that one.

"Mattie, let Sally have her simple joys," I chastened.

"But where are they taking our friends?" Mattie asked.

"I do not know."

"Is it God's will?"

"Yes."

"But I miss them!"

"As do I." I squeezed her hand. Her soft little mitten was as delicate as a kitten's paw.

Mattie scrunched up her face and shook her little head, tears creeping down hollowed cheeks that had once been as rosy and round as apples.

I supposed with only Ashpelon and two warriors, we wouldn't eat until we reached the French fort, however far away it was. I prayed the French would take pity on us, feed and clothe us, and bind our wounds before they set us to work in their houses, gardens, or barns.

I had my girls, so I could endure this, but I did not trust they'd remain with me. Our captors were often capricious. If they had a rhyme or reason for anything they did, I often failed to comprehend it.

The French would want us to convert. To be rebaptized Catholics. To learn their language, as the Algonquians had. Changing us, as John Elliot did the Natick Natives, teaching them English and Puritan ways. Would we, the Puritan English captives, be pale-skinned heathen in the eyes of the Catholic French?

If Ben was coming, he was too late. Unless he'd brought an army or a king's ransom, the Algonquians and the French would fight to keep us. None of us could claim the value of Mary Rowlandson, the wife of a wealthy minister in Lancaster. We were not worth the cost. Not to Hatfield or the colony.

I supposed all my husband had to bargain with was love.

Chapter Fifty-Six
BEN

The storm had frozen the lake solid at the edges. Farther out—where it was not solid black, but blue—'twas only slush. I used the oar handle to test it and prayed not to hear the splintering crackle warning of impending doom.

We carried our canoe and trod lightly at the lake's edge when it was too frozen to paddle. When the lake water allowed, we forced the prow through slushy ice with our oars. Neither was ideal, but either was easier than struggling on foot through the snow.

Lake Champlain was different from Lake George. I knew it was longer, broader, islands like a peninsula dividing it in half, Iroquois to the west, Algonquian to the east. Yet when we started upon it, at the southern end, it was no farther from shore to shore than Lake George. The mood of this lake was different, though. Perhaps my fears were altering my senses, but it seemed barren and desolate. The flat, snow-covered land vanished into the gray sky with no mountains to embrace us.

"Bit of a dismal place, isn't it?" I asked. "No wonder we're the first Englishmen to see it."

"Are we?"

"Well, no, I suppose our wives and children may have seen it before us if they passed this way."

"Do you see any traces of them?"

"No." I adjusted my hold on the canoe.

"Blame the desolation on the Crone of Beare," Stephen said.

"You mentioned her before."

"Yes, The Goddess of Winter. A legend from my Irish mama."

"Pray, tell. I like a good story."

We carried our canoe on our shoulders, and it muffled his voice, making it echo within the birch bark.

"*Cailleach*, the Crone of Beare, has many faces, many names, but the way I heard it, she has two sides," Stephen began. "One side, the one we see now, is the Goddess of Winter, reborn every *Samhain*—"

"*Samhain*? All Hallows Eve?" I asked.

"Aye. This isn't a godly tale, Ben. So, on October 31st, she leaves her home in the mountains and walks across the land, bringing winter storms, ice, snow, and death. Some say she is the daughter of *Grianan*, the little winter sun."

Stephen paused to adjust his hold on the canoe.

"There are two suns in this legend?" I asked.

"Old Celtic calendar. The Big Sun returns on *Beltane*, May Day."

"And the crone has two sides?"

"She can change from a terrifying hag in the winter to a beautiful young maiden in the summer."

"Hmmm. Go on."

"So, in the winter, she is armed with a *slachdan*, a powerful wand, which she uses to shape the land and control the weather. When she hurls her wand, she creates rocks in Ireland and rearranges the coasts of Scotland."

"And here?"

"I'm not sure, but it is said she has existed for eternity, linked not only with winter but also rivers, lakes, oceans, and mountains. She rides on the backs of wolves or reindeer. Some say she's also the goddess of the hunt."

"What does she look like? You called her a terrifying hag."

"That's the droll part—or horrific—depending on your nerve. She is a blue-black giantess, with two faces; one looking into the world of the living and the other to the dead, and her blue mouth shows fangs like a boar's."

I stopped and looked back at him. "Thank you, Stephen. I will thank you again when I wake tonight screaming from nightmares."

Our night passed uneventfully, disturbed only by the thrumming and growling of the lake ice. I remembered no nightmares upon waking. The fair weather held—if by fair, one settles for enough sunlight to discern day from night, and the bitter wind blowing at less than gale force. We fished and hunted to no avail and finished every scrap of dried corn and pemmican. I worried we might succumb to hunger and cold before making it off this massive block of ice. Our fingers and toes were hot and numb with frostbite, our eyes tearing, our noses running and freezing on our whiskers.

On our fourth day on the lake, we came upon a wigwam. We'd not seen any Native people, but this looked Mahican made, and it made sense to make camp there. Thanks to Stephen's Winter Goddess, the daylight hours had dwindled, and we spent far more time by the light of the fire than that of the sun.

Inside the wigwam was a dead fire, cold for many weeks,

but someone had left behind a satchel. Opening it, we rejoiced to find a flask half-full of brandy and a half dozen biscuits, frozen but fresh smelling once we thawed them on the fire.

"I needed this," I took a swig and passed the flask to Stephen.

"Warms the blood."

"Calms the spirit."

We slept better that night than in many, and though dawn was only a glimmer amongst the shadows, I awoke refreshed. I'd hoped to travel a fair distance that day, and we started off portaging on thin but solid lake ice. Presently, to our frustration, the rising sun melted the ice just enough to make it treacherous yet not enough to pass in our canoe. Quite a lot of snow had fallen the night before, so walking seemed foolhardy.

We found a spot to rest beneath the trees beside a jumble of boulders and small slides of rock, undoubtedly cast there by the Irish Crone of Beare. We sat and talked of idle matters. Fond childhood memories, people we'd met on this journey, the cobbler's trade, England and Ireland—anything to take our minds off our impotence.

"Soon 'twill be Christmas. And then Saint Stephen's Day," Stephen said, unfolding a leaf of paper. He kept a calendar, admittedly a wise idea.

"You have your own pagan day?"

"Catholic, Ben. Mama named me after him. The young men in her village called it Wren Day."

"Wren? Like the bird?"

"Yes. A gang of lads found a wild wren and tormented the poor thing with stones until they killed it. After that, they tied it atop a pole decorated with ribbons. The older lads disguised themselves behind straw masks or blackened their faces with coal and carried the wren from house to house. At each house, they sang a song about the wren."

"Dear Lord, you aren't going to sing it, are you?" I asked, laughing.

Stephen laughed. "I would, if you'd pay me. The villagers would pay the lads for their songs. Or throw cold pea soup at them, if they were that sort."

"What did they do with the money?"

"They used it to hold a dance for the entire village."

"I suppose I can understand how, in a country haunted by the Crone of Beare, you'd want some frivolous and diverting traditions, even if they did involve drunkenness and dead birds."

There was a rustle in an old oak tree a stone's throw away. Stephen and I both reached for our guns. Something moved in the waning light, but in the brief time it took me to prime and cock my pistol, the rustling ceased.

"Indians?" Stephen asked.

"More likely, raccoons," I said, yet I approached the tree cautiously.

I heard skittering and scratching above my head, a great chirping and commotion as three raccoons scrambled out of the hollow tree. I dispatched one with the butt end of my gun, but the other two escaped.

"Dinner!" I cried, carrying the raccoon to our fire by his striped tail.

"I've never had raccoon," Stephen said. "Is it tasty as the muskrat was?"

"Better, more like beef. It does need to spend some time on the fire, or it is bitter."

"Raccoon for breakfast it is," he said and helped me skin it.

Chapter Fifty-Seven
MARTHA

RICHELIEU RIVER, CANADA
NEW MOON

We followed the river's west bank. Ashpelon seemed in no haste now that we'd reached Canada, and he let me set the pace. With my baby coming within a month, I had to move softly so as not to slip, and stopped to "gaze upon a rose" every hour or two. I wore my loosely laced waistcoat and apron high and foolishly longed for a bedgown.

We traveled only a few hours each day. There was scant sunlight, and I was exhausted from hunger, cold, and my condition. At each camp, we built two small wigwams; one for Nìbi Wàbà, my girls, and me, and the other for Ashpelon, Kenompāe, and a warrior whose name I learned was Mooi. My loneliness slowly overcame my anger, and I conversed with the Natives again, to the extent their English allowed.

Fort St. Louis at Chambly was situated below cascading falls, its French flag fluttering above a tall wooden stockade. A French soldier in a brown coat, hat, and full armament guarded the gate. The sight filled me with hope—at last, a

Christian outpost. As we approached, the soldier raised his musket to his shoulder.

"*Indiquez votre identité et la raison du voyage,*" the soldier ordered.

I was surprised to comprehend a few words, some sounding similar to English. He was demanding to know who we were and why we were here.

Ashpelon responded in an equally confident tone. "*Je m'ap-pelle Ashpelon, un chef algonquien. J'ai des prisonniers anglais à vendre.*"

"*Il y avait d'autres membres de votre compagnie ici hier. Un kilomètre de plus, il y a un petit village,*" the soldier said, lowering his gun.

Other members? My pulse quickened in hopes Hannah might be found not far off.

Ashpelon spoke French. I do not know why that surprised me; I suppose because I could not. It made sense, as he was an Algonquian with ties to Canada, and in light of his plans for us from the beginning.

They exchanged a few more words, and we continued onwards. Past the fort, we came upon a cluster of small houses. Most were but one story, built of logs, though two were of river stone and half-timbered. Smoke drifted from the chimneys, and I wept to see Christian homes again. Homes that remained in place through the seasons.

The village gave way to scattered farms. An elderly couple offered Ashpelon a bottle of rum and a Spanish dollar for us, but he refused.

"How much are we worth to you?" I asked, hoping the price was reasonable but not insulting.

"A woman of intelligence with child? Three young girls? Much."

I smiled at the comforting scent of stews and soups cooking, the soft mooing of a cow in a barn, and the dark lacework of branches in a snowy apple orchard. I was eager to return to this familiar life. A farmer brandishing a gun halted us, and he and Ashpelon again held a conversation in French.

"Mommy, are we going to stay here?" Mattie asked.

"I do not know, love. I hope so."

The man approached, smiled at me, but shook his head.

He and Ashpelon spoke for a few minutes more.

"He cannot afford my price for you and the girls," Ashpelon said. "We will ask again in Saurel. But he sees you are to have a baby and wants to bring us some food."

"*Merci, monsieur*," I said, using the only French I knew.

The man went to his house made of stone, and in a few minutes, he and his young wife returned. She murmured words of comfort, laid her hand gently on my belly, clucked her tongue, and glared at Ashpelon. Gently, she wrapped a blanket around my shoulders and handed me a basket with a linen cloth. I smelled freshly baked bread, ripe cheese, and apples. She bent and gave each of my girls a small piece of maple candy.

"*Merci, madame, merci*," I said to her.

The French couple bade us sit on their stoop and eat, and our captors hovered nearby. My girls and I devoured one of the two loaves, half the small wheel of cheese, and all the crimson apples. The farmer's wife handed us each a cup of hot tea, and in my gratitude for its warmth, I burned my tongue, unable to wait until it cooled.

We pushed on through more wilderness. I insisted my girls ride upon the sled whilst I trudged atop the snow with the cumbersome snowshoes. At times, my womb clenched like a fist, a sharp pain. I prayed my babe would wait until we reached someplace safe and warm.

On the third day, we came to a cluster of wigwams near the river, a fire burning in their midst. What Natives were these?

"Mommy, it is Holly and Sammy!" Mattie cried, breaking free of my grasp on her hand.

"Wait, Mattie!" I cried as she ran toward the camp.

But it *was* Holly and Sammy. And Hannah.

"Hannah!"

We stumbled toward each other and embraced. I squeezed her tight, not wanting to let go of her warmth. I stepped back and smiled at the bloom upon her cheeks.

"How long have you been here?"

"About a week. The Indians spoke to some French nearby, and none could afford us but said they'd raise the money in haste. So here we wait," she said.

Ashpelon strode into the camp and spoke to the Natives. They kept glancing our way. All three of my girls ran off with Hannah's children, and I tried to keep them in sight.

"Do you know anything about the others?" I asked as we walked farther into the camp.

"We crossed paths. I think they are not far off," she said. "I still do not know whether they will resolve to sell or keep me. For now, they have given me back my children, so I am blessed."

"I feared I'd never see you again once they separated us. 'Tis so good to see you safe."

One of the Native women called to Hannah. She embraced me again and hurried away. I called back my children, and they returned somewhat reluctantly.

I longed to spend the night here, but Ashpelon insisted we continue.

My heart was lighter now, knowing Hannah and her children were alive and well, though I worried over Mary and the rest. I eagerly looked forward to Saurel, praying the other captives were there. Ashpelon let me ride upon the sled when I grew tired and pulled me himself, no doubt because he knew he'd get a better price for us if the girls and I appeared well-tended.

When we stopped so I might "gaze upon a rose," I asked him again about the orphans. "Your people killed their mothers, so Hannah, Mary, and I watched over them. We could do that still."

Ashpelon shook his head. "Your husband, your town, owes us a debt," he said. There was sadness in his voice, in his eyes.

I glared at him but remained silent.

Ashpelon clenched his jaw and lowered his eyebrows. I waited for him to compose himself.

"Your husband led attacks against my people," he said.

"He is a scout, a guide, not a leader," I said, realizing I was mincing words.

"You deny he played a part in killing many?"

"In retaliation for your attacks upon us!" I cried. My voice was righteous. My conviction wavered.

Ashpelon pounded his fist into the palm of his hand. I trembled but stood my ground.

"You English think we have no rights, no feelings, yet do not look at your own reflections. Yes, my band stole your cattle —because they trampled our corn, and we were starving! Now that you have known hunger, can you not understand?"

"'Twas not only that, but —"

"But to avenge the theft of your animals, your men massacred us. Hundreds of our people at Peskeompskut. Hundreds! Women and children!"

His words broke through. I finally believed him. Women and children. I choked back a sob.

I asked then, even though the truth dawned.

"And how will our orphaned children repay our debt to you?"

"We are thinking of keeping them."

"No! You cannot!"

"We can. They will be happy with us."

"But they are English, they—"

"We will speak no more of it," Ashpelon said, and walked away. I stood there seething with anger. It infuriated me he had the power to end every one of our conversations.

After three more days, we reached Fort Richelieu at Saurel, situated on a hill overlooking the rivers and a lake Ashpelon called *Lac de Saint Pierre*. We climbed to an earthen rampart, where two soldiers stopped us at the main gate.

Again, a discourse in French. Apparently, the guards ordered Kòkòkòho, Keompae, and Nìbi Wàbà to remain out o' doors, before opening the gate and escorting the rest of us to the gallery.

"We are meeting with Captain Pierre de Saurel himself," Ashpelon boasted.

I prayed fervently that I would finally have a home beyond the threat of tomahawk and starvation.

The handsome captain walked briskly into the room. He wore a russet coat with many buttons, the gray lining showing in his deep upturned cuffs. Black and gold ribbons adorned his gray hat and the shoulders of his coat, and matching ribbons tied his breech cuffs and boots. A white sash swept diagonally from his right shoulder to his waist. His brown periwig fell to his shoulders, and his mustache was tinged with gray.

"Ashpelon." He nodded, ribbons fluttering.

"Captain." Ashpelon bowed.

How did these two know each other? Furs? Missionaries? War?

"Who have we here?" de Saurel asked in English, nodding to me and bending down to see my girls, his gloved hands on his knees.

"English," Ashpelon said, "captives taken in battle. We have come a long way and hope this woman and her daughters would make suitable servants for one of your people."

Ashpelon's lie angered me. Taken in battle? Hardly. Although I supposed we were prisoners of war. I bit my lower lip, squeezed Mattie's hand, tightened my hold on Sally, and tried to smile. There were worse fates than being a servant to a French captain's family.

"I'm certain they would, but you have caught me at a poor time for trading. France is for once at peace with the Algonquian and Iroquois tribes, the Mahicans, and the English. My charge is maintaining that peace. I doubt taking English captives into servitude would better our cause," said the captain. "How many captives do you have?"

"Eighteen. Three women, two men, the rest children, but—"

"Is there a search party? A ransom?"

"No," Ashpelon replied.

Another half-truth.

"Eighteen. Hmmm."

"I am only concerned with selling these four," Ashpelon said.

Five, I thought, feeling a kick.

The captain turned to me. "Where is your town, madame?"

"Hatfield. On the Connecticut River, in Massachusetts Bay Colony," I said.

"You have come so far. You must be courageous and exhausted."

I nodded.

"You will find most French are kind. We are Catholic, though. There is a mission here, within the fort. Your new master will expect you and your girls to be baptized as Catholic if you wish to have any rights as citizens of New France."

I did not know what to say. I couldn't imagine denouncing my faith and taking on the vanities of the Catholic Church, which was far more sullied by idolatry and indolence than the Church of England.

He turned to go, then stopped.

"What is your name, madame?"

"Goodwife Martha Waite."

He raised his brows in surprise. "Waite? I recall the name from years ago. Was your husband in the fur trade?"

The captain knew both Ashpelon and Ben. It seemed impossible.

"He never traveled to Canada," I said.

"No? But I have been to both Albany and Springfield."

I nodded. "My husband and I met in Springfield."

He stroked his jaw, thinking. "What did you do before, in your town? Hatfield?"

"Cooked, cleaned, and tended the garden, the poultry, sheep, and cows. Spun wool, knitted, sewed, and made soap. Canned and dried the harvest. I read my Bible and kept the Sabbath. Cared for our three children, and taught my oldest to read," I said, squeezing Mary's hand.

"You can read, madame?" Captain Saurel gave me another appraising, though not unkind, gaze. I nodded.

"Come sit in my office," he said, motioning us to follow.

I sat with Mattie and Mary upon an upholstered settee, holding Sally in my lap, and the captain sat behind his desk. Ashpelon warmed his hands by the fire burning in an iron stove. I gazed in curiosity at maps of New France and New England hanging upon the walls. The captain cleared his throat, leaned forward, and steepled his fingers in front of him.

"I was granted a seigneury: a large stone farmhouse, fertile fields, and orchards. I hold a high position with the Comte de Frontenac. I am descended from French nobility," de Saurel said, not in a boastful manner, only stating his value as I had done.

"I married my wife, Catherine, nine years ago. She is a good woman, a good wife. However, the Lord has not seen fit to bless us with children. She is lonely, and I am growing old."

I held my breath, hoping this was leading to my salvation.

"We have two men to work our farm, but I think my wife

might welcome the help and company of a young, intelligent woman such as yourself, Madame Waite," de Saurel said, smiling at me, "and she would adore your three girls," he paused and shot Ashpelon a look, "and the new baby on the way."

I waited, knowing this decision was not mine but his and Ashpelon's. Captain de Saurel stood and turned to Ashpelon.

"Ashpelon, I will pay her ransom. She and her children will live with my wife and me in our home," de Saurel said, and then turned to me. "Madame, you will be employed as our servant, as will your daughters when they are older. If you convert to Catholicism, you will become a citizen of Canada. You will have your own room and board, and your daughters will be free to marry."

It did not seem a horrible fate. But I'd be forced to relinquish my faith, and never be able to return home. What if Ben came for me at last? Would the captain release me? Could I bear a life without Ben's love?

Sally squirmed in my lap, and I handed her the last piece of candy the farmer's wife had given us.

"I have French Louis XIV sol pieces, Spanish dollars, wampum, furs. What was your English ransom demand?" the captain asked Ashpelon.

It was as if I weren't there or was but a horse at the market. Would they check my teeth to judge my age?

"Ten pounds each," Ashpelon said. He'd raised our price.

"I will give you the equivalent of twelve pounds each, including the child she is carrying, but in exchange for my largesse, you must swear an oath to keep the rest of your captives in good health and to find them homes here, in my seigneury," de Saurel said. "Do not take them farther north."

Bless you, captain, for adding those conditions.

"Sixty pounds?" Ashpelon pretended to consider this. "I will need to talk to the others, without, so they can help ensure the bargain."

"Madame Waite and her girls stay here with me until you return," the captain said.

"But—"

"Those are my terms."

Ashpelon nodded, took one last look at my girls and me, and left.

"Now, Madame Waite, it is Christmas! Let me get you and your children some of our holiday cake, *Buche de Noel*, and some tea, perhaps?" He smiled kindly at us and rang a small brass bell.

I smiled back at him.

"Yes, please."

Chapter Fifty-Eight

BEN

❧

CANADA
DECEMBER/JANUARY

"The Richelieu River at last!" I exclaimed. "And it is the farthest landmark our little map describes. Asserie writes, 'From here, follow the river.'"

It had been a slow two days' journey through the deep snow, leaving Lake Champlain behind us.

"Seems frozen solid, at least alongst the banks," Stephen said. He heaved a large stone at the glassy surface, which skipped across with a chirping sound.

"Time to abandon our canoe, no point lugging it with us anymore." I laid it upside down in the snow beside our trail.

"Perhaps someone else can use it?"

"I hope so. 'Tis beautifully made."

I wondered if Asserie might someday travel this far and find his canoe.

'Twas flat land, easy to travel, but it still took us three days to reach Chambly. Packs of wolves roamed the woods, howling at night. Rattle mice swooped low, catching invisible bugs. The blue of the sky was a dim memory, hidden behind mountains of clouds. No French forts, no farms, not even a wigwam to be found. The river ice thinned as the river's speed increased alongst its downward course, so we walked upon the snowy banks of the western shore until we came to the end of the rapids, where the Richelieu River widened into a pond.

Fort St. Louis at Chambly was impressive; strongly built, surrounded by palisades three times as tall as a man and a crowstep on three sides. We approached the soldier who guarded the gate.

"*Qui va là?*" he asked, raising his gun once we came within shouting distance.

"*Messieurs Waite et Jennings, pour parler au capitaine, s'il vous plaît?*"

"*Pourquoi?*"

"*Nous recherchons nos families,*" I hoped my French was correct.

"English women and infants?" the guard asked. "With Indians?"

"Yes!" I cried. "You speak English!"

"A bit. Two companies. Here, a week past. They went north to the village."

If it had been possible to run in the deep snow, we would have. As it was, we came upon the village in a quarter of an hour and began knocking on doors. An older man and his wife said they'd tried to buy a woman and her three daughters, but the Indian refused.

My heart pounded with hope and excitement, and I wept in relief and joy.

Other people we encountered also said they had seen *un ou deux compagnies d' Amérindiens* and English. The size of the companies and the number of Natives and English varied in the telling. Many had refused to open their doors to strangers, but one man said he'd seen them at the farmhouse of Monsieur and Madame Garron. He pointed out the way.

I knocked on the weathered oaken door, and a young

woman greeted me. In my rusty French, I inquired about my family. Had she seen them?

"*Oui, une femme enceinte et trois filles,*" she said, inviting us inside.

"Martha and my girls were here! They're alive!"

"Praise be to God!" Stephen said, embracing me.

I collapsed with relief and exhaustion into the nearest chair.

I asked her how they seemed. She said cold and hungry, so she gave them food, tea, and a blanket. She did not know where they had gone, but they were heading north, perhaps to Saurel? I was closer to them than I'd been in months.

"*Merci, Madame, merci,*" I said to her.

"Ben, ask about Hannah and my children," Stephen said.

"*Avez-vous vu d'autres anglais?*"

She shook her head no.

Stephen hung his head, his eyes downcast as we walked away.

"They split into several parties. Hers may just have taken a different path or stopped at different places," I said, hoping to reassure him.

"Maybe the other bank of the river?" he asked hopefully.

"Perhaps. I think Saurel lies on the other side, so we'll need to find a place to cross at any rate."

'Twas bitterly cold when the sun set, and we spent the night in a ramshackle trappers' hut. In the morning, we found a narrow stretch of the river frozen solid from bank to bank. We crossed to the eastern shore, where I finally saw in the snow what I'd been seeking for days.

"Stephen, look! Footprints, and marks from sled runners!"

I let out a whoop of joy to know I was so close to finding them, that I'd soon hold Martha in my arms and embrace my girls.

All day, we tracked them, barely stopping to rest. Deep moccasin footprints, larger but even fainter snowshoe tracks, the sharp ribbons from the sled. Even one spot of snow tinged slightly yellow, making me smile. My dear pregnant wife and her frequent need to relieve herself.

At twilight, we found an abandoned Nipmuc camp, and signs that it was used only a day or so before. Bewitching, the twists of time and fate leading us here in the footsteps of our loved ones. I could almost see my wife and children in the light of the fire or the shadows cast by the waxing crescent moon amongst the trees.

Exhausted, we built a fire, crawled inside a battered wigwam, and tried to sleep.

The Natives had no idea we pursued them, I was confident, for they'd made no attempt to hide their passage. Stephen's spirits increased when we found more footprints of all sizes and marks from the runners of several sleds. I prayed it wouldn't snow or thaw so we could continue tracking them. Stephen and I were bursting with excitement, but trepidation kept our expectations in check. While the certainty of finding our loved ones increased, the intricacies of their redemption weighed more heavily.

Much remained unknown. Would we find all the captives? Had any met with harm? If they'd been separated, could we reunite them? What if they had already been sold to the French? Was a letter of credit worth more than the paper it was written on, or would we need to draw arms against the Natives, or find our payment refused by the French? My thoughts whirled like a tornado on a stormy sea until I finally fell asleep.

We woke at dawn and broke camp. No more than a couple of hours passed before we stumbled upon an inhabited Nipmuc camp. In a clearing beside the riverbank, smoke came from the hole in a wigwam's roof. We approached almost sound-lessly, guns primed, cocked, and ready.

Two warriors appeared, also brandishing weapons.

"Keep your gun on them. I'm going to lower mine," I told Stephen. I lowered my gun slowly and set it at my feet.

"*Eshqua? Mukkoies?*" I asked. Woman? Children?

The warriors looked at each other. The taller one asked, "You English?"

"Yes."

"*Nummagumuu. Wuttinnumin.* French."

I told Stephen, "He says they sold them as servants to the French."

"How many?"

An Indian held up three fingers. "One *Eshqua*, two *Mukkoies*."

"One woman and two children—your family, Stephen!"

"Or Mary Foote's," Stephen said, his voice flat.

Both women were dark-haired, each with a daughter and son. But Hannah was taller by far.

"Tall? *Eshqua Qunnuhquitugk?*" I asked. Was the woman like a tall tree?

"*Nukkies.*" Yes.

"He said the woman was tall, Stephen," I said excitedly, hoping he'd take hope.

"*Tonnoh?*" I asked.

The Indian pointed northward. "Hour. *Wetu. Eglisse.*"

A house only an hour from here, near a church. Surpris-ingly, they let us pass.

We spied the wooden spire and cross of the church first. The wooden farmhouse sat on a slope above the river, smoke rising from the chimney into the gray sky, a stone barn beside it. We had eight guilders and the raccoon and muskrat pelts remaining between us. A farmer emerged from the barn and paused when he saw us.

In French, I told him our story. He said he'd paid two

guilders, a bottle of brandy, a pocket watch, and some farm tools for Hannah and her children. He and his wife had two sons to work their farm but wanted someone to help with the house. He was disappointed, but of course, we had come so far, and of course, it was the Lord's wish to reunite them with their husband and father. He accepted two guilders and the muskrat pelt.

We were halfway from the barn to the house when Hannah opened the door. Stephen ran to her and took her in his arms. By the time I reached them, he was embracing Holly and Sammy, and the farmer's wife was bidding us to come inside, out of the cold.

The story tumbled from Hannah, the most recent events first. Monsieur et Madame Dubois had traded for Hannah, and when she'd told them of her boy and girl, they insisted her captors bring them, too. Hannah last saw Martha and my girls a few days ago at the Nipmuc camp. They were with the sachem, Ashpelon, a Native woman, and two warriors heading north. She broke the news to us of the deaths of Sergeant Plympton, Sam Russell, and little Molly Foote.

We sat around the table, and the farmer's wife heated some water, bade us warm our hands and feet, and served us hot bean and onion soup and fresh bread. Hannah sat pressed against Stephen, her head resting on his shoulder, his arm tightly around her. The farmer's sons joined us, two lads in their early twenties, and Stephen and I did our best to share our story, our questions, and our utmost gratitude.

In French, the farmer's wife, Madame Dubois, tried to apologize to us.

"The *Amérindiens* told us her husband had died or been killed. They spoke French, and Hannah did not, nor did we wish to tell her the terrible news. I am so happy you are alive," she said, nodding to Stephen. "We knew she was with child and hoped to offer her a safe home."

"Please do not think ill of us," the farmer said. "We gave

her light tasks, knowing her condition. Cooking, sweeping, and caring for the chickens. She showed my wife how to make medicines from our dried garden herbs."

"What are they saying?" Stephen asked me.

"Hannah has been very helpful to them." I translated the rest for him. "Stephen, you should stay here with your family. I can go on alone on the morrow. Praise be to God I will find Martha, my children, and the others in Saurel or thereabouts."

"Is it safe for you to go alone?" Stephen asked.

"We are at peace with France at the moment, and the Natives gain nothing by harming me, not if they still have captives to ransom."

I explained our plans to the Dubois, and they welcomed Stephen to remain with them indefinitely and invited me to stay the night. Saurel was a four days' journey.

Presently, the daylight was gone, the candles were lit, and the farmer and his wife went upstairs to bed. The farmer's sons, Francois and Jacques, insisted on giving up their room and bed to Hannah and Stephen for their *"réunion d'amor"* and threw some mattresses on the floor by the fire for themselves and me. I lay awake for a time, filled with happiness for Stephen and longing for Martha, trying to pay no heed to the tender moans and whispers from the other room.

I woke to another vicious winter storm, feeling feverish and faint. I tried to convince myself it was God's will, and Madame Dubois ministered to me with extra blankets, hot soup, and clean handkerchiefs. But I chafed at being so close to reclaiming my family, yet unable to do so.

Hannah shared more of her story, though she was still terrified. Like a soldier after a battle, she was tormented as I had been after the Falls Fight. Her voice trembled, and

Stephen kept a protective arm around her, encouraging her to tell us whatever she could. Her words put me at ease somewhat. The enemy had not tortured their captives nor defiled the women, and it seemed their killing of Sergeant Plympton may have been a mercy killing. But the captives were suffering from cold, hunger, and exhaustion.

Martha and my girls had been alive only days before, and I prayed they were safe from this horrendous storm.

I set out four days later when my fever broke and the storm eased. I followed the St. Lawrence River, stopping at every wigwam and farm and using every language I knew to ask about my wife and girls. There were hints, here and there, just enough to keep my hopes alive. The Fort at Saurel was the last one on the river. The promise of it illuminated my path like the beacon of a lighthouse in the fog, but I was lonely without Stephen and made more so by the silent wilderness.

Perhaps because of the deep snow, or because they had the land to themselves, I saw more wild animals during the next three days than anywhere else on our journey. A moose browsed beneath the trees on the far side of the river, raccoons scolded me from the treetops, and I flushed up several ruffed grouse and snowshoe hares in my passing. I'd eaten well at the home of the Duboises, and they'd replenished my provisions, so I was not intent on hunting. Perhaps the animals knew it and felt no need to hide from me.

At last, I reached Saurel just after dusk. A bell rang at the mission church within the fort, and I realized it was nearing Twelfth Night. Dying sunlight gilded the partially frozen rapids of the Richelieu River, where it emptied into the St. Lawrence. A nearly full moon peeked above the trees.

The fort would be locked up tightly until dawn, so I knocked on the door of a farmhouse. The farmer let me spend the night in his barn, and I lay on a pile of fresh straw outside the stall of an inquisitive cow, the soft clanging of her bell lulling me to sleep.

Chapter Fifty-Nine

MARTHA

SAUREL, CANADA
BUTTER CHURNING DAY AND LAUNDRY DAY

I hummed a ditty as I churned the week's butter.

> *"Come butter, come*
> *Come butter, come*
> *Peter stands at the gate*
> *Waiting for a buttered cake."*

When at home in Hatfield, I'd swapped out the name Peter for that of one of my girls, but they were busy with Madame de Saurel's daily French lesson. Seated at the table, their legs dangling, they repeated various phrases and answered questions. I liked to listen to the rise and fall of the language, in rhythm with the dasher in the churn. In time, I supposed I'd learn French, also.

"*Bonjour,*" said Madame de Saurel.

"*Bonjour,*" echoed my three girls.

"*Marie, comment allez vous?*"

"*Très bien, merci, et vous?*" said Mary.

"*Très bien! Bon, Marie!*"

Madame had asked permission to call my girls by the French equivalent of their given names. Or rather, she had asked her husband to ask me. It seemed a small request in exchange for their kindness and our redemption from the Natives. Still, Mattie was upset about it.

"*Martina, comment allez vous?*"

"My name is Mattie."

"*En Français, s'il vous plaît.*"

"*Je m'appelle* MAT-TEE.

Mattie looked over at me, pouting, arms crossed. I shook my head and glared at her.

Sally's lessons were more straightforward, and her name needed no translation.

"*Sarah, combien?*" Madame de Saurel asked, holding up her index finger.

"One. *Une,*" Sally said

"*Bonne! Y maintenant?*" Madame asked, raising a second finger.

"*Deux!*"

"*Oui, maintenant?*"

"*Trois.*"

"*Oui, trois. Trois jeunes filles,*" Madame de Saurel said.

A snowstorm had kept us housebound since I came to live with the de Saurels, but after nearly a week, the sun shone, and a few hardy birds chirped in the trees. I was settling into my new routine. Today was the day for churning butter. The morrow was laundry day, and the day after that was the mass before Twelfth Night, or in French, *l'Épiphanie.*

Monsieur and Madame de Saurel had invited us to *l'Épiphanie* Mass with them, but I had declined. Epiphany was a holy day, and I asked to wait until the next Sabbath. I needed time to think, and to discuss my conversion.

We would gather here after Mass to celebrate. It was all so new to me, the language, the religion. God had swept his chessboard clean twice, plucked me up, and set me back down again, first with the Natives and now with the French. Each life was strange to me, a new game with new rules. Blasphemous thoughts, but they neatly fit my mood and circumstances.

I was deeply grateful to finally have a house and three meals a day of food I did not have to dress and skin. I was glad for a safe place to bear and raise my new babe and for the Christian company. Yet I felt like a stranger in a strange land, for I'd grown accustomed to the Nipmucs and Pocumtuck ways. And not a minute passed without my longing for Ben. This place would never be home without him.

Captain de Saurel, at my entreaty, said he would send word to Governor Leverett and Le Compte de Frontenac, explaining the situation, asking if a search party had been sent, if there were any means of returning us to Hatfield. He meant well, but it was evident from his brief mention of it, the sorrow in his eyes, that he did not believe it would be possible. And so I set that hope aside, knowing that my God must have a plan far greater than any I might envision.

Their lessons done for the day, I bid Mary make the beds and told Mattie to lay the table for supper. Madame took plates, linens, and knives, and I set them on the board for Mattie. Madame asked me a question in her best English.

"Marta, please, teach English? For me?"

I pondered why her husband had never done so, but perhaps she hadn't required English before nor conveyed a curiosity to learn. I wanted to know if she'd been born here or in France, how old she was, how she'd met her husband. It was not my place to ask as her servant, nor could she yet understand my English. But we could discuss such things if I were her English teacher. Perhaps the task would make me feel more at home.

I began with lessons similar to those Madame taught my

girls: introductions, numbers, and names. I couldn't help but learn some French at the same time.

"I was born in Springfield," I said. I patted my chest, my round belly. "Where were you born?"

"I was born in Quebec," she said, pronouncing each new word slowly.

The next day, after I had washed and pressed the linens, petticoats, cuffs, and collars, we continued our English lesson. I learned Catherine de Saurel was my age, twenty-eight, but her husband was twenty years her elder. She had married at nineteen, an arranged marriage. She was happy but still longed for children.

She asked me about Ben.

"Your—how do you say—man?"

"Husband," I said, smiling.

"Yes, your husband. His name?"

"Benjamin. Ben." It startled me that merely speaking his name brought tears to my eyes.

Catherine laid her hand on my arm and offered me her handkerchief.

I dabbed at my eyes.

"He is a good man?" she asked.

I nodded.

"*Tu es désolé?*" she said.

Désolé, like desolate. "*Oui.*"

I handed her back her handkerchief, but she waved me off.

"Your girls—Marie, Martina, Sarah. Good girls." She glanced at my belly.

"The *bébé*, boy or girl?"

I shrugged.

"I think, girl. Four good girls. Like mama. *Thé?*"

I rose to put the kettle on.

"*Non.*" She placed her hand on my shoulder and went to make it for us both.

We drank our tea in silence, and then, she brightened.

"*On fait la galette! Viens!*" she said, taking me by the hand and leading me to the kitchen.

I was still amazed this home had a proper kitchen and three fireplaces—one in the keeping room, one in the adjoining kitchen, and one in the bedchamber of the master and mistress upstairs. The downstairs bedchamber I shared with my girls had a big bed and a little wood stove, and it seemed like heaven after months in the wilderness.

"I teach you," she said.

I knew Madame de Saurel must be lonely, with no children of her own and her husband busy with his many duties as Seigneur and captain. I had taken for granted my life as a farmer's wife, the comfort of knowing Ben would be home for supper each day, rarely away on business. I ached to have that life back again—though I supposed the threat from the Native people would remain forever.

We cut fresh butter into flour, added a pinch of salt and a cup of water, and kneaded the *pâte feuilletée*. While the pastry rested, we mixed butter, sugar, eggs, and ground almonds for the filling. Catherine rolled out two circles of dough, placing one in the pan. I spread the filling and was about to put the second circle of pastry on top when she stopped me.

"*Non, non! C'est Galette des Rois!*" she said, handing me a silver charm shaped like a chubby baby about the size of my thumb.

I looked at her questioningly, and she pointed to the edge of the pastry.

"Ici. *L'enfant Christ.*"

Now I understood. I set the charm atop the almond filling before I placed the top crust. Catherine crimped the edges, decorated the top, brushed it with egg, and put it in the fire's oven to bake.

"*L'enfant Christ en la galette, pourquoi?*" I asked. Each word was an achievement.

"How do you say, it is a surprise? For a person." She pronounced it like sur-preez, but I understood.

❧

I rose early, before the sun. Before they departed for Mass, Catherine left me a list of what to prepare: A lentil soup, a leg of lamb on the spit, and a stew of carrots, parsnips, and turnips. She had written it in her neat hand in French, with little pictures of the foods, and also provided a book of recipes, all of which were helpful.

Mary and Mattie finished their chores and washed, and I dressed them in the clothes the de Saurels had given us, simple clothes from the families of their two farmhands, Gilles Daniou and Claude Courtois. After I had the lamb and the cooking pots on the fire, I put on a gown Madame had given me. She was taller and more ample of bosom than I, yet I was fain to undo the lacings and abandon a corset entirely. The low-cut silk bodice and high-waisted skirt were vertically striped in ivory and gray, with lace at the cuffs and the neckline. It was the fanciest dress I'd ever worn and would have cost Ben a severe fine in Hatfield and earned me a day in the stocks.

I assumed Madame and Monsieur would dine first, and the girls and I would eat after with Gilles and Claude, as we always did. But when they returned from morning Mass, Captain de Saurel looked at the table set for two and laughed.

"No, Martha, today is a celebration! We all sit together!" he said.

I set three more places.

"The children, too! What is the word in English, merry? Yes, we make merry!"

He removed his periwig and undid his pigtail, revealing natural dark hair that brushed the ruff of his doublet, and handed me the wig, hat, and long coat. Catherine unwrapped her lace veil and removed her cloak, giving both to me. I stifled a gasp when I saw her dress. The low neckline of the blue brocade bodice bared her neck and the tops of her shoulders, and all was edged in lace and ribbon. She lifted her looped-up skirts, and her husband pulled out her chair for her.

The eight of us sat around the table. Gilles and Claude had changed from work clothes to their Sunday best, and the de Saurels looked like royalty. We bowed our heads for grace before we ate our soup, passed the lamb and vegetables, and broke the bread. Madame complimented me on my cooking. We drank wine from a glass carafe and beer from an oak tankard.

I cleared the table, placing the dishes in the tub to soak.

"*Maintenant,*" she exclaimed, "*la Galette des Rois.*"

She sliced it into nine equal portions.

"Pierre," she called to her husband. "*S'il vous plaît?*"

She spoke to him rapidly in French.

"Oh, yes, Martha, I am to explain the tradition of the King's Cake. The youngest—Sarah—passes out the cake, one piece to each of us. Whoever has the piece with the Christ child is King or Queen for the day and may pick a companion to be their Queen or King."

"Sally, you have a special task today. You will pass out the cake," I said.

Sally smiled and picked up the first plate of cake as though it were made of glass, setting it in front of Monsieur de Saurel.

Chapter Sixty

BEN

SAUREL, CANADA
JANUARY 6

I overslept well past dawn. I awoke briefly when the farmer came to milk the cow but fell back asleep, exhausted from travel and illness. I rose long after the sun and hastened to Fort Richelieu at Saurel, berating myself for my slothfulness.

Fort Richelieu was impressively situated on a hill overlooking the confluence of the Richelieu and St. Lawrence Rivers and Lac de Saint Pierre. In the daylight, the fort was more massive than I had expected, a square of tall timber with diamond-shaped bastions at each corner, embrasures for cannons, and smaller loopholes for guns.

I climbed the hill and spoke to the French soldiers protecting the main gate. The guards remembered several *Amérindiens* and an English woman and children from about a week before. They weren't sure, but perhaps Captain Pierre de Saurel himself had taken them in? Considering the seriousness of my strait and my feverish condition, they resolved it was within their authority for one of them to escort me to the home of the captain.

Overcome with joy, I struggled through the snow ahead of the soldier, spying the three chimneys of the mansion above the snow-clad firs, smoke rising into the crisp blue sky. The crunch of snow, the pounding of my heart, and the exhalation of my breath were loud in the silence. A stone's throw from the house, I heard voices, laughter, and merriment from within. The soldier called out to me to wait, but I paid him no heed. I broke into a run, newly light on my feet and bursting with hope.

Chapter Sixty-One

MARTHA

"Monsieur, why did we cut nine pieces?" I asked once Sally had served us all. "There are but eight of us."

"*Oui*, Martha, the extra slice is *la part du Bon Dieu*, the part for a good God. It is a tradition to set that piece aside lest a stranger or person in need should come to our home," Monsieur de Saurel explained. "Place it by the creche, *s'il te plaît*."

The creche was an assemblage of daintily painted porcelain figures of the Christ child, Mary and Joseph, shepherds, a lamb, a donkey, and now, three Wise Men bearing gifts. I laid the plate with the extra slice of galette beside the Wise Men.

Just then came a pounding on the door. I went to answer it.

Chapter Sixty-Two

BEN

❧❀☙

SAUREL, CANADA
EPIPHANY

At last, I reached the front door, grasped the brass knocker and pounded.

The door opened wide. It was her. She gasped.

I pulled Martha into my arms, breathed in the scent of her. Stepping back only for a second, I gently cupped her face in my hands and gazed into those green eyes, liquid with tears, traced the curve of her smiling lips, and kissed her deeply.

The soldier coughed loudly, and we stepped aside to let him pass.

"Captain, sir, I apologize for the intrusion," the soldier said in French, "but this man says, well, it appears, he is this woman's husband."

I kept one arm around Martha's waist, and she drew me inside. I doffed my hat.

"Bonjour, captain. I am Benjamin Waite, here to claim my wife and children."

Chapter Sixty-Three
MARTHA

REUNION

I pressed against Ben, clinging to his warm, solid strength. Loving the steady beating of his heart and the safety of his arm around me. I did not let go even when Captain de Saurel rose from the table to shake his hand, not until Madame pulled another chair up and bid him sit with us.

By then, our girls were running to him, clambering into his lap, throwing their arms around his neck, squealing in delight. I served him a plate of lamb and vegetables, and Captain de Saurel poured him a goblet of wine. Madame made a pot of coffee and another of cocoa. I pried Sally from Ben's arms and sat her in a chair. Mattie and Mary returned to their places at the table, chattering excitedly, telling Ben many details of our time amongst the Natives.

Madame poured the coffee, and cocoa for our girls with peppermint cane stirrers. With deep joy, I sat speechless beside Ben at the table. He took my hand in his, rubbing his thumb gently against my palm as he briefly summed up his journey to find us. Our love overwhelmed me. I couldn't staunch my tears.

"I am eternally grateful, captain, that you gave my wife and children a home and ransomed them from the *Amérindiens*. So many dreadful fates might have befallen them."

"It has been our pleasure," the captain said, "and I want to assure you, I had no idea any English still searched for them. It is astounding, the journey you describe. Albany, Le Lac Champlain—over 200 *lieue ancienne*! And you found your family!"

Ben gazed at me, misty-eyed. "Love never fails. And my wife endured a similar journey. She is also incredible."

His words set me to sobbing anew. I glanced at my girls, but they were cutting apart their cake, searching for the surprise they'd been eager to find.

"I believe you—and your wife, children, and kin—are the first English to travel this far north. And in winter, no less," the captain said.

"I had to find them, for I know no life without them. And I had a good friend beside me."

Ben took another bite of his stew. He was hungry. With a stab of sorrow, my gaze rested on the sharp planes of his jaw, the knobs of his collarbone. He'd lost weight.

"This Stephen? He is nearby?"

"Yes, with his wife and children at the Dubois farm. Three or four days south of here, north of Chambly. There is a little wooden church."

"Ah, yes, I know it. The Church of Saint-Ours. I am glad they took you in, and your friend's wife and children."

"Hannah is safe? And Sammy and Holly, too?" I asked.

"Yes, love, they are well." Ben drew me closer and addressed the captain. "I realize there's a question of payment. I have a letter of credit from Boston, I—"

The captain held up his hand.

"Whenever you are able and whatever you can afford, Monsieur Waite. We are only sorry we will lose such a kind woman and such precious girls," he said, glancing at his wife, who gave us all a weak smile.

I cleared Ben's plate quickly and returned to his embrace. He sipped his coffee and kept his arm around me.

"Meanwhile," the captain continued, "we should discuss what must happen next." He took a sip of coffee. "How many captives were taken?"

"Twenty-one, seventeen from my town of Hatfield, four from Deerfield, though one escaped, and—"

"Excuse me," I said, "there were some . . . deaths."

Everyone looked at me. Ben squeezed my hand. I picked up my cup of *cafe au lait* with shaking hands.

"Hannah told us," Ben said gently to me. "My wife is right. There are only seventeen now, including my family. Three of the captives were killed."

"I am sorry," the captain said. "Seventeen then, ten unaccounted for."

"Yes, ten captives I must find and redeem by ransom," Ben said.

"I could send soldiers?" the captain offered.

"Thank you, yes, one or two. We have guns; perhaps you might spare us some ammunition?"

"Of course, whatever you need."

Ben and the captain discussed strategies for the redemptions, converting the letter of credit to a currency Ashpelon's band would accept and ensuring our kin's safety until we returned to Hatfield. I only half-listened, oblivious to all but the warm, strong presence of my beloved husband, whose devotion and heroism had saved us.

"Mommy, nobody found the surprise," Mattie said, frowning at me as though I'd failed to deliver on a promise.

I looked around the table. "Did anyone find the Christ child?"

All shook their heads. Ben raised his eyebrows in question.

I went to the creche and picked up the extra slice of

Kings' cake, set aside for a stranger or someone in need. I smiled and brought it to Ben.

"It is a tradition here. We cut an extra slice for any visitor who might arrive. *La part du Bon Dieu la Galette des Rois*," I said.

"You speak French now?" Ben said, smiling and taking a forkful of cake.

"Madame de Saurel is teaching me, *oui*."

Ben stopped chewing, removed the silver charm from his mouth, and placed it on his napkin. "*L'enfant Christ*," he proclaimed, holding it up.

"Daddy is the King, Mommy!" Mary said, laughing.

"You have to choose a Queen!" Mattie added, excited despite her envy.

Ben smiled and took both my hands in his. Even the girls hushed.

"Madame Waite, will you be my Queen?"

"Of course," I said, and he kissed me.

The winter sun was nearly gone, the light beyond the window panes a pale violet.

I could wait no longer to be alone with Ben.

"Time for bed, girls. Mary, help Sally with her clothes," I said.

"But it is still light out o' doors!" Mattie complained.

Ben frowned at Mattie. "Do not argue with your mother, Mattie. She and I are tired. We need our rest."

"Good night, Daddy!" Mary said, giving him a big kiss on the cheek.

"I love you, Daddy!" Mattie said. "I knew you'd find us!"

"Night, Daddy!" Sally said.

Madame de Saurel excused herself and headed upstairs, and Gilles and Claude retired to their room at the rear of the house.

I disentangled myself from Ben and excused myself from the table. I put the girls to bed on a pallet on the floor, covered them with the feather tick, and put a flame to the wood in the stove, which cast a soft glow in the room.

"Why may we not sleep with you in the bed?" Mary asked.

Mattie snorted. "Because Daddy is going to sleep there, right, Mommy?"

"Right." I settled Sally in between the two of them.

Ben and the captain were still deep in conversation when I returned. I cleared the rest of the plates and lit the lanterns. Donning my coat, I walked behind the house and used the privy, then returned and washed up in the *salle de bain*. It was a separate room adjacent to mine, with a big copper tub and a porcelain wash basin I'd filled with hot water before dinner. It was still warm. Madame had left clean towels and some small items for my use. I chewed a pinch of dried mint and dabbed perfume where I wished.

I removed the lovely dress and hung it in the armoire, then shed everything else except my linen shift. As I unpinned my hair and let it fall, the last brave rays of sun splintered through the window shutters. I undid the cords tying the bed curtains to the posts, and let the charcoal gray damask envelop the bed. Cozy under the warm woolen blankets atop the feather-tick, I waited.

Ben came to me, his footsteps soft on the floorboards.

I listened to him undressing and imagined what I couldn't see. Pulling off his boots to set them gently on the floor by the stove, his nimble fingers unfastening the hooks and eyes of his buff coat, the buttons of his shirt. His hard, muscled chest soft with hair. A tug on the cuffs of his breeches, his long bare legs. A gentle splashing of water.

He opened the curtains. Firelight caught the gold of his hair, shadowing his face except for his indigo eyes locked on mine. He lowered himself gently beside me, kissed me so tenderly it was like the brush of a feather against my lips.

"My God, Martha, how I've missed you," he whispered.

"I love you so," I said, my voice breaking. "My every thought, every day, was of you."

He kissed me again, deeply, running his hands through my hair. I unbuttoned the front of my shift, and he cupped one of my breasts in his hand and kissed my throat. His other hand found and stroked the secret part of me only he knew, where the slightest touch opened me to him like a flower blooming. Our breaths came in gasps, and shudders rippled through my loins. I bit the pillow to stifle my moans, and then Ben slipped inside me, clenched my hair in his fingers, and pressed me against him, consuming me, until the heavens exploded.

We lay in each other's arms for a long time afterward. The moon rose. I traced the lines of Ben's jaw, his beard new and soft under my fingertips, the hard muscles of his chest still glistening with sweat. He laid his head on my bosom, rested his hand on my belly, and laughed when our baby moved. I touched his cheek and found it wet with tears, and tenderly kissed them away.

Chapter Sixty-Four

BEN

LEAVE-TAKING
JANUARY 1678

I wanted to stay forever in bed with my wife in that soft, warm home. Three days passed in ecstasy before I could bear to tear myself away, and then 'twas only because Stephen Jennings appeared at the door.

"You found me," I said, slapping him on the back and laughing.

"I learned my tracking skills from the best," Stephen said, coming in and hanging his hat on the peg by the door.

Martha embraced him, introductions were made, and handshakes all around. Stephen, the captain, and I sat by the fire, whilst the women and girls retreated to the kitchen to tend to dinner and leave us to our discussion of negotiations and ransoms and the governor of Quebec.

"Gentlemen, what do you envision next?" asked Captain de Saurel.

I was still reeling from my joy at being reunited with my wife and girls, humbled by the benevolence of my God. It was difficult to feel that any other matters required my attention. But Stephen deferred to me with a nod, so I spoke.

"First, we need to find the remainder of the captives and ensure their safety," I said. "Then, present the colony's letter of credit to the governor of New France, Frontenac. Finally, we must secure the safe passage of everyone home to Hatfield." I counted on my fingers for clarity. "Stephen, have I omitted anything?"

"There is the small matter of the births of our children," Stephen said, his eyes sparkling.

"No small matter," the captain said, smiling. "When do you expect them?

"My wife told me she is due in a fortnight. Stephen?"

"Late March, a week or more past the new year."

The captain considered for a moment.

"Let me send a soldier or two with you when you seek the captives, to ensure the safety of all and impress upon the *Amérindiens* the local authorities are involved," he said.

"Excellent."

"Your visit to Lord Frontenac in Quebec is most definitely required. I am not authorized to oversee your ransom negotiations, nor do I have access to funds for such purposes. I cannot spare a soldier to travel so far, but I can send a letter with you explaining the situation."

"Thank you, sir. We have the one from Governor Leverett, but one from you, in French, would be helpful," I said.

The captain nodded. "As to your homeward journey, in some ways that is the most daunting. You and Stephen suffered two months of severe weather and brutal conditions to reach here from Albany. And your wives and children fared no better with the *Amérindiens*.

"With women, children, newborn babes—I do not foresee a safe passage feasible until spring. As Mister Jennings's babe is due in March, it is best to wait until April or May. I'm sure that seems far off, but we want your babes to be born safely here in Saurel. You'll need fair weather for your trip, and the delay will give Governor Frontenac and me time to arrange a detachment of French soldiers to accompany you, thereby warding off any attempt by *Amérindiens* to ambush you on your return."

"Three more months." Stephen sighed.

"Stephen, he's right. With Martha and my children safe, home can be here or Hatfield or a wigwam in the forest."

"Of course," Stephen said, his demeanor brightening.

"I will personally see to it your townspeople are safe," the captain said. "Some will need to remain for a time with the French families to whom they are indentured. Some might even be forced by circumstance to remain with the *Amérindiens* for now, at their permanent camp nearby. Once you have met with Governor Frontenac, we will know better where we stand."

Captain Pierre de Saurel left for the fort to secure a soldier for us, and we changed our clothes and packed provisions for our trip.

"Will you be back after you find our kin? Or straight on to Quebec?" Martha asked, helping me with my buff coat and handing me my hat. Our familiar routines now precious.

Her eyes melted me every time. I kissed her gently, my arms on her shoulders.

"We will have the soldier with us to convey to the captain the state of our kin. I must continue to Quebec once we find them," I said. The prospect of leaving her again squeezed my heart.

"So, this is goodbye again," she said, biting her lip and blinking back tears.

"A fortnight. Perhaps a bit longer, depending on the weather."

Martha gazed up at me. "I love you, Ben."

I could barely speak. "And I, you." I wrapped her in my arms and kissed her.

"You will miss the baby," she said.

"I will miss the birth, at which I would be completely unnecessary. I recall I fainted at Sally's," I said, hoping my levity lightened both our hearts.

"True." She laughed. "Girls, come say goodbye to your father!"

Captain de Saurel returned with Sergeant La Fleur, his rank displayed by the white sash beneath the twelve apostles of his ammunition belt. We shook hands with Captain de Saurel, shouldered our packs, and thanked Madame de Saurel again for her generosity. I hugged my three girls, kissed my wife once more, and we set off.

It took surprisingly little time or effort to find the first five of our kin. All were safe in the homes of fur traders and tenant farmers—Quintin Stockwell, Mary Foote and her son, Nate, and Noah and Sarah Coleman. Quintin and Mary were overjoyed to see us, although their new masters were, by turn, either astounded or disappointed. Quintin was writing a journal of his travails, which I longed to read when he was done.

Sergeant La Fleur made it clear to the French that by his authority and that of Captain de Saurel, they must continue to treat their new servants kindly and give them up willingly for ransom. Stephen and I spoke with Quintin and Mary, reassuring them of their safety and planned redemption and taking note of their suspicions of where we might find the remaining captives.

Basing our search on what we learned, we crossed the frozen Richelieu River and walked in the gentle snowfall alongst the western shore of Lac de Saint Pierre. Captain de Saurel and Quintin said the Natives spoke of a fort there, a permanent camp and longhouse, where they planned to spend the winter, regardless of the situation with their captives.

We found them quickly enough, the smoke from their fires beckoning us to their camp in the forest beside the lake. Before drawing closer, Stephen and I checked to be sure our muskets and pistols were at the ready.

The woods parted on a clearing. A stockade of birch trunks stood like sentinels against us, yet the gate was open. We approached cautiously, our guns drawn, but the entrance was unguarded. Inside was a sturdy longhouse, smoke wafting from a hole in the thatched roof.

As far as we knew, the sachem Ashpelon, who'd designed the attack, killings, and ransom, was within this longhouse holding the remaining five captives—the two Abbys, Obadiah Dickinson and his son Daniel, and Matthew Kellogg. Captain de Saurel said their transaction at the Fort had been respectful.

I knew I must somehow set aside my rage and approach Ashpelon in peace, for anything less would risk the captives' lives. Yet when I stood outside the longhouse, within feet of my enemy, my civility deserted me. Having spent the past four months in impotent fury at Ashpelon and his band, my anger was a rogue wave threatening to swamp us all. My heart pounded, my hands shook, and sweat dampened my shirt.

I couldn't promise what I'd feel or do once I came face to face with the one who'd slaughtered my kin and taken my family from me. Though I'd read the line from Shakespeare's *Julius Caesar* but once, it rang in my ears now: "Cry havoc, and let slip the dogs of war."

Stephen placed a firm hand on my shoulder.

"Ben. Steady."

I barely heard him, my weapon and hatred aimed at the entrance to the longhouse.

"Ben!"

I lowered my musket only slightly.

Sergeant La Fleur stepped ahead of us to announce our presence. He stood between us and the longhouse, his musket on his shoulder. *"Je m'appelle le sergeant La Fleur, du régiment de Carignan-Salières. Je viens en paix parler avec le sachem Ashpelon!"*

"I come in peace to speak with the sachem, Ashpelon," I translated in a whisper to Stephen. Excited voices came from within, and the flap opened.

A Nipmuc sachem, shorter and younger than me, emerged. His long black hair fell from below a beaded headband, his rank of sachem signified by a cluster of eagle feathers. He was gaunt beneath his deerskin tunic and leggings. In a gesture of peace, he held up his hands to show he had no weapons.

I held his gaze. In it, I saw a strange mix of disbelief and resignation. Our fates forever joined and yet at odds.

"Benjamin Waite," the sachem Ashpelon said evenly, folding his arms across his chest.

I wanted to kill him. Not a feeling I'd ever had toward anyone before. My heart was racing, and my vision blurred. I raised and fully cocked my gun.

Stephen gripped the barrel of my musket. "Ben."

"*Monsieur Waite, non, pensez aux captifs!*" the soldier exclaimed.

I took my finger off the trigger but kept my musket aimed at Ashpelon's heart.

"Sachem," I said, "do you speak English?"

"Yes."

"I found my wife. My children and the other captives."

Ashpelon was silent.

"We are here for the rest," I said.

Ashpelon nodded.

"You followed us?" he asked. "How many of you?"

"Stephen Jennings and myself," I nodded to Stephen.

Ashpelon shook his head.

"Atian's vision. Two men. The blizzard did not stop you."

I was puzzled by his reference to a vision but replied to his words about the blizzard.

"No, it did not."

"Your people are safe," he said.

"We need to see them. Now." I lowered my gun.

Ashpelon turned back to the longhouse's open doorway and spoke in his language. A young warrior emerged with Obadiah Dickinson, tightly gripping him by the arm, and two Native women appeared holding the hands of the four children.

"Ben! Stephen! Lord is merciful. You found us!" Obadiah said, his voice hoarse. "Are you here to redeem us?"

"Soon, Obadiah, soon," I said. "Are you well?"

"We are ravenous. And some of us, including myself, are frostbitten."

I spoke rapidly to Sergeant La Fleur. He said he would be sure the captives' injuries were tended to and that they were fed.

The Natives took their prisoners back inside the longhouse.

"Do you have the ransom?" Ashpelon asked.

"We have a letter of credit from our governor. We are on our way to Lord Frontenac to fund it."

"I will not accept a letter. English promise much in their letters, but later twist the words like the knot of a hangman's noose."

"I will pay. But you must agree to wait, and the French will ensure it. Sergeant La Fleur, please tell him he must ensure the safety of all the English he took."

"*Ashpelon, je vous tiens responsable de la santé et de la sécurité des Anglais,*" said Sergent La Fleur.

"Tell him what will happen if he does not keep them healthy and safe," I said, glaring at Ashpelon. I could kill him in an instant.

"*Si un mal leur arrive, vous serez blessé.*"

"You do not need to threaten me, sergeant. Mister Waite. I have protected the English prisoners more times than you know," he said. "From starvation, from the cold, even from my own people!"

"Three of them are dead, Ashpelon," I said, glaring at him. "And the count of dead and injured your band left in your wake . . ." I was shooting words at him, like bullets.

"Do you not remember the massacre at Peskeompskut, the Great Falls? You led your soldiers there! You murdered us in our sleep!" Ashpelon stepped towards me and I raised my gun. He stopped, slammed a fist into his palm.

Of course, I remembered. Blood. Screams. The bodies of over one hundred Natives, mostly women and children. I couldn't face that memory. Not here, not now.

"And you have more than evened the score!" I said.

Stephen watched me like a sheepdog does a distant wolf. He was steeling himself for the moment I might do something I'd regret, ready to stop me.

"I must also keep my people safe. I must know that once you ransom your captives, we will be free to go." Ashpelon's voice was strong. Brave.

"And will you go? How do I know you won't return again?"

Ashpelon held up his palms and took four strides toward me. I gripped my musket but kept it lowered, my heart pounding.

"Return? Our days in the English lands are numbered. I have no wish to return. It is too dangerous."

"Dangerous?" My tension dissolved, my eyes brimming with unshed tears. "You killed and wounded women and children, my friends, my family! You say for revenge. But well before our attack at Great Falls, your people killed many. At Hopewell Swamp. Bloody Brook. Springfield." I struggled with my fury, like reefing the sheets of a sailboat in a storm, barely able to maintain control.

Ashpelon's voice was strained. "You see only the battles, only the bloodshed. This enmity began long ago, between your people and mine. At first, in small ways."

His words confused me. Stephen took that moment to speak.

"Ben. Your gun. Give it to me."

Reluctantly, I did.

"Small ways?" I said.

"Boats full of English. Boats and boats and more boats. Bringing guns that replaced our bows and arrows, rum that took our common sense, pestilence that disfigured and then killed us. You turned some of us away from our own stories, our own spirits, put your English words in our mouths!" Ashpelon paced back and forth, his voice rising with each utterance.

I remembered Stephen's words. *Is it naïve of me to ask why we could not share it?* How simple it might have been to live in harmony, if that had been the goal when the English first set foot in this land seventy years ago. If the English had valued peace over land and kept our early promises. If we had treaded lightly and respectfully on land that was not ours to own. If only we'd understood, King Philip would not have been driven to desperate violence.

Ashpelon stopped pacing. Tears streamed down his face. I winced.

"You take and take and take," he said. "Till there is nothing left for us. We fought desperately to save what has been ours since the Great Turtle first rose out of the ocean. If there could have been another way, a peaceful way . . . but you gave us no choice."

If I were Ashpelon, if the tables were turned . . . In Ashpelon's heart, his attack on Hatfield was justice served, equal in measure to our attack at Great Falls. I realized the futility of my anger. Ashpelon and I were merely players on a tragic stage. He was my reflection.

My proud stance wavered. I took two steps toward him, palms raised.

"Ashpelon, I cannot undo the wrongs I've done. The

wrongs my people have done. But I do understand your reasons. And once you release our English, you are free to go."

I stood so close to him I could see the pulse at his temple. The tearstains on his face.

"Your understanding is too late for us. And the understanding of one man is a drop of rain on a dry river bed. One tear shed on a battlefield. A beginning, but not enough."

He turned away and went back inside the wigwam.

The sergeant departed once Stephen and I assured him I'd not burn the longhouse to the ground nor shoot Ashpelon in the heart. He reminded us it was his duty to keep the peace. I reminded him that the continued safety of my family and friends was a grave responsibility. Before I could change my mind, Stephen and I set off briskly up the lake to the St. Lawrence River, which we'd follow for another week.

All the hope, anger, and fear that had propelled me forward was spent. Though our circumstances had often seemed too much to bear, my passion had driven me. I was suddenly very tired. Lost like a sailboat becalmed, with no wind to fill my sails yet still far from a familiar harbor.

Chapter Sixty-Five

BEN

QUEBEC, CANADA
JANUARY 1678

"Have we traveled farther than Champlain did, do you think?" Stephen asked, when we came into view of *Cap Diamant*, the mountain on which lay Quebec's upper town.

"I suppose, although he also traveled west to another lake," I said.

"In the winter?"

"I doubt it."

"So, Comte de Frontenac. A Catholic Frenchman. Why would he help us?" Stephen asked.

"I know only what our Harvard-educated reverends have shared with me, but I believe it has something to do with the never-ending battles between England, France, and the Netherlands for land and the fur trade on this continent, arranged marriages, and secret treaties."

"Sounds sinister."

"If it is to our advantage, so be it," I said.

Quebec had the total increase of God's creation at her

disposal—river, mountain, and access to the ocean. It was possible, I'd heard, for ships to sail across the sea from France, down the Saint Lawrence River to the interior lakes to the west or south to Albany.

I was surprised Quebec's fortifications were not much of an improvement upon those in Saurel or Chambly. Beside her harbor, a simple palisade and the tenaille of a ditch and drawbridge protected a turreted trading post. The drawbridge was down, I suppose only raised if under attack. We presented the letter from Captain de Saurel. It seemed to satisfy the guards, who opened the gate for us.

I had completely lost track of the days of the week, but the guard informed me it was a Saturday, and on the morrow was the Feast of Sainte Antoine of Egypt. Today was a market day, and he advised us to take note of the upcoming Saints' days, as it would be difficult to gain an audience with Governor Frontenac on a holy day.

The liturgical calendar allowed few days for conducting business, but it seemed our first chance to approach Frontenac would be Monday or Wednesday of the following week. After a week on the road, Stephen and I longed to rest and refresh ourselves, so we spent some time strolling about the market in the blessed sunshine.

The houses crowded closely together in the Place de Royal market square, most wooden, a few half-timbered and stone. A bronze bust of Louis XIV, France's Sun King, gazed down on us from a pedestal in the center of the court. We wandered past fur traders' stalls decked with pelts of beaver, muskrat, and lynx, their smell and softness conjuring memories of my youth. Young women called to us, waving bunches of holly and rosehips tied with ribbons. The morning mist trapped the aromas of maple syrup and bottles of Spanish wine, freshly baked baguettes, batards, and pastries, smoked ham hocks and spiced sausages, fragrant orange and blue cheeses. Stephen and I tasted and bought a bit of everything before we traveled the snowy cobblestone paths, searching for an inn.

That night, we washed our underclothes and ourselves in preparation for the Sabbath and our hopes for meeting with Frontenac on Monday. Through the inn's windows, we marveled at the many roaring bonfires melting the snow in the town square. Our innkeeper said the fires burned away the sins of the old year and honored Sainte Antoine, who had done his best to help those with diseases of the skin. I gazed at the flickering flames in the distance and whispered a heartfelt prayer for the Mohawk, Aquinachoo, and the rest of his Turtle Clan.

"May they be delivered from the scourge of smallpox."

Sunday, we woke to the peal of church bells. Neither of us would set foot within a Catholic Church but spent the time reading our Bibles in our room, having neglected that far too many times. Stephen read aloud verses from Deuteronomy.

> *"And thou shalt remember all the way which the Lord thy God led thee these forty years in the wilderness, for to humble thee, and to prove thee, to know what was in thine heart, whether thou wouldest keep his commandments or no . . . Therefore, shalt thou keep the commandments of the Lord thy God, that thou mayest walk in his ways, and fear him."*

"Does seem it has been forty years, does it not?" I said.

"More. I'm utterly exhausted, yet filled with joy and peace now we've found our families."

"One more negotiation and official paperwork, and we can rest."

Monday morning, we left the Place Royal Square on the narrow Rue du Petit Champlain and climbed the icy Quêteux Steps, the "Beggars' Stairs," the quickest—yet upon reflection, the most treacherous—way to the summit of Cap Diamant. At the top of the stairs, we walked the cobbled Côte de la Montagne directly to the Fort of Saint Louis.

The fort was only partially finished, with two parallel walls on the west side, earth and wooden ramparts, and batteries of cannons aimed toward the river. There were two gates, Porte Saint-Jean and Porte Saint Louis. Presenting our letter once again, we passed through one of them. Governor Frontenac's Chateau, orchards, and gardens were safe within stone walls.

Before the third set of soldiers allowed us entrance, they asked for our weapons, which we handed over reluctantly, remembering our experience in Albany. The Chateau St. Louis reminded me of Captain Saurel's manor house, a simply built half-timbered stone building with a slate roof and multiple chimneys. A male servant escorted us into the main hall and left to show our letters to the governor. We stood by the fire, warming our hands.

We met no delays for once, and the servant returned in ten minutes.

"The governor will see you now. This way, please," he said in French.

Louis de Buade le Comte de Frontenac et de Palleau, appointed by King Louis XIV as governor general of Quebec and New France, rose from his chair behind his desk. We introduced ourselves, doffed our hats, and bowed, and he motioned for us to be seated. He was a short, well-dressed man with close-set eyes below a perpetually furrowed brow, a long, sharp nose, and an extravagant mustache.

Ringing a bell upon his desk, he summoned an interpreter, a young Frenchman he introduced to us as Sergeant Monsieur Barrois.

Frontenac read the letter from Captain de Saurel, then

glanced over the letter from Governor Leverett and the letter of credit. He handed all three of them to Barrois. He stroked his mustache with his left hand, and I noticed he kept the other in the pocket of his coat. Once Barrois had glanced at our documents, he and Frontenac conferred and Stephen and I waited, attentive and concerned.

"Your colony does not have the funds at present to back this letter," Frontenac stated. He spoke in French, and Barrois translated to us in English.

"'Twas our understanding funds would be made available when we notify our governor of the captives' safety," I said. "We have done so, but many have been pawned to your citizens for liquor, and the Pocumtuck sachem, Ashpelon, requires coins. French coins."

Again, Barrois translated.

"He and his band intend to remain in Canada, then?" Frontenac asked.

"Captain de Saurel has ordered them to remain in Chambly, pending the captives' release."

"I thought the Duke of York set land aside near Albany for the Algonquians?"

"Yes, sir, but these Natives intend to join the Abenaki to the north in mutual defense against the Iroquois," I said.

He nodded. "*Amérindiens* have chosen sides—Algonquian tribes and Abenaki with the French, Mohawks and some Naticks with the English. I'm afraid it is all a tenuous peace between our countries and their people," he said.

He gave Stephen and me an appraising look. "But you two are not here to discuss the fates of kingdoms. You want your kin returned to you. Wives, children?"

"My wife, with child, and our three girls, and . . ." I nodded to Stephen.

"My wife, also with child, and our boy and girl. In addition, a third woman, two men, and about a half dozen more children. All now amongst French citizens or *Amérindiens*,"

Stephen said, pausing after each sentence for Barrois to translate.

"My family is with Captain Pierre de Saurel," I added.

Governor Frontenac waited for the translation, then raised his eyebrows. "He bought them?"

"He was not aware we were searching for them," I said.

The governor nodded. "I should think not. None would have believed a pair of English farmers could travel 450 miles and find your kin in the wilderness . . . I must say I am impressed by your story. It is incredible, the distance you have traveled, the people who have supported you . . ."

We waited.

"You did it for love," he said.

We nodded.

"I have not had much luck in love myself," Frontenac said, stroking his mustache. "My wife is an intelligent woman, my representative to the king in France, but . . ." He stopped here, perhaps thinking he was revealing more than he intended. "She chose to remain in Paris. We had a son. Shortly after I was appointed governor here, he was killed in the Dutch war. Francois-Louis, only twenty-one. He and I, both skilled at war. Not so much at affairs of the heart."

He removed the stopper from an ink bottle, flourished a quill pen, and smoothed a fresh sheet of parchment on his desk.

"It should suffice for me to extend another letter of credit to you and to sign the one from your governor. The *Amérindiens* should know to accept my word and signature as my troth. They can present this letter to Captain de Saurel if they need coin. Your Governor Andros shall owe me the debt. I am sure he is good for it," he said.

"Thank you, sir," I said.

"I am also giving you a letter to deliver to Captain de Saurel, authorizing him to negotiate on your behalf and granting him any additional men or provisions required to ensure the safety of the hostages. Will you be heading immediately to Massachusetts Bay Colony?"

"I fear we must wait until spring. The snow and new babes," Stephen said.

"I understand," Frontenac said, "I will send a letter to Boston, to your Governor Andros. He will want to know you have succeeded in your great undertaking."

"*Merci beaucoup*," I said.

Frontenac rose and gave each of us a firm handshake with his left hand.

We pocketed our letters, and his servant escorted us out. The guards returned our weapons, and we were on our way.

"Left-handed?" Stephen asked.

"War injury, I think. He was quite the soldier once."

Chapter Sixty-Six

MARTHA

SAUREL, CANADA
JANUARY 22, 1678

"I send for the *sage-femme* now?"

"*Oui!* The midwife. My water. *Mon eau s'est cassée.*"

I gasped as another contraction squeezed me.

"*Toute suite, s'il vous plaît!*"

The pains had begun before dawn. Catherine had wanted to send for the midwife then, but I told her to wait till the sun rose. Now my pains were strong and frequent. I heard her wake Claude and ask him to travel to the midwife's home and bring her back, but first to the neighboring farm to bid one of the girls to come care for my children whilst I labored.

I sat on the edge of the bed, my legs spread, and my feet pushing against the edge of a table wedged between me and the wall. Madame de Saurel had removed the fluffy feather tick and quilts and replaced them with layers of freshly laundered homespun linen. Last night, Claude and Gilles moved the copper tub into my room, and Catherine filled it with hot water this morning. A fire burned cheerily in the little wood stove, heating the room.

I hoped the midwife, Louise, was as skilled as the Hadley midwife who had delivered my three girls. Catherine said Louise had apprenticed with a Quebec woman from a family where many were *sages femme*, or wise women. This babe seemed to be in great haste to be born, and in between the pains, I asked after my children. The farm girl had arrived, Catherine said, and was occupying my girls with games and stories. Their blessed laughter came from the keeping room.

Catherine sat beside me on the bed, held my hand, wiped the sweat from my brow, and offered me sips of water. Ben was not here, and that saddened me. Men were forbidden from the birth room, but Sally had arrived so swiftly that he'd stayed with me until the midwife came. And he had held each of our babes shortly after, taking great joy in them from the beginning.

All three of my girls' births had been blessedly easy, but I worried about this one, the wee babe having endured, as I had, months of cold and starvation, scant rest, and too much work.

"Is there a surgeon, if the babe is breech, or—" I began.

"Shh, hush now, my friends have used Louise many times. They say she is the best," Catherine said.

"But what if there is a problem?"

"Then, yes, there is a chirurgien at the Fort, and we will send for him."

At last, Claude returned with Louise, and she swept in and took charge.

"Madame de Saurel, *plus d'eau chaude, s'il vous plaît, et de la nourriture pour Madame Waite? Des œufs pochés sur du pain grillé?*" Louise said, and Catherine left to do as she was asked.

Louise turned to me, "*Est-ce que tu parles français?*"

"*Je parle un petit peu de français,*" I said.

"Ah, *oui*, English?"

"Yes."

"*Deux mots importants—poussez et se reposez.* Push and rest. *Tu comprends?*"

"*Oui,* I understand."

Louise fetched another bucket of hot water, clean towels, and a plate with a poached egg on toast. I was nauseous, yet Louise insisted, so I nibbled at the food. Catherine knelt behind me on the bed, holding me beneath my arms, murmuring encouragement. The midwife washed her hands in the bucket of water, dried them on the towels, and then washed me. I inhaled the aroma of lavender as she took the stopper from a pretty glass vial, and rubbed the scented oil on her hands, then on me. Gently, she slipped her hand inside me to check my womb.

She spoke French, and Catherine did her best to translate.

"She says it is good, you are widening," Catherine said, "but do not push until she says, '*Poussez.*'"

The pains were sharper now. I clenched Catherine's hands where they rested below my bosom.

Louise said something in French, looked at me, opened her mouth wide, and stuck out her tongue. I understood only the word, "*chien.*"

"She says to breathe like a dog," Catherine told me.

I laughed, releasing some of the pain. I panted, cried, and screamed, and finally, Louise told me to push. Push, and rest, push and rest. A dozen times, maybe more, and at last, the babe's head crowned, and searing pain radiated like a ring of fire. I pushed and rested. With one final desperate push, my babe slipped from my womb and began to cry.

I laughed with relief and joy and prayed to God in gratitude.

"*C'est une fille!*" Louise exclaimed.

A girl.

The afterbirth left me as it should. I lay on the bed, and Catherine plumped the pillows beneath my head and shoulders to prop me up. Louise wiped my new babe with a warm, wet cloth, clamped and cut the cord, and laid her on my chest. Gently, she washed me again, bandaging me with clean towels.

Louise stayed for the rest of the day. After bathing and swaddling my wee babe, she placed her in a cradle Catherine had borrowed from the neighbor girl. She instructed Catherine on all the possible misfortunes that might befall the babe or me, and Catherine reminded me to tell her at once if I grew feverish or if there was much blood or pain. I was grateful to have these two women with me, caring for me. My little babe gazed up at me, and I put her to my breast, and although my milk was not yet in, she nuzzled there like all babes do.

"What will you name her?" Catherine asked.

"Canada." I smiled.

Ben and Stephen returned from their expedition when Canada was three days old. By then, the blood on my bandages was no longer bright scarlet, and our baby was nursing contentedly and often. Stephen stayed only long enough to wish me well before leaving for the home where Hannah waited.

"Canada?" Ben looked up at me, holding our wee babe in his arms.

"Yes, are you in favor? She can always remember, when giving thanks to God she survived, how much you risked rescuing her," I said, stroking my babe's downy head.

"And how much you risked protecting her. 'Canada.' I like it! All our Biblical names, all the Marys and Samuels have become a bit . . . tiresome."

I was confined to bed except to use the chamber pot, but Catherine and Ben tended to my every need.

To think I'd worried I would give birth in a wigwam in the

snow. Captain de Saurel assured me had that been the case, *Amérindien* women were quite skilled at delivering babies. I thought of Nìbi Wàbà. She would have delivered our babes if we had not been sold to the French. Strange, my thoughts. Part of me missed her, curious where and how she was.

Ben sat beside me on the bed, stroking my hair, holding my hand, and watching Canada nurse. He helped Catherine with Canada's shifting, bathing, and swaddling several times daily. He held her tenderly and spoke to her in whispers. At night, he lay beside me, my back against his chest, his arms about me, his face buried in the nape of my neck, and he was the first to wake when our new babe cried, bringing her to me to nurse.

God had shepherded me through the valley of the shadow of death, and now my life overflowed with blessings. Yet despite my gratitude, worries still pricked my mind. I grieved for Catherine, who could not have children of her own, and for Mary, who had lost her child. I feared what would become of the orphans still living in the forest with the Native people and those left behind in Hatfield. My thoughts strayed to the Algonquian children, whom Ashpelon had said were killed at the Great Falls battle.

A fortnight after Canada was born, I was no longer confined to bed. On a bright, clear February morning as all our little girls slept, I invited Ben to walk with me in the garden. I asked him to bare his soul. I would not be at peace without the truth.

Chapter Sixty-Seven

BEN

❧

Saurel, Canada
February 5, 1678

We sat on a wrought-iron bench beneath the bare apple trees, black branches like a crone's gnarled fingers clawing at the bright blue sky. Icicles hung from the twigs, melting in the sun, dripping like tears. Martha held my hands in hers and took a deep breath.

I waited. I knew she was troubled. Of course, after all she'd endured.

"I love you, Ben. So very much. What I need to ask, and your reply, won't change that," she said, gazing into my eyes.

I gripped her hands a bit tighter. My palms were clammy. What did she mean to ask me?

"I love you, too," I said.

"I can no longer ignore the secrets between us," she said, her voice so fragile.

"Secrets?"

"About what happened at the Great Falls and all that befell me with the Natives."

I frowned. "I've told you about the battle."

"Only what you thought I could bear to hear."

My wife was no fool.

"What more do you want to know?" I asked, a sudden shiver chilling me.

"Ashpelon said—"

"Ashpelon?" I said bitterly. "Do you favor his words over mine?"

She flinched, then pulled her hands from my grasp.

I reached out to her, but she folded her arms like a shield against me. My heart thrummed in fear.

Her voice was firm. "Ashpelon said he knew the Native people at the Great Falls. He said they camped there to fish. They stole our cattle because they were starving. They waited there for our response to a peace treaty."

I heaved a sigh. "That all may be true. Peace negotiations were held. But the ambush at Bloody Brook, and Richard's murder at Hopewell Swamp, surely you cannot forget. You must know it was not just about the cattle. They killed your father!" I was angry now, feeling cornered.

Martha blinked at the mention of her father, and I regretted my words. But she continued, her voice steady.

"Ashpelon said your army ambushed them in their sleep, that they were unarmed, that it was not a battle but a slaughter." Martha's voice faltered, and she took a deep, trembling breath.

Though I dreaded her next words, my heart grieved for her.

"He said you killed children." She stated it as a conviction, and her green eyes brimmed with unshed tears.

I looked away toward the captain's house, the smoke drifting from the chimney. I wanted to be anywhere but here. To flee, to cut and run. But I couldn't escape my conscience.

"Ben, did you kill children?" she asked.

She was risking it all. I took her hands in mine, and kissed them. My heart nearly broke that she allowed it. She waited as

I chose my words. I had to speak the truth. Our love demanded it.

"I killed no children," I said, "but others did, and I have kept much from you."

She sucked in a breath, and her eyes filled with tears.

"I could make excuses for what we did, give you a hundred reasons, but you deserve better," I said.

"I've heard falsehoods and boasts often from you and other men. I want your truth."

I looked down at her hands in mine, then off toward the river.

"It isn't an easy story to hear. Or to tell."

She waited, holding me captive with her trust.

"We knew the River Indians were unarmed," I said. "'Twas not a secret. In fact, it was an advantage we sought, but most of us —"

"You, Ben. Your truth."

I began again.

"But I chose to overplay the threat of the warriors at the other camp across the river. I chose to ignore the evil we were complicit in, the imbalance of power."

She bit her lip but held my gaze. I longed to hide but pushed on, as was my nature.

"Once we were there, and Captain Turner gave the command to fire, we—I—became a hellhound, unleashed. I remember loading and firing and reloading my gun over and over. Musket balls flew past me, severing the air," I said. I was reliving it, telling her what I saw in my mind's eye, and feeling the same terror and revulsion anew.

"I shot an elderly man, then broke the arm of a young warrior. I could barely see through the smoke, but I heard the screams, the explosions, the roar of the water. We threw their fish into the river and set fire to their wigwams."

I was shaking, and squeezed my eyes shut. Martha interlaced her fingers with mine, her grasp tightening.

"Three women came at me with clubs. I gripped my broadsword and slashed at them with no more thought than I'd swing a scythe cutting wheat. "

I broke down, sobbing, and paused to catch my breath.

"There was so much blood, Martha, and screaming, and by then, I was not even thinking, just fighting, attacking. I think I threw down my sword, or sheathed it again in my scabbard. I do not remember. I pointed my gun through the door of a wigwam. Inside was a Nipmuc mother, holding her wee babe."

Martha waited for me to go on.

I gathered up the memories to lay before her like a sacrifice.

"'Twas the wee babe's crying that stayed my hand, for it seemed I was listening to our Sally crying out at night for comfort, and it was as though I awoke to the sound. I realized who I was and what I was about to do, and I froze. My finger was on the trigger, but I did not fire. The woman pleaded with me. Begged for her child's life. I lowered my gun, and I ran."

Now Martha embraced me, stroked my hair, and held me close. I clung to her.

"You spared them."

"Yes."

What I'd kept hidden so long demanded now to be exposed in all its horror. "I cannot be absolved, Martha. I was part of all of it, and others killed many children that day."

Martha was silent, as though my confession had knocked her cold. There it was. She'd seen my feet of clay. The part of me that was broken.

"I forgive you," she whispered, her face wet with tears. I gripped her hands like a drowning man.

"But one more thing puzzles me," Martha said, biting her lip.

God, what now?

"Why did you not bring the fallen back home? Why are they buried in the wilderness?"

"Martha, there are some things in the world women are not meant to know," I whispered.

She pulled her hands from mine, stood, and hurled her next words at me like stones.

"Things women aren't meant to know? Do you mean things such as abduction? Imprisonment? Starvation? A child drowning in the icy water? Another buried in the wilderness? A dead man burnt upon a fire? I know all those things now!"

She was furious with me, and rightly so. I had finally shared my pain but had not taken hers as my own. I'd wanted to believe that by rescuing her and my kin from their captors, all would be restored. But her heart held buried secrets, too, and I had not searched for them.

I stood and took her in my arms, and though she did not resist, she did not yield. I murmured to her endearments and words of love. At last, she softened.

"I was so terrified, Ben."

"I am truly sorry. Whatever you need from me . . ." I murmured.

Martha nodded. "I need to speak of it."

I brushed her tears away with my thumb.

"They staked us down in the night like trapped animals. Killed Sergeant Plympton because they feared his hallucinations. And though I hoped and prayed you'd come for me, I thought each day I might die, that our girls would die. I survived. But the dark places in my spirit, the empty hollows of your heart, the unspoken truths . . . those I cannot endure! Our marriage cannot bear it!"

I was stunned by the cascade of her emotions. I held her and hushed her as I would Sally after a nightmare, and when she finally stopped sobbing and laid her head against my chest, we sat again.

"You were incredibly brave, my love. And kept our daughters safe. And it will trouble you for a long time, but you are safe now."

She looked up at me. "And what of the dead at the Falls?"

"We did not bring our dead back to Hatfield because we were forced to bury them where they lay. Their bodies had been . . . mutilated. Scalped."

Martha gasped as if I'd struck her. I felt as though I had.

I owed her the complete truth.

"When the River Indians returned to bury their dead, they found the same." I stopped. I couldn't go on.

"Did you violate the dead?" Martha whispered.

"Again, no. I promise you. But I'm an Englishman and must share the blame for what we did." I seemed unable to hold my tongue. "Our actions led to the attack on Hatfield. It is my fault you were taken."

"No, no, Ben. Ashpelon's reasons were many. Revenge, yes, but much more."

We held each other for a long time. It began to snow. I wrapped my great coat around her and held her close to my heart.

"There you have it. The truth." I tipped her chin up to gaze into her eyes. "I love you, Martha. And I promise I will listen to you, not just your words, but your secrets."

She kissed me but did not reply.

"Now that you know everything, can you still, do you . . .?" I couldn't finish.

"Ben, yes, I love you. I still love you."

She kissed me and whispered, "Always."

Chapter Sixty-Eight

MARTHA & BEN

HOMECOMING
SPRING 1678

Hannah's babe, a girl, was born in early spring. Hannah and Stephen named her Captivity in remembrance of what she'd survived, just as Ben and I called our babe Canada, for the country where she was redeemed. Names giving thanks to God.

The spring came slowly, in fits and starts, with sunshine and snow showers and birds singing, river ice cracking and heaving and sending frozen chunks floating downstream, ewes giving birth to bleating lambs, and hens clucking in glee as they laid eggs once more. Canada smiled for the first time.

Mattie insisted on teaching Catherine de Saurel English by taking her through the lessons in the picture book. I spent many joyous hours listening to them. One of their favorites was Lesson IX, "The Earth."

> "In the *Earth* are high *Mountains,* Deep *Vallies,*
> *Hills* rising, Hollow *Caves,*
> Plain *Fields,* Shady *Woods.*"

Ben took charge of the spring planting for Captain de Saurel, or Pierre, as he insisted we call him. Each morning, Ben left with Claude and Gilles, whistling a jaunty tune. He said he missed farming, and the de Saurels needed the help. After dinner, though, Catherine released me from my duties, and Ben stayed home with us. We enjoyed our time together as a family in recreation, something we'd never had the chance to do before nor likely would ever have the chance to do again.

I borrowed a cittern from Catherine's friend and was happy to find I still remembered how to play. Catherine encouraged me, for she also liked to sing, and the four of us gathered around the fire many evenings, singing ditties in French and English. Ben taught the girls to play hopscotch and London Bridge, Jackstraws, and Knucklebones. Mary taught herself to cross stitch, Mattie learned to skip, and Sally made friends with the barn cat's new kittens.

Hannah, Stephen, and Captivity visited us at the de Saurels, or we visited them at the Dubois farm, on most Saturdays once the spring thaw made the way passable. Mary Foote, her son Nate, and Quintin came and stayed for supper. Mary held Canada and Captivity tenderly, and Quintin and I spoke at length about everything from Ashpelon to frostbite to Sergeant Plympton's tragic death. It was good to share the memories. To bear witness.

Some of the Natives came to see us one day in late April. Not Ashpelon. But Kòkòkòho, Nìbi Wàbà, Neepânon, and her husband Wekoñtam. Catherine graciously sat them at the table, and we shared our dinner with them. Ben and Mattie were disgruntled by these unexpected guests, and they ate silently and fled to the garden after they finished their meal, but Mary and Sally were happy to see their "friends." The Native women brought gifts of rabbit furs for the babies and took salt pork and bread back to their camp. I was strangely sad to see them go.

Ben and I relished our private moments getting to know one another again, softening the raw edges left by months of separation and secrets, cold and hunger, kissing away the tears, soothing the remnants of horrors and anger, sharing the wondrous miracles we'd seen and the dark places that had nearly swallowed us whole. Praying and making love and cleaving one to the other.

The first day of May, which Stephen called by the Irish name of *Là Beltane*, is a festival of spring. The apple blossoms bloomed white as snow, and the hillsides burst with magenta fireweed, yellow dandelions, and hedges of wild pink rose. It was the day on which we prepared to leave Saurel. We knew we must go before the third of May since 'twould be impossible on the busy Feast of the Two Apostles, Saints Philip and James. Hannah and her babe were well enough to travel, the rivers overflowed their banks, and it was time for us to make our way home again.

BEN

Lord Frontenac paid the ransom and sent an escort of six mounted soldiers under the command of Sieur de Lusigny from Quebec. Captain Pierre de Saurel engaged two soldiers from the fort, and two more met us at Chambly. A pair of horses carried the makings of our tents and bedding, and another two pulled a wagonful of our provisions. There were extra mounts for the women and children to ride when they tired of walking. It was slow going.

The French, Dutch, and English were enchanted by our story. People gathered on their doorsteps and looked up from tilling their fields to wave happily to us when we passed by, cheering our good fortune, wishing us a *bon voyage* and a happy homecoming.

We hugged the shores of Lake Champlain and the rugged forests of Lake George, finally following the Hudson River, one of the few rivers Stephen and I had crossed but not yet traveled. As Stephen had once remarked, the rivers did all seem to look the same. The difference was this one led us home.

At Albany, we bid farewell to the soldiers from Chambly and Saurel and four of those from Quebec, but two continued on with us, having business in Boston. I learned later that Captain Salisbury wrote to Governor Bruckholds to complain about our return passage through his colony under French escort. Salisbury's primary concern was not for our safe travel but that his colony should not be expected to cover our "expenses." Governor Bruckholds replied yes, Salisbury should pay our expenses, and if he was so worried about the French, he should have sent his own men with us to Springfield.

We stayed five days in Albany to rest and refresh ourselves. Stephen and I and our families stayed again at the inn of Volckert Janse Douw and his wife. The rest of the English and the two French soldiers were taken in by others in town, including Captain Salisbury's clerk, Bram Jacobssen; the family of the guard from the prison boat, Pieter Smit; and the Albany Indian Commissioner, Robert Livingston.

I wrote a letter to Hatfield at Albany and sent it with the two French soldiers. Although Benoni Stebbins, Major Pynchon, and even Timothy Cooper had informed my friends and kin of all that had befallen us, I needed to ask them for their help.

❦

Albany, May 23, 1678

To my loving friends and kindred at Hatfield

These few lines are to let you understand that we are arrived at Albany now with the captives, and we now stand in need of assistance, for my charge is very great and heavy; and therefore any that have any love to our condition, let it move them to come and help us in this strait.

There are three of the captives that are dead—old Goodman Plympton, Samuel Foote's daughter, and Samuel Russell. All the rest are alive and well and now at Albany, namely: Obadiah Dickenson and his child, Mary Foote and her child, Hannah Jennings and three children, Abigail Allis, Abigail Bartholomew, Goodman Coleman's children, Matthew Kellogg, my wife and four children, and Quintin Stockwell.

I pray you hasten the matter, for it requireth great haste. Stay not for the Sabbath, nor shoeing of horses. We shall endeavor to meet you at Canterhook; it may be at Houseatonock. We must come very softly because of our wives and children. I pray you, hasten then, stay not night nor day, for the matter requireth great haste. Bring provisions with you for us.

Your loving kinsman, BENJAMIN WAITE

At Albany, written from myne own hand. As I have bin affected to yours all that were fatherless, be affected to me now, and hasten the matter and stay not, and ease me of my charges. You shall not need to be afraid of any enemies.

Connecticut soldiers under Captain Watts met us at Canterhook, New York. They escorted us with much military pomp and circumstance to Springfield, but not before kin from Hatfield met us halfway. They brought our horses and food and an outpouring of love and gratitude.

John Coleman scooped up his children in great joy. Samuel Foote embraced Mary. She held Nate and the wee son she'd left behind and shared the tragedy of little Molly. Obadiah and his son were reunited with their Sarah. Fatherless and motherless children were gathered up into the arms of aunts and uncles.

Reverend Wise announced the governor's declaration of a day of fasting followed by a day of feasting for the first week in June. Martha's mother and stepfather, her sisters and brothers, took us in for the night, and Major John Pynchon came to greet us all. Our redeemed captives splintered off to their families and kin and headed home to Hatfield.

That beautiful Saturday morning on the 29th of May 1678, we rode triumphantly down Hatfield's main street. Dooryards overflowed with our neighbors and kin. Stephen led his horse Raven, carrying Hannah and Captivity, and I led Scout bearing Martha and Canada. The rest of our children skipped around us.

We'd been away so long that those not taken or killed on that infamous September day had rebuilt not only their homes, but ours as well.

At the Jennings' house, Martha dismounted. We passed a quarter hour embracing friends and promising to join them at the Sabbath sermons and dinner the next day.

When we finally reached our own home, Martha took one look at it and burst into tears. "'Tis just as it was, Ben!"

I choked back my feelings. "Glad to see the stockade encloses it now."

With Canada in her arms, Martha ran with our girls up the path to our front door.

"Mommy, Mommy, we're home!" Mary squealed.

"Martha!" I called.

Martha paused on the doorstep and, handing Canada to Mary, told the girls to go inside. She turned to look at me, her hand raised to her brow to shield her eyes from the sun. I threw Scout's reins over the fence post and walked up the path.

On that glorious spring morning, I held my wife in my arms on the doorstep of our home. Bending down, I cupped her face in my hands. Our kiss was sweet and tender, followed by another, just as lovely but more fervent. Martha rested her cheek against my chest.

"Your heart is racing," she said.

"Only for you."

She smiled. "Thanks be to God, and to you, that we are home at last."

"Love never fails," I said.

We walked inside our home, hand in hand.

Chapter Sixty-Nine

ASHPELON

CANADA
SÉQUAN, MANY MOONS LATER

It is Séquan, when the water runs again. Many moons ago, the French paid us for the remaining English in Sun King gold coins and wampum belts, in furs, guns, and firewater. It is time for us to seek refuge with the northern tribes by Lake Pohenegamook. It lies in a sliver of rolling, forested land separating the English from the French, the Abenaki from the Iroquois. No man's land.

I hope it will remain a wildland where any people who wish may build fires and tell stories in the winter and fish in the spring, grow corn in the summer, and hunt bear and elk in the autumn. I hope these things but fear in my heart and the whispers of the spirits that it cannot be so forever. The men from across the water—the Dutch, the French, the English – will continue to come here. They will take and take until nothing is left for us.

I have a story to tell you, a story I started in the winter of our journey with the English but never finished. Now it is time to share the rest of the story with you, as my people head north, and the English we lived with for a time head south. All of us going home.

This is the story about the long-ago time when people lived always in the early red morning, before sunrise, before the land was peopled as today.

Glooskap, the Great Chief, went very far to the north, where all was ice. He came to a wetu, and there he found the Great Giant of Winter. Glooskap entered the wetu and sat down, and Winter handed him a pipe and told him tales of the olden times.

The spell of the Frost came upon the Great Chief, and while the Giant Winter talked, the Great Chief nodded and fell asleep. He slept for six months. Then the spell left him, and he awoke and went upon his journey. He hastened toward the south, and at every step it grew warmer, and by and by the flowers sprang up and talked with him.

At last the Great Chief came to where all the little folk were dancing in the forest. Their Queen was Summer, the most beautiful of all women. The Great Chief seized her, and by a clever trick, he kept her. For he cut a moose hide into a long cord and ran away with Summer.

The Chief traveled on until he came once more to the lodge of the Giant Winter. But now he could not be charmed. He was stronger than Winter, for he brought the Summer with him.

We will take the summer with us to the land of cold and ice, and there, we will gather by our fires and tell our stories. My favorite story will be about the brave Sachem who avenged his people. He captured the enemy for a time and then let them go, as one throws fish back into the river when they are small, hoping for a better catch the next season.

For one can never know the end of a story. It can circle back, like the deer or the hawks or the orange butterflies, to begin again when you least expect it.

Acknowledgments

Thank you first of all, to my daughter, Emily Potashnick, for your thoughtful alpha reads of my first drafts and your honest advice, support, and patience during numerous discussions about my novel. I always learn from your compassionate perspectives on human rights and sensitivity as they apply to historical events. Also, thanks for the website, public relations, and marketing. I love you.

Much appreciation for my friend of many decades, Linda Kristiansen. You were an astute and devoted alpha reader of my first draft and offered insights and suggestions that improved my work, and praise that kept me going.

Heaps of gratitude to my beta readers and fellow authors, Chrissy Hicks and Jim Ditchfield, who read every line, encouraged me, and provided honest feedback. Chrissy, you helped me dig deep for emotion and really understood my characters. Jim, you caught any errors in historical details, and entertained me with your many stories of Australia. I wish you both luck with your upcoming novels.

A special thanks to my cousins, Steven and Kent Wiley, for reading specific chapters at my request and advising me on matters relating to your respective areas of expertise, anthropology and weaponry.

Thank you to romance author Laura Taylor, my first editor, for believing in *Hatfield 1677* long before that was the title, and offering friendship and wisdom in your read-and-critique groups and many conversations. You have the most beautiful reading voice of anyone I know.

To enable me to publish a book about events that required care and multiple perspectives, I am indebted to Sarah Elisabeth Sawyer for her online course, "Fiction Writing: American Indians" and her "Native Reads Analysis Workshop." Sarah, thank you so much for making yourself accessible and being so generous with your time and encouragement.

I am grateful to Stacey Parshall Jensen, my sensitivity reader, for helping me see through the veil of white privilege to the tragedy of what European colonists, including my ancestors, did to First Nation people, and how I might best present that within the arc of my story.

The launch, or relaunch, of my career as a fiction author is largely due to the Southern California Writers' Conference and the friends I've made there, to all the agents and writers who read and critiqued my chapter submissions, and to everyone in the SCWC Rogue Read and Critique Groups who shared support and critique long past midnight. Thank you.

Thanks also goes to The History Quill and their fabulous, five-day, February 2023 online Writers' Convention; to The Manuscript Academy and hosts Jessica Sinsheimer and Julie Kingsley for your workshops, classes, agent meetings, consultations and #MSWL; to Autocrit, for Writing Academy Zoom courses with delightful host Daniel Kaplan; to the San Diego Writers' and Editors' Guild for their "Highest Recommendation" evaluation of an early draft of *Hatfield 1677*; and to Shut up and Write and the fellow writers I met through their Cary and North Wake County Chapters.

Honor is due the National Park Service and the archeological study at Peskeomskut— "Turner's Falls"— for your ongoing work with and for the Nipmuc and Pocumtuck First Nation to honor those killed in the massacre. A nod also to the town of Montague, whose webpage for the village of Turners

Falls begins with a conciliatory memorial to those First Nation people.

For the legends told by Ashpelon, many thanks to the Library of Congress, https://www.loc.gov, for two books in the public domain. "How the Flying Squirrel Got His Wings," from *Indian Nature Myths* by Julia Darrow Cowles, copyright 1918; and "How Glooscap Found Summer," from *Glooscap the Great Chief and Other Stories* by Emelyn Newcomb Partridge, copyright 1913. I excerpted and paraphrased from both.

Thank you to all the authors, editors, publishers, and survival videographers for the invaluable information they provide online, and to Google maps, for allowing me to plunge my readers into a time and place nearly 350 years ago, and take them on 400-mile long journeys through the wilderness.

Eternal gratitude to Acorn Publishing, especially Holly Kammier, for believing in me and *Hatfield 1677*. Thank you to my publication coordinator Leslie Ferguson for patiently guiding me through all the steps of publication. Thank you to my cover artist Damonza for the beautiful cover, my proof-reader Kat Ross for your eagle eyes, and everyone else on the Acorn team.

Thank you to all my newfound cousins, also descendants of Benjamin and Martha Waite. I hope this novel honors them in your eyes. We wouldn't be here without them.

Finally, my deepest gratitude to you, my readers. I hope you find *Hatfield 1677* engaging, thought-provoking, and memorable, and that it leaves you firmly believing that love never fails.

Laura C. Rader
Author
Lcrwriter.com

Historical Notes

This novel would not have been possible without extensive research accomplished through online sources, as well as help from many archivists, librarians, and historians.

When possible, I referred to primary source documents. These included letters between Benjamin Waite, John Pynchon, Governor Andros, and Captain Salisbury; the captivity narrative of Quentin Stockwell; and the translations of John Elliott's Bible, among others. (Hough, Franklin B. *Papers Concerning the Attack on Hatfield and Deerfield by a Party of Indians From Canada September Nineteenth, 1677.* The Bradford Club April 1859, from the archives at Albany, NY.)

I also relied upon Douglas Harper's marvelous Online Etymology Dictionary to ensure my English language was authentic for the Restoration period, the Nipmuc language resources of David Tall Pine and other members at nipmuclanguage.org., and the ongoing work of Larry Spotted Crow Mann, at whisperingbasket.com, a gifted storyteller, author, and Native American cultural educator.

A full bibliography can be found on my website, lcrwriter.com.

The day to day lives of the late 17th century Puritans were

often grim and tedious, although not as grim and tedious as those of their Pilgrim forbears. Literature other than the Bible, especially poetry, was available, and prohibitions against music, dance and celebrations were rarely enforced. Although their religious faith still guided them in all things, their humanity was evident in the small daily pleasures of Puritan life and their strong community and family ties.

Hatfield 1677 is a work of fiction, and I did take some liberties with the facts:

Although most Puritan men and women could read English, the children's book *Orbis Pictus* was published in Latin in London in 1654 and not translated until fifty years later. Martha could not have read it in 1677, but it was the first children's picture book and primer in America.

It was against Massachusetts Bay Colony law for men to physically abuse their wives, although wives could be publicly whipped for adultery. Hannah's abuse at the hands of her first husband is my creation, although other events surrounding Hannah and her family are based on historical record.

I found mention but no evidence that Ashpelon was related to Massasoit, or to the natives slaughtered at Peskeompskut, although he was the sachem who led the raid on Hatfield.

The circumstances of the deaths of "Molly" Mary Foote, Sam Russell, and Sgt. Benjamin Plympton are purely my own speculations, although their deaths are a matter of record.

I would love to hear from my readers, and I will do my best to reply to you. To contact me, please visit my website, lcrwriter.com. If you loved this novel, please share a review on Amazon or Goodreads, and recommend it to your friends. Thank you.

Laura C. Rader

North Carolina

2024

About the Author

Laura C. Rader earned a BA in psychology from San Diego State University, where she minored in history and took creative writing and literature classes. She drew on those passions in her thirty-year career as a history and English teacher of elementary and middle school students. Now a full-time historical fiction writer, Laura also enjoys studying genealogy, attending neighborhood book club meetings, taking forest walks with her Rough Collie, and visiting her adult daughter in Brooklyn. Originally from California, Laura lives twenty miles north of Raleigh, North Carolina.

Hatfield 1677 is a work of historical fiction inspired by a story Laura discovered about her ninth great-grandparents while researching her family's genealogy.